6-05

unimaginable
ZERO

Date Due

D1114219

Also by LESLIE STELLA

Fat Bald Jeff · *The Easy Hour*

unimaginable
ZERO summer

a novel

LESLIE
STELLA

**Three Rivers
Press** NEW YORK

Published in the United States by Three Rivers Press, an imprint of the
Crown Publishing Group, a division of Random House, Inc., New York.
www.crownpublishing.com

Three Rivers Press and the Tugboat design are registered trademarks of
Random House, Inc.

Library of Congress Cataloging-in-Publication Data
Stella, Leslie.
Unimaginable zero summer : a novel / Leslie Stella.—1st ed.
p.   cm.
1. Bookstores—Employees—Fiction. 2. Class reunions—Fiction.
3. Friendship—Fiction. 4. Women—Fiction. I. Title.
PS3569.T37972U55 2005
813'.6—dc22   2004019701

ISBN 1-4000-8102-5

Printed in the United States of America

Design by Karen Minster

10 9 8 7 6 5 4 3 2 1

First Edition

To James Franklin
·   ·   ·

Thanks to Noah Lukeman,
Caroline Sincerbeaux,
and the boys in
the Downers Grove clubhouse:
Steve, Willie, Pete, Al, and,
as always, Chris.

Happy families are all alike;
every unhappy family is
unhappy in its own way.

—Leo Tolstoy,
Anna Karenina

Where is the summer, the unimaginable
Zero summer?

—T. S. Eliot,
"Little Gidding"

unimaginable
*ZERO*summer

one

they met at one of her father's swinger parties. People were determined to like any story that began in such a way, so Verity had given up explaining that her dad was not *really* a true swinger; he had no fishbowl in which his guests could deposit their keys, yet one could not ignore the revolving cast of ladies with whom he kept company.

Verity sampled the homemade onion dip. *Not bad.* It had taken Tex years to master the basics of loner dad cuisine.

Behind her, an unfamiliar male voice spoke. "There's the onion dip, but where are the other delights?"

She turned around to face a man of squinky appeal: warm brown eyes, a tsunami of wild auburn curls, charming beer belly, bowling shoes. "What?"

He bit his lip. He had not planned what to say after that sure-fire come-on. "Er . . . I . . . Herb Alpert and the Tijuana Brass? That album?"

"Whipped cream," said Verity. "The Herb Alpert album is *Whipped Cream and Other Delights.* Very nice. I just got one at the thrift last week for eighty cents. It was an old college radio station copy, and the girl on the cover had been sliced up with an X-Acto knife."

"Oh. That's, uh, too bad."

"No, no, not at all. The vinyl was in decent shape; all I want to do is play it, not worship it." She ate more onion dip, just as a thick, coiled hair made its descent from the tsunami next to her into the bowl. They both watched it, fascinated.

"I'm sorry," he said, retrieving the errant strand with a contrivance concocted of plastic cocktail swords and toothpick umbrellas.

She dipped the chip and said, "It's okay. Your hair looks reasonably clean and I'm not all that particular anyway."

He stared at her in amazement. Who was this girl with the record player and blasé indifference to hygiene? He had to know.

She obliged. "I'm Verity Presti. Tex, our swinging single host, is my dad." Her gaze traveled over to her father, who was engaged in a train wreck masquerading as a three-way fox-trot with two wanton senior citizens. She glanced back at the squink. "Who are you?"

He replied, "I met your dad through a flyer posted at the Koffee Kup in Chicago that read 'Experienced dentist, Downers Grove—will clean your teeth in my home in exchange for yardwork.' I got six years' worth of plaque and tartar scraped off, and then I went out in the yard and created a yew topiary for him shaped like a heart. I guess he was pretty pleased with the shrubbery, so he invited me to this party. He said it was going to be 'a swinging little soiree,' but I had no idea . . ." His voice trailed off as the fox-trot threesome convulsed nearby.

Verity watched them, too. "He's harmless. Just lonely."

He reached for her hand and said, "My name is Charlie Brown."

Verity considered telling him about the onion dip on the front of his trousers, but figured with a name like that, he had enough problems.

Shortly thereafter, Tex retrieved a brass urn from his fireplace mantel and stepped into the center of the family room. He clutched the urn tightly, smiled sorrowfully, and cleared his throat. *Here we go,* thought Verity, and she addressed the onion dip with renewed vigor.

"I'd like to make a short speech," he began, "a tribute, really, to my dear, dead Thelma." Tex raised the urn so that all could see Thelma, or Thelma's vessel, more clearly. "She was a wonderful wife and mother, and when she passed on she left me and my daughters abandoned and heartbroken, of course, but richer for having known her."

Tex's stable of calcified sexpots made sad, sympathetic clucking noises as they moved in for the kill. Men who paid tribute to their wives, even dead ones, were rare creatures.

"She must have been small," someone remarked.

Guests took turns consoling Tex, patting his back kindly and then, unsure of what complicated etiquette dance Emily Post had devised for the situation, patted the urn, too.

"It's not as though you can wait around at the crematorium and then you're presented with a quality urn in some kind of ceremony," Tex explained. "Sure, that's what everyone thinks, but in reality, you have to buy the urn yourself—they don't tell you *that*—and then the ashes arrive whenever Cletus or whoever is running the incinerator that day gets around to sending them. And the delivery itself—well, just imagine the shock: the doorbell rings one morning, and you're faced with the thought, 'I'm standing here holding my spouse in a box sent certified mail.' They just weren't very sensitive." The ladies surrounded him, dosing him with good intentions and fellow feeling and tequila and homemade guacamole (elderly swingers love homemade guacamole). The urn somehow made its way back to the mantel, where it perched on the precipice with its lid askew.

Charlie paused as he lifted his beer to his lips and turned to Verity. "I'm awfully sorry. I didn't know."

Verity clinked her beer bottle with Charlie's and said, "My mother's not dead."

two

it began with the ridiculous, at one of those cocktail parties they lived to have. Craig arranged his Belgian beers in the wine refrigerator, then set the Pilsner and Weiss beer glasses along the countertop. Would people know which glasses went with which beers? He stood back and regarded his handiwork doubtfully. If someone wanted a Stella Artois and all that were left were glasses suitable for a Hoegaarden, he'd never forgive himself.

"Do you think these are okay?" he asked his wife.

Carolyn said, "You have nine thousand glasses. Everything will be fine. Just repeat the calming mantra I taught you." She listened for the baby, hoping she would not awake at the tone of hysteria creeping into Craig's voice.

"Yes, but Will's coming and you know how he likes Chimay Rouge, but I only have two Chimay glasses, so I wonder if I should just hide them until he gets here, or—"

He continued on this road for some time. Carolyn chopped vegetables and wondered if it was too late to change her husband's personality. Lately he had been acting like the depressed oval in that animated Zoloft commercial, which just could not be good for his chi. But she did not want to begrudge him this one interest, this one peculiar and tedious interest in Belgian beer. Of course, he had not always been this neurotic, but ever since the arrival of that new project manager last year, Craig's capacity for insecurity and diffidence had reached critical mass. Each time he had been passed over for a promotion, he acquired new glasses that bore etched names no one could understand, like

Corsendonck and Rochefortoise, and he kept them wrapped in acid-free tissue in a locked cabinet until such events transpired that warranted their use.

"Nice!" he exclaimed suddenly. "Blanche Steendonk! I forgot I had this." He withdrew a bottle from the back of the wine fridge and adjusted the coolant setting to 40.1 degrees, optimum temperature.

The baby had had enough of Brussels' finest and began to wail. Carolyn, in the middle of slicing crudités, paused and rested the heels of her palms against the cutting board. She tapped the point of the knife on the board and turned her gaze to Craig. He rearranged the bottles in the fridge and felt her eyes upon him, but did not move.

"I'll go up," Carolyn said.

The doorbell rang. "I'll get it!" Craig called out and ran to the front door.

Will was the first to arrive and was given a Chimay glass in exchange for his jacket. He was cautioned to hold on to it while Craig admitted other guests. Will poured himself the appropriate beer and sat on the couch, wishing someone would get rid of that smooth jazz playing on the stereo. Why was smooth jazz always on the stereo in this house? It had been playing the last time Will had been there, in March, when he had come over to watch the war on TV, but the baby had been crying so much that it was difficult to follow the play-by-play. He would wait five minutes to see if anyone would dump the smooth jazz, then he'd have a go at it himself. Five minutes—wait patiently—then get up casually and change the station. He had the whole uncontrollable rage thing going on again this morning and did not want a repeat. The entire day had turned out to be moderately bad, mostly because someone had stolen the wash he was doing at the Laundromat— from the washing machine, no less. He suspected this one guy who had this look about him that said, "Give me a reason to kick your ass." So Will did, and the cops were called, but he got out of there through the back door and ran all the way to Kmart, where he bought enough underwear and T-shirts to get him through the week. After he reached his apartment, he realized he had bought a five-pack of irregular tighty-whiteys that he would have to return because they were stained, and that's when he put that hole in his wall.

The girl who had sat down next to him repeated her question. "I said, so what do you do?"

Will said, "I'm a karaoke jockey," and the girl nodded and then got up and left.

carolyn materialized at some point after that. She brought Will a plate of mini French-bread pizzas and sat down next to him, trying to arrange the intricate layers of her artfully ragged skirt around her. Will had not realized until then how hungry he was—it had taken all afternoon to patch the hole in the wall and clean up the mess—or that he hadn't eaten anything since last night.

Carolyn crossed her legs—she was barefoot as usual—and swung her foot back and forth, her anklet of tiny Indonesian prayer bells tinkling softly. She inclined her head toward her feet with a beatific smile—the bells complemented the smooth jazz wonderfully, and everyone knew that smooth jazz was good for balancing the chakras—and said, "Isn't that a relaxing sound? It always reminds me of that spring I was in Jakarta, helping the natives assemble jewelry for export."

"Yes, you sent me a postcard from the Jakarta Hilton. Roughing it, as I remember."

Carolyn said, "Without the jewelry sales, we might not have been able to afford to dig and set up the village's new well."

"You helped dig the well?"

"Of course not. It was important that the villagers 'own' the project, so we had them do all the labor."

The jangling of the prayer bells irritated Will, and he laid a rough hand on her ankle. "Could you stop clanging for a minute?"

"The 'clanging,' as you put it, is good for balancing the chakras. This is a replica of the same exact anklet worn by Gwyneth Paltrow, down to the pavé diamonds, and everyone knows how serene she is." She slipped her foot out of his grasp and swung it with gusto. "You could do with a little serenity yourself. Unless you've decided to attend that rage-o-holic primal scream therapy I told you about."

Will thought if he was going to be stuck in some room with a bunch of men, he'd rather be screaming at them than with them, preferably with his hands around someone's neck.

"I suggested it to Craig, too," Carolyn said, "but he only screams when I fool with the coolant setting of the wine fridge." She watched her husband cross the room, carrying a tray of sweating beers in elaborate bottles. He wore a nervous, stretched smile that looked like a frown. "He needs a good, solid scream, not these frail little freak-outs."

Will said, "Craig had a pretty serious freak-out when you left for Jakarta, having to watch baby Kronos by himself."

"Please." She waved away his words. "My mother was here and did everything, and Kronos was a perfect baby. Anyway, speaking of Craig's freak-outs, now he's been freaking out all week about the Downers Grove reunion."

"I can imagine," said Will.

"Are you going?"

He glanced at her. It was hard for him to visualize far-off events, like the high school reunion two months away. "Maybe. You?"

She nodded. "Did you know Kronos is entering ninth grade there this fall?"

He wondered how many of their other classmates at the fifteenth-year reunion would have a fourteen-year-old preparing to attend the same school. "I wonder if Stan's going. I haven't seen him for years."

"I heard he got married."

"Another one bites the dust," he replied automatically. But

Carolyn merely gave him the tiny pitying smile she gave all of their single friends.

She said, "I want to see Verity. I hope she's still around."

He swallowed the last of the minipizza, which was dry and had sharp crusty edges that irritated his esophageal lining, but then what *didn't* when you suffered from eternal acid reflux? His stomach churned and he knew he would have another beer. "Yes," he said. "I hope so, too." He did a quick calculation in his head: sixty-three days and sixteen hours and ten minutes until the reunion. That was a long time and now that he had made up his mind to go, he knew he would obsess compulsively about the event until it arrived. He saw Craig pass through a group of zombies from his office and he snapped his fingers. "Craig," he said, pointing to his glass. "Hit me?"

Like an eager Labrador, Craig grabbed the glass and fetched another Chimay. Familiar twinges began in Carolyn's jaw as she watched her husband scuttle into the kitchen, and she noted to herself that the radishes on the vegetable platter were terribly bitter.

Will would go to the reunion and if his luck would ever turn, he'd see Verity and Stan, and Craig and Carolyn would be there, and maybe he could figure out how things had ended up the way they had, and it would only take sixty-three days and sixteen hours and nine minutes more. He smiled. See, one minute was gone already.

an hour later, Belgium had exhausted its significance for the night, and Craig began the all-important, repeating-maudlin-things stage of public intoxication. He told Will how sorry he was they never got the chance to watch the war on television together because of the baby.

"Don't worry about it," Will said. "There'll be another one."

"God, I hope not. Carolyn's back on the pill. She gave up holistic birth control, which, by virtue of the baby's arrival, has not really worked out that well."

"I meant another *war,* not another baby." Will had only thirty minutes to sober up before he had to drive back into Chicago from Clarendon Hills for work, and he could not face sobriety with Craig getting mawkish all over the sofa. "Listen, what's with this nonalcoholic jazz? I hate it. Can't we change the station?"

Craig looked forlornly at the stereo. He hated it too, and was *sure* he must have told Carolyn at some point that he hated that station, but it was the only music that calmed the baby during her nightly tantrums. Craig wanted to try having the baby listen to his old CDs, the Psychedelic Furs and Ultravox, but they were locked away in a storage unit somewhere, and Carolyn had never given him the key.

"I don't think she wants me to change the station," he said.

Will did not rebuke his friend for his flaccid response and tactfully changed the subject.

But Craig interrupted him; he leaned in and said, "She threw away all my kitchen magnets, Bettie Page and the robot from *The Day the Earth Stood Still.* And I can't find the address of where the Furs or the Young Fresh Fellows are. The storage unit, I mean." He liked the feeling of the blood rushing to what he was sure was a tumor the size of a grapefruit in his gut; he liked that it proved none of this was in his imagination. He said, "Every time I leave the house, she removes every visible sign that I live here."

Will's shift at the bar started at ten; he drove back to Chicago drunk and nobody stopped him.

three

stan tore around the corner, narrowly missing an old woman in the crosswalk.

"Would you watch out?" Laurel yelled. In the backseat, their boy began to cry. "Oh, don't cry, Sebastian. Look, Mommy's okay. Mommy's smiling! Mommy's not mad at Daddy. Stan, turn around and smile at Sebastian to show him we're not angry."

"I can't turn around, I'm driving the goddamn car."

"Don't *swear* in front of him, you moron."

The light turned green, Stan hit the gas, and the Subaru tore off, tires squealing. Chunky baby chew-books in assorted stages of fug flew around the backseat. He sailed through two red lights, cut off slow elderly drivers, and passed on the double-line all the way to the sitter's house, his menace undercut by the BABY ON BOARD sign.

The sitter was not pleased that they had shown up half an hour before their scheduled time, but she was not surprised because it had happened before.

Laurel unbuckled the boy from his child seat and rushed him to the front door. "Sorry! Stan had an early meeting and forgot to tell me until this morning—he's such an idiot—and our other car is in the shop, and I have to be at work by—"

"Come on, Sebastian." The sitter grimaced and took the boy's hand.

"I'm sorry," Laurel repeated, silently adding, *Please don't take it out on my child.* She smiled sheepishly at the woman but felt like kicking in the door and running through the streets foaming at the mouth like an escaped mental patient. Laurel's days had mutated into hours-long fixations with pleasing the sitter and dying to be cut some slack.

Sebastian wandered into the house without a backward glance and plopped himself in front of the television.

Laurel cleared her throat and tried to smile at the sitter, who was trying to close the door in her face. "Thanks. Um, just reminding you, Stan and I prefer that Sebastian watch only public TV, and only for an hour or so."

"Oh," the sitter said. "Which station is that?"

Before Laurel could answer, the door closed in her face and she jumped back in the car. "Drive; drive!" she screamed at her husband. She swore softly to herself, then loudly, as no little ears were in sight. It was depressing how much better that made her feel.

Once she arrived at work, her mood plummeted from the temporary high brought on by unrestrained profanity. She was only two minutes late, but she'd already missed one call, and her boss stood waiting at the reception area. She opened her mouth to explain, but he held up a hand to stem the flow of excuses.

He said, "What does any of that have to do with me? I hired you to be a receptionist; all I ask is that you're here on time to answer the phone."

Before she turned on the computer, she caught sight of her reflection in the dark monitor and nearly wept. She looked half dead, and the appearance of her hair—a tangled underbrush greasy at the roots and desiccated at the ends—made her want to split her scalp down the middle and peel back the sides of her head like a rubber mask.

She had only eight more hours to go and would earn nine dollars each of those hours, and when she thought of it that way she could not believe seventy-two dollars was worth scalping oneself, but of course, as Stan said, you had to add it up, day after day, and then it would start to make sense.

At this same time, Stan himself was adding up the hours of his day and doodling hangman nooses on his desk blotter. No one was more surprised than he to discover that he was actually good at his job, which was the most depressing thought he'd had in weeks. To have aspired to a career in revolutionary tract publishing, or rock music, or fringe-documentary making, only to discover that you could not make a living at any of those things and were in fact perfectly cut out for middle management was enough to send you for the Leonard Cohen records and a glass full of Drano. Anyway, he rationalized, the bass guitar was too heavy and he always got a kink in his neck after playing, though it was nothing compared to the gargantuan hod of pulsating fat forming between his shoulder blades as he sat, hunched, shrimplike, at his computer.

He'd been promoted four years ago, right before Sebastian was born, and he'd beat out all those dolts in the production services department, too. Like that was something to be proud of.

He relayed the thrillsville news of the promotion to his wife. "Well, I guess I now serve as the single point of accountability for all major cross-functional projects sponsored by the Operations Group, effectively interfacing with the Enterprise Program Management Office and other functional Program Management Offices. I also manage project activities affecting or involving the Operations Group that are part of larger, non-Operations programs."

She said, "That doesn't make any sense."

He said, "I'm a project manager."

"Did you get a raise?"

"Yes, I got a raise, but I have no"—he searched for the phrase—"no cultural capital."

She said, "We can't live on cultural capital. Can I quit when the baby comes?"

He told her no, of course she couldn't quit, he wasn't the president of the company for Christ's sake. He knew Laurel entertained the notion that one day she could quit working and become a full-time poet, a "spoken-word artist," who would recite verse in a bored, black-turtleneck voice at some squat palace or spontaneous freak-gathering spot in Chicago. Life with her post-partum blues was a picnic next to life with a poetry slam partici-pant. This was not callousness, he reminded himself, this was survival. And callousness, too.

Stan opened up his e-mail and went to the calendar, blocking off dates during July for the dinner party and August for the Downers Grove reunion. He was surprised Laurel had agreed to his idea of the party, given that she had never met any of his old friends and was not a big fan of people in general. But, he sup-posed, she occasionally wanted to please him and perhaps wanted to meet some of these people he had talked about over the years.

"Do whatever you want, jackass" is what she had said. Stan and Laurel had been married for six years, and the irony of their names was not lost on them.

He'd contact the DGS alumni coordinator later and get the ad-dresses of Craig and Carolyn, Will, and Verity. He expected that, like many of their classmates, they had all probably moved to Chicago after college, and he momentarily felt the dull ache of jealousy. Oh, he knew they'd rag on him for still living in Down-ers Grove, for his "failure to launch" (the phrase they used for those poor bastards who never left town), but they'd see that he was no longer a mess, that he had a son and had been married for six years, and that suburban life was just as enriching as the city, was just as fun, was just the same seething cauldron of marital accusations and disappointments as anywhere else in the world.

four

verity had accepted much about her life, and with a fair amount of grace considering the void that it was. She accepted her father's unconventional means of dealing with his divorce, she accepted the divorce itself, and she accepted the double duty it demanded on birthdays and at certain family events. Verity even reconciled herself to her career, such as it was, as a cash register operator, or "clerk" as the bookstore called it, which bestowed further Bartleby-esque desperation upon the job. Five years after that inauspicious meeting at the swinger party, she and Charlie were what her dad embarrassingly referred to as "an item," despite a series of personal and professional setbacks that resulted in Charlie's permanent residence in his parents' duplex apartment, and she accepted this. *So I'm a clerk and the daughter of a swinging retired dentist, so what? I accept all that, yet at the same time these are things that are difficult to brag about at a high school reunion,* she thought, staring at the envelope on the table, nestled amid the rest of the day's bills and junk mail.

"Do you know what today is?" she asked Charlie.

"Sure. May twenty-ninth. Ascension Day: the anniversary of when our Lord returned to the mothership."

"Of course; I'd forgotten. But it's also the day that marks the beginning of the end. Take a look at what I just got in the mail this afternoon." She tossed the envelope in his lap and turned to her friend, the refrigerator.

"Ah, yes. Your fifteenth-year high school reunion." He lay back on her sofa and read over the card. "I blew mine off. Wonder where all those jag-offs are now? Oh, well. It's easy to cast asper-sions on the rabble from the triumphant summit of my childhood bedroom."

Verity found the enemy of womankind, low-fat yogurt, in the back of the bottom shelf, a spot ordinarily reserved for her simu-lated pudding treats. "I hate you, refrigerator."

"Are we going? I think it would be fun," he said. "After all, you can learn a lot about a person when you see her in her old high school setting."

"You want to learn something about me? Here." She retrieved the 1988 Downers Grove South High School senior yearbook from her bookshelf and opened to the appropriate page.

"Geez," he said, studying it.

"Believe me, I know."

"Where did I get the idea that you were a cheerleader?"

She shrugged. "Masturbatory beer commercial fantasies?"

He read the notations under her picture. "Hmm . . . AV Club, Home Ec . . . Good God: Mock UN, too? They should have just put 'awaiting the Internet' by your name." Charlie knew what he was talking about; his own high school experience had included Chess Team and Future Scientists of America. "On the other hand, even then you had those sexy cat's-eye glasses. I've always had a thing for cute, new-wave nerd girls."

High school . . . sock hops and whatnot. Verity could not recall if they had actually called their dances "sock hops"; perhaps they were "mixers" or "canteens." Her group of friends, the band geeks and drama club fags—an affectionate slam among friends, connoting nerdliness more so than sexual orientation—had loved the sock hops, and would pogo to anything the DJ played, even Cinderella or Bruce Springsteen. With teenage cynicism they had scoffed at the pep rallies, the sentimentality of year-end student council speeches, and any sport that required a ball and strategy. This was how she remembered those years, in isolated chunks, in earthworm segments, chopped off at both ends, wriggling for a while, then lying still. She had not hated high school, just plodded through it, a four-year bog, hoping for something more interesting on the other side of the swamp.

"I'm not sure going to this reunion is such a hot idea," she said.

Charlie sat up on the sofa. His shirt had become untucked and revealed a cute mound of beer belly. "I can understand that you don't want to go, but what about me? What about me getting to see Downers Grove South High School and all those people you always talked about, and your locker, and where you changed into your AV Club uniform?" His eyes rolled back in his head, rhapsodic over the image.

Attending a school with the word *Downers* in the name should have prepared her for the days of slog she now enjoyed at the bookstore and for acting as quasi caretaker of her lonely dad in his weird dating scene, but one of Verity's earthworm memories was her optimism that real life would improve after high school.

"Let's go," urged Charlie. "It's not until August, and that will give me plenty of time to make up a plausible career to tell your friends about. Maybe I'll say I'm a Web developer."

"But you don't know any of them and I haven't exactly kept in touch the last fifteen years myself."

"All the more reason to go. Plus nobody will know I'm lying about my job. I think you could probably tell the truth about your career; it's okay."

"What career? I'm two steps away from pushing around a grocery cart piled high with garbage bags of salvaged treasure."

"But still, I don't think anyone would make fun of you."

"No, you're probably right," she admitted. "There's nothing to make fun of, because there's nothing there. I'm the most unperson on the planet."

"You know," he said, "I looked forward to lying and bragging at all my own reunions, but I chickened out of attending each time. Don't deprive me of this one opportunity to make something of myself. Come on; it'll be fun. We need some fun." He dragged out the last word, and Verity fiddled with the fraying hem of her blouse.

"We have fun," she said. "Didn't we just go to one of those alkie promo nights at Tuman's Tavern?"

"Yeah, but there weren't any blond identical twins to be found anywhere. Just a guy in a blue grizzly bear costume handing out glow-in-the-dark key chains."

Charlie was a good boyfriend in all the important ways and she felt guilty for dragging him down to her fundamentally morose level. She looked at his eager face, at the pit stains on his too-small baseball jersey, and told him she'd think about it.

Mr. and Mrs. Brown had decided to name their son "Charlie" and drew no associations from the lovable loser of *Peanuts* fame and their thirty-five-year-old son, currently back home with his collection of software T-shirts and his Klingon bible and hundred-sided dice. At the swinger party years ago, he had told Verity about his job as a programmer, flaunted his geek pride in being a "dot-com thousandaire." *Cool,* she'd said, wondering how the urn episode would affect this burgeoning relationship. He shrugged self-deprecatingly, honesty winning out: *At least,* he'd said, *I'm a thousandaire on paper.* It was hard not to fall for earnestness coupled with nerdly good looks. She sat on the thrift-hell sofa and curled into his armpit. The shirt bore a crusty yellow sheen, but Verity didn't mind.

He said, "I stole your last pudding treat."

"That's okay. I guess I shouldn't buy them—what the hell are they even made of?—but they're my guilty pleasure."

He chuffed her lightly on the shoulder. "That's silly, guilty pleasure. Who in the world is above their own taste?"

Verity picked velour lint dreads out of her sofa and said nothing. That *was* a silly phrase, and not among her usual arsenal of rhetoric. How could she be above her own taste? She lived in an apartment full of junk, each piece of furniture and clothing, each semifunctional appliance, each weird and wonderful tchotchke rescued from garage sales, thrift stores, church bazaars—all of it cataloged, fairly neat, and loved.

Charlie checked his watch. Verity worked the second shift at the bookstore on Thursday nights and would have to leave soon. He'd take the Chicago Avenue bus with her and then get off downtown to transfer to the Red Line for the long trip home to Rogers Park. His mother was making turkey meat loaf tonight, and his stomach started to growl. Verity, in no rush to get to work, curled closer to him and nuzzled his neck.

Charlie was aware of a sudden and urgent stirring in his trousers. How could this be happening mere moments after thinking of meat loaf and his mother? What kind of a sicko was he?

"Meat loaf," he muttered, instructing his brain to send the appropriate message into his pants.

"Excuse me?" said Verity. She had felt the sudden and urgent stirring as well.

"Meat loaf," he said louder, staring at his lap.

She grinned. "That isn't even a single entendre, bub," she said and nuzzled all thoughts of meat loaf and mama right out of him.

barnes & noble sat on a corner downtown near the Water Tower, and its three floors remained busy from open to close. A seven-year veteran of the store, Verity had once thought of Barnes & Noble as a stepping-stone to grad school or even owning her own bookshop. She now thought of it as a building she would enter every day until she died of despair.

It was typical of Charlie to ride all the way with her to work, then take another train home. Tex always said, "That guy is a real gentleman." She knew he was a real gentleman, a real gentleman who lived with his parents.

Team Leader Joe approached the checkout desk and chastised her for sitting on a stool behind the counter. "I think we've discussed—oh, maybe a hundred times now—that it does not look very businesslike for the team to be perceived as slacking off. It creates a sense of unease in the guests when they see seated clerks." Exasperated, he ran a hand through his perm and stomped off. Verity rose from her stool and silently grabbed her own throat and choked herself. A guest with book in hand watched warily.

"Easy, there," cautioned fellow clerk Bob. "Our workman's comp doesn't cover self-inflicted strangulation."

"How about murder?" asked Verity. The guest handed her the book and looked for affirmation in her eyes, as did so many who bought this, Dr. Phil's latest.

"I get the feeling we have a Dr. Phil book quota, like cops giving out speeding tickets at the end of the month," she muttered.

The guest departed and Bob sneered at the Dr. Phil display dump. "I'd like to kick that mustache into the back of his skull. *Self Matters.* Please. Since when?"

Bob—unkindly known as Van Gogh around the staff room due to an ear wound sustained during Vietnam—made Verity's tenure at the store less demoralizing. His dislike of the customers, his refusal to call them "guests," the obscenities he jotted down and passed to her whenever someone asked for the inspirational books, his homemade T-shirt that read "I served in Quang Tri '68 and all I got was this stupid T-shirt and my ear blown off," and the misanthropy that extended to all except his wife, two of his children, and Verity Presti, combined to form an acid-tongued, blowhard personality with a soft, marshmallow filling. Had he advertised for love in the personals and carried around an urn of cigarette ashes, Verity would have called him paternal.

"Bob, I'm going to have a thrombo. I just got an invitation to my fifteenth-year high school reunion," she blurted.

"Do not go," Bob said. "Case closed, thrombo averted."

She sank back onto the prohibited stool and gently banged her head on the counter. "Suddenly, I feel old."

"Oh, get outta here. *I'm* the one who's now wearing bifocals whenever I'm awake, which is really breaking down my elaborate denial mojo about getting older. You're just gearing up for a nightmare, midlife crisis-inducing class reunion. Don't go if it bothers you so much."

"I don't want to, but Charlie does. He thinks it'll be fun."

"Well, yeah, it's always fun to go to other people's reunions and laugh at the losers and get tanked. It's not fun for the reunionees."

"No kidding. My great passion in life is thrifting, Bob. That's not the kind of thing you can bring up at a reunion. 'What have you been doing all these years?' 'Oh, well, I picked up this fantastic portable bowling alley at the Salvation Army and I also have a closet full of crocheted beer-can hats.' It *is* impressive, yes, but only to a small portion of society."

"You don't have to impress those jackasses! Who the hell are *they*?"

She sighed and picked at her cuticles. "I know, I know. But here's the thing: I don't feel like explaining myself to people I haven't seen in fifteen years. Nobody would understand that I'm satisfied just being a bookstore clerk."

Bob looked over his bifocals at her.

"I *am* satisfied," she insisted. "I mean, fine: I may have considered getting my master's in English literature once, but the thought of scrutinizing Pope, Swift, and Johnson day and night charmeth me nay. I'm not good at it and I wouldn't fit in with literary types." She gestured around the store at the customers to make her point. As she did so, a man approached the counter with a copy of *Chicken Soup for the Soul*. He stared at her while she rang up his purchase, then said, "Thanks, chubs," when she handed him his receipt.

Outraged, Bob tried to hop the counter, hit his knee, and let loose a flood of vulgarities. Verity told him to forget it; he was on disciplinary probation for chasing customers out of the store, and she didn't want him to lose his job.

Her imagination clicked on; the old creative AV enthusiast with perfect attendance woke up. As she watched the customer walk away, she wondered if it was possible to look up his address from his credit card information. She would show up at his front door dressed in a nice suit as if she was someone important and then she would walk in and shoot him in the stomach. She'd choose a small-caliber gun, perhaps a .22; he wouldn't die, but the impact would put him on the floor and make a mess of his insides and his carpeting. Then she could drag him to the banister of his staircase, handcuff him to the railings, and call his wife to inform her that her husband had been shot and was near death. Then she would rip the phone out of the wall and go home.

Bob said, *"Chicken Soup for the Soul,* my ass. I'd like to take a pot of boiling chicken soup and shove it down his fucking throat. Anyway, Verity honey, I can't see you in the competitive world of grad school. You're way too nice."

charlie saw a beautiful woman on the El ride home, the kind of woman he could instantly fall in love with if he was not already in love with Verity. She had dark hair past her shoulders, thick and wavy but not at all like his own fright wig. He wanted to say she had nut-brown skin but decided that sounded unflattering and maybe even racist; it drew attention to the fact that she was black—not that it mattered—but maybe dwelling on her race was not good form. But then neither was leering at her, and he felt ashamed and guilty for being so hormone-driven, and he looked out the window as punishment.

Yet she was so beautiful. He stole another look; he could not help himself. As the train jounced along he felt his jowls jiggling. Halfhearted anger boiled in him at the thought that a gorgeous woman like that could never love an ugly mug like him, which was beside the point as he already loved someone else and she loved him, and God knows Verity was beautiful, just in a different way.

The woman on the train must have felt neurotic eyes burning into the back of her head; perhaps the hair on her lovely, slender neck stood up, a psychic warning that someone mentally unwell was afoot. She turned slightly to look at Charlie, but he immediately hid his face in his book, afraid she would think he was leering, or that she would see his dead tooth.

He got off the El at Jarvis and walked home. He had eaten a

cheeseburger at lunch and now had cheerleader fat guilt. Also those chocolate doughnuts that looked so good in the staff cafeteria that morning didn't really look that good after sitting on his desk all day, but he had eaten them anyway. Diet pills didn't seem to help with the stress-eating that came with temping at some hellhole place that had no intention of hiring you. He once asked Verity to find him a book at the store, *It's Not What You're Eating, It's What's Eating You,* but she just looked at him like he was crazy or must be joking, so he pretended he was joking because, let's be honest, who wants to date a man who reads obesity self-help books? Life as a shut-in seemed more and more attractive. Charlie mused about potential strategies he might try in order to qualify for Meals on Wheels and never have to leave the house again.

"Charlie!" his mother bellowed the second he set foot over the threshold. "You left your room a disaster area! If I've said it once, I've said it a million times: just make the bed, just clean up once in a while."

He took off his shoes and placed them next to his father's orthopedic clogs. "Sorry. I was running late."

"What's new at sea? They're catching fish," she replied.

A man had been murdered in their apartment more than fifty years ago, at least as the Rogers Park lore would have it. This went a long way toward explaining his home's omnipresent negative atmosphere, his mother's unprovoked aggression, and the reason his life was going nowhere. Ghosts could do that to you— hold you back, haunt and torment the living, of whom they were so envious; he'd read about it. The day after he became a dot-com casualty and moved back into his parents' apartment, he saw the apparition disappear into the vent above the stove and his father said, "He's been lonely here. Misery loves company."

He turned toward the stairs, but stopped when he heard the unmistakable sound of an oven mitt being thrown down, gauntlet-style. "Now where are you going? We're eating in five seconds."

He said, "Just going to change my shirt and wash my hands."

"Thank God I did the laundry, or else you wouldn't have a clean shirt to change into, not that I mind."

Charlie did not know what this meant. Should he *not* change his shirt, *not* go upstairs? For guidance he looked to his father, who was carefully laying a game of solitaire on the family room table, an exemplar of ostentatious nonintervention.

"The turkey meat loaf is getting cold!" his mother screamed, and threw the oven mitts in the air.

team leader joe announced in an uncharacteristic display of generosity and morale-building sentiment, "Free fishwiches on your break."

Verity's dinner hour came at eight and by that time the lone fishwich left on the plate had assumed the condition and color of a corpse in livor mortis. But it was free, and she could not resist the siren song of free food left out on a table. She ate her meal, chewing the fish a disconcerting number of times until it finally collapsed into a manageable bolus of gristle, and withdrew from her cardigan pocket the reunion announcement. Funny how simply reading certain words could resurrect memories and emotions she assumed were dead—but to her dismay she found them neatly recorded and wriggling like maggots in her brain.

The memories of Downers Grove South, Craig and Carolyn, Will and Stan, faded as Team Leader Joe barged into the staff room. "There's a lady out here asking for you." Team Leader Joe had a "thing" about friends coming to visit his team at the workplace, but this old broad outside looked like she had money to burn and plus she was holding a giant box of Godiva chocolates and two copies of *Who Moved My Cheese?*

Verity recognized the woman at the register giving Bob the once-over as one of her dad's swinger friends from Downers. Verity braced herself for the fake smile and extremely awkward hug. She knew Fran was going to make conversation. Suburban etiquette demanded it.

"So nice to see you again, dear. Tex told me you worked here, so I thought I'd pop in," she said. "What do you think of this for his birthday?" She pointed to *Who Moved My Cheese?*

"It's a very popular book," Verity said.

"Yes, and since he's contemplating so many lifestyle changes right now, I thought it was appropriate that we each had a copy. Of course," she added, eyes straying to the Dr. Phil dump, "maybe a different one would be better. Perhaps we could browse the self-help books together."

"I'm not allowed to leave my worker containment field."

Fran paused, then firmly pushed the books toward the register. "About those lifestyle changes? Your dad has intimated that he's ready to settle down."

For years Verity had tried to erect a blockade from her mind to her mouth, but she imploded it constantly. "Please don't say 'intimated' in the same sentence as 'dad.' It's like saying 'grandpa' and 'thong.' I can't even wrap my brain around it." Bob, flaunting store policy, pulled up a stool to watch the show.

Fran misinterpreted Verity's attitude and said, "Oh, don't worry, dear. I have no intention of taking Thelma's place. Gone, but not forgotten, I know all that."

Verity detected vinegar in Fran's words, but smiled suddenly, seeing an out. She said, "My mother's not dead."

"Well, not in the important sense, of course. We all stay alive if someone we love remembers—"

"No, no," she clarified, "she's really not dead, just divorced. She lives in Downers Grove with my stepfather in a restored Georgian colonial. My dad carries around old cigarette ashes in an urn because he can't accept it. It's nothing to worry about; he's not a kook or anything."

Fran goggled while something dry and unpleasant got caught in her throat. The corners of her lips fought the tremors laying siege to them, but eventually surrendered, and she finally mumbled, "I . . . I don't understand."

"Trust me," Verity said, "no one does."

Bob rang up the woman's items before she could escape, and,

head swimming, she clutched her packages and stumbled drunk-enly, soused on too much information, toward the escalator.

Staving off Bob's rash of prying questions, Verity said, "Don't *ask*. She's just one of Dad's ravenous middle-aged girlfriends. According to sources"—Verity shuddered—"Fran's the most amorous of the bunch."

Bob watched Fran negotiate the escalator, her face still frozen in a palsied grimace. He said, "I'd rather have a lap dance from Trent Lott."

Verity straightened up the magazines and Godiva chocolate bars littering the desk, muttering, "I don't know. Maybe he *is* a kook."

He said, "Honey, if my wife died, I'd carry her ashes around in an urn, too."

She said, "Yes, but my mother—"

"I know, I know, she's not dead. But all the same, it's a kind of romantic notion your father has, if slightly twisted. Think you'll be in trouble for outing the urn?"

Oh, she'd be in big trouble with Tex now, for sure. Nothing en-sured his success with the ladies like the widower-with-ashes routine.

five

"so, still temping these days, Charlie?" Tex asked.

Charlie wished Tex would change the channel. At these family get-togethers, Tex cloistered himself in the family room and watched golf on TV until he was dragged to the dinner table. "Yeah."

"Something will open up for you soon, I know it. It's too bad you're not interested in teeth because I still have quite a few friends in the dental industry."

There was a dental industry? Charlie imagined dentists getting blotto at dental textbook release parties and hobnobbing with one another at prophylaxis seminars.

Verity walked in. "Soup's on." Charlie sprang up from the leather sofa and barreled past her into the dining room, a flock of shrill pug dogs in his wake. Tex sat glued to the tube, refusing to acknowledge his daughter, the spoiler of romance, the revealer of secrets.

"Dad?" Verity waited a few moments as her father scratched his ear and stared up at the ceiling, obviously primed for another bout of paternal melodrama. "Dad! Come on, dinner's ready."

He said, "I'm not speaking to you."

Verity sent a ferocious gust of wind through flared nostrils.

Thelma stomped into the room and shouted, "Dinner is *ready!* Get in here." She stood with her hands on her slim hips, glaring.

Tex faced a quandary. He was determined not to speak to his daughter, and as usual he refused to speak to his ex-wife, but he was hungry. He unleashed his fury on an innocent pro golfer in eleventh place, screaming, "Shanked it, jerko!" at the television. He charged past Verity and Thelma and threw himself into the chair next to Charlie at the table. Thelma looked at her daughter, perplexed.

"He's not talking to me, either, Mom," she said.

"Oh," Thelma replied. "You told someone about the urn, didn't you?"

The dining room at the Rasmussen home was tastefully decorated in shades of genteel lameness. The table and chairs, antiques with well-worn mahogany patina and turned legs, gave off a sort of folksy opulence, not too *too*, of course, but still quite beautiful and "family oriented," as Thelma liked to say. The chandelier, huge and brass and intense, cast both light and deep shadows on those who sat beneath it. The rug (Tex could describe it with his eyes closed, so often had he studied it while Thelma spoke) cost more than Verity's car, and its crimson and navy Oriental design camouflaged years of pug-related bodily functions.

Charlie helped himself to the salad and wished there was some meat in it. Out of his periphery, he saw Tex fiddle absently with his knife, pointing it in Thelma's direction, and he thought to himself for the hundredth time that of all the divorced couples he knew—sadly his own parents were not among them—Thelma and Tex were the most peculiar. The first time he came to dinner at Thelma and Dick's, he was shocked to see Tex in the family room.

Verity had explained. "Mom feels bad that he's all alone and has no one to eat with, so she invites him to Sunday dinners and holidays, and he always comes; he just won't acknowledge her presence." Charlie had stared at her in befuddlement.

Over time, Tex had grudgingly brought himself to address Dick, as in "You've done wonders with your rec-room paneling, Mr. Rasmussen," calling him by his surname when any other fool would get much more pleasure out of snarling *Dick* at the end of every sentence. But Tex was not vulgar, just sensitive and resistant to his plight as a reluctantly divorced gentleman.

Tex took a mouthful of salad. Mmm, raspberry vinaigrette with celery seeds, his favorite. He glanced at Dick. "The salad is wonderful. Please send my compliments to Mrs. Rasmussen."

Dick, game as ever, smiled at Thelma and said, "Mrs. Rasmussen, Mr. Presti sends his compliments regarding the wonderful salad."

Thelma, usually more than happy to blast Tex out of his courteous communication system by addressing him directly, decided to have a little fun herself. "Oh, thank you, Mr. Rasmussen, but please tell Mr. Presti that it was actually Miss Presti who made the salad."

"Mr. Presti," began Dick, but Tex cut him off.

"On second thought," Tex amended, "it could use a little meat."

Verity rubbed her temples while pugs salivated on her sneakers.

"The dressing is good," agreed Thelma, glancing at her daughter, "but a bit sweet and oily for my taste."

"Mom, where's Diana?" Verity asked.

Her mother barked a short laugh. She explained that her disappointment of a daughter was not interested in "bogus family dinners" and had retreated to the basement, where she was probably at this moment listening to the type of music that made children kill themselves.

"Cool," said Verity.

Thelma drummed her fingernails on the tablecloth and wondered, not for the first time, how Diana—her and Dick's daughter, not a single chain of Tex DNA in her—could have inherited so much of the Presti bad attitude.

Verity thought about her young half sister and felt a moment's flood of relief that she would not have to interact with her today. She supposed there were a lot of siblings who had nothing in common, who shared some blood and nose shapes and eye color, and nothing of themselves. There must have been hundreds of women like her who also viewed the birth of said sibling as the event that finally pushed one's dad over the edge into insanity. Thousands.

After dinner, Verity cleared the table and Thelma brought out sugar-free Jell-O for dessert.

Verity wobbled the gelatin. "Mom, do you have any whipped cream or anything?"

"Well, I'm sorry my dessert isn't good enough for you *as is,* but we don't use whipped cream in our home; it's not exactly nutritious."

Dick, ordinarily a good sport about the constant presence of his wife's relatives in his house and her abnormal relationship with all of them, banged his fork down on the table. "Oh, for God's sake, Thel, get the girl some Cool Whip. We have a whole tub of it in the freezer."

Thelma blinked at Dick, and complicated layers of ice chilled the room. She rose, retrieved the Cool Whip, and set down the plastic container in front of Verity with a spoon. "Have at it."

To Thelma's consternation, the family waited patiently for their turns with the tub, too. She watched it make its route around the table and said, "It's just that . . ."

Oh, Jesus God! Verity ground her teeth, emitting a creaking groan heard around the room. "Yes, Mom, it's just that what?"

"Now you don't have to get snippy, but it's just that I know it's hard to get healthy when you eat too much sugar, that's all." She spread her arms wide with an innocent smile to show just how painless her helpful advice could be.

"I'm not on a diet; thanks anyway." She spooned another heaping glob of Cool Whip on her Jell-O; no one had ever slathered whipped topping with such pornographic zeal.

"Diet? Who's talking about a diet?" Thelma's voice rose to an unnatural pitch, as it did whenever she lied. "I'm just talking about good habits for life. I'm talking about *health.*"

"Really? Health? That's interesting, because I've been thinking I might take a knife and disembowel myself. It would be a great relief to feel the contents of my guts falling out of my body onto the street, plus I'd lose some weight."

Thelma gasped. "What is the matter with you? All I was talking about was good health—"

"Mom, all you ever talk about is losing weight. I'm not skinny and I don't care, so just get over it."

Dick returned to ignoring everyone, as he had heard this specific discussion a number of times and was no longer interested in refereeing. Tex, however, was determined to become a full participant in the scene they were evidently having and scanned the room for an ally to whom he was currently speaking.

"Charlie," he said, "would you please tell Mrs. Rasmussen that Miss Presti is beautiful just the way she is?"

"Uh . . ." Charlie's mouth was full of Cool Whip.

Luckily, Verity felt a wet nose on her ankle and saw a chance to change the subject. "Hi, Snaps," she said and bent down to pet the little dog.

"That's Nipper," admonished Thelma. "Snaps is right here." She pointed to one dog amidst a heaving mass of identical animals eating out of the Cool Whip bowl on the floor. Verity fake-smiled and Thelma did the same. All was forgiven. Dick and Tex sighed with relief and pushed their chairs back from the table. There was a buzzing in Verity's head as she watched Thelma feed the dogs from her plate. In this house, all was always forgiven.

six

will met verity in the cafe-
teria sophomore year. He and Stan walked in together and entered the part of the cafeteria known as the Dark Side, as it was
dimly lit, lacked sufficient tables, and stood divided from the
main dining area. It was a well-known bit of DGS trivia that some
students preferred to take their meals in the Dark Side to avoid
the discussions (reputed to be long, sports oriented, and hostile)
that characterized meals in the cafeteria.

"Who are you meeting?" Will had asked him.

"These girls from my Psych class. We've been assigned a group
project." Stan spotted them in the darkest corner and waved.

The first thing Will noticed about Verity was that her lunch
tray was piled high with Funyuns, and that she had a creepy mad
scientist/sexy Belinda Carlisle thing going on.

"This is the superhero I came up with." Stan sat down and slid
a notebook toward the girls. "I don't have a name for him yet, but
he's a metaphysical emotional warrior. He uses his emotional
powers to combat evildoers who make citizens unhappy."

"This is your Psych class assignment? Making up super-
heroes?" Will asked.

Stan shrugged. "What can I say? Mr. Reese is a progressive
guy." He cocked his head at Verity. "We're very accelerated in
that class, aren't we? Of course, we're advanced in so many
ways." Then he winked at her, a ridiculous gesture coming from
any other fifteen-year-old boy, but one that looked preternaturally
cool on him. Pink spots appeared on her cheeks, and she shoved
her glasses up the bridge of her nose with one finger. He asked

her for her ideas, but she shook her head and began to bounce a Hacky Sack from palm to palm. She tried to cover her notebook with her elbow. "Come on, Verity," Stan said, "I can see you have something written there. What is it?" He gave her the flirty half-smile that always worked.

She looked down at the pages, and her cat's-eye glasses slid down the bridge of her nose again. A muscle twitched in her jaw, accompanied by a long, grating creak.

She said, "Bruxor."

Stan blinked. Flirty smile gone. "What? What is that?"

"Bruxor. He grinds his teeth."

"Teeth grinding is his superpower?"

"Technically, it's called bruxing."

He stared at her. "What does he do? How does he help mankind by gnashing his teeth?"

Verity bobbled the Hacky Sack in her hand a few times, then closed her notebook. "I haven't gotten that far yet."

Will suggested, "Maybe Bruxor's grinding is supersonic. The noise drives evildoers insane."

"Great. Clearly, we're going to get an F." Stan turned his attention to the other girls.

Will looked at Verity, at those bright green eyes that had trained themselves on Stan with an unreadable expression. "I think it's a good superhero. Bruxor. Sure, why not? I'll tell you something, I wish I had super tooth-gnashing ability."

She opened her mouth and popped out a clear plastic mouth guard, the molar edges worn down. She said, "I'm great at it."

Having reached an impasse on the heroic capabilities of Bruxor, they parted ways after lunch. Will spotted Verity at the end of the day on the quad, reading. She explained she was waiting for her friend Carolyn, who was under the bleachers at the moment with her boyfriend, Craig.

Will said, "The bleachers, eh? There's something about firmly established sexual relationships between sophomores that makes me want to throw up."

"Funyun?" she offered him the remains of the bag.

It was early October and the late afternoon air had turned chilly. Verity pulled out of her backpack a candy pink cardigan and slipped it on. One sleeve dangled four inches below the other.

"Little trouble with the pattern," she explained, then kicked a Hacky Sack at him. They talked, and he tried to volley it with her for a while, but her every shot went flying into the buckeyes at the quad's edge, when she managed to make contact with the bag at all.

"You made that sweater?"

She shrugged: no big deal. Will noticed that whenever she shrugged, the movement drew attention to what he could only think of as an astounding rack. He tried to ask her other ambiguous, shrug-inducing questions. "Not too many girls know how to knit, do they?"

"I can knit, thanks to Home Ec, but I'm not good. I get distracted from the pattern. Sleeves are the worst. That's when I lose my enthusiasm and throw the thing in my closet with guilt-ridden finality."

"Well, can't you fix the mistakes?"

She paused, letting the beanbag fall to the ground at her feet. "I don't know how, and anyway I'd rather just move on. I knitted my dad a sweater vest for his birthday. It was supposed to have a tooth on the front, you know, with bloody roots, like it had just been yanked. Except when I added the red yarn to the pattern for the blood, I forgot what I was doing and added the stitches onto the top of the tooth instead of the roots. So it turned out to be a tooth on fire."

Will could not imagine why the bloody tooth was somehow preferable to the tooth on fire. "Seems like a lot of hard work down the tubes."

"No, he wears it. He thinks it's got 'panache.' His dental patients think he's nuts, but in a lovable way."

Coppery sunlight filtered in through the trees, and a cold wind blew in from the north. Verity tied the pink sweater around her head, explaining that uncovered heads accounted for 80 percent of body heat loss.

Will cleared his throat, preparing to ask her out, when she kicked the bag up into her own face, knocking off her glasses.

"I'm an idiot," she said, retrieving the glasses from the ground.

"No, you're not. I've done the same thing myself."

"But you don't even wear glasses," she said.

"I meant—"

She waved off his words. "Yeah, I know what you meant." She looked off toward the school exit and said, "Great. There's Stan, he's waving. Laughing, too. Nice. 'Yes, it's me. Yes, I did just kick myself in the face with the Hacky Sack.' " She pantomimed the conversation across the quad. " 'No, go ahead; laugh! It's funny, everybody laugh! Look at the monkey, she's a goddamn idiot.' " She turned to Will. "I am *such* a desperate dork."

"Maybe he didn't recognize you."

She pointed to the pink sweater wrapped around her head, evidence that no one else could be mistaken for this desperate dork.

"Oh, right. Well, why do you care what he thinks?" But even as he said it, he knew. This is how it always was with Stan. In answer, Verity put her hands over her heart and slowly lifted them, lowered them, lifted them again. Thump-thump. Then she gave a careless shrug, grinned crookedly, and resumed her summit with the beanbag.

Will watched her, and warmth flooded his face while a mistral rose up in his chest like the beating of wings. He smiled in the slanting rays of fading light. She was the worst Hacky Sack player he had ever seen.

seven

"verity is another word for truth," Tex had told her when she was young. "I picked out your name because I always want us to tell each other the truth. Understand?"

Tex kept up his end of the bargain by occasionally calling her *bella paffuta*. "The words mean 'beautiful fatness,' but it's like saying, 'pretty, chubby girl.' It's a compliment." He learned this and other complimentary Italian phrases from his own father, who had been an immigrant. Verity had never met her grandfather, but she felt that she would have disliked him.

Tex's own name had been conferred upon him in his twenties, by friends who teased him about a pair of green shit-kickin' boots, back when the suburbs boasted few men in cowboy attire. The move from John to Tex was seamless, and even his own parents made the switch without a fuss. At least, that was his story, and everyone knew Tex always told the truth.

Charlie entered Verity's apartment and found her struggling to pull a handkerchief shirt over her head. Of all the clothes she had made, this one ranked high on Charlie's list. It had been patched together from antique hankies, some monogrammed, some embroidered with colored borders or flowers, all of them constructed of sheer, lightweight cotton. Okay, you could see her bra through it and the neckline was cut very low, but that was not all Charlie liked about it; the shirt itself was cool and completely original.

"Little tight," she said, forcing it over her chest. Her dark blond hair flashed out in static and clung to her eyeglasses.

"No such thing." He watched her apply bright red lipstick

(girls putting on lipstick drove him wild) and brush her silky hair into a little flip. Ohhh, he groaned inwardly, sex-kitten librarian-type girls . . .

Verity turned from the mirror. "What's the matter? You look like you're having a stroke."

He regained his composure and adjusted his pants.

She continued. "Listen. Don't be mad, but my dad wants to come out with us tonight."

"Oh. All right."

"I'm sorry, it's just that he's been dating some new screwball he found through the personals and he wants to introduce us, and I can't bear it alone."

"He's bringing a date? That's fine, I guess."

"Wait," she said. "It gets worse. They want to go to a kara-oke bar."

verity and charlie stood outside Kit-Kat Karaoke in Buck-town, waiting for Tex and his date to park her car. Calling out encouragement and direction from the curb, Tex guided her gigan-tic SUV into the spot with a series of undecipherable hand motions.

"Good job!" he exclaimed as she bumped the VW Bug behind her and turned off the engine.

"Good God," muttered Verity. A bumper sticker on the SUV read ANKH IF YOU LOVE ISIS.

Tex made the introductions. Carol, a tall woman with short, dyed red hair, subaquatic in style, shook Verity's hand and smiled. Small, pointy teeth gleamed in the lamplight. Charlie reached for her hand, too, then caught sight of a corn vendor pushing his cart down the opposite sidewalk. "One minute," he excused himself. *"Señor Elotes!"* He chased the vendor, waving a dollar bill in his hand.

Tex said, "All set for some karaoke, babe?" and squeezed Carol's shoulders.

Please don't say "babe," thought Verity. Carol wore black suede trousers, though it was June, and a black silk shirt. Her skin was so pale it was almost transparent, and she wore a large silver moon on a chain around her neck. Tex, in contrast, wore his old flaming-tooth sweater vest and looked as though he had put styling product in his mustache.

Charlie returned munching a corncob-on-a-stick that dripped mayonnaise, salt, and cayenne down his chin. As they headed toward the bar, Verity said, "You just called that guy 'Mr. Corn.'"

Charlie said, "At least I was polite. Anyway, I couldn't resist the pull of the *elotes*. Sweet, heavenly *elotes*."

Once inside Kit-Kat Karaoke, or the KKK as it was more troublingly known, the four of them made their way to the bar for drinks, then to a table in the back. Carol excused herself to the ladies' room and the moment she was out of sight, Tex turned to his daughter with eager eyes.

"Well? What do you think?"

Verity tried to dredge up some enthusiasm for the Isis devotee while Charlie wiped a river of mayo from his lips and gave Tex the thumbs-up.

"Isn't she wonderful?" Tex sighed. "You know, I still carry around the personal ad she placed two weeks ago. I want to keep it as a memento in case we ever get married."

Verity said, "Already you're getting married? You just met her."

"So? You never know." He removed the newspaper clipping from his wallet and gazed at it happily. "We have so much in common. We both like Chopin and clambakes and moonlit walks."

"What are you talking about, Dad? You don't like any of those things. And I've never seen you walk anywhere. You hate walking."

He ignored her. "And she loves wine and dancing *and garage sales.*" He saved this delicacy for last, hoping to impress his daughter.

"Yeah, but is she one of those garage salers who secretly longs to be an antiquer? Because if she is, then that's no good, Dad. Antiquers always think shopping at a thrift store is gross, and if I were you, I'd try to weed out the nose-wrinklers as soon as possible."

Tex continued undaunted, having heard Verity's treatise on thrift-culture reverse snobbery many times before. "The only thing I don't understand"—he took out his reading glasses and peered at the ad—"is what a 'vampire lifestylist' is."

Carol appeared at the table just as Verity choked on her beer and Charlie spewed corn kernels down the front of his shirt.

An announcement came over the sound system, declaring that the karaoke jockey was going on break and would be back in fifteen minutes to take your karaoke requests.

"I think I'll sing 'Oh, Susannah,' " said Tex.

Verity flagged a passing waitress. "Another Heineken, please." A vampire lifestylist? This is what comes of dragging out an urn of fake burial ashes at every opportunity. She scanned her father's neck for bite marks.

"Tex tells me you knitted this vest for him," Carol remarked. "It's very beautiful, Verity. You're quite talented." Tex beamed.

"Thanks." She felt a pounding in her temples. How does one converse normally with a vampire? "I had a little problem with the tooth. It wasn't actually supposed to be on fire—well, it's a long story."

"I *like* it this way," Tex insisted. "It's distinctive. It has real panache."

Carol said, "You know, I've long had a fascination with teeth myself. When your dad replied to my ad and said that he was a dentist, I thought, 'Now, here's the guy for me.' I had just recently had some dental work done and it had taken a while to get my teeth looking just right." She smiled and leaned closer to the small lamp on the table, revealing two extremely sharp and pointed canines. "Not bad, huh?"

Verity asked, "You had those . . . sharpened?"

"Yes, and I had the ends bonded a little. To give me some length."

"Of course." What good are sharp canines without length? The waitress handed her the beer and she shot the tankard at once. Tex proclaimed modern dentistry to be marvelous. In spite of the noise of the KKK, an uncomfortable silence descended on the foursome. Charlie smiled at Carol. Carol smiled at Verity. Verity picked the dried mousse out of Tex's mustache.

Charlie cleared his throat. "I've always considered teeth and dentistry fascinating, too. For example, if I go without brushing my teeth, I find that pop starts to taste bad. But when I brush my teeth, pop regains its great taste. This is absolutely true and I have no reasoning for it."

Something must be said for the sixth sense, because even as Verity struggled to grasp this bizarre unfolding of dental and vampiric secrets, she felt eyes boring into the back of her skull. She looked back over her shoulder and met the gaze of a tall, lean man with a black crew cut and black brow, standing at the corner of the bar. Unsmiling and sharp-featured, he might have been called handsome if not for the thin veneer of hostility in his eyes. Verity began to turn from him when suddenly he smiled, the hostility fell away, and he became Will Demske, former Downers Grove classmate and onetime sort-of flame.

She rose from her chair and made it over to the bar before she blurted out her own orthodontia nightmares. Orchestrating the greeting proved challenging, as she was not a hugger and shaking hands seemed so cheesy. Will, too, wrestled with this same ordeal, evidenced by their eventual compromise: grasping each other's elbows and forearms in a minimal contact embrace.

He announced straight off: "I'm the karaoke jockey here. I just wanted to have that out in the open."

"Don't sweat it; I'm a cashier," she said.

The hard lines at the edges of his mouth relaxed into an easy grin.

She said, "So this reunion thing . . ."

"Yeah," he said, "I'm going. You?"

"I guess."

"You get the thing from Stan?" He watched her closely. Her bearing stiffened and she blinked rapidly, but that was all.

"What thing?"

"Never mind. You will." As he said it, he rested his hand on her shoulder. She let it stay for a second; it was heavy and her pulse beat against it. Then she lowered her shoulder, slipped out from his grasp, and led him back to her table.

Will and Verity happened upon the group in mid oral examination.

"Yes, indeed, I see it." Tex crouched over Charlie and poked around. "A little white bump over number twenty. In the old days we called that a gumboil. Pus drainage from an infection is really what it is."

Perspiration beaded on Charlie's forehead. He appreciated Tex's spur-of-the-moment dental exams, but he had never grown accustomed to another man's hands in his mouth. His eyes traveled over to his girlfriend, who had arrived at the table with a tall, good-looking dude, and felt himself at a disadvantage.

Verity, who was used to Tex's public dental appraisals, made the introductions unself-consciously. "Dad, this is my friend Will from high school. You might remember—"

Tex held a palm up and wrinkled his brow in Will's direction. "Don't tell me . . . chip on a central incisor. No nerve damage. Simple bond."

"Good memory, Mr. Presti." Will smiled, showing him the repaired front tooth. "Still in decent shape, too."

Charlie gurgled in an attempt to dislodge Tex's other hand, which the older man did, and then wiped on his vest.

Verity continued. "Carol, vampire lifestylist," to which Carol shook her head modestly, as though she had been introduced as "genius" or "Nobel Peace Prize winner." And finally, "Charlie, my boyfriend."

Charlie rose instantly, upsetting the edge of the table with his beer belly and spilling the remainder of his drink. *No matter*, he thought; *this is what men did, was it not? They faced up and squared off, and any imbecile could see that this choad Will was slavering after Verity.* They shook hands and Charlie stared up at the other man. He had never realized before how much taller six foot two was than five foot eight.

Even as Will sat down, Charlie could sense the questions boiling beneath the surface. This was one reason he always avoided parties, for that inevitable moment when he'd have to explain to strangers who he was and what he did, and he was goddamned if he was going to do *that* anymore.

"So, Charlie, what do you do?" Will asked.

Charlie had come up with a rather clever way of heading off this particular train. "What do I do? Well, I enjoy painting miniatures of medieval characters and fantasy creatures, playing Dungeons and Dragons, and collecting *American Splendor* comic books."

"Oh," said Will. "So how long have you been unemployed?"

"Fellas, I'm sorry to interrupt," said Tex, "but it seems like I'm the only one in the dark here about this. What is a vampire lifestylist?"

Carol explained. "In simplest terms, I am interested in the culture of the vampire. Books, film, lore. I like the sleek, cool look of vampires, the beauty of death, and the idea of immortality."

"Who doesn't?" Verity gave her the nut-job smile. *Lore,* oh God, no good could come of someone who released the word *lore* into casual conversation, not to mention *beauty of death.*

Unperturbed, Tex said, "Yes, sir. Nothing beats a good Dracula movie at Halloween, I always say."

Charlie was not sure if he should depart from the vampire theme, but took a stab at it. "The ghost of a murdered man lives in our apartment. Did you ever think a three-flat in Rogers Park would be the afterlife? How depressing. But I guess it's better than haunting the South Side. Can you imagine spending eternity in Bridgeport? Your soul would be floating around Thirty-fifth Street, thinking, 'Oh my God! I've been sent to hell!' "

Carol nodded. "Every culture has its own view of eternity." She moved aside one collar of her blouse to reveal a small tattoo above her breast. "This is an ankh, the ancient Egyptians' symbol of eternal life. I embrace their beliefs."

Tex smiled in appreciation, but no one spoke. The exposure of middle-aged, tattooed flesh was not at the forefront of anyone's predictions for the course of the evening.

"And what do *you* do, Will?" Charlie asked, circumventing further revelations on the undead.

Will hesitated. "I'm the house KJ here."

"DJ?"

"No, the KJ. Karaoke jockey. I wouldn't be caught dead—no offense, Carol—as a DJ. I mean, it kind of sucks that I can't choose my own music, but on the other hand, I don't have to endure the adulation of numerous neo-nerds and vinyl-collecting geeks, all making assholish observations and dropping obscure rock references."

Tex asked, "When is the karaoke starting up again? I'd like to sing 'Oh, Susannah.' "

"Right about now," Will said. "My break's almost over and I've gotta run outside. The bouncer told me some jackass in an SUV bumped my VW." He stood up. "So just come on up when you're ready. I don't know if we have 'Oh, Susannah'—"

"Or I could do 'Surrey with the Fringe on Top' or 'God Bless America.' "

"We'll find you something. We have plenty of songs that aren't, you know, in the public domain." He turned to Verity and Charlie. "See you guys at Stan's." To himself he counted down: Thirty-one days and seventeen hours and forty-four minutes to go. To himself he murmured: Verity. Beautiful name, that.

for the third time, Charlie grumbled, "KJ. Like *that's* anything."

Verity fumbled for her key in the dark stairwell. "So what,

Charlie? So what? He's a KJ, you're a temp, I'm a cashier. We're all just trying to get through the day."

"I wasn't prepared," he replied. "By the time we get to this reunion, I'll have it all worked out. I'll have rehearsed what I'm going to say, and I'll be ready for any questions."

Once inside the apartment, she sifted through the mail on the kitchen table. Charlie watched Verity's face as she found the dinner party invitation from that other guy, Stan what's-his-name. She must not have known this about herself, but her eyes changed color like a mood ring, ranging from the murky green-grays of a muddy fen to the soft hazels of the forest floor, to a brilliant aquamarine when she was fired up. Now, reading that letter, they shone like two bright beacons, the panicked glare of a ship lost in the fog. Charlie read it, too, when she was in the bathroom. It was no big deal as far as he could see, just a "prereunion reunion" a few weeks before the official one, then a cocktail party the weekend of, and directions.

She came out of the bathroom and said, "Don't you wonder what other adults think when they see us? The ones who don't know us, who we pass in stores and elevators. In my mind, I look eighteen—young, fresh, and ignorant."

He said, "I don't look at myself much. I'm usually depressed or horrified by what I see. It's like looking in the mirror and seeing the Swamp Thing staring back at you."

"An eighteen-year-old mind-set in a thirty-three-year-old body. How does that come across to people? 'Hi, I've been intentionally ambition-free since college and have only now realized that my life sucks.' I must seem like a fool."

"How do you think I feel? I'm thirty-five and I live with my parents."

She said, "But you have potential. I'm a career sleepwalker." She flung herself into bed and covered her face with the handmade tiki quilt.

Charlie switched off the ceramic pineapple lamp and crawled

in beside her. The sodium light from the streetlamps shed an orange glow into her bedroom, casting the rattan thrift furniture and giant Easter Island head in the corner in silhouette.

"So, should I pretend to be a programmer or a graphic designer?" he asked.

She peeked out from under the tiki quilt and looked for Charlie's profile, but could not find it. "You don't have to make up anything. Temping is nothing to be ashamed of. It's not like you push a hot-dog cart down the street."

Frankly, he would feel perfectly at home behind the wheel of a hot-dog cart, what with its belly full of steamed offerings at his command. But the ghost in his apartment would never allow him that kind of success. He thought about that lanky dude tonight, with his flat stomach and lunatic skinhead glower.

Eventually sleep began to steal over him, to steal his obsessions and release them. "Web developer . . . Java programmer . . . dead tooth . . . gumboil . . ."

Verity bruxed her teeth sideways, but the giant plastic night guard impeded her progress.

Charlie mumbled, "Can a dead tooth throb?" and fell into a deep and dreamless slumber.

eight

"i don't believe it." stan shook his head. "I just don't believe it. Even after all this time, Craig still has to one-up me." He stamped his feet on the welcome mat, on the raised coir letters that spelled out *The Kickels*.

Laurel rang the doorbell. "Don't be such a drama queen."

As Carolyn opened the door, a liquid smile stretched across her face, and she took a step toward Stan, said, "Hey, sugarpants," and hugged him. Laurel shifted the bread loaf in her arms. She had asked Stan before the party what the hosts were like in high school and he had described Carolyn as a cross between a Kennedy cousin and a deadhead.

"Carolyn, this is my wife, Laurel."

Carolyn lunged in for the hug, but Laurel stiffened and clutched the bread to her chest, warding off physical contact. "Nice to meet you. Where should I put my health loaf?"

"Your . . . ?"

Laurel bounced the bread in her hands. "Whole wheat with millet and sunflower seeds and walnuts. Made it myself."

"Sounds scrummy! You can put it on the dining room table."

Craig strode toward them, instantly recognizable by Stan's succinct description, "Bryan Ferry wannabe. Marching band. Ultravox fan club." Floppy, sandy hair fell in a comma above his left eyebrow, parted too far over to the side. He shot his cuffs, displaying the silver monogrammed links. There were more hugs and more introductions, and the health loaf still had not left Laurel's arms.

•   •   •

charlie said, "Your friends sure like to have a lot of parties."

Verity made up a plate of hummus and vegetables. "Have you noticed that hummus is the new onion dip? You wouldn't catch anyone putting out Ruffles and onion dip these days; it's all hummus and baba ghanoush and pita and vegetables."

"Your dad would put out onion dip. You would put out onion dip."

"Yes, we would. But we're a dying breed."

A woman with thick, straight brows and a black bob, wearing a black tunic and striped, Hamburglar leggings came up to them and deposited bread on the tablecloth. "Help yourself," she offered. "It's a health loaf: whole wheat with millet and sunflower seeds and walnuts. It weighs about five pounds and nobody ever wants to eat it, but you're welcome to dig in."

Charlie, no slave to cutlery, lifted the loaf to his mouth and took a tremendous bite, but Verity's eyes strayed to the doorway. Stan had embarked on a self-improvement campaign over the last fifteen years. Gone were the chin-length bangs and mismatched Converse; presumably hidden under that Banana Republic linen shirt were the homespun tattoos. He waved at her with a hand long emancipated from its fingerless glove.

"This is a good loaf," said Charlie, mouth full of millet, as Stan advanced upon them, Craig in his wake. He heard Verity murmur, "Psycho."

He said, "Enjoying a health loaf doesn't make me a psycho."

But Verity said, "Stan Siko," and felt a fizz in her stomach, a vestigial response brought on by the sight of the man she had pursued with magnificent incompetence for three years. Stan smiled, always aware of his best props, revealing a phalanx of straight, white teeth. He said, "You probably don't recognize me without my raincoat and Chuck Taylors and Psychedelic Furs T-shirt."

Verity recognized that he had replaced his patchouli with the same cologne her dad wore.

He embraced her, even as she went for his elbows in her usual manner. Craig ran for his Belgian beer glasses.

"so we figured, why not?" Craig laughed. He passed a drink to Verity, confiding, "Blanche Steendonk."

"Gesundheit," she said.

Stan crossed his leg, rested his ankle on the opposite knee, and spread his palms out on his thighs. "Sure, why not? I mean, we all haven't seen each other in fifteen years, the reunion's coming up, *we* send out party invitations, and the next thing you know, why, there's *your* invitation."

Craig struck a pugilistic pose, arms crossed, and sunk back into his sofa. "So what are you saying?"

"I just think it's curious. We announce we're having a party, and then three days later, you announce yours."

"So? What, you wanted to have the first party? Sorry," Craig raised his voice, "everyone has to go home now. Stan's party should have been first, not mine."

Carolyn tried to diffuse the tension by complimenting the Sikos' health loaf, despite Charlie's bite marks on the one end, but bent her best bread knife in the process of slicing it up. "Mmm . . . millet! Everyone dig into this bread. Use your hands and just, uh, pull it apart. The experience is more organic and earthy that way. Like in Jakarta, we used to share our meals with the villagers hunkered down on the ground. We pulled meat off the bone and passed it around from elders to children and divvied up handfuls of some corn-mush thing. They're a very communal people. And so endearing, the way they don't mind if food falls out of their mouths while they're passing down oral histories."

Stan asked, "You ate food that had passed through other people's hands?"

"No, of course *I* didn't—those people's fingernails are like *E. coli* traps. But I pretended to participate in the meals. No one caught on."

Verity took an extended pull at her beer and longed to change the radio station. From the stereo brayed a Kenny G–like free jazz that brought to mind plate spinning and Greek circus performers. She stole a glance at Stan over her glass and found him staring at her. Disconcerted, she sputtered the beer down her chin. She lowered the glass and wiped her face with the back of her hand. His gaze traveled from her eyes to her lips and back again. He did not smile. An awkward flush suffused her skin as she pretended to be studying the pictures on the wall above him. Had she looked down, she would have seen the wave of satisfaction settle across his face.

She went toward the kitchen to slice the homemade peach pie she'd brought, and lingered just outside the door, watching with amusement as Charlie tested cheeses on a carving board.

"Ick, Muenster," he said, putting the half-bitten cube back.

Laurel stood at the kitchen window, staring out into the dark. "I hate being a fifth wheel," she said. "They all know each other and we're just the spouses."

"I'm not a spouse," Charlie corrected her.

"Oh, living in sin then?"

Charlie contemplated his home life and the sins he occasionally envisioned visiting upon his mother. "No. I'm just the boyfriend." Was that relief in his voice, or sourness, or scorn? It was hard to tell. Verity frowned and leaned in closer for better reception.

"What do you do for a living?"

"It's kind of hard to explain."

"I know what you mean," she said. "I never thought I'd be this age and still saying, 'I'm working as a receptionist for the time being.' Like anything else is ever gonna happen for me."

Charlie looked at her in surprise. He had probably found the one person in this house who would not mock, or pity, his temp-slave status. "What would you rather do?"

Laurel had weathered years of poorly concealed sniggering whenever she revealed her true calling. But she watched this portly dude putting half-eaten cheese cubes back on the serving tray, wiping his hands on the back of his pants, and gave it a whirl. "I'm really a performance poet. I've always felt called to it. Well, I haven't performed in a long time or even written anything decent since my son was born," she admitted. "But that's what I am at heart."

"That sounds cool. I wish I was called to something." He smiled at her and handed her the last block of unbitten cheddar. His fingertips brushed hers, and she gave him a wide smile of cutely crooked white teeth.

"I used to put love haikus in my husband's lunch bag for work, but once he got promoted, he started eating out with the other middle managers and told me not to bother anymore."

Charlie said, "Lunch and love poems go so well together. I wish someone would do that for me." She laughed and patted his shoulder.

Verity felt an unfamiliar surge of jealousy rise in her throat and stopped her eavesdropping. She put an ordinary smile on her face, walked into the kitchen, and said, "You two are missing some really fine jackassery out there."

Laurel said, "Just let me know when Stan and Craig are done with their pissing contest."

"How do you win one of those?" Verity wondered. "What are you judged on? Distance, duration, or penmanship?"

Laurel hooted and asked, "How come I haven't met you before?" She listened to the argument in the living room for a moment, then rolled her eyes. "That's a cool poncho. I like the pom-poms and fringe. Very retro."

Verity twirled. "Thank you, crocheted it myself. Pom-poms are news these days; I don't care what anyone says. Why should I let jag-off fashion designers take them away from me?"

"Sing it, sister."

Verity blinked in astonishment; no one had ever appreciated her defiant use of pom-poms before.

The living room argument had reached a stalemate; apparently

Craig would not apologize for hosting his party first. "Wish me luck—I'm going in," said Laurel.

Verity turned to Charlie, who was making a good show of pretending to be engrossed in cheese. "Coming? What's the matter?"

Panic flashed across his face. "I was trying to practice my lines, but that damn Belgian beer fuzzed my brain and then the loaf woman came in and started bitching about her husband—"

"Oh, really? What did she say? And what did you say?"

Charlie blinked. "What?"

"Nothing. Go on." Verity swallowed. She disliked the vinegary taste in her mouth.

"Anyway, now I can't remember what I ought to reveal about whatever fake job I'm supposed to have. Java developer sounds good, but they'll want to know where I work and what I'm working on, and I've got to have that down; on the other hand, if I just say I'm programming—"

"Oh God, who cares? Don't lie; it will get too complicated."

Her voice was harsh and he shook her off, turning back to the cheese and the imaginary job description beyond his reach. She grabbed her pie plate and left the room.

Back in the living room, Stan made a token conciliatory step. "Well, buddy, I *am* glad we got to see your house, anyway. This is quite a place."

"Thanks," said Craig. "All Carolyn's doing. I just sleep here."

"Is that a—what do they call it—Florida room over there?"

Carolyn said, "It's a solarium."

The word hung in the air, echoing in Craig's ears. He felt the blood rush to his intestinal tumor.

"We have one of those, too," Stan said. "Except we call it a hole in the porch roof."

Craig raised his palms in a gesture of defense, compelled to explain that despite appearances to the contrary, he was only the pauper of Clarendon Hills.

Verity set out the pie in the dining room on some very fragile-looking pieces of bone china. Craig was first in line. He decided to let Stan's comments just roll off him. Although, let's face it, Stan always had it in for him. How did he forget that? Carolyn used to say Stan was jealous of him, jealous of the money Carolyn's father had given them and the way things seemed to come easily to Craig, the way things, like Carolyn, just fell into his lap.

"That looks awesome, Verity," he said. "I can't tell you the last time I had homemade peach pie. You were a good cook even in high school."

Carolyn laid out a collection of antique sterling flatware, all of it mismatched, all of it expensive. She said, "Everyone, just pick out the fork that speaks to you."

the summer before senior year turned Downers Grove into a sweltering, humid jungle. The constant hum of air conditioners sent DuPage County into weekly power outages, and the pool behind Will's house had nightly, drunk, uninvited visitors. Stan slept in a tent in the backyard most of that summer, and Carolyn's parents yanked her off the Dead tour to go to their summer home in Michigan's Upper Peninsula. The Prestis had a generator backup so that even when everyone else lost power, Tex's home dental clinic and his pharmacist's cabinet of gypsum plaster, amalgams, and molding resins remained cool.

Craig had explained to his parents that he wasn't going to the University of Chicago, was not interested in the least in business or law, and in fact he had already filled out the application for the School of the Art Institute. They issued an ultimatum and he left. His parents had given him a used Chevette for his sixteenth birthday, which provided him adequate if stifling and cramped housing during the heat wave of 1987.

The shrubs in the Prestis' backyard were seriously overgrown, and Craig usually found refuge in them. He laid out his towel and sat down to dry off after that dip in the Demskes' pool, a real treat after moving his car from side street to parking lot to side street for three hours.

The kitchen light flicked on. Verity's sister Victory—another of

Tex's titular triumphs—went to the fridge, stood there with the door open, then picked out a few items. Craig's stomach growled. Victory opened the sliding glass door off the kitchen and tossed an armful of food just beyond the patio chairs onto the lawn. What was she doing? Craig crept closer. Then he saw the bright little eyes glinting in the dark and heard the scrabbling of feet across the wooden deck. Raccoons. Victory was the animal nut, that's right. Was that salami? He felt himself salivating, as wild as any creature scavenging that night. The raccoons heard his approach and scattered. Oh, what a windfall: meat, bread, half an apple. He gathered up the food as quickly as possible, but dropped it in fright when a flashlight beam blinded him, followed by a girl's scream.

"Verity! There's a bum outside stealing the raccoons' food!"

Craig tried to make a break for it but slipped on the wet grass. Verity peeked out the glass door, then opened it.

"Craig?"

Sheepishly, he turned back. He'd come down hard on his knee when he slipped, and anyway he was tired of running.

She washed and dried his towel and clothes as he sat at the kitchen table eating a sandwich she'd made. He still wore the grimy Roxy Music T-shirt he'd been living in.

"I'll wash that one when you're done," she said.

"No, it's okay." He flapped his hand in front of him, a dismissive gesture, waited for her to tell him to just go home, that his parents would eventually let him back in.

She said, "Your eyeliner's all smudged."

Rubbing his eyes with the heel of his hand, he pressed tightly until bright blue floaters rose up in his vision. "You can't run away without eyeliner." He tried to laugh.

She put another sandwich in front of him, then motioned for the dirty T-shirt.

He took it off and asked, "Where's your dad?"

Verity said, "Out with your parents." He made a face and swallowed hard. She did not tell him to go home. She said, "Maybe Carolyn can help you."

But he said, "She's going on vacation tomorrow. It's not a good time for her," and that was the end of it. He licked his fingers . . . rye bread, unspecified lunch meat, provolone, lettuce, tomato, mayo, butter, and brown sugar. He closed his eyes and the floaters came back, blue and yellow this time, and he sunk his head into his open hands to muffle the freight train roar in his brain. Eyes shut, hands clamped over ears, the floaters faded to black and the roar became a silence equal to it. This was the best sandwich anyone had ever eaten.

"temping? You're joking." Stan moved over on the couch to make room for Will.

"I wish. I spent a year with Manpower and am still recovering. Temping makes KJ-ing seem secure and remunerative in comparison, and at least at the bar, no one makes me collate, or sit in a supply closet."

Stan agreed. "It sounds horrific. I'd rather be a dishwasher."

Charlie snapped the celery sticks on his plate into small ragged arches. However much he despised being a temp, he suddenly felt an overwhelming urge to defend his so-called career to this pretentious yuppie Stan. He began to breathe in and out of his nostrils with bullish ferocity. Verity, highly attuned to the warning signs of Charlie's ire, ran to get him a piece of pie, which in most circumstances subdued any feelings of rage.

"No, thank you," he said in a clipped tone, as she placed it on the end table next to his chair. "I'm not hungry."

Oh, no. "But it's pie, Charlie. *Pie.*" In desperation, she stabbed a forkful and tried to distract him by waving it in front of his mouth. No good had ever come of Charlie's turning down pie.

He pushed the fork away in irritation. The temp bashing was *over*. "And what do you do for a living, Stan?" he asked.

"I'm a project manager."

Charlie seized upon it. "Oh! So you're a professional babysitter."

Laurel snorted and leaned back in her chair. Stan blinked and forced a laugh, rubbing his chin in a puzzled manner. He asked, "Okay. Well, what do you do?"

Charlie wanted to strangle himself. He walked right into this! His pulse quickened, and his face flushed a dangerous crimson as he mentally rehearsed his speech. Cottonmouthed, he stuttered. "I . . . I . . . well, these days . . ."

Verity interceded. "He's a theorist. For a . . . an Internet company." A what for a what? What? She blanked her face and smiled pleasantly. Her blood pressure soared and beat against her chest, vibrating the pom-poms.

"A theorist?" asked Stan. Charlie turned to stare at Verity.

"Yeah," she said. "A big one."

Will said, "I thought you made Dungeons and Dragons miniatures."

Fighting for composure, Charlie said, "Well, yes, that, too. As an . . . an Internet theorist, I keep company with elves, ogres, orcs, and their close relatives, project managers."

Stan said, "Verity, where did you find this guy?"

She answered, "We met at one of my dad's swinger parties."

And with that deft touch, she turned the conversation in another, less volatile direction.

craig and carolyn's backyard, though small, managed to accommodate a jungle gym and a climbing wall. Charlie swung on a tire suspended from an oak tree branch while Verity pushed him.

"What in God's name is an Internet theorist? Why did you say that?"

"How the hell should I know?" she snapped. "It just popped out."

"What was wrong with me pretending to be a programmer? At least I know something about programming. Now I have to pretend I'm a theorist and I don't even know what that is."

"Well, no one else does either. I'm sorry, but I had to say something. You were just sitting there, you big baby."

"Why are you yelling at me? And whatever happened to, 'Oh, don't be embarrassed of your job, Charlie. Don't lie, Charlie, it'll get too complicated,' huh? Internet theorist!" He wrestled for a better grip on the tire swing. "Don't push so hard; are you trying to kill me? Well, I'm sorry I lost my temper, but I'm really not comfortable around yuppies and rich people."

"They're not really yuppies."

"Please! What is with the smooth jazz? I'd like to kick the speakers in. And did you see what's parked in the garage here? This is the kind of town where you see a solitary woman driving around in the afternoons in a three-ton, military issue, $125,000 Mercedes SUV."

"Why were you looking in their garage?"

He didn't answer, and she swung him hard into the tree, then went inside.

verity followed Laurel and Carolyn into the nursery to peek at the sleeping baby. The mothers spoke in a sort of cooing foreign language that made no sense. Verity looked down into the crib, waiting for stirrings of a dormant maternal instinct, but felt nothing. No particular emotion at all, really, in regard to infants, beyond envy of their sedentary lifestyles and unapologetic "me-first" attitudes.

Even in the dark, the nursery emanated a glow of luxury that, to Laurel's sensibilities, bordered on obscene. The room itself dwarfed her own living room, and opened onto a private balcony and a smaller sitting room. The furniture did not exclaim, "Target closeout sale" or "castoffs from Grandma," like Sebastian's did. The built-in bookshelves displayed an orderly collection of multicolored Steiff bears trucking along, gender-free and race-unspecific dolls, Tiffany's infant cups and teething rings, and dozens of hardcover books, spines unbroken. The mobile above the crib played instrumental Phish.

"I've never seen tie-dyed crib bumpers before," Laurel whispered. "What's her name?"

"Aura. And we have an older son, Kronos. A delightful boy."

Laurel, grateful for the dark, rolled her eyes. Aura and Kronos? They sounded like Godzilla opponents. Not for the first time, she congratulated herself on choosing Sebastian's name. It was solid and no-nonsense, and no one could say any different. Though people tried.

They emerged into the hallway and headed downstairs. "Well, Verity?" Carolyn said. "Are you getting mommy urges?"

"Does craving alcohol count?"

"It might seem daunting at first, but having children is so rewarding. You would not believe the cool baby items I got for Aura, like this stuffed alarm clock that yells at her in Japanese, and this holistic infant health-care set made of recycled rubber and hemp. All at Whole Foods, too."

Laurel muttered, "Whole Paycheck," having shopped there a number of times herself. She cleared her throat and spoke up. "Stan wants to have another kid, but I'm not sure I can handle it."

Carolyn said, "I know what you mean. Our nanny is cutting her hours down to thirty when school starts. It'll be such a drag."

Laurel and Verity exchanged glances. Carolyn sensed this and wanted to say, *Not that I don't want to spend more time with my kids,* because she did. She liked watching informative nature programs on television with them, or escorting them down the aisles of Whole Foods with a running commentary on non-GMO breakfast cereals and organic skin-care products, because that taught them things. It was when she found herself alone with them, really alone, in the house without the TV on or staring at one another across the dinner table that she discovered she was bereft of meaningful knowledge to impart. She said, "Wine in the solarium, anyone?"

Will watched the girls come down the stairs. He wondered how long it would be before someone started in on him about not having a girlfriend. It was not as though he didn't hear it often enough from his parents: *You're thirty-three; what are you doing with your life? Why don't you settle down with a nice girl?* He met plenty of nice girls at the KKK. Nice college girls. No rush, he decided. Fifteen years living in Chicago bartending and KJ-ing provided a decent amount of fodder for the dating manifesto he was currently composing, titled *Four Psychos and a Lesbian.* He pictured a movie deal in his future, with Hugh Grant attached.

The back door in the kitchen banged open and Charlie walked in. Will saw him glance at his reflection in the microwave, try to fix his hair (no luck there), straighten his collar, and suck in his gut. Poor slob. He grinned at him.

"Hey, Charlie," he called out. "I'm working on a manifesto for single guys. Any words of wisdom I should include?"

Charlie considered. "Never keep your industrial magnet collection in the same place as your videotape collection. Don't whistle with pudding in your mouth. Popcorn is a vegetable."

Craig wanted to say men should register for Maalox when they get engaged, but instead offered this bon mot: "Don't buy any car that will embarrass you when taking out one of your future ex-wives on dates."

"This is just for single guys, bud," Will said. "You haven't been single for fourteen years."

Craig said, "I remember what it was like."

after an hour, the girls entered the room, and Laurel flopped down on the couch. "I need a solarium."

Carolyn said, "You can come over and use ours anytime. Sit by the orchids and meditate or just daydream and stare out the windows."

Laurel grimaced and futzed with the back of her slip-on wedge, jamming her heel down into it. She could not believe that Carolyn had asked them to remove their shoes before entering the solarium, so as not to track in housebound bad vibes or some other hoo-ha. If only she had worn socks tonight. The girls had politely averted their eyes from Laurel's big bunions and cracked, yellowed toenails, thick as horns. Verity's toenails were plain and clean, and Carolyn's professional French pedicure shone with high gloss against the bluestone floor. "I don't really have a lot of free time for meditating and staring out windows," she said.

Working moms often reacted to her this way, Carolyn knew. It was okay; each person had her own burden to bear.

Verity was tanked. She had not drunk like this in years. Her stockpile of "I was so wasted" stories remained archived and smoldering, a black box recording retrieved from a wreckage of shame. But everything she had done over the last seven years had been while in charge of her faculties, and so she could blame none of her recent life on alcohol. She thought: *I am now an idiot in plain view, a clerk in totality, fully responsible for all the things I have done and haven't done.*

Charlie wrapped his arm around her waist, holding her upright, and said, "We're gonna get going. Anyone want some peach pie to take home?" Will and Craig ran for the pie. Stan took a step after them, glanced at his wife.

"Laurel?" Charlie offered.

"No, thanks." She waved it away. "I don't like sweets. I don't eat sweets."

Stan frowned and turned away from her. Why not say no and be done with it? Why did she like to advertise her food insanity to a house full of people she'd just met? He said, "She wouldn't eat any of our wedding cake, either."

The front door banged open and a teenage boy entered, his curly hair and blue eyes reminiscent of Carolyn's, his weak chin and sulky mouth clearly Craig's.

"Kronos, say hello to everyone." Craig stood with his hands on his hips, fake-smiling.

"Hi." The boy looked down as he flew through the foyer and up the stairs. The same words, barely containable, hovered upon everyone's lips: Kronos Kickel?

Craig said, "He's really a great kid."

Stan flung his coat over his shoulders. "Don't forget, kiddies, next week is our dinner party."

"How could I forget?" asked Craig. Stan gave him an affable, hard punch on the shoulder, which obligated Craig to hunt for the heating pad and Ben-Gay later that night.

verity had just dropped off to sleep in the car on the way home when Charlie said, "I would never have recognized any of those people from the way you'd described them. None of them!"

She picked up her head and shook both the fuzz and remaining coherence into a mixed jumble. "That was high school, bub. Don't you think people change since then?"

"I bet *you* haven't."

"Thanks."

"I meant it as a compliment," he said. "I'm sure you'd never name your own kid 'Kronos.' "

She yawned. "Kronos seemed like a nice enough boy."

Charlie said, "Kronos booked through the room like a panicked horse fleeing a burning barn. What parameters are you judging by?"

"I dunno. Lack of facial tattoos? It's the best I can do at the moment."

In the back of Charlie's mouth, a tooth began to throb. He wasn't sure if it was the gumboil tooth (number twenty), the dead tooth, or perhaps the molar behind it. All the problems with his teeth had combined to form one pulsing abscess of agony. Steering with one hand, he poked the molar and felt a quick stab of pain and a certain wobbliness, and he decided it was losing its structural integrity. Great. Now it was only a matter of time before that long, slow slide into PoliGrip senility. "I can't imagine how you must have described me to them."

Verity looked out the window and said nothing.

craig watched Stan and Laurel attempt to retract their car from the tight spot they'd found on the street, bumping the ones in front and behind, and setting off a deafening car alarm. Craig smiled and let the curtain fall. "I knew they'd never get that thing out of that spot." He turned to Carolyn, but she had already disappeared.

Stan gunned it. "You know what Craig said to me when we got there? He said, 'I never thought you'd get that SUV into that tiny spot.' He called our Subaru an SUV. It's a big station wagon, it's *not* an SUV."

Laurel said, "Did you get a load of that house? I've never used the word *solarium* in my life, but tonight it was all I could say, 'solarium, solarium.' "

"I know our house is a toxic waste dump, but you don't have to rub it in."

"I didn't say anything was wrong with our house. Jesus, Stan. Our house is fine. Considering," she added meaningfully.

Catching her unspoken criticism of his inattention to his household chores and yardwork, he swore at her silently. Then he asked, "So what did you think of them?"

"Scrummy," she said. "Although I'm pretty sure you never mentioned that Verity girl to me before."

"Didn't I?"

Laurel stared at Stan, his expression opaque and unreadable.

will sped down the Ike all the way home, blowing through the tolls.

at the town limits around the block from Craig and Carolyn's house, a wooden signpost and shingle, erected in 1982, proclaimed: YOU ARE LEAVING CLARENDON HILLS, A NICE PLACE TO LIVE AND SHOP. A beat-up VW slowed down by the curb and discharged two young passengers, who glanced over their shoulders and then reached into their backpacks. The car idled, its back doors open, as the sign swung and creaked in the summer wind. Downers Grove teenagers pelted it with garbage.

nine

band camp attendees assembled in the high school parking lot, divided from one another by instrument class. Diana watched the boys of the percussion section and the drum line, their inherent coolness mitigated only by the occasional tuba player. Even the choad who clashed the cymbals stood on a higher rung of the band camp hierarchy than she, amid the other clarinet losers. The rest of the woodwinds kept their distance, not wanting the contagious ickiness of the clarinet section to contaminate them. Four years of band camp assured her a shot at a college music scholarship for next year, and her eyes clouded over, reflecting on the summers wasted standing here in the DGS parking lot, that far-flung prize in sight.

Worried-looking freshmen picked their way through the formation, the director shouting out placements as inspiration struck. "You, there! Young man in the circus trousers, situate yourself right there, third from last. Girl, girl in glasses, middle of row between circus pants and Asian fellow. That's it."

A glum, chinless boy with electrified hair took his position next to Diana. He wore a red-checked shirt, flood trousers, and red socks. He felt her eyes take in the full measure of his wardrobe. No one understood him, that much was certain; his red-hued clothing homage to Studs Terkel, his disinterest in sporting life and muscles, his love of clarinets and woodwind melancholy, which was beautiful, unlike people.

Diana heard a girl in the row behind making cracks about her torn fishnet hose and purple vinyl skirt. She wondered what everyone would do if she suddenly spun around and beat the girl with the bell of her clarinet, smashing her head with the instrument, holding it two-fisted like a toilet plunger, and then perhaps driving the reed end into the soft flesh of her face. She'd be dragged off, no doubt, kids screaming all around her, freshmen whimpering to go home, the scholarship probably lost, as universities frowned upon such things these days. Another girl joined in, giggling at her red grandma Keds.

The wild-haired boy next to Diana turned to her. He possessed the solemn expression of one who has worn a digital watch to school and lived to regret it. "Those girls," he said, "are rude as pigs."

Diana blinked. The band director blew his ubiquitous whistle and announced that the uniforms were ready for measuring and the sheet music lay waiting in stacks on the table inside the front doors. He used phrases like, "Hustle, gang," and "Chop chop," while teens cringed. Diana looked at the boy and said, "After you pick up your uniform, we get lunch in the cafeteria. I'll be sitting in the Dark Side, if you want to come over there."

"The Dark Side . . . ?"

"You'll figure it out." She headed toward the school.

"Wait!" he called. "My name's Kronos."

"That's okay," she answered. "I'll still sit with you."

charlie prowled the self-help section at Barnes & Noble. With Verity off at her father's, mutilating shrubbery, he knew he'd have uninterrupted time to peruse the career strategy books. Although she supported him in most of his ill-conceived ventures (translating the works of Tennyson into Klingon had been personally satisfying, but no real market value had been established), he was too aware of her disdain for self-help books to risk letting her see him there, amid Dr. Phil and *What Color Is Your Parachute?*

He pulled four career path guides from the shelf and sat in a coffee-stained chair by the windows to page through them. The problem with these guides was that their suggestions were obtuse, way too broad, and generally cringeworthy: public relations?

Advertising? What he wanted was a reasonable-sounding fake career that Verity's friends would buy and that would not make him vomit. He would have to work the untimely revelation of "Internet theorist" into it, whatever he chose.

A familiar voice sounded behind him. "If you want to steal those, slip 'em down your pants and I'll look the other way."

Charlie looked up. "Oh, hi, Bob." Embarrassed, he tried to cover the top title with the overhang of his stomach. It did not work. Bob's gaze moved down to the book and he saw *Your Parachute?* sticking out from below. Charlie looked down, too. Hey, maybe he had lost weight! His current stomach did not mask everything in his lap, as he had expected it to do—in the past, the fleshy protuberance successfully concealed those little packs of doughnut Gems he was always hiding from scavenging co-workers. It had also saved him the time his mother nearly caught him with his only fetish magazine, an erotic sci-fi monthly called *Playbot*.

"You're lucky Verity isn't here to see you in the self-help section," Bob said. "You'd never hear the end of it."

"I know," Charlie said, withdrawing the books from under his blub.

Bob glanced through the titles. "Are you really looking for a new career?"

"I don't know. Not really, I guess. I was just hoping to come up with a good lie to fool Verity's classmates at her reunion. Somehow I gotta be able to explain what an Internet theorist is—oh well, it's a long story."

"Not you, too? God, she was afraid of what they'd think of her clerking job. I'm happy to say I think I straightened her out on that account. I told her, who gives a flying crap what those losers think? It's this line of reasoning that keeps me from opening fire on the customers here."

Charlie said, "These books don't seem to have anything for me anyway. I wanted to find a job that sounds impressive to others without sounding corporate and creepy to me."

"No such thing, son." Bob patted him kindly on the back.

Together, they slid the books onto the shelf. After pushing the last one in, Charlie spied a slim little booklet shoved to the rear of the shelf. Curious, he pulled it out; soft and ragged brown leather covered it, inscribed with Latin words in faded gold type, *Labor Officium Auxilium*. Printed below: *A Guide to Meaningful Work in Our World, by C. Aquilus*. He flipped through it, and the pages fell open to a section headed Shaman/Healer.

"How much is this?" He handed the booklet to Bob, who turned it over, looking for a tag or ISBN.

"No idea. That's weird, there's no price and no bar code. I don't even know how it got here." Bob studied Charlie's disappointed face and said, "Look, just stick it down your pants and walk outta here."

"But what if the beeper thing goes off at the door?"

"So what? I'll just wave you through. The damn alarm goes off every day, and I always wave people through. Let 'em steal from us, what do I care?"

Charlie did as he was instructed and exited the store, the booklet snug in his trousers. The alarm did not go off.

the Dark Side's few tables hosted what the rest of society comfortably envisioned when thinking of "marching band," the strategists of the Chess Team, the Glenn Miller fans, the Saturday night bunco players, the lonely tubist. *That there are cliques within the marching band would surprise society,* Diana thought, considering the semipopular boys of the drum corps and the cute-for-band-nerds flautist girls, all sitting in the bright light of the right side of the cafeteria.

"Excellent!" said Kronos, sliding in beside her. "Mac and cheese."

"Summer band camp lunches are better than the regular school year lunches," Diana said. "I have no explanation for this, but after four years, I know it's true."

"You're a senior? Wow, after four years of band camp, you must be a wunderkind on the ol' licorice stick."

Diana put down her fork and felt a responsibility to set this kid straight, this Kronos, this skinny turtlelike person beside her. "I'm not against it, but I'm just saying: using words like *wunderkind* and *licorice stick* around here are going to get you pummeled. Particularly licorice stick, since everyone who plays the clarinet really wishes they'd taken up the saxophone instead, but their parents wouldn't let them."

"Noted," replied Kronos. "Yet I must defend the clarinet. Those cool, round tones, the sad lower register. I love it and I don't care who knows. Why don't you?"

"I wanted to play the sax, but my mother said the sax was a boy's instrument. I hate the clarinet. It makes me want to throw myself out a window."

"Defenestrate yourself."

She paused. "Yes. Defenestrate myself."

"Yet you stuck with it. That's admirable."

"There's an Oberlin Conservatory of Music scholarship out there for four-year band members. I plan to dump the clarinet and move on to composing progressive, hybridized music. I want to establish a madrigal-influenced ensemble that blends acid/minstrel rock with hard-core rap, called Death Row Tull."

Kronos said, "Nice. I've always thought hip-hop suffered from a dearth of flutes."

Diana looked at him, trying not to let her surprise transmit. She *too* had thought hip-hop suffered from a dearth of flutes! Who was this Kronos?

He looked up from his lunch and said, "You never told me your name."

"Diana."

"Oh. Like the princess?"

"Yes," she said, cursing Thelma and Dick for the millionth time, "like the princess."

A noodle clung to his little chin as a thoughtful expression took over. "I hope you get the Oberlin scholarship, Diana. Although the prospect of college may make one wish to stay in the safe womb of high school a while longer, hoping to stave off—"

Diana stared at the cafeteria exit, watching her reflection in the door panels as they swung out and back. She said, "I am so out of here already, I'll go straight through those glass doors without even opening them."

charlie spent the remainder of the afternoon holed up in his room, poring over the *Labor Officium Auxilium*. The curtains fluttered every so often, though the window was closed. The ghost of the man murdered in the Browns' apartment was interested in Charlie's career trajectory as well.

"Charlie!" Mrs. Brown screamed up from the kitchen. "Dinner will be ready in ten minutes. Wash up! And don't come down in that moth-eaten computer T-shirt, either."

"Busy. Not hungry," he answered.

Mrs. Brown bellowed in reply, but, thanks to the ghost, Charlie's bedroom door suddenly shut. The lock turned. All was quiet and still.

Charlie looked up into the ether and smiled. "Thanks," he said.

tex sat on the patio watching the sealant on his picnic table dry, as Verity clipped the rosebushes against the back fence. Having no sons never stopped Tex from insisting that his children help him around the house and yard. It was good for them to work, to have chores, and if nothing else, at least he had encouraged them to have a healthy work ethic. Not that he was averse to helping them, no indeed. But they had to earn it. What was wrong with that? Gladly he had lent Verity the money for that used 1992 Honda Civic of hers, no problem there, and eight and a half percent interest was quite reasonable at the time. He had taught her a lesson about saving money and repaying loans, yes at a cost, but that was life: anything dear enough to you always came at a cost.

"Am I done?" Verity called to him. "I'm broiling out here." Why had she worn a crocheted vest today? Why? Being made of cotton yarn with plenty of wide-open holes did not mean it provided the ventilation she required out in the blazing sun. She considered taking it off and just wearing the skimpy white tank top she had on underneath, but there are specific kinds of girls who easily wear skimpy tank tops in public, and she was not one of them. There was also a certain amount of ick factor in wearing a skimpy tank top in front of one's dad.

Tex looked over her work. "It's kind of lopsided, Verity. You know I always say symmetry is key in shrubbery."

She could not help but grin. He *did* always say that, and a thousand other sweetly bizarre idioms. "Asymmetry is the new wave of gardening, Dad." She put down the hedge trimmers and made her way across the lawn in search of lemonade. "It'll grow on you."

He frowned. "I'm not much for fads." He checked his watch and said, "You want to pick up Diana from school now?"

She stopped in her path. "What?"

"Diana's at band camp and Thelma and Dick both are at work, so I said we'd pick her up. They'll come get her after dinner."

Verity reached down into her well of avoidance excuses but came up dry. "I didn't know she was coming over today."

"So what? The more the merrier. I'm making a pizza."

The Honda idled in the driveway as the air-conditioning refused to kick in. Verity tapped her fingers on the steering wheel, killing time. She and Diana got along fine, for the most part. Really, it was not a big deal; so what if they weren't close or friendly? It was just the age gap that caused an ocean of prickliness between them. It *must* have been the age gap. Diana had some good qualities, like anyone else.

Verity backed out of the drive and turned toward the school, a mile south. Though Verity had come back to Downers Grove countless times since graduation, she had made a concerted ef-fort to avoid driving by the high school all these years. What was there to see? Cinder block and asbestos memories. The walls painted in shades of inmate-calming blue. The bleachers with their stench of truly revolting sex. And also the kids, their faces shiny and fresh despite the layers of modern cynicism, glowing the way new things do, at first.

A girl with a brown ponytail and torn stockings marched up to the car, swinging her clarinet case, a hideous blue and white uni-form slung over her shoulder. "I've been waiting for like twenty minutes." She threw her stuff onto the backseat and climbed in the front.

"Why don't you walk next time?"

"Why don't *you?*"

Verity said, "That doesn't make any sense."

"Oh, shut up," said Diana, and turned to stare out the window.

By the time they had pulled up in front of Tex's house, Verity had reconsidered her sharp remarks, as adults sometimes will, and made another stab at conversation. "So what's going on these days?"

Diana shrugged and poked a fingernail through the fishnet openings.

"How was band practice?"

"Stupid. Whatever. There's this new kid named Kronos that seems okay."

Verity paused, then said, "His name wouldn't happen to be Kronos Kickel, would it?"

That poor little freak, thought Diana. "I wouldn't be sur-prised."

"I didn't get to see you last time we were at Mom's. How was prom?"

The girl succeeded in jamming her finger up to the knuckle through the hole, then twisted it until the threads made little pop-ping sounds. "It sucked. I didn't know anyone. The chicken marsala was gross, and I felt fat in my dress. I left early by myself, but before I pulled out of the parking lot, I sat in the car for a while and thought about how fucking stupid I am." This hung in the humid air a second, then vanished with Diana as she grabbed her things and slammed the car door behind her.

Tex's pizza had a certain . . . what was the term? Verity sought the right word. Ah, yes, *Carol-ness* about it. Not that it was slathered in blood or sprinkled with the dirt of one's ancestral homeland, but the addition of goat cheese, sun-dried tomatoes, and prosciutto spoke to the influence of sinister forces.

"You'll like this one, girls." He rolled the wheeled pizza cutter through the crust. "Carol always says goat cheese makes everything better, and I have to agree. Well, not everything, I'm sure there are some things that would just stink made with goat cheese. Like Velveeta."

"I can't eat this, Tex," Diana said. "I'm a vegetarian."

"I know, hon," he said, "the prosciutto's only on half."

"No." Diana shook her head. "I can't eat it even if it's only on half. The essence of it will still be on my half; I'll just get sick to my stomach."

Tex stopped the pizza wheel. "Oh. Well, what if you blot it?"

"No, the smell of it will still be there, deep, deep in the cheese."

Verity glared at her sister. "Why do you have to be so difficult? I can't stand people with self-imposed dietary restrictions; you just make life hell for the rest of us."

"It's all right," said Tex. "I'm sure I have other stuff in the kitchen. How about chicken salad?"

Diana pushed her plate away. "I'm sorry, but chicken is an animal, too."

Tex considered this. "Yes, but I guess I don't think of it as being as much of an animal as a pig. A pig I can almost see not wanting to eat—they have feelings, they walk around and observe things,

I believe there can be training of some sort. Certainly, I can almost see not wanting to eat them. Except they taste so good." He gave a crooked, helpless grin.

"You're nuts, Diana," Verity said. "You were shoveling in Peeps last Easter like you'd been living on gruel. You can't say Peeps are healthy."

Diana sputtered, "It's not about whether it's healthy, even though the idea of flesh decomposing in your guts is *totally disgusting and vile.* At least the Peeps weren't alive at some point."

Tex tried to reroute this runaway engine. "I was surprised to see they make Peeps for all the holidays now. There's Christmas Peeps and Halloween Peeps."

Encouraged, Diana nodded. "Yes, they're a vegetarian, multicultural treat."

Verity folded her pizza slice in half and shoveled it in. "Are there Ramadan Peeps?" she asked.

Diana stood up. "Why do you have to be so mean to me? I didn't ask anybody to cook me dinner. I'm not even hungry."

"Blot it," urged Tex. "Come on, it'll work." Why had he varied from his tried-and-true mushroom-and-olive pizza that everyone loved? Poor Carol could not have predicted how tampering with a recipe would devastate his family unit.

On the other end of the spectrum, Verity imagined that Carol had purposely planned this whole scene as a ruse to lure Tex from his family, the goat cheese pizza a manifestation of her black art.

Diana sat down and looked at the table through blurred vision. Who cares about a damn pizza? Who cares? Her own mother barely bothered to make dinner at all and had certainly never made a pizza from scratch. This was nothing to get upset about. Yet . . . there it was: she was upset. She inhaled deeply, restoring calm.

Verity had never been much for burying the hatchet with people; it was easier to just move on. Diana was even more stubborn, and truthfully, Verity had always admired her brand of resistance, that core that would not yield. When Diana went away to Oberlin, Verity knew she would miss her, would miss their fights; in the end, that was all they had. She said, "Diana, if you want, I'll make you a peanut butter sandwich."

Diana shook her head. "That's okay, I'll blot," she said, and set to work on her pizza. "But I'm lowering my moral standards."

the presti household boasted a collection of warm, mismatched, and comfortable furniture. Though the divorce had taken place nineteen years ago, the house remained the same; Thelma had taken almost nothing with her when she left, and no chair or sofa had so much as moved since then. "I like it the way it is," Tex always said. "Why buy new things that don't mean anything to me?" Gold shag carpeting blanketed the living room and family room. A bright red bandanna-patterned wallpaper lined the kitchen. Though Tex had tastefully removed his and Thelma's framed wedding photo, he had kept on the mantel and the bookshelves any pictures in which she appeared with anyone else. "She's the mother of my children," he'd explain. Even if she was a coldhearted bitch.

On the wall above the piano were Verity and Victory's senior photos. On the piano itself were small gold frames with pictures of Diana opening a present at Christmas, the family dogs, one of which still lived in glorious incontinence, and Tex himself at work in the old dental office, a terrified, inverted Dick trapped in the chair undergoing a root canal. Tex smiled broadly in that one, waving an instrument of torture. Verity remembered that the hygienist at the office had always been instructed to have a roll of film ready in the camera, for when spontaneous photo opportunities arose.

Verity adjusted the frames slightly. They caught the full western sun in the evening, and the photographs had faded into colors she associated with the '70s: harvest gold and avocado and muted brick red. It seemed to her as if that time had taken place in exactly those colors; in her mind's eye she saw things happening in washed-out, autumnal hues. The '80s-era photos had not weathered time much better. The fuchsias and teals of the giant, Shaker-knit V-necked sweaters and titanic dyed hair had also dulled. Here, on the coffee table, was a picture of Verity and Victory in July 1986, the girls' bronzed skin a testament to the happy days of SPF ignorance, to the sunbathing success of their Apollo arsenal: silver metallic tanning blankets, foil-covered record albums, swimsuits that allowed UV rays to penetrate, forty-eight-ounce bottles of coconut oil. Verity turned the frame from the sun; along with the other colors, her sister's tan had begun to fade, as if she were a real person standing in this room, months after the end of summer.

Verity heard a noise, a dull thump behind her. The last in the series of Presti dogs—a fourteen-year-old yellow mongrel of inde-terminate weight and parentage—stood two feet from the corner of the room and stared at the wall. Its tail wagged against an ot-toman, then hung still.

Verity knelt down beside her. The dog (proper name Gingiva, unfortunate beast) always had a special hold on Verity, as she had come from what Verity liked to think of as a pet thrift shop, the West Suburban Humane Society on Ogden Avenue. Like the thrift, the animal shelter had perfectly functional goods for sale that had been used, discarded, and devalued. Tex had been the first to show Verity the glories of thrifting fondue pots and Orlon golf sweaters at St. Vincent de Paul in her early childhood, and he judiciously extended his shopping common sense to selecting the family pets. Happy to give a few bucks to the charity, he enjoyed the added bonus of coming home with something weird and delightful, another thrifted thing that had escaped death and re-ceived a second shot at life.

"What are you doing, Gin?" she asked. "What are you look-ing at?"

Gin continued her quiet congress with the white wall.

"This is what she does now," Tex said. He came in and patted the dog on her head. "I often find her just standing in the middle of the room staring. She's old."

"No, don't say that," replied Verity, and she picked up the dog and tried to cuddle her. She used the goo-goo voice that nauseated her when others used it on children. "You're not old, are you, big baby? Just fat and dumb, you lovey thing, you. Oof, really fat. What are you feeding her, Dad?"

He smiled sheepishly. "Biscuits and gravy sometimes. I know, I know, don't lecture me. It's just that it makes her happy. She doesn't have much going on these days."

The pleasure of cuddling the plump animal no match for the damage it was doing to her back, Verity deposited the dog onto the floor, where she resumed staring at the wall. She said, "This is making me sad, Dad."

He put his arm around her. "Don't be sad. She doesn't know."

Verity leaned against her father, breathing in the fusty mingled fragrance of Old Spice and Pepsodent. "But she once knew. How can that not make me sad?"

Tex squeezed his daughter's shoulder, kissed the top of her head. Eldest children had a tough time of everything; they were more sensitive to the mercurial dynamics within families. As soon as they got used to things around the house, life changed: new children were born, dogs died, people left. The eldest were the first ones to enter kindergarten, to go on dates, to take driving lessons, to go off to college. Tex sighed and released Verity from his embrace. It was heartbreaking when your children left home. But then, there were many ways they could break your heart.

In search of Diana, Verity went upstairs, glancing in her old bedroom. Like the rest of the house, Tex had not altered it, banking on the occasional Christmas Eve she'd spend here, perhaps hoping a grandchild would one day nap in this room. Grandchild? An indescribably gross feeling came over her, causing a mild societal shame that quickly dissipated.

Verity's bedroom bore witness to a life defined by the accrual of crapulence. Even as a child she held onto her old lunchboxes, games with missing tokens, outgrown clothing, paint-by-numbers sets of horses in paddocks, candles that had burned down but still contained enough wax for some future, mysterious project. *Don't throw it out!* she begged her mother. *I can still use it for something.* Tied to these belongings were not just hopes hitched to the future, but a belief that keeping items from the past drove old memories deeper. Verity looked around her bedroom. No one could say her memories were not firmly rooted, or did not cast broad shadows.

"So, what do you think of this?" Diana stood in the hallway, arms spread wide. She twirled slowly, exposing all dimensions of the finery that was the marching band uniform, its sequined blue sash and sassy fringed epaulets, its snug white trousers, its obscene patent leather shoes.

Verity came out into the hall. "Besides the camel-toe and the fire hazard?"

"You think it's not flame retardant?" Diana raised her eyebrows in happy surprise. Suddenly the uniform seemed kind of cool.

"Can't you get them to sew some pom-poms on it?"

"Not everything needs pom-poms."

This was one of those universally held truths that Verity had difficulty accepting. "Well, I don't know about that. Consider pom-poms on ponchos, pom-poms on mittens, pom-poms on little dog sweaters, pom-poms on bedspreads—"

"Anyway. Does it look okay, in spite of everything?"

"I guess, considering what it is. My friends were in the marching band, too, and they had to wear those furry beefeater hats." She paused. "You know, I'm going to my class reunion this summer."

"Voluntarily? I can't think of anything more depressing or pointless." Diana practiced a few high steps. "Damn, it's hard to high-step in tight pants." She moved toward the bedroom across the way, Victory's.

"What are you doing?" Verity asked.

"I'm going to check myself out in the mirror."

"Use the one in the bathroom."

Diana stopped. "But this one's full-length."

Verity reached out and laid her hand on an epaulet. The gold cord was rough to the touch and sewn tight. "Don't go in there."

Diana tried to shove past her. "I'll just peek in."

Verity's usually placid countenance puckered in resentment and she grabbed hold of Diana's shoulder. "I said, don't go in there. So don't go in there."

"What's your problem? You need to get over this." Diana's cheeks grew pink, and she stared down at her sister. It was good to be tall when making dramatic pronouncements.

"I don't need to get over anything. You need to get the hell out of rooms you don't belong in." And with that she slammed Victory's door, rattling the china dogs on their shelves, leaving them in solitude to contemplate the moody, kohl-lined eyes of Duran Duran from the wall opposite.

Diana scowled. "It's not a shrine, you know." God, she was sick to death of Tex's house sometimes, with its mantel urn holding the supposed remains of her not-dead mother and the general tomblike quality of all the rooms. Tex was no relation to her and even Verity was only a half sister, and an old crotchety one who never liked her, at that. Why should she have to abide by all the unspoken rules and goofy rituals that kept the Presti family from imploding?

Verity pushed by and went downstairs. What was wrong with a shrine, anyway? Shrines commemorated treasured things that one no longer had. She hoped she would live a long life because she could not bear to think of the distressingly vacant shrine her family would have to erect to her current life: a box containing her Barnes & Noble name tag, bamboo knitting needles, gooey pudding treats. Her stomach gurgled. Pudding treats, she realized, had become a major component of her adult life, part of her own defining crapulence.

She heard Thelma's car pull up in the driveway. Like its owner, it was tiny and tan and had a kind of glossy embalmed look about it. Diana said a quick good-bye to Tex, ignored Verity, and threw herself into the Mercedes. Thelma asked her to stow the band uniform in the trunk, as the spangles looked "strange" and might possibly scratch the leather interior. With Diana and Thelma gone, the house resumed its quietude.

"I better go, too," Verity said.

Tex's face fell and frown lines gathered around his mouth. "Aw, we hardly even got a chance to talk."

She gave a helpless shrug as though it were all out of her hands, that spending more time in this sad little house was simply impossible given her demanding clerking schedule.

"I appreciate you coming over and helping me in the yard today, honey. I've been having a tough time finding people who are willing to trade dental work for gardening. Even Charlie's not interested—I think he's afraid of the pain involved in draining an abscess and repairing his crowns."

Trimming his rosebushes was no great task, she thought. Her whole life was a swirling maelstrom of monotony. At least helping Tex in the yard made her feel useful.

Her father went on. "It's too bad we didn't get to chat. I wanted to know if you had a nice time seeing all your old friends the other night, and if you were excited about the reunion."

A familiar throbbing began in her brain. Despite her given name and all the baggage that went along with it, she usually found it easy to lie to her dad, so eager was he to believe that she was happy and her life fulfilling. But those lies took a psychic fortification for which she could not dredge up the required heartiness today. "It was okay. Oh, you know how it is: everyone's talking about their kids and careers and I'm just standing there like a dummy."

"You're not a dummy! You have a good job in a good bookstore. You've never complained before."

"I never *thought* about it before. I decided I'm just a jerk with a jerk job."

Tex's face flushed and he gasped. "Don't *say* that! How could you say such a thing? You are the least jerky person I know. You are the *opposite* of a jerk."

"I'm glad you like me, Dad. We all know what Mom thinks of me."

"The last time I drove by your mother's, she was standing on the front porch in her pink dressing gown, aluminum foil in her hair from a home highlighting treatment, yelling at the neighbor kids to get off her lawn." He smiled. "So I wouldn't worry about what she thinks. And of *course* I like you. You're smart and kind, and you're a good bookstore clerk."

"A good bookstore clerk? That's like saying I'm a good pedestrian or I floss well. Who cares? It's meaningless."

"No, it isn't," he insisted. "It's important to be a good clerk, and don't even get me started on the flossing. I remember you saying a long time ago, 'I want to own a store that sells cool stuff,' and you're just getting practice for that now. You've always been happy around books. One day you might own a store, maybe even your own bookshop. You just have to put your mind to it, like Hermie did."

Verity closed her eyes. Tex's admiration of the little elf determined to become a dentist in *Rudolph the Red-Nosed Reindeer* had served as a lifelong tool through which he could instill his values in his family. "Please, Dad. Do you know how humiliating it is not to be able to measure up to Hermie the dentist? Face it: Hermie at least had a talent. I do not."

"Potential," Tex argued. "It's all about potential and realizing what you're capable of." He put his arm around his daughter, walked her to her car, and shared a morsel of dental life-wisdom: "A great man once said, 'You don't have to floss all your teeth; just the ones you want to keep.' "

Gin had followed them outside, strolled halfway into a boxwood hedge, and stopped, only her rear end visible. Periodically she wagged her tail.

"Oh, Gin," Verity said sadly.

"Don't you worry about her," Tex said. "She sees something there, you can bet on it."

"She's standing in a bush, Dad."

"Again, I refer back to the word *potential*," he said. "Some part of her brain remembers that chipmunks like to dig under these hedges. She sees potential in that boxwood shrub."

Verity prepared to back the car out when Tex motioned for her to stop. He leaned in her window and said, "Everyone has potential, Verity. Some elves really are meant to be dentists, and some disenchanted retail clerks with college degrees are meant to own bookstores."

ten

laurel stared down at sebastian and the carnage of broken toys and smashed graham crackers embedded in the living room rug. He had just undergone a grand mal tantrum, his blood vessels a visible and throbbing blue network down the center of his forehead. They stood out from his skin like the veins of a racehorse in the prime of condition.

The child had collapsed, panting and wild-eyed. Scratches spidered his arms from his own thrashing as well as Laurel's unsuccessful attempts at gentle restraint. A welt rose on her cheek, a result of the Thomas the Tank Engine missile lobbed from ground zero, and a ragged chunk of dark hair, scalp thankfully unattached, lay on the floor between them. Guests were due in sixty minutes; Stan had not yet come home from work; the oven was cold; a brown, spreading stain inched out upon the rug. Laurel's gaze traveled over the wreckage and came to rest again on her son, whom she regarded with a growing, familiar sensation of fear and dislike.

She used the plaintive voice that all the parenting magazines said not to use. "Sebastian, we're going to have a party tonight! Don't you want to have a party? Please help Mommy clean up the living room."

Outraged at this request, Sebastian let loose with a howl of primal anguish. But daylong tantruming was hard; he lay back on the floor and whined, pausing only to launch trains at his mother's head as she tidied up the room around him. Sleep came over him and as soon as he conked out, Laurel retrieved him from the floor and carried him to his room. She watched him in his bed for a moment; even in sleep, red gullies scored his puckered, angry little face. She thought he looked like a dried-up, rotten apple. A six o'clock nap only spelled trouble for the latter part of the evening, but there was nothing else for it; she had to shower and cook. In a pinch, she could depend on Baby NyQuil later, if the need arose.

Roast in cold oven, check; vegetables ready for baking, check; sugarless pumpkin pie, cooled on counter, ready, check. She flew into the bathroom, turned on the shower, and cringed at her reflection in the vanity mirror, at the red lump throbbing on her cheek. She would say nothing about it; it was too embarrassing to admit that her own toddler had assaulted her. She brightened momentarily as she stepped into the stream of blessedly hot water: perhaps everyone would think Stan had done it. There would be pity, unspoken and therefore unjustified, but she'd take it. Pity was vastly underrated.

charlie first held the white button-down (gift from Mother) in front of himself, eyeing his reflection in the dresser mirror, then switched its position with a brown knit polo shirt. He supposed the brown shirt was more fashionable—he'd bought it at Target—while the white shirt had come from the Gaslight Men's Shop, a locally owned business patronized by Mrs. Brown and four other senior citizens in Rogers Park. A faded and sedate dinosaur, stuck to the corner of the mirror, watched in critical silence. In comparison to the white shirt, his teeth would look even more rotten, more dead.

The ghost watched sorrowfully from the foot of the bed. He had considered himself quite dapper in his day and missed wearing clothes. Charlie had the same build, the same unfortunate dental tragedies, the same predilection for dark and somber earth tones. The ghost made a movement with what had been his arm and suddenly the button-down fell off its hanger into a large dust bunny next to the bed. Charlie looked down at it and decided it was just as well; brown clothes were clearly the right choice.

He sat on the edge of the bed, pulling on brown socks with worn-out heels. The mattress, a twenty-year-old cheap twin, sagged under his heft and threatened to drag him down into its quagmire depths of bedbugs and horsehair and conspicuously stained ticking. These things in this room were his; at least, they were provisions courtesy of Mr. and Mrs. Brown. Childhood memories, furniture, the dinosaur stickers, the Intellivision in the back of the closet, blue and white wallpaper of baseball diamonds and men with bats. In his old apartment, the one on Western Avenue in that cold and verminified three-flat, he had had things of his own: a lumpy futon, a TV tray table, an upholstered rocking chair, all rethrifted now. The last rays of the evening sun filtered through his window, refracting through the clear polyhedron dice on his nightstand.

Charlie moved to slip the *Labor Officium Auxilium* into his nightstand drawer and noticed the sunbeam glinting off the gold type on the cover. He had come to regard author C. Aquilus warmly, as a friend he could count on to guide him in choosing a fake career. But having read and reread the chapters on career opportunities for demagogues, high priests, monks, botanists, and bards, he began to daydream about actually changing career paths—or at least delving into sideline possibilities. Particularly enticing to him was the shaman/healer section, which detailed many methods for exorcising evil spirits. That ghost was to blame for Charlie's failure in life, he was sure of it. It wanted him to stay here in the apartment forever and share its anguish. C. Aquilus had practically said as much. He hesitated, holding the book aloft above the nightstand. There was something familiar there . . .

He pulled his old high school Latin-English dictionary from his bookshelf and turned to the A section. Aquilus: swarthy, dark, brown-colored. Brown. Like his clothes. Like his name. Like his teeth. If this wasn't a sign he should take the book's suggestions seriously, well, then, what *would* be? And what did it matter anyway? He connected with the *Labor Officium Auxilium*'s message, with his new friend C. Aquilus. Charlie smiled and put the booklet away. The color of his parachute was brown.

"Are you eating dinner here or not?" Mrs. Brown hollered from downstairs.

"No, Mom," Charlie yelled. "I told you I was going out with Verity."

Earlier, Mrs. Brown had shoved into a beige pair of "comfort walkers," the flesh spillage of her ankles smothering the top perimeter of the shoes, and she now derived a perverse enjoyment out of the pain pulsating from her feet, swollen and bloodless as larvae. She tapped one toe and thought of all she had suffered: the corns, the hammertoes, the bunions, the hemorrhoids (during all four pregnancies), the stretch marks, the varicose veins, the curious burning in her gut whenever she watched Mr. Brown lay a game of solitaire on the family room table.

"I certainly don't see how you can afford to go out to dinner on your salary. It's just foolish to waste your money. Unless she's paying, and frankly I can't see how a cashier can afford it either. You two ought to spend less and work more."

Charlie headed down the stairs and charged through the foyer. "We're going to her friend's house. It'll be free, so don't worry."

Mrs. Brown stepped aside and let him pass. "Is that what you're wearing?"

The smell of Hungarian goulash wafted in from the pot simmering on the stove. All three Browns felt a cold spot move through the foyer, heading for the kitchen. The ghost, having made his wardrobe preferences known to Charlie, now turned his attention to supper.

Charlie grabbed his keys from the Peg-Board hanging by the hall mirror. Mr. Brown timidly followed him out the front door and tried to shove a ten-dollar bill into his son's hand. Charlie looked down at the money and blinked, then shook his head and tried to hand it back.

"Please," said Mr. Brown. "I want to."

when verity heard the doorbell buzz, she leaned out her front window and called down to Charlie that she'd be right out. A real intercom would have been nice, but her landlord could not see the point in such a security system.

"Wouldn't you feel bad if you buzzed in a rapist or a murderer?" He countered her one intercom request with this infallible logic.

For the first time in a long while, Verity had stood confounded at her closet. The secondhand 1940s dresses, hand-knit sweaters, and flattering-to-every-shape A-line skirts that rounded out her wardrobe seemed suddenly lacking tonight. It wasn't that she had developed a case of unexpected low self-confidence, but rather that she wished she had clothes that would allow her to blend unobtrusively into the group of people she was about to see. At the bookstore, it didn't matter what she wore; all saw her for what she was—a clerk—and no Armani dress or sackcloth could change that. She chose a pair of jeans (she could not think of the last time she had appeared in public in jeans, but they were ubiquitous and this particular pair semicomfortable) and a short-sleeved vintage blouse, pig pink in color but lightweight, roomy, with a darling march of silvery gray diamonds around the collar. Everyone wore jeans, utilitarian, stiff, and singularly unmatched for discomfort in the female-garment world, but perhaps in these dreary dungarees no one would look askance at her and start questioning exactly what it was she'd been doing with her life the past fifteen years. People in jeans were just like everyone else, living the same ordinary, desolate lives. *There was much to be said for fading into your surroundings,* she thought; *much that could be accomplished when no one looked your way.*

Verity checked her reflection for the last time. She nodded in satisfaction; she was bland and unassuming, and even the thrifted cat's-eye frames were, she felt, modest and plain, lacking the rhinestones rimming her other pair. The entire effect was sort of a makeover in reverse. Just once she wanted to see a movie with a renovation scene where the extroverted victim is made over into a sedately dressed girl and coached to be a quiet, introspective, yet friendly and thoughtful individual who was not assumed to be a freak because she'd rather prowl the bargain bins for satin hostess aprons than go to parties.

"Pink," Charlie said approvingly as she slid in next to him. "Very nice." He glanced down. "Are those . . . ?"

"Don't say anything."

He pulled out onto Chicago Avenue and headed toward the Kennedy. "Well, it's just that I've never seen you in jeans before."

Verity sighed. "They don't make jeans that fit Italian girls' butts."

"But you're only half Italian. Thelma's WASPy."

She admitted, "I may have inherited her Germanic objection to emotional exhibitions and her Scottish penny-pinching ways, but my butt is all Italian."

Thank heaven for small mercies, thought Charlie.

"What do you think of my shirt?" he asked. "Too brown? Should I not have worn brown pants?"

Brown shirt with brown stripes, brown pants, brown bowling shoes. "No, it's just the right amount of brown."

"The pants are kind of itchy," he complained, squirming in his seat. "I'm all chafed."

"They're probably Sanfor-Set permanent press poly. Sanfor-Set clothes are soaked in ammonia to keep them from wrinkling and synthetic fabrics are chemically treated and then baked in an oven. No wonder you're chafed."

"You bought them for me! You bought me ammonia pants."

"But they only cost a dollar seventy-nine." She watched the cars fly by on the highway. "Maybe I should have worn brown— it's a good color for introverts. I think we introverts get short shrift in modern society and pop culture. People are always trying to get us to strip down and get out of the library and put aside our knitting needles."

"Actually," Charlie said, "I don't think we're technically introverts. I think we just don't care for people very much."

Verity turned to him with that wide, demented grin she could not quash whenever he said these things that were so right and true. There could not be a better boyfriend than Charlie Brown.

the siko house, gleefully referred to as such around the subdivision, boasted that pastel blandness of its near-identical neighbors, which made the homophonic "Psycho House" appellation that much more disturbing. Skinny maple saplings stood squarely on the parkways; in twenty years, they might cast shade. Each driveway, barely thirty feet of cement, led up to a double garage hosting an SUV or two, an array of mint recreational equipment, and a snowblower. On blustery winter mornings, the men waved to one another over the din of their snowblowing engines during the three minutes it took to clear their driveways. A broom or child's red plastic snow shovel served to clear the front steps.

As Stan moved Sebastian's toys into the garage, he decided that his shoulder muscles had atrophied from four years of extreme inactivity. He used the leafblower to clean off the grass clippings left on the driveway, exposing thirty feet of concrete cracked and off plumb, just like the rest of his house. Every driveway on his block had also cracked, and the siding on each western wall had faded and buckled, drawing away from its skeleton. Each house had seemingly gone up overnight, quickly, crappily, a tiny tree in each tiny lawn, each front door sagging in a permanent curtsy to the street, a happy family in each happy home. Of course, they weren't all *identical;* some houses were beige while others were white, Stan admitted, and there were other differences, too, interior ones that you would never know existed unless you were invited inside, or glimpsed them through the windows late at night, which you could not help but do sometimes.

•   •   •

carolyn proclaimed the Siko house "cozy," and Laurel's jaw twitched. Stan gave Craig the tour.

"Two minutes is all it takes to view this dump, stem to stern," he said.

"It's nice," Craig said. "You did a good job remodeling the bathroom." Some company had remodeled the bathrooms in Craig's house; he wasn't sure who, only that one day he came home and the master bath was peach and stunk of Fruitopia.

Carolyn glanced at Laurel and noticed the welt on her cheek. "God, Laurel, what happened to you?"

Laurel tried to implicate her husband with an inclination of her head and wild eyebrow movements, but Stan ruined it.

"Our kid threw a train at her head," he said.

"Oh no," Carolyn clucked in sympathy. "Luckily I always carry stress-busting lavender eye sachet soothers in my purse." She fished around in her Dooney & Bourke bag. "Here they are. Lavender grown in Provence, mulberry leaves, eucalyptus. And in the prettiest silk cases, handstitched by cloistered French nuns." She set the bags in the freezer for a few minutes.

Laurel said, "You use these?" She could not imagine Carolyn defending herself from an attacking baby Aura, though maybe that weirdo Kronos pushed his mother around. Yes, he had that dangerous post-Columbine air about him.

"All the time," Carolyn assured her. "They're only fifty dollars an ounce. I go through them like bottled glacial spring water."

"So your kids beat on you, too?" Laurel gingerly applied the cool sachet to her cheek and closed her eyes in bliss. In a moment she would have to announce that she had ruined dinner.

"Well, no," Carolyn said, rather apologetically. "I use them whenever I have to wait more than five minutes in the acupuncturist's office. I get nervy when people aren't on time." She brightened. "But once Aura threw up all over the nanny. It was a real mess for our housekeeper to clean up, but I know both women appreciated the sachets I let them borrow afterward."

Stan glanced out the front window. "Two cars just pulled up. There's Will, and there's Verity and that other guy."

"Charlie," said Laurel. Hectic spots of color appeared on her cheeks and she checked her reflection in the toaster.

Carolyn said, "The single people are always late."

Charlie opened Verity's door and extended his hand to help her out. "More yuppieville," he grumbled. He saw a piece of newspaper crumpled up and lying near the curb. "Rich people are always throwing garbage out the window."

Verity asked, "Do you even know what you're talking about?"

Charlie escorted her to the door and rang the bell. "Not really. But I know what I don't like."

Will strode up behind them, clapped a hand on Charlie's shoulder. It sunk deeply into the layers of his flesh, like the hand on that NASA-quality mattress commercial. "Hey, it's the Internet theorist."

White dents appeared on either side of Charlie's nose and capillaries exploded in his cheeks. He would need food soon, and the health loaf wasn't going to cut it.

Laurel opened the door, tears swimming in her eyes. "Hello," she said. "I forgot to turn the oven on."

Stricken, Charlie grasped her hands. "Our dinner?"

"Ruined." She sputtered a sob and choked the word out. They followed her into the house. "I turned the one oven on for the vegetables but forgot to turn the one on with the roast beef."

Charlie groaned. God hated him. Why couldn't the vegetables have been in the cold oven; why? Fate's cruel jokes always knocked him senseless.

Verity consoled her. "It's okay, Laurel. We'll figure something else out."

Laurel sniffed and turned to her. "Can you help me cook something quickly?"

"Sure," she answered. "If it's dessert. I'm only good at desserts."

Laurel rummaged around in the refrigerator as Craig and Stan soberly regarded the carcass of cold raw beef sitting in the roasting pan on top of the stove. "I have lentils and brown rice syrup and tempeh."

Verity glanced at Charlie, who had begun to mop his brow. "Or we could order out," she suggested.

Twenty minutes later, they had decided that only the take-out menu from Kombu King could appease the omnivores, gourmand vegetarians, and health goons gathered in the Siko kitchen.

"Hey!" Laurel brightened. "I still have a sugarless pumpkin pie for dessert."

"Oh, good," lamented Charlie.

Stan said, "Laurel, would it kill you to just put a little sugar in a pie, for Christ's sake?"

She retorted, "It's a *vegetable*. Who puts sugar on vegetables?"

"If you're serving it in a pie shell after dinner, it's dessert."

She looked around at the unenthusiastic faces of her dinner guests. "But this way you can really taste the pumpkin."

"The taste of pumpkin is offensive and unpleasant," her husband said. "That's why people put sugar on it."

Carolyn suggested a tour of the house while they waited for the food. Laurel put her hands on her hips and gave a horrible imitation of a smile. Tour? What tour? *Here's our kitchen, there's the living room connected to the dining room, and upstairs our child is sleeping off a tantrum where he beat me with a train. Deep breath, okay* . . . "This is our dining room. Stan just put in new double-glazed windows—I only had to nag him for two years—which offer great protection."

Will asked, "From the elements?"

Verity asked, "From bugs?"

Laurel stared at them. "From potential child abduction."

Everyone nodded and moved into the next room.

"Oh, let me handle this one," said Stan. Laurel threw up her arms and rolled her eyes. "Yes, see this little nook off the living room? The one strewn with every movie tie-in and PVC nightmare toy known to mankind? This was supposed to be my den.

Of course, we needed more room for the toys, as they could not possibly all fit into Sebastian's bedroom, the basement, and the yard. But I'm not bitter." He folded his arms across his chest and looked wistfully into the playroom.

"For crying out loud, I said we could change it sometime!" Laurel yelled.

Verity glanced into the room. The gears of her brain started humming. "A den. Hmmm. I see a lot of possibilities here, Stan. Every guy needs a manly room."

"Yes, we do," he agreed.

Carolyn said, "Craig has a den with really nice leather club chairs and a walk-in humidor and a Bose stereo system. It's where he goes to escape me and the kids." She tried to laugh, but there was bitterness in her voice, a sour and sudden jealousy that closed up her throat and set her lips into a thin, hard line. Why were men always allowed to hole themselves up in cozy little enclaves whenever they wished, but mothers had to make themselves available at all hours for homework help and snotty noses and mediating tiffs between the household staff?

Craig thought about his den, that room where he sat by himself with the lights off, getting drunk.

Verity said, "The den of the 1950s is really a lost room. These days, the best you can hope for is a home office, and that's not really the same thing. I have about a hundred *Better Homes and Gardens* magazines from the forties and fifties and they all agree: a man needs at least a corner of his own."

"Yes, yes!" Stan grew excited. "Just a corner, is that too much to ask?"

She went on. "But here you have a whole nook. There's a lot you could do with this nook."

"Like what? Can it be done on a budget?"

"I don't know how to do anything not on a budget." She tapped her fingers against her chin, thinking. "Give me a few days and I can come up with a real plan. Of course, there are some basics to go on for the Manly Den, based on what you like.

Cowboy themes were popular in the fifties, mostly for boys, but you can still transpose some western object-based stuff into the modern Manly Den, if that's your thing. There's always the fishing motif or the north woods cabin or the cocktail theme—cheesily overused these days, but still viable options. Shellacked cedar plaques, the kind with bad epigrams stenciled on, just scream out 'Manly Den.' And best of all, this can all be obtained at the thrift."

Stan said, "We have a souvenir driftwood clock from the Wisconsin Dells. Will that work?"

"Perhaps. Is Jesus etched onto it anywhere?"

"No."

"Good. Because Jesus, God love Him, just doesn't fit into the Manly Den decor."

Stan smiled, admiring her expertise. "My den is in your hands. Even if you fill it with useless garbage from the thrift store."

"Useless garbage? I must disagree. My apartment is full of the most wonderful crap you've ever imagined. Portable miniature bowling alleys, rotary dial phones, Hawaiian records, boomerang tables, tea towels from 1947, combo cigarette dispenser/Bibles, mugs that say 'Mug,' big-eyed waif jigsaw puzzles, pink Melmac sugar bowls, homemade ceramic reindeer, photographs of strangers. Take a look around my place sometime: if it's fabulous and I own it, it came from the thrift."

Verity stood there, pink-cheeked and breathless. Her vocal cords ached; she had "thrift throat," a condition common to culture junkers. Her eyes shone bright and brilliant, green as a cat's. Charlie smiled at her encouragingly, pleased to see her one often-suppressed fondness oozing out. Carolyn smiled at her, too. She had forgotten this eccentric side to Verity's usually phlegmatic personality.

Rubbing his hands together, Stan jerked his head toward the toys in the nook and said, "I can't wait to clear this shit out."

A cloud darkened Laurel's forehead. "It's time to pick up Kombu King."

• • •

will and verity set off in his VW to pick up the food. As was expected, Craig and Carolyn didn't have any cash on them. There seemed to be some natural law about the richest couple in any group never carrying any money.

"I guess we can use my credit card," Craig had said unhappily.

"Oh, forget it," Will replied. "I'll float you."

"I'll pay you back."

As he drove, Will thought of the story Craig had once told him, about the time Carolyn's parents had paid for the bathroom remodeling and ignored Craig's requests for plain tile and no ruffles. When Craig paid for his own remodeling he could choose his own colors, his father-in-law had said, and everyone laughed.

Will said, "No problem," and bought the Kickels' Kombu Surprise with his KJ tips.

Verity held the take-out bags on her lap. She had not ridden in a car with a man other than Charlie or her father in a long time, not counting the time she had to drive Bob to the emergency room after a bad fishwich incident at the store. "Do you think the Kombu Spareribs were a good choice? It said, 'Chef's recommendation' in the menu."

"Are they real spareribs or spareribs made from kombu?"

"Can you make spareribs from kombu?"

Will said, "You can make anything from kombu." He glanced over at her. "I don't think Charlie looked too happy when you volunteered to come with me."

Verity had decided to accompany Will after she had heard Laurel admiring Charlie's brown polo shirt, proclaiming it to be "frightfully handsome" and so complementary to his brown eyes. He had mugged like a bashful schoolboy, and Laurel had picked stray fabric pills off his elbows. It was a sickening display.

"He'll be fine," she replied to Will in as natural a voice as she could muster. "He's good with strangers. He dragged me to Blues Fest last year and we got separated, and when I finally found him, he had made friends with a group of Polish tuck-pointers.

The language barrier was not a problem, as terrible blues music transcends all cultures."

"It's sad, ironic commentary that the very worst Chicago blues—that horrendous Bruce Willis rubbish—is mostly what you'll hear at Blues Fest. God, how I hate it."

"Me, too! I hate all the festivals."

"Really? I hate them, too! I hate the music and the food and the people."

She relaxed in her seat and grinned. "I forgot how much we had in common, Will."

He had, too. Suddenly, he got this inexplicable, perfect calmness in his head; it felt nearly as intense as his best rages. "Well, even so, maybe we shouldn't have left Charlie alone with all those married people."

"I hadn't thought of it that way," she admitted. "They may try to sway him over to the dark side."

Nothing wrong with the Dark Side, Will thought. After all, the high school cafeteria was where he first met her. "Weddings don't always have to lead you down the path of ruin."

Abruptly, a new thought entered her head. "You know, my sister once thrifted a wedding dress at the Salvation Army for like six bucks. And it wasn't one of those twinkly blobbo affairs, either; it was a column sheath of ivory silk, handmade by someone's nana. What a score. She would have worn it, too."

Will swallowed uncomfortably. "I always felt bad I didn't make it to her funeral, Verity."

The smell of the Krispy Kombu Tidbits drifted up from one of the bags, the delicate deep-fat odor twined about her like a creeper vine. "It's okay, Will. You were away at college. But, man, you should have seen that dress. It's probably still in her closet, but if I go rooting around in there, my dad will cry."

"Still a shrine, eh?"

"Yeah. For someone who hates God, he's very religious."

• • •

they spread their Kombu Krap all over the Sikos' dining room table. The idea was for everyone to share, but nobody wanted Laurel's green mess health platter, and Carolyn declined everything but the Kombu Surprise, which was just a bowl of kombu, which evidently was the surprise.

"Sparerib?" Verity offered Laurel a dripping, juicy bone.

"No, thank you."

"Sorry. I forgot you don't eat meat."

"Oh, I eat meat," Laurel said, "I just don't eat anything with a sugar glaze. Or any sugar, actually."

Is this why I have no friends? Verity wondered. *Because I can't freak out over fattening food?* That could not be it. There had to be plenty of other girls in the world who, like her, ate sugar and junk sometimes and got on with their lives. Victory had been that way, unobsessive, laid-back, fun. No sugar? Why not just cut out beer and sleeping in and schlocky monster movies while you're at it? Sure, just expunge all the little pleasures that mitigated life on this hideous planet.

Stan helped himself to one of the spareribs. "God, I'd love to have just one day free of the sugar police."

Laurel felt her cheeks redden. Why should she have to feel embarrassed simply because she ate better than everyone else? It was a hard road getting to where she was right now, made far more difficult by the kind of mother she was stuck with. Nobody understood the paradox of growing up female and Jewish. Every day it was, "Eat! You're all skin and bones," and then, "Hey, don't eat so much! You want to get fat?" And Stan, that bastard, didn't have to roll his eyes with his little snarky comment. Oh, he was always rolling his eyes and getting irritated with her. It wasn't *her* fault she had to eat at the same times every day without varying from the routine by even one instant; she had a low blood sugar problem for God's sake! At least, that's what it felt like. She'd have had it diagnosed by now if Stan's HMO wasn't so lousy.

"Don't forget," Craig said to Will, "I'm paying you back for mine and Carolyn's food."

"It's fine; quit worrying."

"No, I insist." His voice rose in hope. "Come over sometime this week and I'll have cash."

Will threw down his Kombu Hot-Fat Friedling. Everyone stared at him, no doubt pitying the poor KJ who had to shell out his pennies for richer friends. God, he was sick of pity, of people looking down on his job and finances and lack of serious romantic entanglements. "Look, I can afford the twenty bucks, if that's what you're thinking. I'm not broke just because I'm Polish and grew up in Westmont."

"I wasn't saying that at all," Craig began.

"Please, I know what everyone thinks of me, and I don't really give a damn, you know? So I'm a KJ, so what? At least I'm not a slave to a corporate swine."

"Like me?" Craig and Stan asked simultaneously.

"Sparerib?" Verity offered one to Carolyn, hoping to diffuse the tension.

"Well, I'll lick off the glaze, but I don't want to eat the meat," she replied, and proceeded to do so as the men watched in blissful fixation. Laurel bit down hard on her fork; Verity choked loudly on her Coke, but no one could be bothered to whomp her on the back. It was not that difficult to redirect men's attention. All you needed was meat and a woman capable of meaningful interaction with a sparerib.

"Sucked pretty well clean, if I do say so myself," Carolyn said afterward, wiping the sauce from her mouth. "Now who wants my meat?"

kombu king thus vanquished, they retired to the Siko backyard for after-dinner drinks. Craig brought a bottle of wine and poured a few glasses while Will retrieved two six-packs of Fat Weasel Ale from the fridge, both having been apprised of Laurel's home alcohol zero-tolerance policy ("Bring your own, if you must"). Frankly, she was not thrilled that people were drinking in her house at all, but Stan pointed out that as they were all outdoors, no one was technically drinking in the house.

Several webbed chairs had been set up on a slab of concrete abutting the back of the house. A tree in the last throes of Dutch elm disease stood wasted and black in the corner, threatening to thunder down upon a plastic playhouse and rusted jungle gym. Carolyn and Craig exchanged glances; what terrible antienjoyment the Sikos must suffer sitting out here in this scorch of suburban blight. On the other hand, Will, Verity, and Charlie relished an evening spent outside without the usual urban accompaniment of gunfire, Mexican oom-pah-pah music, car alarms, and intermittent screams.

"I would like this someday," said Charlie, surveying the grass patch and dead tree. "This . . . outdoor area."

"It's called a yard," said Stan.

Charlie nodded. All this suburban lingo was hard to keep track of.

Laurel got up to refill Carolyn's water; though she had Volvic in the fridge, she derived a perverse pleasure out of filling the glass from the tap.

Stan watched his wife disappear into the house, then turned to Verity. He stretched his legs out lazily and clasped his hands behind his head in a practiced move; the posture made his pecs and shoulders look bigger. "So I'll call you soon to get started on my Manly Den."

"Okay."

"We'll make an evening of it. You'll drag me from thrift store to thrift store, I'll acquiesce to your good taste. It'll be just like old times."

Old times? Verity frowned. *Does that mean you'll flirt with me when nobody else is around and tell me things about my face and bod that nobody ever says and put your hands on me in some innocent but embarrassingly stimulating way and never kiss me? And kind of ignore me but not really when other girls walk by, in that way that makes me feel alternately silly, invisible, and then grateful when you finally turn around and look at my face, all that light and fake interest in your eyes? Great.* But even as she thought this, a cold thrill stole through her blouse and circled her spine in its grasp.

Old times? Will scowled at Verity, then rolled his eyes and chugged his beer. *Like every other weekend of senior year when you would come over and get drunk and tell me what a shit Stan was for tormenting you, and why did he toy with your affection, and why couldn't he be a decent guy like me? And then you'd lay against my chest while we watched reruns of Merv Griffin, with me sweating and breathless, Levi's a ridiculous pup tent to which you were thank God oblivious, hoping my father would not come down the stairs, hoping I had enough Bacardi stashed under the stained and pitted sofa bed to get you to transfer some of that misplaced affection. Which you finally did, then pretended it never happened.*

Old times? Charlie looked from Verity to Stan. *What old times?*

Laurel returned, and talk turned to the upcoming reunion, particularly to the cards sent out by the alumni committee requesting information on the attendees' current professions.

"This is going to put a cramp in my style," Will complained. "I can't walk around the gym with a name tag introducing me as 'Will Demske, KJ.' Why do we have to reveal this kind of thing? It'll totally eclipse the fact that I didn't get fat and I still have all my hair, which is far more significant."

All eyes strayed to Charlie.

"What else would you put?" asked Craig.

"I don't know, but no one would understand how KJ became my career. I barely understand it myself."

Stan said, "Well, if you're not putting down 'KJ,' I'm not putting down 'project manager.' I sound like a dud. A boring, lifeless, pencil-pushing dud."

"Yeah, but if I don't put down 'KJ,' what will I put?"

"You're always going on about that single guys' manifesto

you've been writing," Stan replied. "Why don't you put down 'essayist' or 'crank'?"

"Because if anyone asked me about it, I'd embarrass myself since I can't correctly pronounce a lot of the big words I know."

Craig cleared his throat. "I already sent mine in. I put down 'activist.' "

Will said, "How are you an activist? You proofread content for a pharmaceutical Web site."

"I'm active in the, uh, social sphere. I participate in causes. I donate blood, and once Carolyn and I escorted women going into Planned Parenthood."

Carolyn set down her wineglass with force. "I didn't know you put 'activist' as your career. Now what am I going to put? I was just going to say 'mother' and leave it at that, but if you're going to be a damn activist, I can't be just a mother."

"So put down 'activist,' too. Or activist-hyphen-mother," her husband suggested.

"Can we do that?" Carolyn looked around. "Can we hyphenate? Because if Craig here thinks he's an activist, I'm *at least* as much of an activist. Or I was, at any rate."

"Honestly," Stan said, "I've been thinking all along how I'd like to get back into playing music or fringe documentary-making. I might as well put that down. Sure, it may start out as just a hobby, but I think I can parlay it into—"

Laurel could not hold her tongue anymore. First the alcohol, now this. "What's wrong with project manager? Suddenly it's not good enough? I'm sick to death of you complaining about work. Most men would be grateful to even have a job, and if you think for one minute that you can quit working to be a rock musician or something—"

"Don't worry, nobody's quitting anything." Stan tilted his head and regarded his wife through narrowed, dark eyes. "I just want something else for myself."

She said, "And how come all they care about is your profession? What about marital status and kids?"

Carolyn said, "That's not fair to the gay or transgendered alumni."

"We have transgendered alumni?" Stan asked. "Cool."

Charlie spoke up. "What about Laurel and me? Will we get name tags even though it isn't our reunion?"

Verity said, "On the card there was space where you could fill out the name of your spousal equivalent. I guess we could put a career title for you in there, and while we're at it, we might as well cram in our current gender/sexual orientation/political affiliation."

Will said, "I think White Sox/Cubs affiliation is a stronger binary distinction for some people than gender."

Charlie said, "What about PC/Mac loyalty? I have to use a PC at work, but at heart I've always been—"

Laurel looked at Stan. "You put 'poet' for me. Poet-mother. No, mother-poet. Mother should come first, I suppose. Or mother–spoken word artist."

Charlie looked at Verity. Now it was time to announce what all his research had been leading up to—C. Aquilus would be proud. "And for me: urban shaman."

There are probably no two words in modern English that can cause silence to descend so rapidly upon a group discussion of real and perceived career failures as "urban shaman."

"What about your Internet theorist job?" asked Will.

Charlie replied, "I can sympathize with Stan about wanting something more for yourself. About how you have your drudge job, and then you have your passion. Shamanism is something I've been reading up on, primarily to banish the ghost in my parents' apartment—you may have heard something about that—but I really feel called to it. Community life is so splintered these days, and I'd like to make a difference to the social circles I travel in, such as they are." He looked at the men and women gathered around him and nodded in satisfaction. "Yes. 'Urban shaman' it is."

"But what is it?" asked Verity.

"It's spiritual." He said no more. The vocation was new, and frankly he hadn't worked out every niggling detail yet. But he remained convinced that his parents' apartment was haunted by the man who was murdered there fifty years ago, and that's why his life was such a mess. If only he'd had an urban shaman to exorcise the place, he might have made something of himself by now.

charlie grasped the steering wheel as tight as grim death to keep from floating out of the car. What was this weightless feeling? This absence of chains, of gloom? He felt it as soon as he announced his intention to pursue his vocation, which truthfully had been heretofore only a glimpse of a dream. The corners of his mouth crinkled up, begetting unfamiliar spasms in the lower half of his face. He touched his curving lips gingerly. Charlie was happy.

Verity, not so much. No one appeared surprised when she revealed that she filled out her alumni information card with "Bookstore clerk. What else?" Why lie? She knew who she was.

Off the expressway ramp, Charlie idled at a red light and poked around in his mouth. "Ow," he said. Something bad was happening in there. He poked it again, as addicted to tormenting his teeth as he was to worrying about them.

"Take a look," he begged. "It's number thirty-one."

Verity obliged. Children of dentists often found that the non-dental public considered them almost as good as the real thing.

"Well?"

She said, "Have you ever seen those pictures of houses after a tornado, how the sides and roof and everything is gone, but the foundation is still there in the ground? That's how your tooth looks. The sides are busted and there is only the substructure in the gum. But now it, too, is breaking apart. One piece looks like it's broken off from the root but is still attached to the gum, so it won't come free without a fair bit of pain. At least, that's my diagnosis. How did this happen?"

"Last night I experimented with pulling my own teeth. The filling just popped off, sticking to the three pieces of gum I was chewing. And it's one of my main molars, too. I'm torn up about it. Maybe I should lay off the gum and the Sugar Babies?"

"If you keep performing your own dentistry, pretty soon you're not going to be able to eat at all. The light's green."

Charlie drove off. This sounded a great deal worse than he had expected, though it might help him lose weight. Could Tex even fix such a problem in his home clinic? Probably not, and anyway he'd need five acres of yardwork-worthy land with which to barter an even exchange. Another dentist, no matter how marginally qualified, would charge a lot of money for this kind of repair, and he had a lot of expenses at the moment, what with the shaman equipment he needed to procure and Verity's birthday coming up in August.

Yet, though he cited to others and to himself the prohibitive cost as the reason he had avoided getting his teeth fixed all these years, deep down he knew his real problem with the insane amount of dental work he needed was this: he was afraid of the pain. Even though Tex was a gentle dentist, he'd only ever cleaned Charlie's teeth before. Never had Tex actually had to use . . . *instruments;* the kind that plugged in and made horrific noises and obligated the dentist to shield his face with plastic jockey goggles. He supposed one day he would just have to bite the bullet, providing he had any teeth left at all by that time, and just go to an oral surgeon with a vial of Valium, but for now the possible expense excused him from setting up an appointment.

Charlie glanced at Verity, at her blond hair in its continual state of static frenzy, clinging to her lipsticked mouth, the ill-fitting glasses she continually shoved up the bridge of her nose. He'd wait on ol' number thirty-one. *Worst case,* he reasoned, *I can have my teeth replaced sometime in the future. I cannot forgo my new career path, nor can I undo not buying her a birthday present.*

Perhaps the idea of his tooth-as-blown-apart-house-foundation implanted itself in her mind, because Verity then said, "I'd like a house someday."

"Really?"

"Yeah. Not like the one we just escaped from, I mean. Just a regular old house that looks different from all the other houses on the street. A place for me and my junk."

He said, "I'll buy you a house someday. With its own outdoor area."

"Really? Cool. This urban shaman thing of yours must be very lucrative. Wanna tell me about it?"

"Soon," he promised. "You work second shift tomorrow, right? Maybe you can help me buy some shaman-type accoutrements before work. I'll just leave my job a little early."

"Okay, but I don't know any good root-and-herb stores."

"Well, I was thinking first of a cape. I need a cape. It seems like something a shaman should have."

Verity said, "I agree. Does it have to be new?"

"Of course not. I like to think the essence of the previous wearers would add to the mystical qualities."

The bookstore clerk, happy at last to have a project at hand, turned her head to feel the wind sail through her open window. "Tomorrow," she said, "we thrift."

eleven

she plunged her hands deep into the racks and walked down the aisle, pausing only when the right fabric slid over her fingers. Summer having entered its humid, sweltering zenith, certain fabrics—old rayon, silk, linen—drew her, hypnotized her with their cool promise of days sipping lemonade on the front porch, of nights dressed in kick-ass muumuus, tipsy on girlie drinks, dazzled by tiki torches.

Verity had in her mind a list. The actual, physical list resided somewhere in her apartment, but she knew its contents as well as she knew *The Forbidden Sounds of Don Tiki* songbook, or the inflated rate of Six Million Dollar Man metal wastebaskets. A thrift store is an everyday treasure hunt, and the list of things she needed had grown to epic proportions. She knew that people who thrifted with her for the first time were always amazed at the amount of stuff she needed. But what was the point of paring down a list to only a few items? That only increased the chances that you would find nothing, that you would leave the thrift heartbroken and empty-handed.

"Ah," she said suddenly, stopping in her path. "Silk." She lifted a hanger from the rack and beheld a gorgeous yellow robe embroidered with blue peacocks and mulberry trees, fastened up the front with green silk knots. She held it up to Charlie, stretching the garment's shoulders to his. "I think it'll fit! Wow, did a woman this big really wear such a flashy dressing gown? What an awesome person she must have been."

"It's a lady's robe?" Charlie tried to push it away. "I can't wear a lady's robe."

"Who cares? Look at this stitching: it's quality hand embroidery. There's a lining! Everything is intact! Why has no one snatched this up? Where has it been all these years? Who first owned it? It's so excellent, I feel like crying." She closed the space between her and Charlie; her thrifting radar began to echo and she saw other shoppers eyeing her find.

"But it's a *lady's* robe, Verity. I don't see how I can conduct my rituals in women's wear."

Verity led him through the aisle, still holding tight to the robe, and asked, "What kind of rituals? You still haven't told me what an urban shaman is."

A thoughtful expression crossed his face and he searched the heavens, or rather the Salvation Army's acoustic ceiling tiles, for inspiration. "As we all know, shamans in general—or is it shamen? Shamans, shamen. Hmm, neither sounds right. This is something I should know, but the resources are slim."

"Maybe the bookstore has *Shamanism for Dummies*."

He went on. "Never mind. The shaman, according to ancient lore as well as the definition I found on the Internet, is part priest, part sorcerer, a seer, healer, and prophet, who can enter into a trance state and call upon benevolent spirits to fight against malevolent ones. The shaman executes justice, heals the body, and saves the soul. As an *urban* shaman, I plan to do all this while focusing on the plights common to us city dwellers."

"Like what?"

"Well, I could spiritually cleanse apartments for new tenants, cast spells of protection against evil landlords; perhaps I could even christen new coffeehouses and Laundromats."

Verity said, "I don't think 'christen' is the right word."

"All right, inaugurate, bless, whatever. First off, as you know, I'd like to evict the ghost in my parents' apartment. It's all his fault I'm only a temp and will never be promoted; why he has it in for me in particular, I'll never know, but perhaps he just feeds off my suffering. From there, I'd like to get into hosting shamanistic rituals in public parks for the community. I mean, they let homeless guys sleep there, why wouldn't they let an urban shaman do his thing? I'm all about goodness and light; I would never hurt anyone in my rituals. Of course, I haven't figured it all out yet, but you can't advertise for shaman mentors easily. This is going to be a fly-by-the-seat-of-my-cape operation anyway."

Thus reminded, he pulled from the rack a long black robe, shiny and thin polyester with a deep hem and flowing sleeves. "Nice!"

"That's a graduation gown." Verity gently replaced it on the rack; the kiss she suddenly planted on his lips made a lovely, muffled *ptch*. She felt as surprised as he at her unexpected public display of affection. "Okay, I think I can really see it, bub. I do. You're going to be an enormously successful urban shaman and it will make you happy. You're lucky to have been called to a vocation."

He put his arm around her. "You can be one, too. You can have Wicker Park and I'll handle Rogers Park."

"No, thanks," she said. "I have no calling."

They continued shopping, pushing the wobbly grocery cart down the narrow aisles. In the toy section alone they found voodoo charm sticks (cute shrunken heads impaled on skewers), a plaid bowling bag, and a cracked crystal ball.

"I don't need those things," Charlie said.

Verity made check marks on her mental list. "These are for me."

bob rested his elbows on the desk, staring at Team Leader Joe, willing an embolism. Team Leader Joe tapped his hoof by the front checkout counter, staring down Verity as she strolled in ten minutes late. "Late, Verity. Unacceptable. Clement here has had to wait to punch out."

Clement, his giant red Afro bobbling above bloodshot stoner eyes, hitched his thumbs into the belt loops of his rodeo clown trousers and smiled sleepily. "No sweat, man."

"It *is* sweat," Team Leader Joe protested. "I've said it a hundred times: the team must never arrive late to work. Without punctuality, we have chaos." He stormed off, a spitball lodged in the back of his perm. Bob slid a straw back into his shirt pocket.

After punching in, Verity took her place behind the counter next to Bob.

"Here's one," he said, starting a conversation in his usual way. "They hired a new café worker today, a fat shithead also named Bob. Guess how he suggested they differentiate us? He persuaded everyone to call me One-Eared Bob, while he's Regular Bob."

"Jag-off. They're all jag-offs. I hate working here," Verity said.

"*Aha!* I knew it." Bob was triumphant. "What happened to 'Oh, I'm satisfied just being a bookstore clerk'?"

"I lied."

"Good," he replied. "I like what I've been seeing. You're lying, you're ambling into work late, you're freely admitting to hatred. I sense great things from you, Verity."

The tray of fishwiches made their weekly appearance in the break room. Verity had two, the first of which had a Band-Aid stuck to the underside of the bun, discovered, unfortunately, midbite.

"Do you really need two of them?" Team Leader Joe trundled in, accusatory. "How about saving some for the rest of the team?"

Mouth full of fishball, she tried to explain it was necessary due to the used medical dressing confiscated from the previous grotesquerie, but he held up his hand. "Save it. Your break's over anyway, and I have a new task for you. Maybe it will spark some interest and entice you into showing up on time."

He led her out to the floor and pointed to the two tables of new fiction. "We're trying to unload some of this dreck and I came up with a fantastic idea. Our store is going to have a book club and you're going to run it. Some of these novels have reading guides, some don't. You'll figure it out. Also consider the books on the two-for-one table. They're not selling as well as we'd hoped."

Verity looked through the books on the tables. Many of them had soft-focus images of portions of women's bodies. Never a whole body, just legs or a headless torso, cut off by artistic cropping at the top of the cover. Sometimes a whole body appeared, but the model's face would be obfuscated by a suitcase or title box or cigarette pack.

Other books seemed geared toward manly men, not to be confused with the Manly Den and its excellent admirers, but bombastic men keen on a life of hard drinking and ugly truths and other sensitive shit, at least as espoused by disenfranchised writers with six-figure advances embarking on thirty-city book tours.

She returned to Bob and related her new drudgery.

"You mean you'll have to interact with customers *outside* of our worker containment field?" Bob held steady to the cash register for support. "They might touch you. There might be conversations."

"Yes, I know," she said. "Although I don't actually object to running a store book club." She should have been shocked to discover this but found herself relaxed and even energized, the kind of high brought on only by a prospective project. "But why can't I choose the book myself? Why does it have to come from those three tables?"

"Because that's what they're pushing."

She shook her head, firmly positioning her glasses back in place. "No, I didn't see anything I particularly liked over there. A book club should be challenging. I can do this, but I need to select my own book. I can't ask people to read and discuss some hokey family saga or any other media-sanctioned, misguided publishing venture." She paced behind the counter, kneading the hem of a polyester blouse straight from the Norman Fell line. "It should be the equivalent of an Olympic sport. It should be a literary Olympiad."

"Go west, young woman." Bob turned her away from the three tables and steered her toward the morass of identical fiction shelves. "Thomas Pynchon to your right. *Finnegans Wake* to your left."

Twenty minutes later, she stumbled triumphant and sweaty

from the stacks. It was not, after all, *just* a project. It was a project that gave her the means to drive customers, assorted doofi all of them, out of their minds, for in her hands she grasped a test of raw patience and endurance. A newer translation, but still the tangled subordinate clauses, convoluted sentence structure, and rambling chapters on pastry and sleeping remained. She rejoined Bob behind the counter and slammed the enormous box set down in front of him, whereupon he studied it for a moment, then nodded.

"Proust," he said. "Splendid."

Verity smiled blissfully. "Yes. *Remembrance of Things Past.* Book club members will weep and blaspheme and rend their garments. Some will hate me. It will be glorious."

Bob asked, "All eight volumes? What's that, about four thousand pages?"

"Give or take."

"And what if Team Leader Joe is not enthralled by the rambling work of obsessive French dandies?"

She said, "Team Leader Joe can bite me."

the rest of the evening passed in a haze. Verity was consumed with the idea for the book club; *her* book club, something of her own. First she had talked Charlie into getting the awesome yellow silk robe; now she had the chance to foist Proust on an unsuspecting consumership. The reunion looming in mere weeks seemed less creepy now that she could brag about being a book club organizer. She considered this infinitesimal promotion; sure, it might not be much to your ordinary productive citizen, but it was a giant, lovely step for career sleepwalkers.

on verity's sixteenth birthday, Tex took her and Victory out for a celebratory evening of putt-putt and ice cream. Some families had beloved vacation spots, others had certain sports in which they all excelled; the Prestis had a definitive list of favorite miniature golf courses, and topping it was the excellent Par-King, medieval-themed home of All-Sinatra Wednesdays and the twice monthly Hot Dog Night.

"I thought you were coming out with us," Will complained. "You could watch us skateboard around the train station fountain and then drink beer over at Stan's house."

"My dad's taking me out," she said. "We're going to Par-King."

"Come on! You're old enough to ditch your family. It's *your* birthday, after all."

"You don't understand. This year my birthday falls on an All-Sinatra Wednesday *and* on Hot Dog Night. It's unprecedented. He'll be crushed if we don't go." Their family unit had disintegrated only two years previously and Thelma was expecting a baby with her new husband, Dick. Much rested on every encounter Verity had with her father. His emotional well-being hovered daily between recovery and nervous breakdown.

"Can you believe it?" Tex fairly crowed as he bustled the girls into the station wagon. "Hot dogs, Sinatra, and a birthday, all at once. How lucky we are."

Other teens might have responded with an eye-rolling *whoopee*, but Verity and Victory, sensitive to Tex's forced single-dentist status and his perch on the precipice of complete mental collapse, just smiled at each other and playfully punched their father in the shoulder.

"Wow, sixteen, honey," Tex said as he pulled out onto Fifty-fifth Street. "I know a lot of girls would like a car to commemorate such a milestone, but I . . . I . . . things are just not . . ." His voice trailed off, reflecting on the mess of his life.

"I don't care, Dad. I don't want a car. I don't even like driving."

"But still! I just wish I could give you a car on your sixteenth birthday, a nice red one that you could easily make the monthly payments on. You deserve a wonderful present and birthday."

Verity said, "I *am* having a wonderful birthday. I'm really looking forward to my hot dog and bashing a golf ball through that clown's teeth."

Tex started to cry. What kind of birthday was this? What kind of father was he? What a sad-sack idiot, sobbing at the wheel, their so-called mother nowhere to be seen, no presents (he couldn't drag himself off the couch to get to the mall), no cake (Thelma had taken her mixing bowl).

Victory looked in panic from her sister to her father. "Dad, don't cry! You're veering all over the road."

"I can't help it." He ran a sleeve under his nose. "I'm sad."

Verity looked through her purse and found a handkerchief, a beautiful vintage one that had a pair of lime green cowboy boots stitched in the corner. Gratefully, Tex took it from her and wiped his eyes. He gazed at it before handing it back. "That's a real nice hanky, hon. You know that's how I got my nickname, right? My old green cowboy boots?"

She knew. That's why she paid three dollars for a used snotrag at a marked-up estate sale. "I'm going to collect a bunch of different ones and make a shirt out of them."

Tex sniffed again. "I'll go halvsies on a sewing machine with you once I get back to work and pay off some of the bills." His lip got wobbly and a strangulated howl escaped his throat.

"It's okay, Dad." Verity patted him on the back and tried to ignore the blood roaring in her ears, the exquisite ache of watching a parent cry. A hole opened up in her.

The car came to a halt in the Par-King lot. The smell of hot dogs eventually drew them out.

An adenoidal teen in doublet and hose sighed as they paid him their fee. "The King welcomes thee. Here ist thou free hot dog ticket. Pray thee selectest a putter and Day-Glo golf ball, and takest no more than six strokes per hole. Snack bar closes at ten."

From the tree-mounted speakers came the strains of "Summer Wind."

"I love Par-King." Victory smiled dreamily, then whacked her ball into the eye socket of a giant fiberglass chipmunk. "Maybe I'll buy it one day."

Tex waggled at the tee, setting up his putt, and crooned along with Sinatra.

Verity thought it would be nice to own Par-King. Attached to the snack bar was a half-timbered Tudor-style banquet hall, often rented out for parties, that would make a fabulous home. "It would be great to have complete control of Par-King, Vic. You could live in the banquet hall."

"We all could," Victory said. At fourteen, she still harbored some familial fantasies.

"Not me. I'm going to own a store and move downtown."

Tex's ball took a wrong turn through the windmill and ended up in the moat. "Golf is a game of inches, girls. And more are lost on the putting green than won on the fairway." He reached in the water and pulled out his ball. Something green and stinky hung from it. "What kind of store, Verity?"

"I don't know. Something cool that sells cool stuff."

With some embarrassment, he hit from the ladies' tee. "When the time comes, I'll help you secure a low-interest loan. I'm glad to hear you're thinking about a career. It's important to plan for the future. You don't want to be thirty-five and thinking, 'What am I doing with my life? What happened to me?' "

The last verse of the song floated through the air. Tex swayed with his putter and sang softly. *"And still the days, those lonely days, go on and on."*

But by the end, his voice splintered. *"My fickle friend, the summer wind . . ."*

He stopped swaying. His hand passed like a shadow over his face and he wept.

Victory put an arm around Verity. "Happy birthday," she said.

but verity wasn't thirty-five *yet*. She was a glorious thirty-three, two full years away from the period of gloom that Tex had warned her about. It was perfectly fine to be a nothing at thirty-three.

Team Leader Joe pulled her away from the counter and directed her toward the café area. He told her to mop up, even though the employee handbook clearly stated that only café workers were expected to maintain café-area cleanliness. This was her punishment for tardiness. New employee Regular Bob—tumescent, evil—smirked at her and handed over the mop and bucket.

"Have fun," said Regular Bob. "Oh, and there's a bunch of smashed scones in the corner over there. Don't miss 'em."

Verity scowled at him, at his gray fishwichlike pallor and tubular body. How could one Bob be so righteous, and another be so disgusting? She glanced down at his name tag. It read BOBB. She could not quite explain the delicious sensation that rippled through her after viewing the ridiculous spelling of his name.

As she scrubbed the tile floor, she heard Bobb chatting away on his cell phone, which, during work hours, was clearly against the rules of the employee handbook. Alternately he cooed at, then browbeat, the caller, no doubt someone female and masochistic. He shouted and swore, then evidently tried to charm her with a nauseous, one-sided tide of vulgarity. Customers moved away from him.

"Hey, Bobub," Verity barked. "Put your cell phone away. Nobody cares about the mad drama going on in your life."

Bobb paused in his woo-pitching. "It's pronounced 'Bob.' The last B is silent."

He resumed his flood of frightening filth, explaining to the unseen, wireless troll the sundry acts of varying legality they would perform in the sanctity of Bobb's kitchen, bathroom, and, if time allowed, bedroom balcony. Oh God, the very idea that some woman would willfully rut with this human fishwich! In protest, her stomach threatened to dislodge the free dinner she'd just eaten. Befouling the café area seemed appropriate, despite the progress she'd made with her mop and bucket.

She had slopped gray water over the smashed scones when it occurred to her: she was actually much closer to thirty-four. Her birthday was just weeks away. Thirty-four was so much closer to thirty-five that it practically obliterated all memory of thirty-three. She felt something rise up in her chest and flap its wings. She *loved* being thirty-three. It was a mystical number, just like the Rolling Rock commercials insisted. It was the age when Jesus got the boot and returned to the mother ship; the number of degrees of initiation for the kooksville Freemasons; the number of elements in the "Tree of the Sephiroth" of the Kabbalah; the number of years King David reigned in Jerusalem. What the hell was thirty-four? Nothing! Thirty-four was when ob-gyns began warning you about your advancing maternal age. Thirty-four was the age for dead-eyed soccer moms to drive their SUVs through the streets, for men to consider hair plugs. It was twelve months away from saying, "What have I done with my life?"

Suddenly the golden light of an untapped future, a burnished and beautiful thirty-three, began to slip away from her.

she took the Chicago Avenue bus home. The passengers after second shift were no more peculiar or aggressive than those earlier in the day, but they did exude an aura of resigned hopelessness more plainly than the morning commuters. Her seatmate was a garden-variety seat hog. He held a newspaper spread out in front of him, overstepping the invisible boundaries of personal space, and he had wedged his briefcase in between himself and her. This whole posture ran counter to Verity's own bus-riding etiquette, which involved squeezing as tightly as possible next to the window, piling your belongings on your own lap, and staring at nothing. The man flipped a page of the paper, and as he did so, his arm hair brushed against her. She drew herself further into the aisle and tried to rub the sensation from her skin; arm hair contact was much more disturbing and intimate than actually being elbowed.

She got off at Damen even though her apartment was technically closer to the previous stop. The corner at Wolcott and Chicago sucked, and picking her way through the assortment of gangbangers and urinaters and men who made that peculiar slurping sound through their teeth was to be avoided whenever possible. Her building, once a perfectly respectable brick four-flat, had been painted that strange shade of landlord gold twenty-five years ago and had entered its associated decline ever since. The first floor housed a discount store featuring very little of thriftdom and much of cheapo peddling: satin-look couches in mauvey shades, thousands of Hallmark Precious Moments knockoffs, giant bags of tube socks, and other items recently birthed from the sweatshops of Malaysia. The occasional find redeemed the shop in Verity's eyes, so she made allowances for the preponderance of dollar-store garbage.

Main door unlocked, she quickly made her way up to the fourth floor, past the heavy-metal Asian dudes' apartment on the second and the fireman with the friendly pit bull who was coming out of his flat on the third.

"Hey," he said.

"Hey," she answered, the rules of urban neighbor decorum thus met.

Not one of them knew any of the others' names. The apartment buzzers were marked only 2, 3, and 4. Someone from number 2 had drawn a Viking helmet next to the numeral.

She threw down her bags, deposited her keys in a bowl made out of an Allman Brothers record, and flicked on the dining room lamp; it had the unfortunate screeching eagle base and Spirit of '76 patterned shade found in every thrift in America, but whatever mysterious process that made lamps light up when you shoved a bulb in the socket seemed to work, and that made it all right. Better to light one ugly bicentennial lamp than to curse the darkness.

Ice cream called. She spooned up a big bowl of Snickers flavor and retired to the living room to turn on the stereo. Yes, Esquivel was unmatched for perfect aural ice cream accompaniment. Verity drew the curtains, their tropical floral designs in green and maroon and cream eminently soothing in the soft light of the living room bowling-pin sconces. Now, who to spend the evening with? The June 1951 issue of *Better Homes and Gardens*? One of the hundred back issues of *ThriftScore*, the thrifting zine? A Kennedy assassination conspiracy tract? *The Woman in White*? *Crockpot Cookery for Singles*? Verity perused her bookshelves and wondered what it would be like to have friends.

The phone rang, its beautifully harsh tone unique to heavy, black, rotary-dial models. Verity plopped into the green vinyl telephone chair, expecting Charlie or some relative caught up in familial high drama. Stan, she was not expecting. "Oh! Hello."

"Hi," he said. "Busy?"

Of course: ice cream, the hi-fi, xeroxed leaflets, it was all waiting for her. "No. What's up?"

"I was just thinking about my Manly Den, and I am all pumped to do it. I cleaned up all the kid's toys and it's ready to be made manly, and I was thinking since I work downtown anyway, I could just meet up with you after work tomorrow and we could go looking for stuff."

"Are you whispering?" she asked.

"No," he whispered.

They set up a time and place to meet. She had asked if Laurel was coming, too, but Stan said that someone had to stay home and watch the kid. Verity hung up and went back to her ice cream. In the past, whenever Tex was mad at Gin for some canine infraction, he referred to her only as "the dog," as in "The dog just rolled in something dead," or "Will someone get the dog out of my home clinic? It just stepped in Mrs. Percy's impression tray." So it was "the dog," just like "the kid." Only now, Tex bawled when he thought of calling Gin "it," "the dog," or anything other than her given name. No matter if she peed all over her dog bed or got lost in the yard or asked to go out ten times a night.

Verity decided to sew Gin a soft bandanna collar lined with jingle bells. That way, Tex could track her down more easily when she wandered around in soporific dementia. A warm gratitude spread over her, having multiple projects to work on. She drew up a flyer for the book club and planned to copy it tomorrow at work, cut out a pattern for the collar, and then retired to bed with a notebook, listing possible items for the Manly Den.

The pineapple lamp cast an amber arc upon the wall, bathing the framed pictures upon it in golden pools. Unlike the thrifted photos mounted in the tiny hall between the kitchen and dining room (the Hallway of Strangers), these photos boasted only family and friends. Or friend, as the case was. There was Charlie, drunk on the Dodgems at Six Flags, there was Tex at a long-ago Easter dinner, wearing a purple plaid sport coat and '70s-era Tom Selleck mustache. And there, setting a humane trap for the Downers Grove raccoons, was Victory, crouched on all fours and grinning. The largest photo, framed in semirealistic bamboo, showed Victory crocheting beer-can hats, seated on a picnic blanket with baby Gin. Verity stared at it; she could not help it. The pineapple lamp shed gorgeous light on her sister, an almost sunny beam. Her hair had been dirty blond like Verity's, but lemon juice that summer had brightened it. She painted her mouth with that awful brown lipstick everyone wore in 1990, but on her it had not been too gruesome. She smiled earnestly in the picture, as she always did in real life, a friendly soul to her core.

That terrible lump grew in Verity's throat, that Ping-Pong ball of electric despair. Silence blanketed her room; even the howls of horror from the Chicago alleys stopped. Esquivel ended. The window fan circulated more hot air. Something closed up in her. "I still have you as my sister," she said. But she felt silly talking to a photograph and turned to the opposite wall. *I have these memories. I live in a house full of junk, and all of it is tied to other memories, and other people, to strangers and family.* She turned off the pineapple lamp; the new blackness muffled all thoughts of old history swirling around her, and of this experimental future she had begun toying with, leaving her in the solace of now. Nothing comforted like the dark; not even the past had such quiet power.

•   •   •

charlie sneaked down into the kitchen for a midnight snack. He opened the fridge and took out a Tupperware container of left-over elbow macaroni with slightly curdled cream sauce. He felt something cold and weightless brush against his arm. The ghost hovered at Charlie's shoulder while he scarfed the contents in the sickly yellow cast of the fridge lightbulb.

"Cut it out," said Charlie, hunching over the macaroni tub.

The ghost took a respectful step back, imagining the scent of pasta delicately curling up to where his nostrils would be. He knew that sauce, what was it called again? Oh yes, béchamel, though Mrs. Brown's unorthodox recipe called for past-its-prime buttermilk.

Charlie felt the ghost withdraw. It had obeyed him; he had said, "Cut it out," and the ghost had moved away. Charlie straightened up, put the macaroni back, and tightened the sash of his robe. "He fears me," he said. "I am an urban shaman."

the next morning, Craig's cubicle phone rang, so the project manager took a break from dragooning him and stepped away.

"Craig Kickel."

"It's Will."

Craig glanced behind him. Personal calls were frowned upon at the office, and even if they weren't, the onion-skin cube walls afforded no privacy in which to take them.

"Are you busy?" Will asked.

"Just proofreading content."

"Oh? What drug?"

Craig scrolled down the screen. "An antipsychotic. This one is supposed to be good because it doesn't make the psychotics gain weight like the other drugs."

"Samples?"

Craig said, "How I wish that handing out antipsychotic drugs was part of the incentive package here."

"Well," Will said, "here's the thing: were you serious about that 'activist' nonsense the other night?"

Craig's cubicle wobbled as the zombie on the other side bashed his head against the shared divider in a daily ritual of frustration. Thumbtacked photos of Kronos and Aura fell into the crack between the desktop and the fabric wall. "Not really," he said.

"Excellent. There's got to be more to life than pretending you're an activist. I've been thinking: what reason is there for us to be stuck on this hamster wheel? I mean, what kind of lives are these? Things just happen and we let them happen, and the next thing you know you're having panic attacks or beating up guys in Laundromats or bathing with a toaster. There's more to life than just working and drinking Belgian beer and remodeling bathrooms over and over again. I don't know about you, but I want something for me. Something meaningful, gratifying. Something that will make a difference."

"What did you have in mind?"

"I think we should start up the Lousy Dates again."

Craig paused. "Our old band? The Lousy Dates can make a difference in the world?"

Will ran his hand over his crew cut and across the stubble on his chin. "Well, my other thought was maybe we could host a radio show and rip apart modern music. I think we have faces well suited to radio."

"I don't know. Eventually we'd just be two forty-year-old music dorks having petty squabbles that men half our age have outgrown, about topics we're too old to be discussing."

"Well, yeah. It could be very entertaining. But I still would rather start up the Lousy Dates again. You have a better idea?"

Craig stared at the manila folders scattered on his desk, each one a clone of the others, all containing equally depressing production schedules for the various drug-Web-site launches; he looked at the Outlook appointment alert calendar, which popped up every half hour announcing more dreary meetings in which he understood nothing; he regarded his Ziggy mug and the ring of dried false creamer that had become one with the glaze. "I have no better ideas," he admitted, "but Carolyn locked my drum kit away in the storage unit and I don't know where it is."

it was settled then. Will spent the remainder of the day trying to clean his wreck of an apartment and forgoing his usual pre-work nap. He ate dinner in front of the TV and then reclined in his chair, folding his hands across his stomach in satisfaction. Stan was in, Craig was in. All that remained was getting the drums out of the storage unit, but he seriously doubted whether Craig had the guts to talk Carolyn into it. He, Will, might have to intervene. The truth of it was *anyone* could handle Carolyn better than her own husband.

He glanced at the clock; time to get to work. He threw his leather jacket on and slammed the door behind him. It was Ladies Night at the Kit-Kat Karaoke. *But then again,* thought Will, *when he was KJ-ing, when was it* not *ladies night?*

He had not seen Verity and Charlie at the club since that first time. Why not? He just assumed they, or rather she, would come back again to visit. Wasn't she interested in pursuing their friendship, in picking up where they had left off? She was not a shy person, it couldn't be that, but then again she was a private one; she kept to herself. That might have explained her continued absences. She was never, of course, an extrovert or outgoing type of girl, but in high school she at least showed some interest in being with him. Maybe not *being with* being with, in the normal way men expect, but that's not to say he ever ruled that out either. There was a time, yes, rum had been involved . . . well, better not think of that now. He warmed up the crowd with a disturbing, Nick Cave–like rendition of "I'm Not a Girl, Not Yet a Woman."

Victory Presti had been in an accident and had died and he had not come back for the funeral. Within two years he had transferred from Illinois State to Eastern to Western, each one of them a shittier state school than the next, so he had been anxious, stressed. He had failed something at that time—geology possibly—just when he heard the news from Carolyn. He sent word, or rather condolences, through Carolyn, explaining his messy circumstances and inability to get away from school for the funeral. Verity understood; everyone understood. Everyone said they understood.

But he had met Verity for drinks two years later and saw her at the other end of the table as through a kaleidoscope— fragmented, flattened, and far away. He'd tried to invite her to come down to the city and hang out sometime; he said he had two new roommates who were nice, a guy and a girl, maybe they could all go out.

She shook her head and said, "I'm sorry, I can't. I don't have any room."

"Room? For what?"

"For any more friends." She pushed her glasses up on her nose, blinked a few times, then looked toward the exit. No reproach or malice in her words, only resignation. That evening did not end there like that, but Will could not remember anything that came after.

A nubile young thing walked up to the KJ booth. Will saw the house DJ scowl in jealousy from across the bar. Of the two of them, Will usually attracted the most girls at the club because the DJ was too busy showing off his red vinyl imports to the reverent geek brigade. Like those East/West Coast rap wars one was always hearing about, the KJ-DJ animosity at the KKK ran high. The nubile young thing smiled and greeted him. She was one of the Thursday night DePaul crowd who slummed it in Bucktown every week.

"You didn't show up at Blues Fest," she pouted. "We all had a big blanket spread out and sangria and everything."

"Sorry," he said. Blues Fest? Had he really said he would meet a bunch of college kids at Blues Fest with its hopeless smattering of Bruce Willises and families with screaming babies? "I hate Blues Fest."

"How could you hate it? It's fun."

"It stinks," he said. "The whole Chicago festival scene is terrible. Each one is the same: greasy food, cops swinging their big batons everywhere, and it's either one hundred degrees or it's raining. Especially vomitous is the way the white people dance and the look of surprise on every blues guitarist's face as he solos those four chords over and over."

She said, "The blues is like an art form."

Will made a dismissive *psshh* sound. "Please—those twelve-bar limitations? Some art form. Nothing's ever new! The newest invention was that gaudy hammer-on, hammer-off technique Eddie Van Halen made famous on 'Eruption' over two decades ago, which he stole anyway from Melvin Taylor. I have better things to do with my time than watch an art form develop at glacial speed with the jag-offs from Alsip and Bridgeport."

The nubile young thing took a sip of her drink and said, "I also love the Dave Matthews Band." Her friends pulled her away for a group trip to the bathroom and she waved good-bye.

A man with a sad fringe of last-hurrah hair in the classic horseshoe pattern approached the KJ booth and selected "Lady" as his song.

Will groaned. "Styx *again?* That's three times tonight. I can't listen to any more Styx. Was that guy who sang 'The Renegade' with you?"

The man, unaccustomed to karaoke challenge, nervously looked from the six-foot-two karaoke jockey with the angry eyes back to his table of fellow middle-aged combovers. "I like Styx. They're . . . they're kind of kitschy."

"No, they're not. I'm sorry, you can't like Styx in an 'ironic' way. You can't like them because 'they're so bad, they're good.' Either you respond to Styx or you don't."

"Fine," said the man, trying to be a sport as the bored audience ran for the bathroom and the bar. "I respond to Styx."

Will said, "How can anybody respond to Styx?"

The man said, "Can I just sing my song?"

Will sighed in irritation and waved him forward. "Fine. Sing your fucking stupid song." The man ascended the stage and loosened his tie. Pathetic, the way he crossed his fingers and waved them hopefully at his friends. The majestic arena-rock chords of "Lady" began and Will signaled the bartender for a double bourbon.

As he had every night for the past several weeks, he scanned the crowd for a glimpse of Verity. Oh, what was the use? She was not going to show up here, that much was certain. So what then? Will watched the fat choad with the microphone sway on stage. *That could be Craig one day,* he thought, *the poor slob.* He thought, *That could be me.* Will slugged back his drink. He wasn't going to rot here forever—if he owned his own bar and KJ equipment, he'd quit here in a second. He was on the cusp of new things, of launching a life, of reuniting the Lousy Dates. If Verity would not come to him, then he would go to her.

The Styx fan finished his performance with closed eyes and a fist brought down sharply in triumph. At some point thereafter, the nubile young thing returned to Will, sufficiently drunk for whatever adventures lay ahead. She selected her song and he pushed the appropriate buttons. Twitching her hips, she smiled at him as she began to sing. He admired her infant-sized DePaul shirt, thrusting pelvis, and gooey, oozing sexuality, but decided at that moment to go home alone, because despite her obvious charms, he found he could not forgive her for liking the Dave Matthews Band.

twelve

1986

tex asked victory to fix dinner that night, then retreated to his bedroom and closed the door.

"What do I make?" she asked her sister. "Can we just have grilled cheese again?"

"It doesn't matter," Verity said. "He's not going to eat whatever you make anyway."

Thelma had gone into labor and arrived at Good Samaritan about an hour earlier. Dick had called and promised to keep the girls updated when their new brother or sister arrived. Verity was stuck with the unenviable task of relaying this information to her father.

"So it has come to this," he'd said after she told him, hands on hips, staring out the kitchen window.

"It was bound to, Dad," she said, "what with the nine months of pregnancy and all."

He walked over to the fireplace mantel and took down the photo of him and Thelma on their wedding day. He looked at it, ran his finger along the mother-of-pearl frame, and slid it into the back of the board game cabinet. Then he went back to bed.

Later, Victory flipped the grilled sandwiches and confided to Verity, "I'm kind of excited. I like babies, and plus I always wanted a little brother or sister."

"Dad put away the wedding photo."

"No!" Vic spun around. "I don't believe it."

Verity nodded. "I think he just realized she's not coming back."

"Maybe he'll remarry one day."

"Ha! What kind of nut would have him? And the last thing we need is a stepmother, Vic. We lucked out with ol' Dishwater Dick as a stepdad, so obviously our good fortune is exhausted. You know any woman who'd come into this house would start bossing us."

Victory bit her lip. She was not the type to mind being bossed; she could not reconcile herself to the forced lady-of-the-house duties she shared with her sister. Sometimes she thought it would be great to come home from school and have someone else cook dinner for all of them or do the laundry or take them shopping or something. Someone else to console her weeping dad every other day would be nice, too. Victory could not explain to her friends why they could never come over: that her dad had not worked in months and rarely changed out of his bathrobe; that he often cried in bed at four o'clock in the afternoon, refusing to eat; that once a week he threw Thelma's old bite impressions out the bedroom window, then scurried outside after them, gathering them up in the pockets of his robe, having changed his mind.

"You're burning them," Verity said, nodding to the blackened sandwiches.

Later that night, Verity informed her sister that Will was coming over.

"We're gonna watch a movie, maybe work on Trig homework but probably not since he's bringing beer. Don't tell Dad. You can hang out with us."

Victory ran upstairs to put on makeup and change her shirt. When she came back down, her sister stared at her painted face and said, "Oh, my God. You like him!"

"No, I don't!"

"You do," she said. "You love him."

Victory colored. "Well, so what? I just think he's cute. Anyway, he's in love with you."

Verity furrowed her brow, shaking her head. No, nobody was in love with her. Sometimes with Stan, she felt like he was coming on to her, but let's face it: she knew she was too hopelessly awkward for anyone to have a serious crush on. She was the girl guys talked to about the girls they really liked.

Will walked in later wearing a Ramones shirt, a frown, and a black eye. Verity had stopped asking where his sporadic wounds and injuries came from once she met his father, because only a dummy would not be able to put two and two together there. Will blew off his friends' questions in that department. But still, he liked how Verity always offered their extra bedroom to him in case he ever needed it.

"*Silent Night, Deadly Night Part Two,*" he said, holding up the slasher film's VHS cassette.

"The sequel?" Verity asked. "But I never saw the first one. I'll be lost."

Halfway though the movie, the three of them on the family room couch, Verity felt Will's arm across her shoulders. He had been moving it infinitesimally closer over the past twenty minutes and had only now made nonchalant contact. Verity thought it felt nice, so why should she move? She had once clumsily grabbed Stan's hand while they were walking back from Barth Pond one night, and he'd said, "Aw, you're sweet," then slid out of her grasp immediately. She'd never do that to a friend.

Will rested his fingertips on the back of her neck and she stole a sideways glance at him. Was he in love with her? No, couldn't be. If someone was going to be in love with her, she decided, it would have to feel different than this. *She* would feel different—amazing. Beautiful. Something other than the ham-fisted dork that she knew she was.

Tex ambled around the kitchen in his bathrobe, poking through the cabinets. He was not really hungry, but maybe a little snack would settle the roiling tempest in his gut. Verity hid the empties under the couch.

"Want something to eat, Dad?" Victory called out.

"No, honey, I'm just looking around."

Verity said, "Dick hasn't called yet, Dad."

He said, "I don't know what you're talking about." Then he took the Yellow Pages and thumbed through them. "You kids have any idea how I'd go about buying an urn?" There was no listing under "U." He stuffed the book under his arm and shuffled back upstairs.

With the last teen slaughtered, Verity switched off the TV. Victory checked her watch and asked, how long did it take to have a baby anyway?

"Today's the day for the new little halfling, eh?" Will asked.

"I'm kind of excited," Victory said, for the second time that night.

"I know, I know," her sister answered. "You're excited, Thelma's excited, Dick's excited. Whoopee for everyone. Nobody's thinking about Dad. We're all getting something out of this except for Dad."

Victory said, "Maybe he'll like the baby."

"I hope it's a boy," Verity replied darkly. "That's just what Mom deserves. An evil, stinking, wretched boy." She looked at Will. "No offense."

Around midnight, she peeked upstairs and saw the light on underneath her father's bedroom door. She returned downstairs, signaled to Will and Vic that she'd be back in a minute, and brought Tex up a plate of fruit and cheese.

"I'm not hungry," he said, flipping through the channels on his TV.

"But you have to eat something today," she said. How many times over the past few months had she said this to him? All those days, would he not have eaten if she didn't bring him food? She could never leave the house for more than eight hours or he'd starve to death.

The assortment of grapes and sliced apples and cheddar cheese made his mouth water and he reached for the plate. "Maybe just a nibble, since you went to the trouble."

"It wasn't any trouble," Verity said and sat on the edge of the bed. She swallowed, breathed in deeply, and decided to just come out with what she had to say. "Dad. She's not coming back. You know that, right?"

Tex found a rerun of *Barnaby Jones*. He said, "This is a good one. They don't make TV like this anymore."

So unfair. Verity, who usually loved to hide from reality and avoid addressing problems and fixing things, was stuck sitting there, speaking the truth, and her father wasn't paying a bit of attention. She grabbed the remote from his hand and turned off the set. "Did you hear me?"

"Put that back on. That's Buddy Ebsen." He reached for the remote, but she held it behind her back.

She frowned and spoke roughly. "She's in the hospital right now having a baby with her new husband. She left us. She didn't want us."

"Don't say that!" he cried.

"It's true, and if you don't accept that she's not coming home, I don't see how we're ever going to get over any of this and move forward."

Tex gave a violent shudder and buried his head in his pillow, sobbing. Victory heard the commotion and dashed up the stairs. Will, sensing Presti family melodrama, opted to return to his own home, hoping his father had drunk himself into a dead slumber.

Victory hovered at the doorway, watching the scene unfold. "Daddy," she said, "you're scaring me." She sat next to her older sister and said nothing else.

"We're a family," Tex blubbered. "We don't leave each other. Your mother is gone. But it wasn't anything we did. It would be easier if she'd just . . . died."

"Dad," Verity began, but he cut her off.

"Let's say she's dead. Come on."

The sisters looked at each other.

Tex rubbed his eyes with the heels of his hands, long lines of snot and drool and tears crisscrossing his face. He sounded cracked and brittle, a tinny, old man's wheeze. "Girls, I need to hear you say it. We weren't left on purpose, we're still a family."

Victory stifled a cry and hid her face behind Verity's shoulder. Verity held her dad's hand and responded woodenly. "Okay. She's dead."

The phone rang and she dove for it. She said, "Great," and "Yeah, I'll tell everyone," and "Congrats," and hung up the receiver, bruxing. Victory raised her eyes timidly and even Tex held off bawling for a moment.

"Goddamn it," Verity said. "Another girl."

thirteen

as a gift from the corporation, two large boxes of Krispy Kremes sat on the cafeteria tables the next morning. The Meyers-Briggs tests, administered earlier that year, confirmed that these workers could be kept docile with doughnuts. As the crowd dove for the treats, the percolator, and the Cremora, Charlie bowed his head and clasped his hands in front of him.

"Wait a second," cautioned one of the secretaries, holding up her finger. "The temp's praying. Let him finish."

"It's not really a prayer," Charlie admitted. "It's a traditional blessing-chant, altered for use in the modern office."

"Well, let's hear it," said the head of IT. Everyone held their doughnuts in midair.

Charlie cleared his throat, closed his eyes, and raised his hands before him like a surgeon awaiting gloves. "May the sweetness of these doughnuts never be overshadowed by the sour taste left in our mouths from the absurd corporate restructuring of the IT department, nor by the lack of last year's Christmas bonuses. May they fill our bellies and our souls and keep us from the hunger that drives us to compose death threats, ransom demands, and manifestos on company time."

Charlie's coworkers continued to hold their doughnuts aloft as they exchanged glances. The head of IT shrugged. "Works for me," he said and bit into a cruller.

"Amen," said the secretary.

"Please." Charlie held up his palm in a peaceful, Jesus-y gesture. "No religion. This is a nondenominational service."

Back at his desk, he could barely contain himself. This, his first foray into shamanism, had proven a success. No one had called security, no one had shoved him aside in a frenzied run on the doughnuts, no one had laughed at his blessing-chant. True, he wished he could have worn his new yellow robe in this inaugural ritual, but the company had a strict dress code. He ran his finger over the silver tie clasp that Verity had found in the Village Thrift jewelry case near the cash registers. One end of the bar boasted a little etched shield and sword; the other was engraved with the words, "Bristol Renaissance Faire." He smiled, looking down at it. It was the next best thing to wearing his robe; it was almost like having Verity with him.

"what . . . what the hell is this?" Team Leader Joe sputtered, waving the Literary Olympiad Challenge flyer.

Verity paused in her tidying up of the Godiva rack. "It's for the new book club."

"Proust? I told you to choose a book from the front display tables."

"Well, I know Proust may seem a little intimidating, but I think people will really get into it, especially once they ride out the infamous chapter on falling asleep. Plus I'll bring cookies—madeleines, of course—and coffee, so—"

"I don't give a rat's crap about cookies! Now, you get over to those tables and pick a featured fiction title." He grabbed her elbow and pulled her away. Verity flung her arm out of his grasp; his team leader claw blistered through the fine cashmere of her sequined cardigan, which could not withstand rough handling.

"Here!" he bellowed, pointing at the array of trade paperbacks. "Any one of these will work."

She said, "But I don't like those. They're all about some woman who dates the wrong man and it takes the whole book for her to realize that. Why can't they write a book about a woman who already has the right guy? I don't think I can run an effective book club if I don't believe in the product."

"What is the matter with you? 'Believe in the product'? We're trying to sell some books here. That's what we do; we're a bookstore. I don't care if you 'believe' in them." Team Leader Joe's perm quivered in agitation. Then he caught sight of that catchall, that savior of bookstores, that messiah of the mass market. "I've got it! Now, you can't possibly object to this." Sweeping his arm grandly toward the dump, he cried out: "Dr. Phil!"

Verity goggled. It was like an insane-asylum nightmare, where every open door revealed some fresh horror. "Are you out of your mind? I can't lead a book club discussion on Dr. Phil. His brand of psychology is based on hillbilly platitudes and a Magic Eight Ball."

He leaned in, nostrils hot and wild. "Dr. Phil is the best lifestyle strategist that *television has ever seen.* You're starting off the book club with him. Case closed."

"But it's an advice book. You can't have a book club with—"

Team Leader Joe cut her off. "Are you listening? This is the book."

The dream of her beloved project disintegrated. So much for leading the customers into the dark forest of Proust, of Joyce, of Castaneda. Now they'd be chatting about life laws and getting real, all while the gleaming dome of Dr. Phil shined down on them from the book club flyer, like a beacon for morons. "No. I won't do it." Her heart beat hard against her old sweater.

He began to tick off her transgressions on his fingers. "Tardiness. Defiance of my book club mandate. Insubordination. You're on thin ice. I suggest you do as I say, and I won't mention this on your employee record."

From the checkout counter, leaning over as far as possible while still within the boundaries of the worker containment field, Bob signaled her with a flurried wave and shining eyes. He ignored the line of customers and sent his message to her via one raised middle finger and jerked his head in the direction of Team Leader Joe: *Screw him.* Then Bob smiled and gave Verity a thumbs-up.

She acknowledged Bob's plea with a brisk nod. "I'm sorry," she said to her boss, "but that dog just won't hunt."

"fired?" asked Stan. "What do you mean?"

Verity removed her sweater—now that she was permanently out of Barnes & Noble, she would no longer have access to any regular air-conditioning in her life—as they walked along Grand Avenue toward the giant, three-floor Salvation Army on Des Plaines near Halsted. She told him about the book club fiasco.

"And he fired you just for that?"

"He did give me the opportunity to apologize and do everything his way, but I wasn't having it. Even though by law they have to give me two weeks to get out, I'm just not going back."

"Wow!" Stan was visibly impressed. "You're like a, a suffragette or something."

"I did suffer," she admitted.

She thanked God for the gigantic building of junk. It was the only thing staving off her impending sense of doom, the desperation that rose in the chest of each person who found herself jobless in a Bush administration. True, there was some money in her checking account—all was not completely lost—but there were no prospects on her horizon.

"What are you going to do about work?" Stan asked.

She said, "You need a manly recliner," and marched over to the La-Z-Boys.

He followed her, eyeing the velvet-look monstrosity. "How am I supposed to haul that home?"

"There's plenty of room in your SUV."

"It's *not* an SUV," he protested. "It's a large, modern Subaru station wagon."

They amassed an arsenal of manly stuff: hunting prints, a fake birch-bark wall clock, a tiny cigar store Indian, a stuffed and mounted crappie with badger teeth, a latch-hook rug of bouncing golf balls, a somewhat battered silver cocktail shaker and tray, a globe with black oceans.

"You will need a recliner at some point," advised Verity. "And make sure it really reclines, not just tilts back in that 'don't want to be too obtrusive' way of today's furniture. You'll want to go horizontal. Space considerations be damned."

"I haven't bought a piece of furniture from the Salvation Army since college." He regarded the assortment of recliners doubtfully. "They probably smell weird."

"So clean it. You gotta get over this fear of used items," she said. "Most of life smells weird."

Suddenly a memory came to Stan of a time the Sikos visited a garage sale on their street. Sebastian saw a greasy, stained SpongeBob doll on one of the tables and reached for it, but Laurel swatted his hand away.

"No, dirty," she had said. "Smelly, disgusting." Sebastian pouted.

"Aw, just let him have it," Stan said. "It's only a dollar. We'll throw it in the washing machine."

But Laurel had argued that SpongeBob was plebian in addition to stinky. Sensing dissent among the governing body, the boy launched into a campaign of whining and begging.

"No!" she had snarled suddenly. "It's dirty and stupid, Sebastian. Why do you want a smelly, stupid toy? Are you a smelly, stupid boy?"

"What's the matter with you?" Stan stared at her.

Laurel had four dollars in her pocket. She bought a book of Sylvia Plath poems and read aloud on the way home the poem about Sylvia eating a bag of green apples, which represented pregnancy and the impending birth of her child, she said. "This way, Sebastian will get some culture." She looked down at her son. "Isn't this better than some old stuffed toy? Isn't it? Sebastian, I asked you a question."

The child held his father's hand and said nothing, eyes on the white toes of his sneakers. The ice cream man trundled down the street in his truck, the canned melody of "Home on the Range" ringing out. Children emerged from their homes, tearing out to the curb, laughing, falling over one another, dollars in their fists. Sebastian never raised his eyes, since he had never been told what an ice cream man was.

As Stan waited in the checkout line, Verity wandered to the back of the store repeatedly, each time bringing back with her some new treasure. He smiled at her. "I guess you'll have to cut down on your compulsive thrift shopping until you find a new job."

She stopped and stared at him. "What do you mean?"

"Well, just to save money."

"Hey, I can always find another job. I may not *ever* be able to find another Reaganomics dartboard."

He looked down at the other purchases in her basket. "And the wig head?"

"I need that, too." She regarded him in baffled amazement.

"I'm just saying that if you add it all up over a period of months, you'd be surprised to see how much you spend on useless items. I could create a database for you to track purchases and create a real budget—"

"No, no. I don't want to know. I don't want to look at 'the big picture' and nickel-and-dime myself into a bleak and barren future. It's better to consider things on an individual basis," she said, picking up a Ziploc bag of old keys from a manual typewriter. "As in 'This only costs eighty-nine cents.' "

He handed his items to the cashier one by one. "I guess if you don't have kids and a wife and a mortgage, you can afford to do that."

Verity fumed. This was that age-old defense that married people always used, half in smug pride for their responsible and adult lives, half in envy for the seemingly careless, slacker lifestyle of their single friends.

She said, "That argument is so tired, Stan. Our lives are equally bad in different ways, okay? Nobody's world wins the 'sucks most' award. You have stuff I don't have, I have stuff you don't have." She thought of the phrase that she had used with Charlie: *"We're all just trying to get through the day."*

He handed the cashier a ten-dollar bill, then gathered up his booty in the white plastic grocery bags. "I disagree. If you fail, you only ruin your own life. If I fail, I ruin my family's life as well."

"Oh, please! Fail, ruin. What are you talking about, money? So what if you fail? So what if you're poorer than you were before? It's not like you'll ever end up living in a subway tunnel; you'll just have an apartment instead of a house. You'll have to take your kid to the park instead of buying him a bunch of stupid toys. You'll have to eat at home instead of in restaurants. You'll work in a shitty store instead of a shitty office. Everyone's life stinks! You have a family to go home to every day; I can be a thrift store spendaholic. Get your joy where you can."

He begrudged her common sense. Grousing bestowed a sense of righteousness and peace upon him that the actual act of living never could. He grumbled, "You'll see what I mean one day."

Verity got in the Subaru and rolled her eyes at the ingratitude some people had. Stan would never appreciate how terribly rare the globe with the black oceans was.

"here it is," Verity said as Stan pulled up in front of her building. "Thanks a lot for the ride."

He looked up at the horrible four-flat. Garbage blew in from the street and clung to the door and threshold. Glowering dudes sat on the front steps of the adjacent houses, and in the distance a baby cried. A man stumbled by, his hand outstretched, his eyes rheumy and free-flowing with milky fluid. *No doubt a homeless subway-tunnel dweller,* thought Stan.

Verity glanced at him, recognizing that look of horror. She had seen it strike Thelma's face on her occasional visits, threatening to undo recent Botox treatments. She had even seen a similar expression from Tex when he came to call, as he liked to sit by the front window in her apartment and keep an eye on his car. A peculiar sensation gnawed at her gut. *It's not shame*, she told herself.

"You live here?" he asked.

"It's okay inside." God, how pathetic she sounded! She couldn't stand the shade of apology that had crept into her voice. What should she be sorry for? What shame was there in living in a place you could afford? It wasn't as though it was a dump or a freak squat. It just wasn't very clean or modern or kept up. Nothing terrible had ever gone wrong with the plumbing; they had had no robberies except for the time the lock on the front door jammed. Numbers 2 and 3 seemed like congenial neighbors, whoever they were. "Come on up," she offered.

Stan smiled that lazy, crooked grin that had worked wonders in his past. Verity missed it, so intent was she on proving her perfectly acceptable lifestyle: *Once he sees my fondue fork collection and my 101 million 101 Strings record albums, we'll see who's the freak.*

"Wow," Stan said upon first sight of her pad. Though packed from the sloping ceiling to the wide-board pine floors, the place was actually fairly orderly. It looked like a cool store. "Hey, what's in here?" He poked his head in her extra bedroom.

"That's the 1950s," she said.

"Everything in here . . . ?"

"Yes. Everything is from the '50s, documented, authenticated, and dusted regularly. I hang out in here whenever I want to return to simpler times."

"Oh. That's neat."

"Neat?" Her eyes bugged out and she planted her fists on her hips. "You have no idea how hard this was to construct. You just can't *buy* this stuff anymore. All the fifties crap is gone from the thrifts. All of it, gone! Fortunately, I started in high school and my dad rented out part of his dental office to me for storage. Now I'm lucky if I can find one fifties cigarette lighter or can opener in the stores."

"I didn't know. Maybe I should have decorated my Manly Den in a 1980s theme. That way in thirty years, it would be cool."

Verity beamed at him with new appreciation. "You may have the body of a project manager, but your brain has the makings of a hard-core thrifter."

Aha, thought Stan. *So she has noticed my body.*

He declined her offer of pudding and invited her to sit beside him on the couch. He could practically see the waves of heat rising from the floor of the attic apartment. A glistening line of perspiration soaked the hair at her temples, and her cheeks flushed with the hue of crushed roses. After all these years she still had, Good Lord, an astounding rack.

Suddenly Verity became aware of the heat and white teeth and Stan's wily ways. There was something at once flattering and sad about the way he stroked her arm, how her hair stood up at the slightest brush of his fingertips. She had felt this before, this simple touch that was more intimate and disturbing than actually being groped.

When he reached for her face, she stood up awkwardly and said, "I have some things I have to get to tonight, so . . ." It was a lame excuse, but she was not one for scenes.

Stan had not really expected anything from this, nor truthfully had he planned what he would do if she responded. But it was important, he felt, to try. "Oh really? What kind of things?" he asked, then quickly shook his head. "Never mind. I'm a jerk. You can say I'm a jerk, it's fine." He shrugged with a silly grin, as though his behavior was beyond him.

Her face now smooth and blank, she lifted her eyebrows and said nothing.

He stood. They were not touching at all, though it was hard to be sure with the heat heavy on their skin. He would have been more comfortable if she had slapped his face and called him a pig. As it was, her feigned ignorance of his pass agitated him. "Go on, tell me I'm a jerk. You can be honest. Isn't 'Verity' supposed to mean truth?"

She turned from Stan, then beckoned him to follow her to the door and down the stairway. She said, "Well, Siko, we can't all live up to our names."

It was, of course, just as the front door closed and she waved good-bye that she realized she had locked herself out of the building.

Guys on the neighboring stoop watched her blaspheme and kick the door. Well, there was nothing for it: she'd have to ring 2 or 3. First she tried the fireman, as she had at least a passing acquaintanceship with him. No answer. She regarded the Viking helmet on 2's buzzer plate, then pushed the button. Nothing there either. Her watch said 6:00; perhaps they were all on their way home from work, unless the fireman was on one of his night shifts, or the Viking-buzzer Asian dudes enjoyed some vague, slackery employment situation, and therefore merely wandered the streets without the constraints of job or family life to bring them home.

To pass the time, and to assuage the gnawing, jobless guilt in her gut, she walked a few blocks north and filled out an application at Blockbuster. She had gotten halfway through the personality test portion of the application process, when she decided it was not worth it to lie so much, filled in the rest of the circles in a pleasant pattern, and then headed home. Again she rang the doorbells, to no avail. She sat on the front step, trying to avoid the bodily function stains around the threshold. At 7:00 she thought, *Hey, at least the heat wave is breaking.* A quick and cool breeze blew in from the north and dried the perspiration rings under her arms. At 7:05, the cool breeze whipped up into a tempest and brought with it a sewer-flooding rain. The guys on the stoop next door dashed inside their house, passersby fled down the sidewalk with newspapers and Jewel bags over their heads, a frightened dog ran into traffic and then disappeared down the center of Winchester Street, goblins on his tail. Verity tried to rush into the dry shelter of the discount store on the first floor, but the proprietor, having sold out his stock of mismatched tube socks, had closed up for the evening.

Okay—she counted off her predicaments on her fingers, just like repulsive Team Leader Joe had done a few hours before—unemployed, locked out, caught in the rain. Verity knew this about herself: she was a crier. Not a public crier, not a drama-queen crier, but a private huddled-under-the-tiki-quilt crier, a lone crier, a lonely crier. The streets were deserted now, and she was as alone as she could be out of doors. She flattened herself against the door (impossible, given the aforementioned astounding rack) and let her tears mix in the rain. She no longer needed age thirty-five to start questioning what had gone wrong in her life. Thirty-three and eleven-twelfths was a fine time to start.

"Excuse me." A man loaded down with grocery bags tried to get his keys in the door. "I have to get in."

"Two?" asked Verity. "Two?"

"I'm sorry," he said. "I know it's raining, but I can't just let people in. We had some robberies here."

"No," she said, pushing into the entryway, "I live here."

He removed a pair of eyeglasses from his shirt pocket and put them on. Verity noticed they were huge gold-tone squarish frames, the kind that went for a dollar in the thrifts these days, so outdated were they. He blinked. "Four?"

"Yes." She sighed with relief. "It's me, four. I locked myself out." She wiped her eyes with the heel of her hand. Two saw the wet streaks and red nose and thought perhaps it wasn't all rain. "Thank you so much. I was out there for a long time."

"That's okay," he said, shifting the bags.

"Can I help you?" she asked, indicating his groceries.

"If you want."

She took one of the bags from him and nearly ripped her shoulder from its rotator cuff. "Oof. Whatcha got in here?"

He started up the stairs and answered without turning back. "Chain mail. Come on."

Two opened his door and took the bag from her, setting his belongings down just inside. Whoa . . . on level ground now, her gaze traveled up. A very heavy and wide man, he stood over six feet tall, with a brown, broad face and thick black hair cut in a sort of proto–Rod Stewart fashion. "Well, thanks for the help," he said.

"Thanks for letting me in. I'm Verity."

He stuck out a meaty paw adorned with horned skull rings and a digital watch. His grip was surprisingly gentle. "Eddie Loa." He watched her eyes travel over to the aquarium against the wall. "And that's my blue-tailed skink," he explained. "My lizard, Eggy. If you cut its tail off, it'll just grow another one. But I would never do that."

"See ya," she said.

As she trod up the stairs to the fourth floor, she heard the opening strains to some Celtic nightmare death metal music. It began at full volume, then suddenly softened, as though someone had quickly turned the dial down, knowing other ears were listening.

"charlie brown." Even as he said it, answering his phone for perhaps the hundredth time during this long temp gig, he heard his cubemates chuckling. The hilarity over his given name would never end.

Verity blurted out the news of her joblessness. Although glad to be finally shut of Team Leader Joe and clerkdom, she had never been unemployed before, and due to Tex's insane work ethic, she found herself at sea on this, the first day of her liberation.

"You quit?"

"No, I was fired," she corrected him. To most people, quitting was preferable to being canned, but to Verity it was better to be fired; she was willing to work if allowed to do things her way.

"Ahhh, unemployment," he replied, leaning back in his office chair. "Please allow me, sitting here beneath the cold hum of a thousand fluorescent bulbs, to envy you. Live the dream, Verity, live the dream! For all of us on the inside."

"I can't live the dream, CB. I have to find another job. I won't be able to collect any slack benefits because I was fired for insubordination."

Charlie said, "That sounds so awesome!"

"But at least I dropped off an application at Blockbuster last night," she said.

"Why?"

"I don't know. I like the shirts." Jesus, even she couldn't believe the new depths to which unemployment had sunk her. "Anyway, I'm going to have a big greasy breakfast now at DeMar's, then I'm going to look in the want ads. But first I was hoping to get an urban shaman blessing. You know, to help me find a job that won't kill me."

"Thank you for believing in my humble powers and my oft-misunderstood vocation. Interestingly enough, I've been compiling some fascinating information on a cool ritual that may be of some use in this area. Let me get my shaman PDA out and look it up. Yes," he read from his notes, "here it is: Okay, first thing you do, you slaughter a sheep and bring me the blade bone—"

"What?"

"Oops, my bad. That's not for unemployment, it's for something else. Oh, here, I found it. It's a simple blessing, designed to aid you in your job search."

"Lay it on me. Should I kneel down or fold my hands or anything?"

"No, just look out the window and imagine yourself happy." He began. "Gods of power, gods of light, steer Verity on the path to fruitful employment. Help her find work that is satisfying to the soul as well as the pocketbook. And also has a good dental plan, if it's not asking too much."

She waited, unsure if there was more. "That's nice. Amen—er, I mean, thanks."

"I'm sprinkling pencil shavings around my chair and also leaving half a chocolate doughnut as an offering on my desk altar."

Verity smiled. "Half?"

"I got hungry," he admitted. "It takes a great deal of intestinal fortitude to be an urban shaman in modern society."

charlie had bought himself a Day-Runner. He marked off a block of time for the coming evening, as a coworker in the cafeteria, having heard about his shaman prowess with the doughnuts the other morning, asked if he would mind using his oneness with creation to help find his lost dog.

"I hope you can locate her psychically or whatever. She ran out the door during yesterday's storm, and I was out all evening and night looking for her," explained Pete, the coworker. "I don't have any sick days left or I wouldn't have come in today. I . . . I can pay you."

"Certainly not!" Charlie replied. "This is my gift to the planet, and I refuse all inedible forms of payment."

Suddenly interested colleagues leaned in to eavesdrop.

He went on. "But I have to confess that locating lost pets is new for me. I'll have to do some research today at lunch, but I'll do my best this evening to help out."

"I believe in you," said Pete.

sebastian threw a toast crust in his mother's hair. Laurel picked it out absently, then ate it.

"I can't believe it," she said. "She really walked out of her job over the book club disagreement?"

Stan nodded and gulped more coffee. "Yeah. She said something about not compromising her moral standards. Can you imagine? In this economy, walking out on a job?"

Although Laurel had said almost those same words to Stan at their party, chastising him for even toying with the idea of quitting his job, somehow it seemed kind of impressive that Verity had been fired for sticking to her anti–Dr. Phil principles. It was thrilling to know that somehow, some people still had moral principles and were being punished for them. "Maybe I'll call her."

Stan put down his coffee. "What do you want to do that for?"

"I don't know. To be nice?"

This wasn't good. "What do you want to do that for?"

"Why do I want to be nice to her? She just got fired! What's wrong with that?"

He snapped and unsnapped his briefcase several times, rising from his chair. "You just can't go around calling people willy-nilly. I saw her, we got the Manly Den stuff, she's fine. She probably doesn't want to talk about it to a stranger."

Oh, so she was a hostess when he wanted a dinner party, but a stranger when she wanted another woman to talk to. She said, "You better get going. I'll take Sebastian to day care."

verity picked up the ringing phone, tossing the keys into her bowling bag satchel. She was pleasantly surprised to hear Laurel's voice on the other end of the wire.

"I heard about your job," the other woman sympathized, offering her condolences.

"It's fine. I hated working there anyway. The only thing I'll miss is my coworker Bob."

"Verity?" Laurel's voice rose. "I really wanted to tell you that I think it's just so wonderful, the way you got fired."

"Thank you."

Laurel tried again. "No, that didn't come out right. I mean—"

Verity said, "I know what you mean. And I thank you."

"You're lucky," she said. Her words all ran together: "Now you can seek out something meaningful. God, I'd love to do that, even if I had to keep my job. No way around that, I guess. I wish I could figure out how to start up something else. Like the poetry thing. I don't know. There's no poetry scene in Downers Grove, but I always think if we lived in the city, I'd be able to join a writing group or take a class or something. I don't know how to find anything like that."

"Art is a noble pursuit," Verity said. "And you're right, there probably are more opportunities in the city than in the Grove. But I know someone who can help you find your . . . your path to, you know, whatever. He's really good at that. I just hope you're open to fake chanting, sham rituals, and the earnestness of a true believer dressed in a lady's bathrobe."

verity ordered the Deuces Wild at DeMar's and opened up the *Sun-Times* to the "Help Wanted" section. Though no listings specified "Seeking spineless cog" or "Zombies only" or "Looking for next link in our chain of indifference," it was obvious they offered the exact same hellishness as her old job. Time to move forward, she decided. Thirty-five was only thirteen months away.

"Four?"

She looked up into the face of yesterday's savior, Eddie Loa. "Oh! Hi, Eddie."

"I can't remember your name," he said.

She tried to examine his wardrobe without staring: black long-sleeved T-shirt with undecipherable white letters on it, black jeans held up by black suspenders, a defeated and dead waistband lolling about his sizable midsection, and black boots strung with red-spotted shoelaces. "It's Verity," she said.

"As in truth."

She said, "It's just a name. My dad calls himself Tex and he's never been south of Peoria." She invited him to sit down.

He slid into the seat opposite her. "I haven't seen you in DeMar's before. I eat breakfast here every morning before work."

"This is my first day of unemployment," she said, indicating the "Help Wanted" section.

"Have you considered temping?" he asked.

"I don't know, maybe. I put in an application at Blockbuster, but I don't expect them to call me, as I most certainly failed their personality profile." She mulled this over. "It's depressing to fail the psych test for Blockbuster," she decided.

Eddie said, "Sometimes I think I would have made a really

good slave. When a job is severely restricting and I am told exactly what to do, I can function in that environment. But when I have a lot of choices, I am at a complete loss as to what to do because everything must come from within me and 'within me' is like a blank piece of paper. It's flimsy and disposable and not worth anything."

Verity thought, *I've got to introduce this guy to Charlie Brown.* She asked, "So what do you do for work?"

He straightened up in the booth and replied with dignity, "I'm the receptionist at my aunt's beauty parlor."

DeMar's marginal air-conditioning unit could not sputter out enough BTUs to adequately cool the customers, and Verity began to fan herself with the newspaper. Eddie's black garb seemed to absorb, then radiate, extra heat. "Pretty hot in here," Verity commented.

"Yes," he admitted. "But I'm not the kind who can wear shorts."

"That's how I feel about tank tops."

"I don't really mind sweating," he said. "Not purposeful sweating, like when you're working on a chain-mail loom outside. It's the sweating uselessly that I object to, the sweating for no reason. Take today, sitting at the counter eating my pancakes—no, I did not like sweating then."

Considering that at this time of day she was usually fielding questions regarding the Godiva candy bar display or the Left Behind religo-crackpot series, she decided she enjoyed this conversation about sweating very much.

Verity closed up the want ads and said, "Actually, it's my first day of unemployment because I was fired from Barnes and Noble." She recapped her job history, avoiding certain details that led up to her dismissal. Not everyone's moral code included hating Dr. Phil.

Eddie said, "Well, if you're looking for another bookstore job, why not check out the Hog? He's always hiring."

Her expression asked the question.

"You don't know the Hogbutcher Bookstore on Evergreen? It's all used books and it's only been open a year or two, but it's a decent place. The owner lets us play Dungeons and Dragons there every Sunday night."

"Why is he always hiring?"

"Because he's always firing. It's still worth looking into."

She said, "Maybe I will."

"Bye." He stood up abruptly. "I have to go to work now. We have a permanent scheduled for ten o'clock."

verity headed north on Damen. Sunshine stripped the sidewalks stark and bare, divesting all the color from the cityscape. A few resilient honey locusts puffed out some oxygen, wheezed on the bus exhaust fumes, dropped black pods all over the street. Could one bookstore really be that different from another? Bosses were the same everywhere; all might not be greedy or inept, but when it came down to it, they could tell you what to do and like a child, you had to just take it. Verity marveled at the notion that, after all these years, she might actually be antiauthoritarian. That was kind of cool. Still, one had to earn a living.

She had not walked this far up Damen in a while. There were not so many pierced pincushion people down in her edge-of-Latin-Kings-territory/Ukrainian Village neighborhood, nor on her block were there as many neo-nerds and drummers milling about in the middle of the day, smoking and cynicizing and not working. Next to a sprawling, abandoned apartment complex on Evergreen stood the modest, two-story building housing the Hogbutcher Bookstore. A long, hand-lettered sign ran above the store entrance. On one end of it was a painted representation of a pig divided up into its meat constituents, on the other was a stack of wheat.

She gazed up at the sign and felt a ripple of trepidation; this was no corporate chain. Her jaw creaked as she bruxed. Peeking in the front window, she saw dirty floors and wild, crooked bookshelves. Tacked to the front door was a placard warning off "religious solicitors and anyone selling Greenpeace." A cat lounged in the window seat, licking itself with great fervor.

Pushing open the door, the words to the famous poem ran through her mind.

> Hog Butcher for the World,
> Tool Maker, Stacker of Wheat,
> Player with Railroads and the Nation's Freight Handler;
> Stormy, husky, brawling,
> City of the Big Shoulders . . .

"Chicago." She always liked how Sandburg ended it with laughter, even after all the bareheaded brutality and wickedness of the earlier stanzas.

the owner, an older man with long, greasy, gray hair, sat down with her at a table in the back of the store.

"So how'd you hear I was hiring?" he asked.

"My neighbor suggested I come down and talk to you."

"And who's that?"

She swallowed. Could she say, *A guy I met yesterday for the first time after I locked myself out of the building*? "Eddie Loa."

He looked at her blankly, then his face brightened. "Oh, Chain-mail Eddie! The big Samoan dude. Nice guy. So what experience do you have?"

She related her seven years of Barnes & Noble history. Ugh, his corporate nemesis. The bookstore owner grimaced and involuntarily marked a black strike against her.

"Working here would be nothing like working there," he grumped, but he took note of her reaction—visible relief, softening of the lines of her forehead, and a new twinkle in her green eyes. He reserved judgment on the black mark. "And I can't pay much. Nine bucks an hour. No benefits, sorry, but I'm working on it. One day, maybe."

"Okay."

He could not make up his mind. On the one hand, he needed someone right away. On the other, how likely was this Barnes & Noble chick going to stick around, given that the last employee booked outta here the first time the rats came up through the baseboards? Not to mention last year's tragedy with the book club . . . he pushed that memory away.

To buy himself some time, he handed her his business card and said he'd think about it. It read: HOGBUTCHER BOOKSTORE. HOT COFFEE, USED BOOKS. CARL SANDBURG, PROP.

"Carl Sandburg?" she asked in surprise.

"Hence the store name." He held up his hand. "But don't start; I've heard it all my life. Born in Chicago with a name like Carl Sandburg, you develop a short wick."

She pocketed the card. Someone else who ought to meet Charlie Brown.

Verity sensed that the interview had drawn to its conclusion and that the impression she had left was, like most of her first impressions, void. Desperate for a second consideration, she said she was available immediately, as she no longer worked at the old store.

"Why'd you quit?" Carl asked.

Here we go, thought Verity. Though a valued few like Charlie would understand her preference for being fired rather than being a quitter, she knew others might not get it. But after the botched Blockbuster psych test, she could stand no more lying. She knew who she was, and it was only a matter of time before Carl Sandburg and the alumni committee and every last acquaintance of hers figured it out, too.

"I was fired," she said.

Carl waited for her to continue.

She exhaled slowly. "I was fired because I disobeyed my manager's orders regarding our store book club."

Carl tensed. "You ran your store's book club?"

She nodded. "He insisted I use a Dr. Phil book for the first discussion and I refused. It was a matter of lowering my moral standards, which, trust me, has never even been an issue before, but suddenly, somehow, I now have principles." She jounced her shoulders in a helpless gesture, resigned to this principled fate, this terminal specter of disease. "It's not that I was afraid to run the book club. But I guess I kind of have a problem with Dr. Phil."

She wasn't afraid? God, if she only knew. . . . But Carl Sandburg liked that spunk and said, "You're hired."

fourteen

tex led carol on a tour of the house. Up until now, she had only seen the kitchen and family room and home clinic, but he felt it was time to open up everything.

"You've passed by the living room, but you've never had a chance to actually experience it," he said. "We hardly ever used this room. Notice how erect the shag still is."

Carol noticed.

"After Thelma di—well, you know—I put plastic covers on the furniture. Verity made me get rid of them all. I guess she thought they looked stupid, but I just wanted to preserve what I had. Honestly, they *were* kind of sticky in the summer if you sat on the couch wearing shorts, plus Gin always slid off and bonked her head on the coffee table, so it was for the best."

"Who plays the piano?" Carol asked.

"Nobody. Nobody anymore."

She looked at the pictures lined up on top of the instrument. She commented on the cute array of past dogs, complimented Verity's nice smile (Tex said, "All due to that mouth guard I made her wear"), and teased him about his 1970s mustache. She pointed to the photo of Diana opening a Christmas present and asked, "Who's this?"

Tex blinked and chewed the inside of his cheeks. He shifted his weight from one foot to the other, trying to extricate himself from his web of deceit. How could he explain who Diana was if Thelma was supposed to be dead? In all his swinging days, he had never let any of his lady friends venture this deeply into his life, or his living room. "The daughter of a patient," he said.

Carol moved to the frames on the coffee table. "Oh, this is a nice one," she said, picking up the picture of Tex's two daughters in 1986. "Here's Verity, so this must be Victory, right?" Tex nodded. "What a pretty girl she was, and she looks like she was a very happy person, too. I'm sure I would have liked her."

Tex said, "Victory had a streak of silliness that was just delightful. She kept us in hysterics all the time! And she was sweet and kind and loving. The most loving child you ever met. Not that Verity wasn't loving, she was, she *is,* but sometimes the eldest has trouble letting herself be as carefree as the younger ones. And of course with everything that's happened, it's no surprise that Verity has become more . . ." His voice failed him. Anything he could say about his daughter's personality would sound disrespectful, especially to someone outside the family. What words could he use to describe the sorrow he felt all these years watching Verity close up, withdraw, go backward? Since Victory's death, his other daughter had been suspended in somnolence, floating in a deep pool of inertia.

She said, "How terrible to lose a wife and a daughter within a couple years."

"And for Verity to lose a mother and a sister." Well, Thelma *was* lost to them, lost to abandonment; it amounted to much the same thing—worse, even, because at least in death you still had love.

He continued. "Oh, those girls were wonderful friends. Not just good sisters, but real friends whose differences complemented each other, real soul mates. I always thought how lucky they were to have been born in the same family, even if they only shared eighteen years together. Some people go through their whole lives and never find a soul mate."

Carol laid a hand on Tex's shoulder and said, "I know."

Fire rose in his throat. He was unused to speaking aloud these feelings, and equally unused to scanning others' faces for reactions. His memories were his to recall in his own way; he could not stand when they flooded in haphazardly, in currents he had not chosen. He took the photo from Carol's hand and set it back on the table, smiling briskly.

Carol closed her eyes, drinking in the atmosphere. As a vampire lifestylist, she was more in tune with the vibrations and psychic ambience of places than others were. She said, "This room has a very sad energy."

"Well, I haven't vacuumed in a while," Tex said and led her out.

Upstairs, he showed her his own room, making a few mild insinuations about the comfort of his mattress and the softness of the sheets. Carol poked him in the ribs playfully. Then he walked her toward the bathroom, proud to show off where he had laid the tile himself with only minor mistakes you could hardly even notice.

But Carol had stopped midway down the hall. "This one's Victory's room," she said.

"Yes."

"I could feel it. What pleasant vibrations emanate from here."

Tex touched her elbow, then guided her backward. "Carol, I'm going to have to ask you not to go in there."

"I understand. It's just for family."

"No," he said. "Nobody goes in there. Well, I go in to dust and vacuum, but that's it. If people start going in there, touching stuff, moving things around, all the memories will get jumbled up."

Carol searched for the right words. "If you don't want me to go in her room, Tex, I never will. I have no quarrel with that. But what you must understand about energy is that it's not affected by mere *stuff*. Stuff comes and goes, people die or move away, carpets get replaced, walls are repainted. But the places themselves retain the essence of those who lived there. She is everywhere in this house. You feel her. People don't truly die if someone loves and remembers them."

A mallet pounded in his brain and a feeling of lightheadedness washed through him. He said, "I have to tell you something about that urn . . . ," but his vision darkened and he stopped talking. He held onto the wall to keep from falling off the planet.

Carol led him across the hall to Verity's room and sat him on the edge of the bed, instructing him to put his head between his knees. "You're just feeling faint," she said. "It's very hot up here and we haven't eaten dinner, and here I am just stirring up old memories for you. No wonder you don't feel well." She made him rest a few minutes while she fetched him a glass of cold water and a wet washcloth for his forehead.

"I'm sorry," he said finally. "I must be hungry. And it *is* hot up here; I don't like to run the air-conditioning too much." He took off his shoes and socks and lay back on Verity's bed. They both looked at his bare toes. "My feet are clean," he said apologetically. He wiggled them around.

She rubbed his ankles and asked what he was thinking.

He wanted to tell her the truth, but the truth was a shady thing. So he said, "Oh . . . I was just thinking about the time I had cellulitis and the doctor had to draw a line around my foot. If I look hard enough I can still make out that line, not because it's still there, but because it's burned into my memory. Sometimes I can just about make out a pink splotch. Sometimes my foot feels like it's purple and throbbing." Behind closed eyelids flashed images of home, the girls, the dogs, the rooms that stayed untouched, a happy family, an urn of cigarette ashes standing sentry on the fireplace mantel. Tex said, "Inside of me is turning out all wrong."

charlie reread the section on exorcising ghosts and readied his materials. Hand mirror, check; glass of water with dogwood leaf floating in it, check; white handkerchief, check; copy of his parents' lease, check. He arranged the items on his makeshift bedroom altar (stacked Krispy Kreme boxes covered with his mother's hairnet, the king of clubs playing card, and a blue candle) and silently practiced the incantation, visualizing the ghost leaving them, going into the light. Suddenly, his eyes flew open. The candle flame flickered and went out, the curtains blew, the hairnet sagged. He checked the window: still closed. That was funny. Next to him on the bed a soft indentation appeared. The setting sun cast golden pink beams that danced through the oak leaves outside their building, dappling his bedspread in circles of moving light. A cool spot had settled above the indentation next to him, and he felt calm. From down in the kitchen, the smell of baking meat loaf, the kind with hard-boiled eggs shoved inside, rose through the floor vents.

The ghost felt sad. It had been so long since he had eaten food. And of all the food he remembered from his life, none looked or smelled as divine as Mrs. Brown's.

If anyone understood the allure of food unreachable and off-limits, it was certainly Charlie Brown. "I'm sorry," he said to the cool spot hovering over his bed. "I didn't know you felt that way about Mother's meat loaf."

Exactly how the ghost's sentiments were conveyed to him, Charlie could not say, but he felt sure of them—this was why the murdered man had stayed with the Browns so long: the food. As if a signal sounded in his brain, he quite suddenly stopped himself from relighting the candle and stared at the indentation on the bed. Charlie Brown had spent the last several years in this apartment, this boyhood backward bedroom; a temp, a drifter, a soft and goo-filled grizzled loser, blaming the ghost for his lot in life. "It's not you holding me back," he said finally. "All along, it was never you. It was always me."

The ghost nodded what would have been his head, though no one could see that motion, that gentle inclination; he dipped down toward the floor vents and absorbed the rising meat-loaf aroma, eyes closed in rapture.

Charlie gathered up his exorcism tools, put them away, and would never interfere again with the ghost's questionable taste in mortal pleasures.

• • •

craig bounced baby Aura on his knee, which made her giggle and burble spit bubbles down her front.

"Thanks for watching the kids," Carolyn said, applying petal pink lipstick in the powder room. "Do you know where everything is? Do you have any questions?"

"I'm not a teenage babysitter, Carolyn. I think I know how to take care of my own children."

She glanced at his reflection in the mirror. Right. "There's formula in the fridge. Don't let Kronos watch TV all night and if the baby cries when you put her down, just ignore her. It's the only way she'll learn to go to sleep by herself."

"I'm not a moron."

She ran out of the powder room, grabbed her Kate Spade handbag, and slipped into a soft pair of cherry Prada mules by the front door. Her blond hair, newly highlighted, was pulled back into a casual twist at her nape, and a stray wisp curled suggestively down the back of her neck. A tie-dyed silk dress clung to her slim figure and revealed a fine set of chakras. The whole effect exuded luxury, but in an Earth Day–celebrant way, thanks to Ralph Lauren's new "hippie chic" line, and Carolyn was all over it.

Craig appreciated the fine-boned beauty of his wife, her almost floral prettiness, even her boogity-boogity New Age witticisms and prayer bells. At least she involved herself in community concerns like the DuPage County wetlands conservation project, which was more than he did. Was it his fault that nothing interested him? Was it his fault that he had no skills or talents?

"Will you be okay?" she asked, hand on the doorknob.

"Of course!"

"Well, don't get your chi in a bunch. I just need a girls' night out."

"Go on, it's fine," he said, turning his head toward the door just as it clicked shut.

Outside, Carolyn breathed in the fresh air of Clarendon Hills. It smelled like solitude.

kronos tried to practice "Baby Elephant Walk," but lost his enthusiasm after the rousing eighth bar, which was no surprise considering that the clarinet had a very low harmonic role in the song and was clearly an afterthought by the arranger. He had suggested "Gonna Fly Now" to the band director, but the band director did not cotton to freshman suggestions. Thumbing through the rest of the music, Kronos decided to give "Beer Barrel Polka" a whirl. Three-quarter time was definitely his favorite, its cheery liveliness made only more beautiful by unexpected minor chords.

His dad came up and asked if he wanted some turkey à la king.

"I don't think so," Kronos answered. "I am into vegetarianism now."

"You are?" Craig asked. "When did this happen?"

Kronos thought of the glorious Diana and her informative treatise on the effect of meat products on the digestive system, given only yesterday during band practice. Kronos thought of her glorious ponytail and snug white uniform trousers, her glorious sequined sash cascading over her glorious, heaving, shifting bosoms. Kronos thought if this music thing didn't work out, he would like to be a writer. "Yesterday morning," he said. Oops; they'd had roast chicken last night. "Midnight," he corrected.

Craig said, "You could pick out the turkey. The à la king part is still good."

This sounded agreeable to Kronos, who had been a vegetarian for twenty-one hours and already felt persecuted by the cafeteria and the advertising industry.

Craig set the kitchen table, seated the kids, and then reached into the cupboard for his Belgian beer glasses. At least a half-dozen were missing. He flung open the other cupboards in alarm, searching wildly, to no avail. In their place were new hand-painted wineglasses that Carolyn had brought home from Nordstrom's, to complete her set of thirty thousand. She had done it again! First his drum kit, then his record albums and magnets, now his beloved Belgian beer glasses.

"Am I invisible?" he asked the wall. "Don't I count for anything around here?"

Kronos looked up from the turkey à la king he had been dissecting with chopsticks. Aura bounced in her bouncy seat.

Craig turned to face his son. "Kronos, have you ever been to our storage unit?"

"I think I have. I waited in the car once while Mom dropped a bunch of junk off."

"So you know where it is?"

Kronos nodded.

"What about a key? Do you know where that is?"

The boy gestured to the tangle of key rings hanging on the back door Peg-Board. Craig rushed to the board and began separating them. Finally he located an unfamiliar, heavy brass key imprinted with a number. He bobbled it in his hand as a new, decisive surge coursed through his blood.

"Tonight, we ride," he said. "Kronos, pack up the baby." He thrust the keys into the air and made whirling windmill motions with his other arm. "To the storage facility!"

"this one? Right here?" Craig pulled the SUV up to the steel door.

Kronos looked up and down the aisle of identical storage doors. "Yeah, I guess this is the one. It was on a corner. But I can't be sure because at the time I was composing a duet for tuba and clarinet in my head, a commingled Sousa/Artie Shaw tribute, and—"

Craig glanced at Aura. Good, she was sound asleep in her car seat. He banked on having a solid ten minutes before her subconscious alerted her to the fact that the car was stationary, at which time she would unleash a series of brain-bleeding, tortured howls. "Okay, keep an eye on Aura. I'm going in. I may need your help loading some stuff into the back of the car, though."

"What kind of stuff?"

Craig considered. "My life, son."

The key slid into the lock and when he pulled up the heavy door, he found himself gazing at a treasure trove of items he had loved and believed were lost to the vortex of moving from apartment to house. There! His broken, wood-look stereo cabinets. And there: black laminate, self-assembled bookshelves from the Great Ace. Grow lights. Trunks of clothes. Golf clubs in a white vinyl Carol Brady–type golf bag, missing a Big Bertha driver (thrown into the water at Timber Trails years ago). He pounced upon the milk crates of record albums, holding them to his chest for a possessive, furtive minute, then loaded them in the car.

He located the drum kit way in the back. It had not even been taken apart properly, but was stacked in crooked towers against the far wall. No cymbal or drum was covered or protected, except by a thick coat of dust. He nearly wept at the sight of their gold-spangled neglect, but then got himself together and brought them out one by one.

Kronos, bored by the parade of forgotten, broken objects, suddenly snapped to attention at the sight of the drums. Craig motioned for him to come out and help, and he leapt from the SUV to the ground in a hurry. "Whose are those?" he asked.

"Mine," said Craig, handing his son one of the timpani. "We're taking them home."

"I never knew you played the drums, Dad. Were you in the marching band?"

"Yes, I was in the band. Didn't I ever tell you? Same as you, Downers Grove South marching band, and I also had my own rock band with Will and Stan and this other guy, Neal, but he moved to Milwaukee and began a society for pipe-organ enthusiasts. Our band was called the Lousy Dates and I probably even have some pictures of our gigs, if I can find my old photo albums in here somewhere."

"Were you any good?"

Craig detached the cymbals from their stands and carefully

stacked them between old towels. "As a band, we had a little trouble reconciling everyone's influences: Prince, Flock of Seagulls, the Dead Milkmen. I think I myself wasn't too bad. I learned to play from a Psychedelic Furs album, *Talk Talk Talk,* and I remember I had trouble in the beginning because I was afraid to open the high hat when I played. But I got over it."

With the last cymbal in place, Aura awoke with a vengeance, demanding the vibrating forward propulsion that had been snatched away from her unawares. Craig brought down the heavy door, locked up, and headed for home.

Having unloaded everything into the house, he went through some of the boxes until he tracked down the Belgian beer glasses, then poured himself a Rochefortoise. He glanced at his son. "Would you like a taste? Half a glass?"

Kronos held up a palm and shook his head. "No, thanks. It may stunt my growth."

"Being tall isn't everything."

"I know, Dad. I just want to be taller than girls."

"Anyone in particular?"

"No!" Kronos bit his lip in worry. *Please don't let this turn into the Talk,* he prayed. The idea of discussing sex with his father made him want to fall to the floor in anguish. He thought of Diana and her gloriousness, her bitter and jaded attitude, her extremely well-shaped torso, her height, her splendid plans for college and madrigal-rap fusion. High color stole into his cheeks.

Craig set up the milk crates of record albums next to the stereo, but realized with distress that no turntable was in sight. *Well, it must be in one of the boxes,* he surmised, riffling among them until he found the turntable and hooked it up. Kronos scoured through the albums as Aura dozed in her swing, its rhythmic movement and clicking better than any tequila shot.

Carolyn had become pregnant directly after high school, due to Craig's failed intelligence on the Snickers-wrapper-and-7-Up method of birth control.

"We'll get married," he'd said simply after her teary revelation.

"What about the Art Institute?" she asked. "What about our lives?"

"My parents will pay for my tuition, room, and board if I agree to go to UIC or a state college or whatever. I can get a part-time job and we can live in the married students' housing."

She burst into fresh hysteria at the thought of the married students' housing.

Craig had not been interested in currying favor from Carolyn's parents, or asking them for financial help. We could do this on our own, he thought. They could have a civil ceremony at the Du-Page County courthouse, then maybe go on a long-weekend honeymoon to Lake Geneva in Wisconsin. They could have their baby, go to school, and work. People had done it before. And there was plenty of time for art school once they were more settled. Yes, eloping was a good idea—romantic, inexpensive, and exciting. Once they reached the hotel in Lake Geneva, he planned to send word to Will: "Ship me my essential belongings (Young Fresh Fellows records and vintage *Playboy* magazine collection) and sell the rest."

As it happened, Craig and Carolyn did not run away together, they did not visit the county courthouse, and they never saw the inside of any married students' housing. When you're a mild-mannered eighteen-year-old boy and a grown man snarls at you, "You knocked up my daughter, you little asshole. You have no money, no job, no future, and if you ever want to see her or the child, you're gonna do things my way," you tend to buckle under his authority and submit. Carolyn's parents threw her the lavish wedding she deserved and set Craig up in the advertising department of a pharmaceutical company beholden to Carolyn's father. No hotel in Lake Geneva ever received a shipment of Young Fresh Fellows records or vintage *Playboys* because after the wedding, Craig boxed them up carefully and Carolyn stowed them away in the darkest corner of the storage unit rented for insignificant personal effects that did not fit into their condo or lifestyle. The in-laws paid for a proper honeymoon, and the only postcard Craig sent from their trip read: "Married life is great, Will. They say the magic fades, but here we are, just short of a month, and we're as into it as ever."

Kronos, no slouch at math, had figured out long ago the spell that had elapsed between his parents' wedding day and his own birth, and coincidentally the length of time that some of these forlorn objects had lain in storage. He put aside the albums that looked interesting to him and said, "You must have missed playing the drums for so long, Dad. It's been fourteen years."

Craig, no insensitive slouch himself, said, "I preferred playing with my new baby." He picked a record out of the pile, Young Fresh Fellows' *The Men Who Loved Music,* and played a track, "I Don't Let the Little Things Get Me Down," but it made him sad. He showed Kronos the title of the next one he played, "Unimaginable Zero Summer." It was one of those funny-on-the-surface songs that depressed him, reminding him acutely of what he felt after senior year of high school. It all made him sad.

Kronos listened intently. "This is cool," he said. He'd always dismissed this type of music before, but now decided that he *liked* classic rock. Particularly that song title about the summer. Where had he heard that line before? It was in English class, when his eighth-grade teacher had made them read T. S. Eliot poems—"Little Gidding," that was it, about the dead season of midwinter spring, where all growth is arrested in time, a mass of blooming frost in winter, silent, nothing budding or fading. *Where is the summer,* the poet asks, *the unimaginable Zero summer?* "That's from a poem, Dad. A guy's garden is like in a state of suspended animation, frozen into a snapshot of a summer garden, where everything is supposed to be in flower, but it's really only snow and ice—not green, growing things. Nothing changes in it. It's like a metaphor for his crappy life." Craig turned and stared at his son. Kronos said, "Maybe it doesn't mean that. I only got a C minus."

Craig sang along with the lazy lyrics of the song, but stopped at that recurring line, "Face to face with absolutely nothing." That one always got him.

Aura fussed in her swing a little, so Craig lifted her out and held her, swaying to the melodies.

Kronos said, "Sometimes when she cries, I read to her and she falls asleep."

"What do you read?"

"Whatever we're studying in English class. Like that T. S. Eliot poem or *The Chocolate War* or *Lord of the Flies.*"

Craig said, "Don't read her that stuff! She's just an infant. Isn't life bad enough? Do we have to drag darkness into children's stories? You should read her nursery rhymes, things that are cheerful, things for babies."

"I'm not hurting anything. She doesn't know what I'm talking about anyway."

But she will soon enough, Craig thought. He wished his child could just bask in sunlight, bogus or otherwise, for a while.

When Carolyn came home a couple hours later, she found Kronos watching the naked channel and her husband sacked out on the couch with the baby snoozing on his chest. Kronos fumbled for the remote (too late) and Carolyn angrily flicked off the TV. The boy scuttled into his room and shut the door, and Craig awoke with a snort.

"I told you to put Aura down when it's nighttime," Carolyn said, taking the baby from his arms. "It's not good for her to be held every time she falls asleep."

Craig knew all the reasoning behind this, yet he still wanted to ask, *Why? Why would it be so bad to be held every time you fell asleep, to feel arms around you and to hear music and conversation as you drifted off? Why was it wrong to feel secure and comforted and loved when reality subsided and dreams took over?* But he said nothing; he knew why it was wrong: things like that do not last, so one should never get used to them.

fifteen

charlie fastened his robe and plugged a Glade air freshener into his bedroom wall socket. Shamans (the plural *was* shamans; he had looked it up) typically used incense, but Mrs. Brown complained that strong smells gave her migraines. He was due at his coworker Pete's apartment in a half hour, and he felt a mite nervous about performing his first urban shaman ritual outside the sadly comfortable confines of work. He tried to sit cross-legged on his bed, but he was not the most limber of shamans and opted for a chair in the corner. He closed his eyes, breathing in the scent of Glade Melon Madness, and held his hands in a sort of pinched pose above his knees, the way he'd seen Madonna do it.

"Gods of nature," he intoned, "gods of cityscapes, a dog is lost in Wicker Park. Help me return her to her human, and he will praise your names with good deeds shown to others, prayers of gratitude, and offerings of chocolate doughnuts. Thank you."

From down below, a voice cried out into his meditation: "Charlie! The tuna casserole is getting cold!" The ghost booked down the hall.

His stomach gurgled in its usual Pavlovian response, but he thought, *I shall forgo this meal as a sign of my commitment to my vocation.* His stomach protested, but he remained steadfast. Tuna casserole? Please. It wasn't that hard to resist.

He gathered up his backpack, then hesitated as he glimpsed himself in the dresser mirror. Going downstairs and passing his parents, wearing the robe and his striped skullcap (knit by Verity), he realized he might attract some bad vibes, not to mention a heaping dose of ridicule seasoned liberally with Catholic guilt. He considered taking off the robe and stuffing it in his backpack, but changed his mind. *I'm not ashamed of who I am.* He sucked in his gut. *Well, most of the time.*

Mr. and Mrs. Brown waited at the kitchen table. The beige atrocity on their plates wobbled of its own volition, untouched. Charlie strode through the room and said he was going out.

"But the tuna casserole," Mrs. Brown whined. "I made it specially for you." She stopped speaking as her eyes traveled down the magnificent yellow robe. "What in the name of God . . ."

Charlie held up his hand. "Mother, I must ask you to refrain from comment. This is a fairly ordinary robe of the urban shaman variety. It's my new calling."

Flabbergasted, his parents sat openmouthed and stunned. Urban shaman?

"Is it devil worship?" Mr. Brown asked finally. "Because we won't abide—"

"Geez, Dad! No, no! What kind of a lunatic do you think I am? It's just a way for me to help my fellow man by connecting with nature via arcane druidic rituals."

"But what is it? What do you do?" he pressed.

Charlie explained. "Well, tonight, for example, I'm helping a coworker find his lost pet. We'll be chanting and gazing into a divination bowl and deciphering supernatural messages out of smoking debris. I assure you it's very boring, normal shaman stuff."

Mrs. Brown rose up from the table. "Where's the parish newsletter? I'm calling Father Marszewski."

"Mother, I still believe in a benevolent creator. I just want to become a more active participant in my community and spiritual life instead of a Bible-study, pew-bound observer. Goodness by any other name is still goodness."

"Works for me," said Mr. Brown, and dug into his dinner. The ghost hovered in a blissful cloud above the casserole dish. Mrs. Brown sank slowly into her chair and fanned herself with an empty Stouffer's box.

"Now if you'll excuse me," Charlie said, hoisting his bag upon his back and nodding curtly to the Browns, "I have to slaughter a sheep and examine the blade bone."

charlie and pete sat quietly on a couch in the apartment. Pete's girlfriend sniffled from across the room, looking out the window.

"I'm sorry," said Pete. "I didn't know about this sheep thing—"

Charlie waved his apology away. "No, that was my mistake. That's for another ritual. I don't know why I keep . . . well, anyway, we don't need a sheep. We've prayed, we've looked for images in the divination Tupperware, and we've burned stuff. Sorry," he said to the girlfriend, "about your shirt. I didn't realize how close you were standing to the lighter."

She looked down at the smoldering black wreckage of her hem and said, "I don't care. If it'll bring Daisy back, that's all that matters."

They waited a few minutes, looking expectantly at Charlie.

"Sometimes, it takes a while for the gods to answer," he said. "In the meantime, may I make a call?"

Pete nodded and Charlie walked into the privacy of the kitchen to phone Verity.

Once he heard her voice, he whispered in despair, "It's not working! I can't figure out where the dog is!"

She asked, "Did you see anything in the divination thingy?"

"I thought I saw the image of an animal running through the street, but it turned out to be a stain on the bottom of the Tupperware."

"I told you to use a glass bowl."

"I know, but my mother wouldn't let me take one. I'm lucky I got out of the house with Tupperware."

Verity drummed her fingers on her telephone chair, deep in

thought. Something about the phrase "animal running through the street" struck her. She said, "I saw a dog running down Winchester during that storm, and that's only six blocks from where you are. Maybe it was their dog. This one was kind of brown."

"Pete!" Charlie yelled. "What color is your dog?"

"Brown," he answered.

"Yes! It's brown, he said it's brown!" Charlie whispered with excitement.

Verity said, "I'll be waiting outside my building."

Once the shaman contingent reached Chicago Avenue, Verity waved to them and crossed the street. Together they walked down Winchester. Charlie held a photo of the dog in one hand, a chocolate doughnut in the other, muttering to himself.

"Are you a shaman, too?" Pete asked Verity.

She said, "Recovering Catholic."

They made it four blocks, stopping just short of Division Street, when Charlie said, "Huh."

All turned to him and waited. He pointed to a flyer posted on a streetlight and read it aloud, "Female dog found 7/20. Brown, friendly, no tags."

Pete whipped out his cell phone and punched in the telephone number on the notice. He spoke for a few minutes, giving out identifying marks and the dog's name, and held his breath. Verity squeezed Charlie's arm and looked up into his face, which had grown pale and sweaty. Absently, he began to munch the doughnut.

Pete breathed again and tears swam in his eyes. "It's her," he said.

while pete and his girlfriend went to pick up Daisy, Charlie waited with Verity on her front step.

She said, "Nice going, CB. This shaman racket is pretty easy."

He shook his head and held up his palms in humility. "I'm just a channel of Benevolent Creator's peace."

The front door opened and they moved aside for Eddie, who

carried two enormous canvas bags, which he deposited mightily into an old, two-toned Chevrolet. Verity began to introduce Charlie, then stopped, awestruck by the car's unconventional beauty.

"What a kick-ass car," she said.

Eddie regained his breath from lugging the bags, backed away from the hatch, and stood up. "Thank you. She's a 1973 Chevy Vega, all-new overhead cam, aluminum block four, with pistons that run directly in the aluminum cylinders, as you might have guessed."

Charlie said, "I have a white Ford Taurus."

The other man patted his arm in sympathy. "I'm sorry."

"Yes, but I have to park on the street all the time, where birds crap on it and lost Cubs fans do even worse, so it's okay."

"Well, Suzanne's not perfect, either. Her carburetor caught on fire once, but I fixed it."

Verity blinked. "Your Vega is named Suzanne?"

Charlie felt he had to ask for a proper introduction.

Eddie stuck out his hand. "My name is Loa. I live on the second floor."

Charlie said, "My name is Charlie Brown and I'm an urban shaman. I believe I may have directed my friends to the location of their lost dog."

"Urban shaman, eh?" said Eddie. "That's cool."

They discussed Verity's new job at the Hog, and Charlie offered a quick prayer of thanks to the employment gods.

"I start tomorrow," she said. "I'm excited. I hope Carl Sandburg will let me launch a book club decathlon. I mentioned something about it, but he changed the subject. I really think I can finish all the Proust volumes; I've made it to page 103 of *Swann's Way* with only minor cerebral scarring."

Charlie asked, "How was the chapter on falling asleep?"

"Excruciating, but I got through it. I'm now looking forward to the prolonged, microscopic description of the church steps from Proust's childhood."

Eddie said, "I'm glad you'll be working there tomorrow. It'll give you a nice introduction to Chain-mail Night." On cue, he showed her to the canvas bags in Suzanne and withdrew from one of them a small length of fine-meshed metal. "I'm making a tunic for myself to wear on Dungeons and Dragons Night. We have LARPs every Sunday."

Verity glanced at Charlie, her translator of all things geek.

He obliged. "Live action role-playing. Sweet."

Eddie said, "It's just taking a long time. I have to attach every little link by hand and twist it with these dinky little needle-nose pliers to get it to take hold."

Verity fingered the metal weave. "It's really very pliable. Does it come on a skein or a spool?" Eddie showed her the skein of metallic mesh in his bag. Verity's eyes sparkled and she felt the word *project* burn into her forehead. She said, "You could knit this."

"Except I don't know how to knit."

"If Carl Sandburg gives me a dinner break tomorrow night, then you'll be in for a treat, Eddie Loa," she said. "I'll bring my knitting needles."

Eddie looked up and spotted a happy couple and a brown dog skipping toward them. "Looks like you're a pretty good shaman, dude." Charlie beamed and waved at Pete.

Other thoughts darkened Eddie's brow. Could an urban shaman banish the demonic force mere feet away in apartment 2? Eddie doubted anything could, but the sight of the found dog and tears of joy gave him a thin thread of hope.

He said, "I have to get to the beauty parlor now. My aunts are playing whist tonight, and I said I'd wash out the hair traps in the sinks." He took a chance and leaned toward Charlie. "What if I ever have need of your professional services?"

Charlie handed him a business card with his e-mail address and phone number: CHARLIE BROWN, URBAN SHAMAN. AVAILABLE FOR SPIRITUAL CLEANSINGS, LANDLORD CONTROL, AND WEDDINGS.

Eddie thanked him and pocketed the card. Perhaps the reckoning day for evil had come at last.

• • •

"no, no," said Will, "you're completely off the beat. Just listen to Craig and try to follow."

Stan rubbed the area where his shoulder strap dug into his hunchback. "I'm sorry, but I haven't played my bass in a long time. It's not that easy."

"How hard can it be, Stan? You're only playing one note at a time." Will tried counting to ten in his head, that super ineffective way of diffusing rising anger. He looked around at the three-piece setup in Craig's basement, crowded in on all sides by piles of old toys, the Ping-Pong table, the washer and dryer. This was just like high school when they rehearsed in his parents' basement, arguing over Stan's whining or Neal's insistence on organ-based rock anthems.

"Can we practice 'I Ran'?" asked Craig.

Will shook his head. "No Flock of Seagulls! What's the matter with you?"

"I just think it's catchy, especially now that VH1 is pushing all the eighties music again."

"How are we supposed to play it without a synthesizer? I don't think there are even any other instruments in that song."

"I wish Neal still lived around here," Stan said with a wistful glance at the empty space their keyboardist once occupied. "Why did he have to abandon us for those pipe-organ cheeseheads? Why?"

"We never appreciated him," Craig said. "He could have been another Doctor—you know, from Prince and the Revolution?—but we always stressed the power-pop stuff. And now he's a pipe-organ big shot in Milwaukee and we're just a bunch of middle-aged losers in my basement."

Will said, "We're not middle-aged."

Lifting the bass from his aching shoulder and resting it against the wall, Stan took a seat on the floor. "What's the point of this? I can't play. Nobody's going to hire us anywhere. People want choreographed dancing with lip-synching now and I can't do it."

"Hey, I never said it was going to be easy for three thirtysomething guys who still worship the Meat Puppets to start a band," Will said, "but it's worth a shot."

Craig asked, "Do we know anyone who owns a bar? We could guilt them into letting us play. I think a personal connection to the bar owner is key; otherwise we might have a hard time securing gigs."

Stan rubbed his flesh hump and said moodily, "Maybe I'm too old to enjoy anything anymore. I feel tired all the time. I'm tired of my house falling apart, I'm tired of my kid screeching all the time, I'm tired of plodding through puddles of misery on my daily march to five o'clock. I just want to get through the day and eat dinner and avoid killing myself. Maybe we don't need the added aggravation of trying to play music."

A panic soared in Craig's chest. He had only just gotten Carolyn's approval for the band practices, not to mention her resigned acceptance of his storage unit knowledge, and he was enjoying the feeling of going forward, even if only in circles. He cleared his throat. "Yesterday at work we had some sort of enforced training session out in Schaumburg, the kind of thing they do to us every couple months or so. We were packed into this conference room and ordered to stand up and shout, 'Act enthusiastic and you'll be enthusiastic!' all while punching the air with one fist, over and over again.

"Later, someone put on a sock-puppet show that illustrated the principles behind 'winning in the workplace.' My workmates enjoyed it and laughed and made profound observations, and then the brass got up to speak. Here's a choice and meaningless quote from them that can in no way be measured or reported on: 'Our hope is to reduce the level of change all of us will have to absorb this year.' They're trying to make us believe they'll be decreasing the amount of work, but they couldn't quite bring themselves to say it." He looked at his friends and said, "I'm dying here, man. I don't care how bad we suck, we need to play."

Stan had never seen him so plainspoken, yet so plainly desperate. How much TiVo and Belgian beer did it take to fill up that empty shell of a man? He stood up and slung his bass strap on and nodded to his friends. The Lousy Dates were back, in all their inept, tone-deaf magnificence.

"So . . . Flock?" asked Craig hopefully.

"Fine! Flock! Fucking Flock!" Will snapped, expelling a mighty sigh. They rearranged "I Ran" for a power-pop trio. Craig thought there was room for a clarinet solo, but dared not say a thing.

the music thumped through the kitchen floor, rattling the cupboard doors and the glasses within. Aura felt the vibrations clear through her bouncy seat and settled back in a mesmerized trance. Carolyn paced the room, unable to sit still for long. Really, she did not mind this new band thing. It gave Craig something to do, something besides complaining about his job and being depressed and ungrateful. After all, she had plenty to do: the wetlands conservation task force, organizing the monthly wine parties with the neighbors, never-ending child care, the book club, the Clarendon Hills holiday charity fund-raiser, not to mention dealing with Kronos's eternal victimization at the hands of every teacher and classmate he'd ever had. Perhaps ninth grade would be different for him, a turning point. People often soared in high school, a new environment full of strangers who had never witnessed the dismal failures of your past thirteen years. This was a valid argument that many people heartily embraced. Kronos, a pragmatist to the death, would never buy it.

Carolyn looked down at Aura, at her little round head and pretty, gurgling mouth and grave eyes, and felt a deep, gnawing, mortifying zero.

"I love you," she said. She rubbed the baby on her tummy and stared out the window.

The guys came upstairs later to feast on the quesadillas Carolyn had made. She herself took one in one hand, the baby in the other, and deposited Aura into her crib for a nap. The child screamed in indignation, and Carolyn shut the nursery door behind her.

"This is just like when your mom would make us sandwiches in high school, after band practice in your basement," Stan commented, mouth full.

"Yeah," said Will, "I forgot about that."

Stan said, "Except it's Craig's wife. Not any of our moms."

The sound of uncomfortable chewing filled up the next minute.

Craig said, "So it's not really the same."

"No, of course not." Will helped himself to another.

A moment or two passed. Stan said, "Still, it's kinda weird when you think about it."

Craig pulled three bottles of Stella Artois out of the wine fridge and found their matching glasses. Thank *God* he had found that storage unit.

Stan, always a low scorer on the sensitivity portion of the compulsory workplace personality tests, finally changed the subject. "Laurel saw Carolyn out the other night."

Craig said, "Yes, I was babysitting. She needs a night of fun away from us every so often."

"Laurel had Sebastian in the car and he was, as usual, throwing a holy terror tantrum, so she couldn't get out to go say hello to her."

Craig longed to ask where this was, since Carolyn threw a holy terror fit herself whenever he asked about her occasional evenings out, but he'd be damned if he'd reveal this little nugget of marital strife to Stan. "That's too bad," he said. "Aura rarely throws tantrums." A tortured scream from the nursery ripped through the walls and somewhere a dog howled.

"Actually," Stan admitted, "I think Laurel was a little envious. She saw her in Starbucks, sitting by herself and drinking coffee, and then later, when Laurel was coming home from the grocery store, she was still in there. Naturally, I got about an hour's worth of 'Why don't *you* ever watch Sebastian and let me go out for a quiet evening?' So thanks a lot, bro."

Craig thought, *Please do not call me "bro."* He realized that of all the scenarios he entertained regarding Carolyn's whereabouts on those "girls' nights" (male strip clubs, bars, expensive restaurants, even coffee klatches where all the women bitched about their husbands), he always assumed that there were actually other girls present.

He recalled the many occasions that he disparaged Starbucks in front of his wife, calling it Fourbucks in deference to the amount of cash he had to plunk down every time he wanted a cup of coffee. He complained about the stained velour chairs and hideous world music and the otherwise unemployable goth Lolitas who rolled their eyes at his inane pleasantries. This was the place Carolyn picked *on purpose* to get away from him and their children.

He swallowed, feeling a tiny pool of bile churn around his intestinal tumor. This was the place she found solace in; why had he never known that? Had there been some moment when she confided her love for Fourbucks and he had snubbed it? Craig recalled with discomfort his martyr tirades against Carolyn when she hid his things in the storage facility; had he dismissed her fondness for overpriced coffee in a quasi-hipster setting with the same insouciance she had shown his beer glasses and drum kit and records? He imagined how she felt every time he mocked her chosen temple.

Oblivious to his friend's moral conundrum, Stan said, "Somehow, you're always one-upping me. Usurping my party planning, letting your wife go out and drink coffee while you babysit—I can't compete."

Craig raised a finger. "Please," he said, "I'm having a moment."

The men helped themselves to more beer and quesadillas while Craig turned things over in his mind. His eyes strayed to the wine fridge and the array of beer glasses in the cabinet. Carolyn might have hid his stuff, but at least she never threw it away. That was something. Maybe his wife did not hate him after all.

He looked at Stan and said, "You should have Laurel call Carolyn; maybe they can meet for coffee some time."

Stan said, "It'll never happen. Laurel guilt-trips herself every time she considers going out alone for an evening, so she never ends up going anywhere. Then she bitches and moans about it, like Sebastian is holding her hostage." He did not mention the time he had come home late from an extra-long day of work to find a broken bowl laying in pieces on the kitchen floor, dried milk and cereal stuck to the linoleum. Sebastian lay sleeping on the couch in a T-shirt, ripped at the collar, stained Baby NyQuil blue; Laurel stared out the small square window of the sagging front door, silent, her hair half-pulled from its ponytail, scratches on her hand. She did not turn when spoken to; she watched the neighborhood life pass by in unimaginable, nothing moments. Stan found hideous, scrawled portraits of his son crumpled up next to the wastebasket, evidently pitched there. He had opened one up—the child looked like a demon baby with great slavering teeth and wild eyes. Underneath it had been scribbled: *My green apple.*

sixteen

cool; it had worked. nothing wrong with lying on a job application if it helped you get the job you were always meant to have. Diana smiled at her ingenuity as she walked through the mall, marveling that all a teenager had to do was put down "McDonald's" on any employment application, and it was like a free, wholesome pass into the working world. Adults saw that name and immediately thought, *Well, if she was good enough for ol' Ray Kroc, she's good enough for me.* Diana skipped out the mall door and into the parking lot, enjoying the warm humid air and the setting sun in her eyes. No one checks references, apparently. What idiots.

Later, she met up with Kronos at Starbucks. She watched him ride up on a girl's bike with a pink banana seat, then waved at him once he entered the café. With glee she related the whole story.

"And your parents are okay with you getting a job?" he asked.

She said, "I'm a C student in a class full of fuckups and whores and my parents have never been prouder."

"Oh," he said. "That's good."

Diana swung the silver rings around her knuckles. In truth, Thelma was not pleased about this job, but not for the usual reasons parents liked to keep teens chained at home. This was hard to explain to Kronos, who probably came from a completely normal family. "I mean, they're not totally against me working. It's just that my mom kind of has issues with me driving and going out a lot. Whatever, it's stupid. I had this sister, this half sister, who died in a car crash when I was a little kid. She was driving home from work at this cheesy minigolf place, and my mom's been kind of mental ever since. I told her I'd ride my bike to the mall instead of driving. She just looked at me with her eyes really wide—you know that trick to keep you from crying?—but she blinked and then walked out of the kitchen and went upstairs. I looked at my dad and was like, 'Can I have this job or not?' and he nodded and then he walked away, too."

Kronos cursed himself for not reading his mother's women's magazines. Did women want to be consoled after relating such stories, or did they want you to be strong and silent? He gave it a stab. "That seems understandable."

"Understandable? My whole life is an empty space. All I want to do is work in a goddamn pet store in the mall and get out of the house for five minutes so I don't murder my parents. My mother is obsessed with buying furniture and step class and her incontinent pugs and she can barely stand to pay me any attention, but when I ask if I can just have a job, she acts like I'm trying to run away from home. There is nothing understandable about her at all; she's insane, and she wears too much blush." Diana took a massive gulp of mocha and then rested her forehead in her hand.

Kronos tried again. "I'm sorry. I didn't mean, uh, what I meant was, anyone would go mental if their daughter died. It's not your fault."

She stared moodily at the baristas. She remembered when it happened, even though she was only four. Thelma cried constantly, deep racking sobs from her bedroom, the door shut. The house went uncleaned, meals uncooked, games unplayed. She remembered Verity wandering around with big, dead, stuffed-animal eyes. *Try to have patience,* Dick had told her. *Mommy isn't feeling well.* Diana knew the cause; she understood that Victory was gone, was not coming back, but no one would say this to her . . . hoping to spare her from a dark and painful truth, no doubt. Why did people think that children knew nothing of darkness? She had climbed on a chair up to the fireplace mantel and taken down, then thrown out, the little framed photos of her sister. The absence of these reminders would ease Victory from her mother's mind and would help turn her attention to Diana again. When Thelma had discovered them missing weeks later, Diana admitted nothing. Well-meaning relatives who had eventually come by to vacuum and dust were blamed; Thelma assumed they had hidden them away, releasing her from the peculiar captivation of pictures, from the torture of seeing her daughter's smiling, nonexistent face every day. Diana remembered all this, and also that her mother began to play with her again shortly thereafter. It was a treachery, and it had worked.

She turned to Kronos. "Each day's the same. Know what I mean? I just sit on my ass night after night in my room, smearing shea butter on my elbows. Nobody cares about my elbows; even I don't care. All I wanted to do was work in a pet shop, and I know I should be glad they're letting me, but now I feel, I don't know, guilty or something. I guess I've been in a shitty mood recently. I don't want to say 'depressed' because I hate that word and everything that goes along with it, but it's just such a fucking ordeal to drag myself out of bed every afternoon."

The boy watched Diana's other hand release the coffee cup and then lie flat on the tabletop. She was such a brilliant clarinetist and had such a horrible attitude that he found her irresistible, so he laid his hand on top of hers.

She let him, even though, she thought, this wasn't that type of thing. His hand was bigger than hers and his fingertip clarinet calluses pressed on her wrist. It felt okay to her and she tried to smile, but the contortion, foreign and hesitant, cracked her lips. Beneath his fingers, her soft hand grew warm. The whole business gave Kronos this sudden, perfect feeling in his pants.

"it's my first night," Verity said, cradling the phone under her chin while trying to apply mascara. "I'm excited, but scared, too. You know how cash registers intimidate me."

"Uh huh," Charlie replied beneath a burble of saliva. He held a cotton ball soaked in bourbon next to his decrepit molar.

"I hope it's not a computerized register. I get lost in all the screens."

"Gaarrghllarrgh."

Damn. She smudged it again. What was the point? Her eyelashes were as thin and dishwater-blah as her hair; wearing mascara only made them look like nesting raccoons. "What's the matter with you? I can barely understand anything you're saying."

"My toof. Ugh, sorry," he said, removing the bourbon-soaked fluffery from his mouth. "I dropped a cotton ball down my throat. My mother swears by this bourbon remedy, but I don't think—"

"For God's sake, why don't you just go to a dentist and get it fixed already? A real dentist," she amended, before he could bring up Tex.

"No. I can't afford it." He thought, rather self-righteously, about the birthday present he wanted to buy her, and how selfless he was to put her gift ahead of his own decaying, rotten, aching molar crisis.

"Charlie, that tooth practically has an exposed nerve flapping around. There's no enamel left. There's just a sad root and two half walls left. Remember what I said about houses after tornadoes rip through them? You're in for a hell of a lot more pain if you don't get it fixed."

Easy for her to say, he grumbled to himself. She never had any problems with her teeth; they were as strong and solid as old ivory. If she only knew how he suffered, hoarding his money for her present, denying himself dental relief. He ignored the semaphore waving from the moral side of his consciousness, the one that hinted that maybe fear kept him from the dentist, more so than financial concerns. He was not afraid! He was fearless! He was a fearless urban shaman.

"I can't talk about this anymore," she said, "I have to get to work. Go to the dentist; don't go to the dentist. I can't help you."

Charlie hung up, frowning as he chewed his chocolate doughnut on only one side of his mouth. Nobody ever appreciated the agony that healers endured.

•   •   •

carl sandburg went off to sort through the overstock and left Verity alone at the counter. With relief, she admired the nice, old cash register, its round, sticking buttons and flag that announced No Sale no matter what the transaction. A gun lay in the traveler's checks compartment, which just goes to show that some bookstores handle customer service in different ways.

"It's not loaded," Carl told her. "It's just to scare off thieves and rabid Iowa Writers' Workshop fans. Also, I had a situation in here when that *Bridges of Madison County* book got popular; I don't want to talk about it, but let me just say that my credo here is 'In few, very specific situations is the customer right.' "

She nodded and bit the inside of her cheeks. She'd have to unlearn everything Team Leader Joe had taught her.

"Where are the dictionaries? I need one for my kid." A man in a Burberry trench hustled up to the counter and tapped his fingers on the glass, indicating how precious the time was that ticked by.

Verity pointed him over to the reference books and he threw up his arms in frustration at the many shelves of encyclopedias, dictionaries, and thesauri ahead of him.

"Can't you just find me a dictionary?"

Carl Sandburg watched from atop the library ladder in fiction.

Verity selected a Webster's *New World Dictionary,* second college edition.

The customer flipped through its stained pages. "What's so great about this one?"

"Well, for one thing I like the blue leather binding—it's cracked in a pleasant pattern and comfortable to the touch—and I also like the wide, labeled craters on the page edges that separate the alphabet into two- and three-letter groupings. Some reference books skimp on the section divisions. I think it's important to have clear and textual markers."

The customer gawked at the publication date. "This came out in 1978! What good is this to me?"

"It's only four dollars."

"I don't care! An old dictionary is worthless."

She said, "It may not have 'bling-bling' or 'killer app,' but all the old words still work."

Carl Sandburg smiled and turned back to the overstock.

Later, when Verity stood below the ladder and handed books to him, Carl said, "So what do you think of your first night at the Hogbutcher so far?"

"I like it. Thanks for letting me put up that sign. It's something I've always wanted to do." She smiled at the picture next to the register of Dr. Phil with the red circle and slash through it.

"My pleasure. It was the least I could do after that squatter from next door rushed into the bathroom and didn't quite make it to the toilet. We do get some unusual messes in this store from time to time."

"It's better than cleaning up Godiva chocolate wrappers and racking up sales for Tim LaHaye or the lifestyle gurus."

"You know," he said, "I love this store. It's the third one I've owned in my fifty-eight years, but it's definitely the best. Ever think about owning a bookstore?"

"I'd love to," she said wistfully. "I know just how I'd decorate it—part tiki, part fifties, part haunted gothic library, all beautiful thrift—and exactly which customers to kick out."

Carl Sandburg nodded in agreement, recalling the halcyon days of his youth when he planned much the same things for his first store.

At 7 p.m., the Chain-mail Club trooped in and commandeered the big table in the back. Eddie waved to her, showing off his new project.

"Nice chain-mail cap," she said.

"Actually, it's called a 'coif with ventail.'"

"Whatever it is, it kicks ass." Was she too old to be saying "kicks ass?" Was there a statute of limitations on juvenilia? The club members helped one another fasten the various chain-mail pieces around their sizable girths, crooning lewd new verses to

"Song of the Volga Boatmen." A fresh, demented smile broke out across Verity's face.

on her break, she had phoned Charlie to tell him about her first night of work and to apologize for rushing him off the line earlier when he began his incessant dental complaints, but he announced that now he had no time to talk.

He said, still a bit stung, "Don't worry about my teeth. I'm sure I'll be fine, and if not, I'll just suffer in silence. I have to get going. I'm meeting Laurel at the Green Mill tonight to watch a poetry slam. I've put together some rites that should help her determine if poetry is the path she should pursue, but I don't know if the bar will let me bring in a stuffed armadillo or handheld recording devices."

"Oh. That's nice." She tried to process this and speak at the same time. "You're going out with Laurel? What about her kid? I thought she never liked leaving him."

"She said Stan's babysitting. Look, I gotta run now."

"But I wanted to tell you about my first night here," she said. "There's no self-help section here! When customers ask for it, my boss points them toward the martial arts shelf. And I'm allowed to use a gun to mediate fanatical customer disagreements."

Charlie said, "You're not the only one with a new calling, you know. I'm about to embark on a mystical journey and all you can talk about is the cash register. *Some* people are actually interested in my spiritual awakening, as well as my tooth woes."

"Oh, like Laurel? Bully for you. And I *am* interested in your shaman shit; who bought you the robe, huh? Me, that's who. And who's been listening to you bitch and moan about your teeth for five years? You go to hear poetry—poetry!—with the wife of a 'yuppie' you can't stand, but I can't talk for two minutes about something going on in my life? I'm very supportive of you, but I can't just take care of people all the time; sometimes I need someone to take care of me and listen to *my* problems."

He said, "Bye, Verity," as he pulled the receiver away. The words slid by like the whistle of a train when it's leaving.

She picked up her knitting needles, those humungo number 17s, and resumed her work on the chain mail, trying not to dwell on the unpleasant conversation they'd just had. She checked her watch. Five minutes left on her break; five minutes left to calm down and decompress. She reminded herself of her good fortune, this exciting new job and the fact that Carl Sandburg let her eat dinner out here in full view of the populace.

Eddie lumbered over, sat down heavily beside Verity, and organized varying lengths of chain mail on the table. She had taught him to cast on the first row of metal stitches and now he attempted the subsequent row of knit stitches. This was not as easy as it looked, but he was getting the hang of it. He complimented her on her prowess. "You think you could knit me a codpiece?"

"Sure, why not?"

"Great," he said. "So how's the shaman these days?"

Verity did not raise her eyes. "Fine," she said as she picked up an extra chain stitch by accident and swore softly to herself.

Eddie said, "I see."

"What do you see? There's nothing to see. Charlie is . . . he's . . ." Where was the pity she would normally feel for anyone duped into attending a poetry slam? "He's going to an amateur poetry reading with a . . . a client."

Links of chain mail hovered motionless in Eddie's hands as a look of horror sank beneath his features. "A poetry reading? For the love of God, why? Why would anyone attend such a thing?"

Verity said, "I don't know. Part of the urban shaman code? They have to help people find themselves."

"Yes, but at a poetry reading? Anyone who finds themselves at a poetry reading deserves to be lost."

"I agree." She jabbed the knitting needle through the metal link and tore into her own cuticle. "Especially poets who don't eat sugar and bore everyone to desperation about it."

"Oh," said Eddie, resuming his chain linkage. "I understand: it must be a lady poet. You're jealous."

Verity scoffed. "You're crazy. I'm not the jealous sort, I'm a very even-keel, unruffled—"

Eddie waggled his index finger at her and smirked.

"I'm not jealous!" she insisted. "That's . . . that's preposterous. Charlie's never given me any reason to be jealous, and neither has anyone else, not that I can even remember dating anyone before him." Eddie raised his eyebrows in question. "I'm sure there was someone, but that one-two punch of being depressed and drunk for six straight years in my early twenties accounts for the blurry memory," she explained.

He looked thoughtful. "I had a similar stretch of alcohol-fueled misery for a while, myself. Quite a few lost weekends, stomach ulcers, episodes of random vomit, and a black hole of social oblivion."

"Yes," she recalled fondly, "the salad years."

"Anyway, jealousy is normal, Verity, and nothing to be ashamed of."

She said, "If I am jealous—and I admit nothing—it is because the health-food performance poetess in question is needy and ignored by her husband and therefore extrareceptive to Charlie's good-natured charms." Acid crept into her voice. "But perhaps as he's so busy with his shaman duties—you know, spiritual career counseling and tracking down stuffed armadillos—he won't have time to flirt."

"Hey, *I'm* never too busy to flirt and I'm the chapter secretary of the Over-35 Dungeonmasters Association of Illinois, the chain-mail coordinator for our little club here, *and* the hair clog specialist at the beauty shop. I hardly have a free minute left over for Norwegian death metal after I squeeze in a little nooky." He smiled broadly, displaying a fine collection of sharp, nicotine-stained teeth.

Verity's break ended and she wandered back to the cash register, ruminating. The bickering she and Charlie had undertaken lately was a new development in what had always been a comfortable, unhurried, lazy relationship. What was wrong with her? Was she really jealous? It so did not fit with her perception of herself. She was the one who gave Laurel Charlie's phone number in the first place, and now she was getting into a mad snit about it? It made no sense. Maybe she just never thought about the two of them actually conversing—without her—and doing things together. But now that she pictured it going on in her head, her imagination began to gain speed. There was no doubt in her mind that Charlie was physically attractive to all women. It was one of those wonders of chemistry that a figure cultivated entirely on White Castle and Charleston Chews could be so steeped in sex appeal, but there it was. She did not like thinking of him in this tawdry way, but could not help it. If he donned the yellow robe tonight, all was lost. No woman could resist its power.

with the store closed at 11 p.m., Carl helped Verity count down the drawer, wash out the mugs, restock books people had left lying around, and clean the coffeemaker.

"I think you did pretty well," he said. "Don't be afraid to laugh at customers who buy stupid books, either. That's part of the fun. At first I made a vow not to stock anything that I personally wouldn't read, but that's like shooting myself in the foot. I'm a capitalist, after all."

She said, "All the Iowa Writers' Workshop authors have been shoved into a bottom shelf by the litter box."

Carl smiled in beatitude, so pleased was he with that setup. "I know; isn't it great?"

Verity broached the subject that had been playing at the back of her mind for a while. "Carl, what would you think about me starting a book club here? I could put up flyers and I think it would help sales of end-of-the-night burnt coffee."

"We had a book club once," he said, then abruptly grabbed a

wad of money from the register. "Six hours today; that's fifty-four bucks. Cash okay?"

Verity took the money and put it in her purse. "Sure." She watched him and said nothing.

He sprayed Windex on the counter and rubbed it with a paper towel in perfunctory circles. "Our book club didn't work out so well," he said. "Do you have to walk home alone? Do you want to take the traveler's checks gun?"

"No, thanks. I have mace and knitting needles." A bad ending to the book club, eh? She dropped it for the time being.

Once on the corner of Damen and Evergreen, purse strap across chest and under jacket, hand on mace in pocket, don't-mess-with-me/judo-champ gait at the ready, she paused. Seven blocks to the south was her apartment, about five blocks to the north was the Kit-Kat Karaoke. She turned north.

will realized that it was only a matter of time before he, as the house KJ, accrued his own following of groupies. Unfortunately, the current batch consisted of six male, midlife-crisis casualties bewitched by his evening kickoff of karaoke AC/DC. They gathered around the KJ booth in their plain button-downs and ironic T-shirts and cargo pants, their bourbons and beepers, waxing nostalgic over the hard rock of their youth.

When he brought up his teenage, heavy-metal bender to the other men, Will felt like he had just presented a party of hungry infants with a massive, triple-sugar birthday cake. They seized upon his Judas Priest confessions, eyes shining, eager to reveal their own binges. At first, they chortled about the metal bands' loutish, circus-style performance routines, but then suddenly they broke out in embarrassingly earnest musical-theory deconstruction. Since tenth grade, all that compiled data about Metallica had lain fallow until someone like Will came along, ready to appraise and dissect *Master of Puppets*. To be fair, he could relate to these audiophiles. He, too, had amassed a mother lode of judgments about the direction of modern music for which unpublished rock critics had no outlet. What good was this vast store of knowledge? It's not the sort of information that helps anyone pick up chicks.

A guy in depressing, triple-pleated pants said, "At home, I've been constructing a shadow-box diorama of a burnout's room, circa 1984." By "home," he meant his parents' house.

This was the type of conversation Will had come to expect at the KKK between his nemesis the DJ and legions of emocore music wonks. Now he evidently had his own following, pathetic middle-aged losers who had gathered purposefully around the KJ booth to see *him;* to express unabashed admiration for his musical taste and what they assumed was a swinging, single-guy lifestyle. They raved about his catalog of Replacements' tunes. They divulged a desire to be the kind of KJ he was, envious of his way with the ladies in the crowd. They shook his hand and touched him with too much familiarity and asked if he wanted another bourbon, ready to share several hours of their lives with him. It was like being a rock star without the money, fame, and product. That they assumed he had a satisfying and bawdy love life, based on the assembly line of KKK honeys parading themselves before the booth, both amazed and saddened him. Well, come to think of it, he *did* have an active sex life; but he was supremely and bleakly disaffected by it.

He nodded occasionally to his new group of admirers, ignoring them for the most part, eyes scanning the room above their heads, then he eventually clammed up and terminated his heavy-metal revelations. He resumed his usual aloofness, followed by an almost aggressive disinterest—he could not help it; he was the sort of person who needed more than a few belts of Jim Beam to feel engaged enough to chat with anyone, and he became distant around wildly enthusiastic strangers. And, like rock star fans, they seemed not to notice his snotty withdrawal and evasive, monotone replies. Were the DJ's groupies this insistent, this obsessed? He tried to differentiate those who were merely chatty from those who were completely insane and likely to plunge a splintered golf pencil into his throat.

Then Will saw her through the crowd, clomping along in black cowboy boots, a fringed skirt, a red blouse, and a boxy gray linen jacket. The mirrored disco ball glinted off her eyeglasses as she approached the booth, and he shooed his groupies away. He saw no lumbering shaman anywhere in the vicinity.

Verity said, "I stopped for a visit and a beer," and explained she had just gotten off work from her new job.

"Nice," he said. "I know where that place is. Right next to the big crack house with all the busted windows."

"Yes, that's how we describe it in the ads."

She paged though the songbook, aware of Will's eyes upon her. As a person who spent the majority of her adult life alone when not working, she was not exactly uncomfortable being in the bar by herself, just uncomfortable with the proximity of people all around her and the propensity for drunks to crash in on her personal space. Not at all like being at the thrift on a Saturday morning, where even though entire families blocked aisles and all the carts were taken, there still remained the likelihood for peace and anonymity, for other shoppers to leave you alone. Even the chattiest fellow thrifter eventually became fixated on buzzing around the store and scoring bargains. Bar-hoppers became fixated on you or themselves and no good had ever come of that.

"Want to sing something?" Will asked. "If so, let's get a move on. The cops usually burst in here around one a.m."

Cops? Verity looked around. Apart from the singing, there appeared to be no criminal activity going on. "Why?"

"The bouncer's a sucker for pretty college girls with laughably fake IDs."

They agreed to sing a duet of sorts (that perennial karaoke chestnut, "Sweet Caroline"), as Verity did not want to be the center of attention. She turned her back to the crowd—like a tremendously untalented Miles Davis—and stood behind Will as they sang.

Afterward, he said, "Not facing the audience was probably a good idea. You're the worst singer I've ever heard, and I've heard them all."

"I know," she admitted. "I sound like a cat with a whistle caught in its throat attacking a baby. Sometimes in my apartment, I'll sing along to the stereo and suddenly I'll catch the sound of my voice and then I have to say to myself, 'Stop. You've ruined it.' "

Will said, "That reminds me. We started up the Lousy Dates again."

"Nice. Have you found a replacement for Neal?"

"No, we're just a trio now. I'm doing the singing, except for our version of 'Turning Japanese,' which Craig handles. He's written a part in it for the clarinet that actually works."

Ah, the clarinet, that underutilized rock-band instrument. "Kronos?" she asked.

He sighed in resignation. "Kronos."

At his break, they took two beers to a table in the back. Will asked if she wanted a shot, but she declined. She'd sworn off the hard stuff, unless it came served in a ceramic volcano or hollowed-out coconut and was accompanied by ice cream, syrupy fruit, three-foot straws, and a lit can of Sterno.

"Less than two weeks until the reunion and the Sikos' psycho house party," Will said, taking a long pull at his Heineken.

Verity dropped her forehead onto the table, banging it not quite gently. Hey, that felt pretty good. She banged it again. "With the help of decent beer, I can just about stand the reunion. I don't think I can stand another night at the Sikos'."

"I like how they bicker in front of everyone and don't care. It's easier to stomach than the Kickels' silent fury."

"Ha," said Verity. "I'll take silent fury any day. Stan told me Laurel phoned him at the health club on his birthday and made him come home because his mother had dropped off a cake at their house, and she didn't want to be alone in the house with a cake. I can't stand high food-drama."

"Aw, women always have weird food issues." He thought of an old girlfriend he had mistakenly shared his life with, and the refrigerator of brown, furred food she had left behind.

"No, we don't. Some of us lead perfectly normal lives obsessing only about our abject failures as human beings, not about thigh fat." She had worked hard to reach her present level of self-acceptance, years she had spent postadolescence disregarding her mother's disapproval of zaftig waistlines, and every time she heard any woman over the age of thirty (especially a woman of fairly normal size) count sugar grams and bemoan her "fat," it drove her nuts. If she, Verity, the borderline high school loner, the present-day hermit with the passion for Melmac and fondue forks and Don Ho albums, could find it in herself to like her bod, then anyone could.

In spite of Will's usual aversion to chronic complainers such as Laurel, he did feel some compassion. After all, she was married to a suburban lothario who seemed to despise her. "I think she has a hard life. It can't be easy being married to Stan."

"That's true," Verity acceded, remembering the episode with Ol' Gropey in her apartment. She paused a beat, then said, "Charlie's at a poetry slam with her tonight, not that there's anything wrong with that, other than it being a poetry slam and her being married to someone who doesn't pay enough attention to her and Charlie being an especially attentive, charming fellow."

Will raised his eyebrows in question.

She tried to explain. "Hey, I'm no dummy; I read Bill Zwecker's column in the *Sun-Times*. I know what happens when a celebrity pays attention to a lonely woman."

He blinked. "Who's the celebrity?"

"Charlie, of course! I'm sure he's really the most kick—the most enchanting urban shaman she's ever met. You know, there's very few of them around, good ones anyway, and women are always dying to get their hands on a first-rate spiritual leader."

"I had no clue that this type of thing went on in the shaman community."

Verity drained her glass, feeling ashamed at this evening's continued outcropping of jealousy. There was probably nothing to worry about; she did not really doubt Charlie's fidelity. It just sucked feeling threatened by a poet.

"so what do i do? Do we hold hands or should I pray or something?" Laurel leaned over the table, choking on the cigarette smoke billowing from the surrounding audience.

Charlie held the stuffed armadillo, pointing its nose toward the stage where a fat man in a ponytail and *Lion King* T-shirt stood at the mike and recited the first lines to his epic:

> *I used to be a gangbanger,*
> *But now I'm just a poetry-reading faggot.*

The armadillo, its little glass-bead eyes sparkling in the nightclub shadows, held its ground. Charlie said, "No, we don't need to do anything; it's all up to him now. I'm using him as a planchette, a barometer for divining messages from beyond. But he's not ready to communicate yet."

"Why an armadillo?"

"He represents the character armor you must bear as a result of antipoetry forces."

Laurel nodded seriously. This was all very thrilling and eerie. She excused herself to the restroom so that she could phone Stan.

"How's everything going?" she asked.

"Great! I've got the Manly Den completely set up now. The stereo's going, I've got *Bitches Brew* playing. It's awesome."

She wanted to tell him about the poetry prognostication afoot, but the right words would not come. Mothers of young children were not supposed to go out and enjoy bars and envision lives of art for themselves. The customary combination of guilt and resentment flooded her heart. She changed her tack to the only one that quelled the feeling. "What about Sebastian?"

A barely perceptible sigh whooshed through the connection. "He's fine. He's asleep."

"Well, I'm sorry, but I'm just not used to being out at night, Stan."

"He's fine, okay? So don't worry. Have fun with Charlie and Verity."

"She's not—" Laurel meant to finish the statement, but stopped short.

"What?" Stan asked.

"Nothing. I better go. I'll be home in an hour or two."

When she returned to the table, Charlie was cradling the armadillo upside down in his arms, his face shining. "A message came through, Laurel! I heard it clear as day in my head! First the armadillo moved a little to the left—I swear, I didn't move it, it moved of its own accord—and it gave a little shudder, then I heard it: *Last call.*"

"Last call?"

"Yeah! Don't you get it? It's your last call, your last chance to pursue this dream. The time is right, but if you forgo this opportunity, you'll never have another one."

Warily, her eyes traveled over to the bar, where the bartender took the evening's final orders and settled up the bills.

Charlie clasped her hand in joy. "I knew the armadillo wouldn't let us down, Laurel, I knew it. He knows what's what, let me tell you, and he sees a bright future ahead of you, plans to make, goals to achieve, and poetry to be written, read, and slammed in the public arena!"

She looked down at his hand; it lay over hers like a warm trout. She said, "This is the most exciting thing that has ever happened to me."

will announced that the final round of karaoke would have a theme: songs of unrequited love. He had spent the better part of the last fifteen years trying not to dwell on his unresolved feelings for Verity, but now that this whole reunion idiocy (thirteen days, nine hours, twenty-two minutes to go) had crept up on him, he lacked the will to continually quash his catalog of stunted and malformed emotions. He endured tearful renditions of "Fifty Ways to Leave Your Lover," "The Break-Up Song," and "Can't Stand Losing You," then abruptly took the mike away from the guy about to launch into "Love on the Rocks."

"Listen," Will said, "I'm talking heartbreak. I'm talking bitter. I'm sick of this hackneyed sap. Give me pain. I want to hear songs with 'You ruined my life, you bitch! Get out!' "

A maudlin-faced woman approached the booth. "How about 'Another Lonely Christmas' by Prince?"

Will considered this, but shot it down. "Well, it's sad, but the love interest dies in that one, so it's not technically a breakup song."

"You can't get more unrequited than loving someone dead, dummy."

"Hey, if you don't like it, then you can go to the unthemed chaos of other bars' karaoke night. I'm looking for 'I want my records back! I'd wish you were dead, except you owe me money!' Next!"

Verity offered a suggestion. " 'When Love Is Found' from *The Muppet Christmas Carol.* I picked up a nice vinyl copy at Goodwill last winter."

"Muppets! Christmas! Only if it has the line 'Start packing, whore! And don't forget the five hundred cat postcards you put up all over my apartment!' "

"It's a very touching song," she insisted. "By the time that one Muppet gets to the last verse and she sings to the young Scrooge that their dreams fell through and it's time to say good-bye, Michael Caine is crying, Gonzo is crying, and I'm starting to get a bit weepy myself."

Will stepped in front of the booth and barked into the microphone. "Hasn't anyone here ever suffered? Have you ever heard

'She's My Ex' by All? That's a *real* breakup song, full of bitterness. Fucking 'Love on the Rocks'! Big deal—by the end of the song, all he wants is a smile? Go to hell, Neil Diamond! All I want is a gun! I'm looking for 'Sweet mother of Christ, just give me the last five years of my life back! And thanks for rolling your eyes every time I tried to bring up my own problems, selfish sick witch! Get out! Go to hell! And take your fucking Pier One crap with you!' "

He kicked his KJ booth, the screen with the words from "Love on the Rocks" still hovering, silent; he threw down the mike and stormed off. The police rushed in the front door then, and Verity ducked for cover.

will pulled his vw up to Verity's building, parked in front, and cut the engine. Well, this was awkward—he had not had to apologize for a rage incident in a while. He said, "I'm sorry if I lost it back there." A burning pit spread out in his stomach. Where were Craig and his Maalox when you needed them?

"Carolyn mentioned you might be taking anger management classes," Verity said. "Or going on a Robert Bly–type retreat, with primal screams and drumming in the woods in your underpants."

"She *what*? No! I'm not doing anything like that. The last thing I need is group therapy. I can handle my personal mindfuckery in my own way, thanks."

She changed the subject, as she was rather good at that. "So how often do the cops come and close down the KKK? We got out of there just in time."

"Maybe once a week. We never lose our liquor license or anything because the owner is friends with the alderman. But you know how Chicago works: City Hall's gotta look like they're trying."

She wondered how Sandburg would have fit that into his "Chicago" poem. Hog butcher no more, soft on liquor license violations, crooked aldermen in the pockets of cheesy karaoke club owners, city of slumped shoulders. She glanced at Will's profile;

he still had sharp, handsome lines despite the smoke unfolding across his brow. "Well, thanks for the ride."

He said, "It's still early." It came out before he had thought it through; what did he mean? Was he actually suggesting that she invite him up? Yes, he decided that was exactly what he was suggesting. He had already turned off the car, so there was no mistaking his intention.

Verity, no stranger to this anymore, wondered how she now managed to attract the very men she got nowhere with in high school. Was it the lone nut persona she had crafted—she, Verity Presti, eccentric recycler of other people's castoffs? Was it the "lure of the clerk," heretofore presumed to be an urban myth? Was it her robust, erotically bespectacled form, her unstyled hair, her crapitude? Although to be perfectly honest, she could not say she had *never* gotten anywhere with Will. She got somewhere once; she just had to get out of high school first. She said, "Remember the Rum Incident?"

"I do," Will said. The Rum Incident had provided a fantastic ending to summer break before their junior year of college, toasting them nicely on both sides. The basement Hide-A-Bed in the Demske home had seen it all: loose springs and soft pillows and softer thighs. Rum drinks flowed freely that night, and in a sense so did Verity and Will, neither of whom would ever flow so freely again. Afterward, while he snored on that lustrously stained and pitted sofa bed, she had snuck out the back door and ran home, fully intending to pick up with him again at the end of term. But months later, the last good day of the fall brought with it Victory's car crash and an end to Verity's plans and potential freeflowing-ness. It was a Rum Incident, a good one, a short one, and finished in every sense.

She said, "It's not going to happen again."

Upstairs, he stopped, as did so many, in her Hallway of Strangers. "Where did you get all these?" he asked.

She said, "Occasionally, I liberate a photo or five from the albums at the thrift. The way I see it, the photo album itself is for sale, not these out-of-focus pictures of Aunt Nilda and the dog, right?"

"So you steal them."

"Oh, I wouldn't rush to a semantic argument with someone who has reached page 103 of *Swann's Way*, my friend. I take care of my good thrift karma by periodically inserting my own photos into other people's albums. The shopper who eventually buys the thing isn't going to know that I'm not related to Aunt Nilda and co. So it all works out."

He teased her. "But what about the person who lays out a dollar for the album? Doesn't he deserve the"—he peered closer at the mounted frames in front of him—"blurry birthday party picture from 1968, or the crying bridesmaid, or the melted snowman?"

She said, "*I* deserve them. I love my Hallway of Strangers; they're almost like family. I'm willing to pay for it in the thrift afterlife if it comes to that."

"Which are your favorites?"

She gazed fondly at the display. "I've always been partial to Sleeping Grandpa. I also like Girls in Garden, circa 1930. Man Eating Hot Dog on Pier is nice, too. I love them all; I can't choose."

"You talk about them like they're real. I mean, real people that you know. They're just photographs."

"They *are* real," she said. "Objects have life; they are witnesses to it."

Will thought Verity had beautiful skin and a fine, feminine figure and a personality unlike any human being he had ever met, and he told her so. He put his arms around her and his lips on hers and she let him, out of tenderness for the Rum Incident and sympathy for his KJ-for-life desperation.

But then she drew back, squeezing his shoulders in a final, definitive gesture, saying, "I love Charlie Brown."

He held on for another moment, then let go. If she had uttered any number of other responses ("We shouldn't . . ." "I can't . . ."

"What about . . ." etc.), he might have pressed it, pressed her. But who can fight true love? There was nothing petty or toying or false about Verity Presti. Goddamn it, she could have been the best goddamned girlfriend ever.

charlie tiptoed into his parents' house. Mrs. Brown snored bulldoglike on the floral sofa. Mr. Brown presumably had disappeared into the ether of his own separate bedroom. Charlie poured himself a glass of milk with two fingers of Scotch—he usually preferred beer or perhaps hot chocolate—but after a taxing night of mysticism and violent recitation by performers in the Gallagher school of poetry, he felt he needed a more powerful calming agent.

Upstairs in his room, he hung up his robe with reverence for his vocation (and fear of Mrs. Brown's fanatical condemnation of slobbishness), lay back on the bed in the dark, and sipped his Scotch milk. The divination armadillo had not let him down. He glanced over at the thing, balancing on its creepy feet, its little eyes surely taking him in, divining something. He wished he knew what it foretold for him, but he could not shamanize himself, this much he had learned. Yet: there had been a moment outside the Green Mill, standing on Broadway, when he had felt that telltale tingle signifying an incoming preternatural message. Buses chugged by and the flickering sign above the Bao Bakery went black.

"I could stay out here all night," Laurel had said, "and just walk for miles and talk about the armadillo's prediction. I can't believe it. This is just so . . . so . . ." Words failed her and she threw up her hands helplessly.

"I know what you mean," he replied. Something about prophecy really started his endorphins humming.

"It's like you believe in me."

Well, he believed in the armadillo. He'd never understood much about poetry or the need to recite it aloud. But Charlie was a sensitive shaman and smiled encouragingly.

An unfamiliar emotion rose up in Laurel's chest, neither her omnipresent guilt nor bitterness. It flopped around in her belly, wriggled like a fish on a line, and spread upward through her lungs, throat, and tickled the inside of her mouth. Laurel was happy.

She had hugged him, he who brought her to this point of transcending mere wifedom and motherhood and administrative assistantship. She felt Charlie must know what it was like to struggle with the need to be more than you were. She meant to say, "You understand beauty." She said, "You are beautiful."

His pulse began to quicken and something awakened beneath his robe. Surely it was a sign from above, or below. But no other message came through, and she continued to hug him, unmindful of the numinous flare-up in his trousers.

"You are the best goddamned shaman ever," she had whispered.

The body in his arms felt nothing like Verity's, and this was difficult to get used to. The chest was ribby with small breasts, the hips wider, the hands bigger, the entire form taller. The hair was a black, thick, Louise Brooks–type bob streaked with cherry red, unlike Verity's can't-bother-to-brush-it-let-alone-cut-and-color-it dishwater flyaways. Laurel's dark eyes glittered with warmth and desire, where Verity's observed with detached watchfulness, bemused and protected behind her cat's-eye glasses.

Laurel squeezed his love handles and rested her head against his chest. Charlie stroked her neck and felt that nothing was so attractive as a woman who wanted him. Oh, God, what was he doing? Nothing was so repellent as a man who wanted a woman who wanted him, but already had a fantastic woman of his own who also, if she wasn't too caught up in her weird world of trashy treasures and familial angst, wanted him. Oh, that made him dizzy. His head, crowded as it was with memorized incantations and computer code and the business hours of the local Dunkin' Donuts, buzzed with conflicting surges of pig lust and guilt and inexplicable chocolate cravings.

Firm kindness, he had decided; that's the trick. Let her down easy without insulting the rather enjoyable chafing embrace going on. "I say this as a friend and as a modestly successful urban shaman: this is wrong." He pushed her away firmly and kindly and smiled. That was easy.

"What's the matter? It was just a hug." An arterial tide crept up her neck and set her face ablaze. Her new and fleeting happiness disappeared, and she went on the defensive. "An innocent hug. What kind of person do you think I am? You think I just go around throwing myself at every hoodoo man who pays any attention to me?"

"Well, no. I just meant that since you're married and have a kid and I'm in a relationship—though I still live with my parents, I consider it a real relationship—we ought not to hug in such a . . . a . . . grandiose fashion. Also, I would not like to compromise my professional standing—I could be ostracized from shaman society. What if people started hugging their dentists? We'd descend into chaos."

She knit her brows and looked around uncomfortably. "Of course, I don't want to jeopardize your standing, I guess I wasn't thinking that a small hug would do any harm. I was unaware the other shamans would look down on that sort of thing."

He explained, "That's because you're not in the industry. If you were, you'd understand that the association between shaman and client is a very dignified—"

"All right, all right. I'm sorry." She crossed her arms over her chest as guilt and resentment, those sorry old jades, jockeyed into position. "God forbid I show a little human affection to the witch doctor."

"I take umbrage at that term, as well as 'hoodoo man.' For thousands of years, my people have fought against those pejorative names in a bid to get the respect and acceptance we deserve from the healer/prophet/high priest community."

All right, maybe she had thrown herself at Charlie, even in a semi-innocent embrace, but she found that she no longer wanted to make room for guilt. Laurel missed that wriggling fish called happiness. She could not stand that those other thug emotions had pushed the newcomer aside. Hadn't she sometimes felt momentary joy with her son and husband? She had felt it tonight at the Green Mill, and outside here on Broadway as the Bao Bakery sign flickered off and on. Perhaps, like a dog, happiness would come when summoned. She said, "I'm sorry I called you a witch doctor. I was upset. I'm not used to being away from my son, and Stan and I have been fighting all the time, and ever since he started thinking about the reunion, he's been wanting to go backward in life, I can feel it, and I want to go forward. Maybe . . . maybe my unbridled passion for spoken-word poetry jams and happiness at hearing the armadillo's suggestion made me a little emotional. I guess I shouldn't have hugged you so passionately. It's just that you were so nice to me."

He relaxed and smiled at her. It was a shaman's duty to put people at ease, to be nice to them, to offer them hope in a faithless, wretched world.

Laurel returned the smile self-consciously. "If we were unattached singles and unencumbered by your vocation . . ." Her voice trailed off in a mist.

Charlie nodded. "I totally would have had sex with you."

he finished the Scotch milk, set the glass on his nightstand, and prepared for bed. Verity didn't know how lucky she had it, not having to deal with the infatuated masses hurling themselves at her feet. It was hard breaking hearts. As a modestly successful urban shaman, he supposed he would have to get used to the attention.

He checked his voice mail before turning in for the night. One message beeped.

"Charlie. It's Eddie Loa. You said to call if I ever had need of your services. So I'm calling. I don't want to get too into it over the phone, but I need a demon banished. This is hard-core exorcism, dude. Can you can handle it? Um, Verity said I should pay you in food. You like Samoan cuisine? My aunt makes great *taisi moa;* it's like chicken baked in banana leaves. Anyway, call me."

Charlie took down the number Eddie left and leaned back on the bed, pensive. Banish demons? That was quite a leap from channeling lost pets and guiding urban poets. He set his chin in resolution. Well, if he had to, he had to. He turned on his side, said a prayer to whoever, and closed his eyes. Mmm, chicken in banana leaves. Hey, his decrepit molar had stopped hurting, and even his gumboil had not throbbed in a while. Funny, that.

seventeen

twenty puppies wagged
their tails as Diana walked into the kennels. She cleaned out each
cage, removed the soiled bedding, and replaced it with fresh
newspaper and ripped-up towels. Against store policy, she gave
every puppy a minute of cuddling, which seriously cut into her
prep and cleanup time, so she always tried to arrive fifteen minutes early. They had no names, and the manager had told her not
to call them anything. Customers liked to pick out names unfet-
tered. Cards hung on the cages detailing what was important:
breed, sex, age. Diana had learned her first day that any medium-
smallish dog with multicolored markings got listed as "beagle
mix." Larger ones of more solid hues were "Lab mix." Barkers
were labeled "poodle mix." Those were the preferred breeds this
year, and so people likely would not mind too much if the animals were mutts. Naturally the purebreds were pushed. They
were parked in the front kennels with the least mangled towels.
Some kid with braces handled the cats, and there was a goldfish
guy and a hamster guy, too.

The manager had said, "I've never had a girl work the kennels
before. You're not intimidated by dogs, are you?" Diana thought
of Snaps and Nipper and Goldie and that other one, whatever his
name was, with their underbites and sharp teeth and inbred mental problems and staunch opposition to housebreaking, and said
no. The pugs were okay; it was not their fault Thelma could not
be bothered to train them or integrate them into the household as
pets rather than wild tenants. Actually, Diana had always liked

Tex's dogs better, especially Gin, with her gentle dopey nature and wide, wagging rear end.

By noon on this, her fifth day, she'd already had her daily visitation from a member of the Pet Store Resistance, as she had begun to think of them.

"Do these animals come from puppy mills?" the woman asked, suspicion wrinkling her brows, fistfuls of literature at hand.

I don't know; probably, Diana wanted to say, but she replied as she had been instructed by the store manager: "They all come from reputable breeders and the purebreds have papers."

"Just because they have papers doesn't mean they were bred humanely." She shoved a flyer into Diana's hand depicting a breeding bitch living in a filthy trailer, surrounded by ill-looking puppies. The woman, more tenacious than the others that week, detailed the conditions of puppy mills and how pet shops furthered this abuse by buying animals from them.

Diana jerked her thumb over her shoulder at the cages. "That's not these guys' fault. Someone has to take care of them." The store manager's keen sixth sense went off, alerting him to activist customers, and he headed over. Diana disappeared into the safety of the kennels behind the glass door.

The barkers were kept back here. Acoustic tiles covered the ceiling and walls in a vain effort to muffle the sound of dog terror, loneliness, and neurosis. Diana could not get used to referring to them as "poodle mix" or "bichon 2." Although strictly against the rules, Diana privately called all the dogs by names from the food court restaurants. It gave her something to say to them each time she cleaned out their kennels. Her favorites back here were Great Steak and Arby. They had nice dispositions despite the yelping. Perhaps in a real home, they would stop their incessant barking. They were all decent dogs in their own way and could not help the weird peculiarities that resulted from constant confinement. Frogurt had a bump on the top of his head from spending too many months in a too small cage; Gyro Hut had crossed, different-colored eyes and big black calluses on his elbows; Taco Bell had a sweet little mouth that seemed to curve up into a hopeful smile every time a person walked by her cage.

Later, at the register, Diana rang up the purchase of a small, brownish "beagle mix" in a new red collar and leash, which bounced up and down on the toes of her new owner.

"Bye, Godiva," she said.

The man said, "She already has a name?" The children with him stopped fighting over who got to hold the leash and stared at Diana.

"No. It was just a name I gave her."

He dangled his charge card just out of her reach and said, "I'd like to speak to the manager."

When the manager materialized, pushing Diana to the end of the counter, the man said, "I wanted to buy a dog that was fresh. You know, uncontaminated by a name, and now I find out this one's got a name, and excuse my language but it *sucks*, and, well, I just want to register my complaint."

"Sir, there must be some mistake. We don't give the products— er, pets—names at Petland."

He pointed at Diana. "She told me this beagle mix is called Godiva, and I don't wanna call it that, but if that's the only name it knows, it seems like I'm getting shoddy merchandise. I've been in stereo equipment sales for twenty-one years and I can tell you I'd never have sold one thing if I did business that way. Not one subwoofer. Not one tweeter."

Straining to comprehend this unprecedented glitch in the Petland consumer relations experience, the manager stuttered, "Well, I can certainly . . . I mean, I see what . . . well, sir, what would you like me to do? Would you rather not purchase this model?"

The children set loose such howls of protest, wrapping their arms around the dog and dousing its furry, mildly flea-bitten scalp with tears, that customers bored with the dead fish in the aquariums strolled over for a gander.

"I didn't say that," the father replied quickly. Then a narrow splinter of light glinted in his eyes. "But maybe you could make it worth my while."

The manager hemmed and hawed while the children continued to weep for the dog, momentarily theirs, that might suddenly be snatched away.

"Would you shut up?" the father snapped at them. "Daddy's trying to conduct business."

Diana felt a rawness burn open the back of her throat. "Don't cry," she whispered to the kids. "Just because I named her doesn't mean you can't, too. People and animals get different nicknames and stuff most of the time, depending on who loves them. In fact, I call my mother's dogs all kinds of names."

Having succeeded in knocking off an additional 10 percent from the price, the father left the pet shop, happy dog, happy children in tow.

The manager whirled upon Diana. "Do you now see the consequences of giving things names? Things that you were told expressly *not* to name, things that are not yours to name in any case?"

"Yes," she said, and thought, *They are not things.*

"Do any of the others have names?"

"No." *None that you'll ever hear, dickwad.*

"Good! Keep it that way! Now get on over to the kennels in back. I need a vomit cleanup in poodle mix two's cage."

In the mall, the dog barked, enjoying the echo and magnificence of her voice, solo, unaccompanied by kennelmates. She had never heard her voice before without the ever-present whining of the dogs on either side of her old cage.

"Come on, puppy," the man said.

"You can't call her 'puppy,' Dad," his son complained. "You have to call her Godiva."

"We are not calling her Godiva!" the man screamed. The dog barked again and tossed her head. It didn't matter. She never knew it was her name anyway.

• • •

verity pushed the peas around on her plate. Butterless, salt-free, from a frozen Birds Eye package, they rolled in half-boiled splendor around the nude, baked chicken breast and came to rest under the tines of her fork, where she stabbed them right through.

"Don't play with your food," Thelma admonished her.

"I'm thirty-three," Verity replied. "I've earned the right to push my peas around, if I so choose."

Thelma sniffed. "Almost thirty-*four*."

"That's right," Dick said. "I forgot, your birthday's coming up."

Tex slipped a piece of chicken to a slavering pug under the table. "We could have a party, honey. Carol makes a wonderful red velvet cake."

Verity looked at her family seated around the Rasmussen dining room table: Thelma, primly eating her peas one at a time; Dick, fighting off another migraine; Diana, reeking of dog kennels; Tex, feeding the pugs, thinking no one could see him. "No party," she said, "no celebration."

Diana covered her chicken breast with her napkin, a burial shroud for a creature gone too soon. "Birthdays are lame. You're just one day closer to death." Thelma stared at her; who was this child?

Verity said, "I don't think of it as one day closer to death. I think of it as one day closer to having my severed head dunked in liquid nitrogen and stuck on a shelf between Ted Williams and Walt Disney."

"You're not serious," whimpered Thelma.

"Why not? After all, at times like these, we should take comfort in religion."

Tex snorted. Since God had taken his beloved daughter, His sacraments deserved a little bashing.

"Still," Dick said, "we could have a little party."

Verity shook her head. "Please, no party. I've got the class reunion coming up, and I don't want to ask for any time off from my new job." She let the words settle in and do their work.

Thelma could not contain her pleasure. Verity never realized how much of a disappointment her Barnes & Noble gig must have been to her mother.

Tex said, "But that was a good job. It had benefits."

"I know, but now I'm working at a different bookstore, an independent one near my apartment."

"Oh," said Thelma, her face falling. "So it's basically the same job, just at another store."

"No, it's not the same! It's completely different. I'm an assistant manager." Oops, that was a lie. But Carl Sandburg did drop some hints recently that he'd need someone trustworthy to take over when he retired one day, which clearly had the earmarks of managership all over it. "I like this place. My boss may even let me run a book club if I can just figure out the deep, dark secret about the previous book club—well, never mind that—but it's a great store, and there's no self-help section, and most of the people who shop there are really interesting. I even made friends with this one guy who lives in my building, and the place is walking distance from home. Also I can eat my dinner in front of the customers, and nobody cares!"

"Oh, you made friends with some guy?" Thelma mimicked. "That sounds a little silly coming from a grown woman."

"It means a lot to me," Verity answered. "I don't have any friends."

"Does the job have benefits?" Tex asked.

"No. No benefits. Yet."

He said, "Even so, I'm glad you like it, honey. Congratulations. Remember we were just talking about how when you were sixteen you said you'd love to own a cool store? And it sounds like this may help you get on track with th—"

Thelma rose from the table and picked up the dinner plates, some of which were still being addressed by their owners. "Well, that's just fine. You're thirty-four, working in a little store in that godforsaken neighborhood you call home, renting a disgrace of an apartment, no closer to being married than you ever were. And you have no benefits."

Verity stomped into the kitchen after her. "I'm thirty-*three* and I like my new job, Mom. I like parts of my life. I'm no different than other people and I'm relatively happy considering the state of the world. Why can't you just be happy for me?"

"Happy? You call this happy?" She yanked on the hem of Verity's handkerchief shirt, yanked the ends of the blond hair that had not been cut in four months, tapped her rhinestone eyeglass frames. "You look like a bag lady. You look like a homeless lunatic."

Verity's mouth dropped open. This from Downers Grove's biggest crank, the chief of the suburban lawn police, the neighborhood patriot who insisted on flying the flag in the most intimidating manner possible. Thelma, who had been caught standing on her front porch in a bathrobe and tinfoil hat, screaming at people to get off her property. This was normal behavior, but she, Verity, was the lunatic? She breathed deeply and counted to ten. What a crock; that stupid technique never calmed anyone down. "Well, Mom, I am trying to be happy. I have a job that I enjoy and a good boyfriend. Maybe we won't ever get married, maybe we will. It's not that important to me."

Thelma wanted to hurl the dishes in the dishwasher, but they were Lenox. "Nothing's important to you. You live like a teenager. You have a college degree and *had* the brains to excel, but instead you just settled for the lazy path. Your father had a thriving dental practice—before that fiasco of a home clinic, which he'll probably get tossed in jail for—your grandfather was a physics professor who wrote textbooks, your aunt has a master's in education, your cousins all have advanced degrees and work in medicine and bioengineering. Even Diana is going to go to Oberlin on a music scholarship and make something of herself one day. You come from a family of academics, and working in a bookstore is your big contribution to the world? You should have done something more with your life; your heritage is that of great minds and hardworking scholars and you never did a damn thing with it. I raised you to have respect for academia. It's part of who you are."

Verity said, "That's why I hate it," and walked out of the room.

Later, Diana found her sister in the basement, curled up in a leather club chair with a pug. The girl took a tentative step toward her and said, "If you're crying, I can come back later."

"I'm not crying," Verity said, wiping the snot from her nose.

Diana sat down in the chair opposite her, across the "game table," which had never seen a game played upon it in its life. "If it makes you feel any better, Mom said the same thing to me when I told her about my first day at the pet store. She said, 'I didn't raise you to clean up after dogs.' Like *that* wasn't obvious from the way the pugs use our family room as their toilet—"

"No offense," said Verity, "but you can't really understand how I feel."

"Why, because I'm in high school?"

"Because you have a future that everyone is excited about. You're gonna do that thing with the flutes and the rap music, you're going to Oberlin, you have parents who are proud."

Diana said, "Tex is proud of you."

Verity sighed. This was true, but there was something kind of depressing about that. "I know, but the thing you have to understand about my dad is that he's just like me. We stopped working after Victory died. Oh, I don't mean 'job' working, I mean living-functioning working. Breathing. Being. We . . . we broke. And now both of us are really proud of each other for just getting through another day.

"I don't know why Mom was stronger," she continued. "Maybe because she had you and Dick. Maybe she was just born that way."

"Mom is not so together. She won't let me drive or go practically anywhere by myself because she's afraid I'm going to get in an accident or die."

Verity said, "But don't you see that that's kind of normal, considering what happened to my sister? She's just trying to protect you; you're the future. Me and my dad . . . we can't go forward. We like living in our memories. We had great pasts." She turned her gaze from Diana to the slant of light coming through the window well. Her eyes were inky as bracken in a winter pond. She said, "Really great pasts."

at the front door, Tex told her he'd drive her home.

"All the way to the city? No, Dad, just drop me off at the Metra. I'll take the train back just like I did on the way—"

"No. I'm driving you home."

Thelma stood in the foyer, drying an already-dry pan with a dish towel while Dick shook Tex's hand and hugged Verity. Diana watched her sister from the top of the stairs, and the girls waved to each other limply.

Tex said, "Mr. Rasmussen, please say good-bye to your wife for us and thank her for the meal."

Dick turned to Thelma. "Mrs. Rasmussen, Mr. Presti sends his regards—"

A sharp and strangled cry rose in Thelma's throat; it sounded like a bawl of fury, suddenly quelled. She threw the dish towel down and flew into Tex's face, screaming. "I heard you, you idiot; I'm right here! I'm alive, I'm not dead, and I'm standing right in front of you!"

Shocked, Tex backed out of the doorway, pulling his daughter with him. Once in the car, he pulled out his hanky and mopped his face, which had gone white beneath his tan. "My word," he said.

It was such a mild invective, so sweetly typical of the dentist who could not bear to hurt his patients, of the man who loved his children and his dog and his hideous flaming tooth sweater vest more than anything on the planet, that Verity couldn't help but laugh despite the film of tears in her eyes.

They had a beautiful past together, but any more than that, they might never have. Verity could see herself in ten years, still accruing crapulence, still in her apartment, and it seemed almost natural. But Tex? A decade from now, still holding mock memorial services with guacamole-bearing, sex-starved senior citizens, still studying the patterns of the Rasmussen rugs whenever Thelma spoke, still staring into the corners, blind, unaware? What kind of daughter was she, letting him live this way for so long? You only get one father your whole life.

She said, "Dad, before you take me home, why don't we go dump out the urn?"

"i'm not going to lie to you," Charlie said. A pall descended over the room, and the tenants of apartment 2 braced themselves for whatever shocking truth lay ahead. "This is my first real exorcism and I can guarantee nothing, but by all that is righteous and good in this world, with Benevolent Creator as my witness, I shall try."

Eddie Loa's cousins cast a wary eye upon their guest. They were desperate to rid themselves of the bad luck that had plagued each of the roommates over the last year, but they had not expected that a portly guy in a lady's bathrobe would be the catalyst.

Charlie plugged his Glade air freshener into the wall, eased back into the chair with a pen and notebook on his lap, sipped the chocolate milk he had brought—strictly for its spirit-summoning properties—and said, "Let's start from the beginning. In detail."

Eddie stood up and began to pace. "Very well. The three of us, my two cousins and myself, have lived here for several years. About a year ago, in order to save money to buy an Xbox, we bunked together and took in another roommate. And there our troubles began.

"He was a seventh-year student at the School of the Art Institute of Chicago, which should have been our first clue, but I had met him at a party and he seemed like a reasonable, normal guy. I said we were looking for a roommate, named the rent, location, et cetera, and he said he was interested. There was one caveat, though: he said, 'I'm a sculptor and need the space, privacy, and freedom to sculpt at will.' I said, 'Sure, why not?' After all, I consider myself an artist, too—well, you've seen my chain-mail garments, Charlie. I brought the guy over, my cousins said he was all right, and a week later, he moved in."

Charlie paused in his note taking. "His name?"

Eddie swallowed, glancing at his cousins. They had stopped speaking that name aloud after the first incident. "Skippy," he whispered. The roommates blanched at the sound of the name they had sworn to bury. One covered his ears, the other made the sign of the cross, then lit a cigarette. Eddie, determined to see this exorcism through, cleared his throat and spoke up. "He told us his name was Skippy Shaftlick, but he may have made that up.

"At first," he continued, "all seemed normal. Skippy went to classes during the day and sculpted here at night. He paid his share of the rent in cash and on time. I asked him once what his job was, but he told me not to inquire into his personal affairs. Well, one day he informed us that his bedroom was too small to be a proper sculpting studio, and that he needed to use the kitchen instead. That was kind of a drag because it left plaster of paris dust all over everything. But you know, whatever; we wanted the Xbox. After a while, though, the stuff just stunk too much, and the dust really bothered my cousins."

"We have allergies," they interjected.

"So I told Skippy to haul the sculpture mess back into his own room. He was incredibly pissed, but he did it. Then two months went by without any rent from him and we had it out right here in the living room: he was screaming and crying, saying we disrupted his art and he wasn't able to think, and he was withholding his rent until his creative juices began flowing again. He dragged his sculpture back out to the kitchen—it was a half-finished bust of a man—and refused to move it until it was done.

So naturally, we moved it back into his room when he was at school and taped a note to its forehead, demanding the rent.

"When he came home that night and found what we'd done, he grabbed a loaf of bread and a jar of peanut butter and barricaded himself in his room, refusing to come out. It was *my* peanut butter, too. After a week, we finally broke down the door and discovered that he had moved out without even telling us. He owed us over two months of rent! But he left behind the sculpture." Here Eddie gestured for Charlie to follow him into bathroom, where he removed a towel from what appeared to be a large pillar. In actuality, it was the bust, a misshapen, evil-looking head over three feet high. From the first glance, no one could deny that features of all three remaining roommates were clearly depicted in the bust: Eddie's glasses and Rod Stewart hair, one cousin's giant ears and Adam's apple, the other cousin's mouth and dimpled chin. Eddie said, "We found a letter folded up on top of the sculpture after we busted into Skippy's room. It read: 'I curse you, jag-offs.' "

Charlie asked, "And since then?"

Eddie threw the towel back over the bust and led Charlie out of the bathroom. "We've all suffered from the following: job loss; robberies; illness; rat infestation; girls dumping us; even Eggy endured a rare digestive disorder, poor little skink; and worst of all, the Xbox broke. Fucking Skippy's Evil Head cursed us, man. And sometimes," he hesitated here, then went on in a whisper, "*it moves.*"

"It moves?"

"Right away we put the Evil Head out on the back stairwell so we wouldn't have to look at its insane hell-mask anymore. The next day it appeared back in the apartment. Another time we put it in the coat closet, and a day later, we found it in the kitchen standing in front of the refrigerator with the door open. One of my cousins tried to move it by himself and drag it out to the Dumpster, but he dislocated his shoulder—the thing weighs like four hundred pounds—and since then we've never been able to get rid of it. It always comes back. At least we've found that it usually stays put in the bathroom and doesn't shake off the towel. Actually, it makes a decent towel rack, but we're still coming down with boils, and last week between the three of us, we had a mugging, a case of shingles, and some nasty dry rot under the radiators. You gotta help us, Charlie. Please kill the Evil Head."

Charlie unfastened the top two knots of his robe and opened the living room window for air. The chocolate milk, long gone, left him bereft of confidence. No urban shaman, he was sure, ever faced such a disheartening task.

After a few minutes of introspection, he said, "Eddie. Others. I'll tell you now that I cannot exorcise this demon today. This is a project the scale of which is beyond my everyday magic. Or whatever. But allow me to do some research, to plan a full attack, to create a contingency plan in case, let's face it, I screw up. May I have some time? A few days or so?"

Eddie looked to his cousins, who nodded in assent. After all, what were they going to do? They had no recourse. There were no Yellow Page listings for shamans.

Charlie said, "Let's see what I can dig up now to help get us started." He whipped out his PDA, perusing the e-books and documents he had downloaded on shamanism, as well as his own stash of personal records and notes. While he scanned the info, he said, "I tried to purge the ghost of the man who was murdered in my parents' apartment fifty years ago. I thought he was the reason my life wasn't going anywhere, but it turns out he's pretty benign. He doesn't cause any trouble, he simply likes the smell of my mother's cooking."

The big-eared cousin said, "You live with your parents?"

Charlie scrolled through a document, then paused suddenly. No, it couldn't be! But there it was, in plain, liquid display. Yes, under the right heading, too: banishing evil ghosts, totems, and devils, and spiritually cleansing rental units under 750 square feet. He said, "I'll amass my ingredients and ready my incantations over the rest of the week, but Eddie, here's something important you can do in the meantime; it's essential to the success of the whole venture." Eddie seated himself on the chair next to Charlie, took a memo pad from his chain-mail bag, and poised a pen above the paper, awaiting instruction.

"I'm ready," he said.

Charlie looked up from his PDA, rested his palm on Eddie's shoulder in a show of solidarity and strength. His brown eyes serious and intense, he said, "First thing, you need to slaughter a sheep and bring me the blade bone."

carolyn sipped her coffee and checked on Aura, asleep in her infant carrier. She tried to fan the encroaching cigarette smoke away from the baby, but it was useless. *Oh well,* she figured; *my mother smoked with me in the womb and look how well I turned out.* The Hogbutcher was probably the only bookstore in the country that had ashtrays out on the tables.

She watched Verity carry on her inaugural book club discussion at the large table in the back.

"I'm really grateful Carl Sandburg let me start up this club," she said. "He seemed reluctant at first, but he did come around eventually, and I hope you'll find it as satisfying as your previous club."

The group of four attendees exchanged uncomfortable glances. One of them took out a tissue and honked her nose loudly, while a dude twirled a hank of dreadlocked hair in nervous spirals around his finger.

Verity stumbled on, nonplussed by their reaction. "So, um, the idea . . . the idea is to select the abstruse, the unfathomably long, the meandering. Even attending the meetings should be a test of raw patience and endurance. I like to think of it as a literary Olympiad, a book club Ironman challenge."

A young woman, her face punctuated by infected holes and

metal rods, raised her hand. "I'd be more comfortable calling it an Iron Person challenge." She had PAGAN 4-EVER tattooed on her neck.

Verity said, "Fine. The literary Iron Person challenge. I was thinking we could start off with Proust. I'm already on page 103 of *Swann's Way*, but we—"

The young woman gasped and her hand flew up to her mouth. One of the men spoke up, and debris fell from his beard into his coffee. "There's something you ought to know," he began with a trembling voice. "The thing is, we already read that one last year, in the old book club. It took about six months, with several palate-cleansing books in between. We used to have a membership of twelve, but as you can see, we four are the only ones left. We underwent an . . . unfortunate circumstance and lost our book club leader."

Verity opened her eyes wide and waited for him to go on.

"You see, our group used to meet around the table in the front window. One evening as we were winding up, engaged in a spirited debate about whether or not to serve fishwiches at the next meeting, a car speeding down Evergreen whirled out of control and smashed through the front window and ended up half in the store, on top of our table, on top of . . ." He stifled a sob here. "On top of our book club! See the cracks in the plaster over there and the patched paint job? Our leader, in an attempt to save our last bottle of grape pop, dove toward the tabletop at the wrong moment—he thought he could make it! He was fearless, that one. Anyway, he was pinned underneath the car and it crushed his skull, killing him instantly. Several other members suffered a host of injuries and broken bones, and needless to say, all the grape pop was lost." He ran a shaky hand under his sniveling nose. "We had just finished *Remembrance of Things Past*. We never did get those fishwiches."

Fishwiches, Verity mused to herself. *It always comes back to fishwiches. Is there no evil they haven't wrought?*

The bearded man said, "We never thought we'd be able to do

this again. The other members, the ones who lived, have either moved away or refused to ever set foot in the Hog again. But when Carl Sandburg approached the four of us and said we ought to give you a chance and maybe move our meetings to the back of the store, well, we felt we owed it to our book club leader not to give up the dream. 'Read!' he always used to say. 'Read, damn it! Read like there's no tomorrow.' Which is kind of a funny sentiment when you consider we'd been slogging our way through an eight-tome series of impenetrable prose, which is not what you would likely pick up if there were no tomorrow—perhaps a slim volume of essays, I don't know . . ." His voice trailed off, reflecting on world's-end reading material.

Verity said, "I'm honored that you would let me carry on the torch of your leader and I'm so sorry that he was killed by an automobile in the store. That's just awful. I had no idea, and I'd understand if you didn't want to get involved in something like this again. If there's anything I can do—"

"We've gone off Proust," the bearded man answered. "But if it's okay with you, Verity, we'd like to take a stab at *Gravity's Rainbow*."

She felt a rare smile stretch from cheek to cheek, the kind that rooted her firmly, if momentarily, in the present. They wanted her, were counting on her. Their old book club leader had been struck down, oddly, disturbingly, over grape pop, but nevertheless in the line of duty, and who knew? It could happen to her, too. Maybe the next time, the car wouldn't stop at the front window and would just barrel on through to the back table until it murdered her as well. Or maybe she'd have a dreadful misfortune with an Iowa Writers' fan and the travelers' checks gun. Yes, anything could happen, but she was willing to put her own life at risk for the cause—books! It was hard not to feel noble. The unaccustomed happiness stretched her face so tightly that it gave her a wonderful ache in the jaw.

If they wanted Thomas Pynchon after all they'd been through, by God, she'd give them Thomas Pynchon.

The group—the pierced pincushion people and their oozing sores and ropes of fur, the men with rubbish in their beards and sandals from biblical Sinai—looked from one another to the woman with the orange Ban-Lon dress and elephant collars, the thick glasses, and the deranged smile of an escaped mental patient. The book club relaxed. They had found their new leader.

"I think I've found my calling," Verity said, plopping down across from Carolyn at the chessboard table. Carl Sandburg overheard and smiled as he piled up books on the counter.

"I used to have a calling," Carolyn said, "but I forgot what it was."

"Isn't it this?" Verity said, gesturing toward the baby.

"I often think of my time in Jakarta, helping the natives assemble jewelry for export. You know, without the jewelry sales, we might not have been able to afford to dig and set up the village's new well. I remember thinking, 'I could do this the rest of my life.' But of course I was just dreaming. I can't do anything like that because I'm married." She shook her head and drew the word out as though it was diseased.

"Having a family is a calling," Verity said, silently adding, *Like I'd know.*

"But what if it's the wrong calling for me?" her friend persisted. "What if I was meant to travel the world like I wanted to, helping the Great Unwashed?"

Verity thought of her book club's members. She said, "The 'Great Unwashed' are everywhere."

"So are the Great Unsold," Carl Sandburg chimed in, stocking more Iowa Writers in their cat-box location.

there is such a thing as an "after the funeral party," though no one likes to refer to it that way. The funeral itself was a mess: the parents sat in separate pews—Thelma with Dick, sobbing uncontrollably; Tex by himself in a black suit with mismatched socks and tan shoes, tears streaming silently into his mustache. Diana had been left at home with one of Dick's relatives. Verity had stood in the back of the church, torn between parental loyalties, until she realized that no one had actually asked her to sit any-where, and neither parent seemed aware that she was missing. She eventually squeezed in next to a grandma, who patted her knee and then asked for water and Kleenex and a less-mangled missal.

Carolyn herded their friends into a pew in the back, behind the family and Victory's own friends and classmates. Her husband, as usual, had been too timid to ask for time off from work, so Carolyn had to do some last-minute wrangling with the boss on Craig's behalf. The fact that she was the daughter of the com-pany's principal shareholder helped. She found a sitter for Kro-nos, canceled her own appointments, phoned Stan and arranged to pick him up from his grotesque apartment above the Tivoli theater, and got the three of them in the car and to the funeral on time.

"Where's Will?" Stan asked as they parked in the lot of St. Mary's.

"He's having a lot of trouble in school and can't leave," Caro-lyn said and directed them into the church.

"I can't come," Will had said when she'd called him with the news. "I'm flunking geology, and my parents are about ready to cut me off."

"This is our friend's sister's funeral. It's your duty. We'll come down there and get you if we have to."

"No! I can't. I'm not good around the bereaved. I never know how to comfort them. I always imagine they're looking at me and thinking, 'God takes our loved one, but leaves you?' "

She said, "Who's good at funerals? Nobody. You're supposed to just show up and be there for Verity. No one expects you to do anything."

"But I want to make her feel better and I can't," he said. "So I'm not going."

After the funeral, Tex refused to come to Thelma's catered lunch. He went home alone and dusted the house, walked Gin, and sequestered himself in the home clinic, poring over the X-rays of Victory's wisdom teeth, as touching to him as any baby picture, and wept for four days.

Carolyn approached her friend on the church steps. "Do you want us to drive you to your mom's, or will you be riding with her?"

"I'm not going there at all. My mom said the caterers are short-staffed and would I mind helping set up and serve for a while? Yeah, I guess I *would* mind, Mom, you jackass." She turned then and let herself into Carolyn's car, sat in the backseat, and stared out the window at the funeral procession.

"What do we do?" Craig asked in a panic, still standing outside the car. "Where do we take her, how do we act?"

Stan said, "Can I take off my tie? I can still grieve without the tie, but I don't think I can breathe *with* the tie."

"Oh, calm down," Carolyn said. "Both of you just act normal, which I understand is doomed to failure, but at least try. We're all going to our condo, and we'll order a pizza and watch a movie or whatever she wants, then we'll take her home or let her sleep over."

Verity overheard this from the open window of the car. She knew Carolyn's suggestion of the "after the funeral pizza party" was not a monumental, difficult gesture. It was not a trial or a big production. It was just one of the countless small, kind things Carolyn did for her during the dark days.

Craig asked, "But what can we do to help? I have no experience with grief; what if she starts crying? The only way I know to make a woman stop crying is to say, 'I apologize,' or 'You're right,' and neither one of those fits the situation. I mean, do we talk about Victory, or try to get her mind off of it, not that she could ever really get her mind off of such a thing, but I'm just saying—"

Stan said, "Hey. I might have some weed."

"That-a-boy," said Carolyn, patting him on the back.

• • •

eddie loa swept into the store, chain-mail gauntlet and gladia-tor tank flying. He cast about for Verity and found her at the chess table, sitting with a good-looking babe and a gurgling baby.

"Busy?" he asked.

She said, "Just discussing squashed dreams."

He pulled a chair. "In that case, I'll fit right in. Listen, I gotta tell you: your boyfriend is one hell of an urban shaman."

"Thank you," she said.

Carolyn nodded. "I knew he'd be good at that."

Eddie explained what had gone down during the Evil Head consultation. "The only thing is," he said, "where am I gonna find a sheep to slaughter? I really don't look forward to doing that at all. I mean, can you even find one in the city? Like at one of those illegal hunting resorts, where they have lions and stuff for you to shoot?"

Verity said, "It seems unlikely, what with the sheep being such a slow-moving, docile animal. It really wouldn't be fair to pit it against a man with a gun. Not to mention the lions."

"That's true," he said. "Can I go to a farm or something and buy one?"

"I don't know. Isn't livestock expensive? Plus where are there farms?"

Eddie looked at Carolyn. "Are there any farms by you?"

She said, "I live in Clarendon Hills."

He said, "Is that the country?"

Verity said, "Maybe you don't actually have to slaughter it yourself. Maybe you could go to a butcher and see if they have carcasses in the back for you to root through, and you could just pull the shoulder blade out of a dead sheep."

"Yeah!" He brightened. "I'll root through the carcasses at a butcher! Now where do I find a butcher?"

Aura's gurgles turned into bone-breaking shrieks.

Carl Sandburg bellowed from the library ladder in the nature section. "Verity! Are you playing that Yoko Ono album again?"

She checked her watch. "My break's almost over."

"Okay, I have to go anyway," Carolyn said, gathering up the yelping infant. "I told Craig I was just running to the grocery store."

"Why didn't you tell him you were coming to see me?"

She said, "I don't want him to think I don't like being at home with him."

Verity walked Carolyn and the baby to the door. Aura let out another raptor scream and grabbed a hank of her mother's hair. Carolyn wrestled it from her grasp, turned to Verity, and said, "Do you ever just want to run away?" She laughed as she said it, rolling her eyes, but the look on her face, abashed, tired, drawn, belied her gaiety.

"Sure, everyone does. And there's always tons of good reasons to." Carolyn looked at her, waiting. Verity lifted her shoulders, holding up her palms. "I guess the trick is finding a reason to stay."

Eddie watched the two women say good-bye at the door. When Verity returned to his table, he asked, "She's a friend of yours?"

"Yeah, from high school."

Through the large front window, they both saw Carolyn unlock the door to her cream-colored SUV, situate the baby inside, and drive off. "I wouldn't have guessed you two were friends. You seem so different from each other."

She just shrugged. Not everyone would be able to understand how long the shadows cast by her old memories were. Verity could confer an entire lifetime of goodwill and human compassion on a person for a single act of kindness.

Eddie asked what she was doing the following night. He said that he and his cousins were going to see a band and thought she'd like to come with.

"Okay, but I've never been to a Norwegian death metal concert before," she admitted.

"Oh, it's really good; you'll like it. Of course, Swedish death metal is also good, I certainly wouldn't disparage that, but I think Norwegian is just a little bit stronger."

Verity said, "Perhaps it's because in Norway they have more weeks of perpetual night than Sweden, and therefore are more depressed and write better songs."

Eddie grinned. He knew he'd been right to invite her.

eighteen

late at night, laurel scrib-
bled into a notebook at the kitchen table. She had found an announcement in the *Reader* for a poets' critique group that planned
to meet twice a month in the city. "I'm going," she told Stan.

"That's fine."

"I mean it. I need this. My soul is starving for poetry, for creative expression."

"It is?"

"Yes. The only way I'm going to feel better about myself is if I
present my work to a group of amateur poets for comment and
evaluation."

Stan, who had concluded long ago that accepting criticism was
not his wife's strong suit, merely nodded in encouragement.
"What are you working on?"

"A collection of haikus detailing my experiences growing up
Jewish."

"But you don't practice any religion anymore."

"Culturally," she said, "I'm still Jewish." She looked down at
her poems, thoughtful. "Do you think *Haiku Jew* is a good title
for the collection?"

"I do," he said.

Afterward, he settled into the Manly Den with a contraband
beer. Moving the boom box into the den was a great idea, he decided, even if the tape from the latest Lousy Dates jam session
sent his son into convulsions. The boy would learn to love it.
Spurred by Laurel's newfound creative outlet, Stan decided to try

his hand at writing some lyrics for an untitled Dates original tune. Craig had arranged most of it, including a really girlish clarinet solo that no one could talk him out of. Though still technically a trio, they had more than a couple songs written for Kronos's clarinet, and were on the verge of becoming a real quartet. He chuckled to himself: the Kronos Quartet. Yes, it was all coming together: creativity, vision, profundity, all that crap, he was into it. His pen moved quickly. In no time he had three verses for "Slippery Steps at the Old-Age Home." He smiled in satisfaction. Art was indeed a magical, monstrous thing.

tex perused the designs in the book at the tattoo parlor. Some of them were very nice, very colorful and lively. Others, not so much. He did not care for the skulls and snakes, nor the girlie figures and wild animals. Though some of the crucifixes and Jesus portraits were quite interesting, he did consider himself a lapsed and angry Catholic, and in any case would not have been comfortable broadcasting religious beliefs via arm art. "What do you think, Carol?"

Carol flipped through another book of designs. "Hearts are always nice," she said, sending him a psychic image of their initials entwined in a red heart. Of course, he did not need psychic abilities to figure out what she meant. Embarrassed but flattered, he continued to look around.

"Maybe Verity will have a good suggestion," he said. "Can I borrow your cell phone to call her?" He examined the phone once she handed it over. "How do I do it?"

She punched in the numbers for him and said, "You should consider getting a cell phone yourself. They come in very handy."

He held the phone up to his ear gingerly, gripping it between his thumb and middle finger. "I'm afraid they'll give me brain cancer."

When his daughter answered, he explained his conundrum. Though loath to imagine her dad with tattooed, sun-damaged flesh, stripped to the waist in a tattoo parlor with the vampire lifestylist by his side, Verity tried to be a good sport and suggested several designs.

He shot down all of them. No roses (those were for ladies!), no yin-yang (whatever that was), no peace symbol (peace was nice and all, but didn't really say anything about him personally), no photorealistic representations of the dog (it would make him sad once she passed on).

"I can't think of anything else, Dad," she said. "And I'm kinda on my way out the door now."

"Well, I need help. Carol said maybe I should get Victory's name on my shoulder. Or even her initials, 'cause they're your initials, too. What do you think?"

Verity thought of the pictures they both had of Vic in their homes, and she knew the bittersweet ache he undoubtedly felt, as she did, in his throat whenever he looked at them. "I don't know. How would you feel staring at it in the mirror every day?"

Silence answered her, for so long in fact that she thought the connection had been severed. "Dad?"

He said, "I loved her so much, honey. But maybe I would think about the accident every time I saw the tattoo, just like when I see her pictures, though I would never take those down, never." He choked back his tears.

"How about picking something that just makes you happy then, like golf clubs?"

"Maybe." He sounded miserable. "I do like golf." Then he said, "I'm sorry I'm the way I am, Verity. I don't think I can ever get over losing her, not that any of us ever will, but I don't even re-member my old self. Why can't I be more normal and levelheaded like you? I don't know how to be an ordinary person anymore."

"Dad, it's a weekday night and I'm on my way to a Norwegian death metal concert with my neighbor, who is having his apart-ment exorcised by an urban shaman," she said. "Every evening I say goodnight to my Hallway of Strangers. My second bedroom is an homage to an era I've never lived in. I only read magazines that were published before I was born, all of my furniture has been sold off from other families' homes, I wear dead people's clothes. How normal am I? We're on equal footing."

diana cradled the phone against her shoulder as she smeared shea butter on her elbows. "I made the mistake of telling my mom about the Pet Store Resistance."

"What did she say?" Kronos asked.

"She said she agreed with them, and that Petland ought to be closed down because they get their dogs from puppy mills instead of good breeders. Of course my sister condemned me too; she hates me anyway and she thinks pets should only come from shelters. I *know* puppy mills are bad, but what's wrong with me trying to take care of the puppies now that they're here?" she asked. "And make minimum wage while I'm at it."

Kronos struggled for a similar parental contretemps. "Today my dad disparaged the clarinet," he said. "He said although *he* didn't feel this way, *some* people regarded it as being a girl's instrument and that he'd be happy to teach me the drums if I wanted."

"The drums?!" Diana shrieked. "Hey, as much as I hate the clarinet, I couldn't stand watching you join the caveman crowd in the drum corps. You might as well play football. It's positively Cro-Magnon."

Diana couldn't bear for him to leave the woodwind section? Kronos lay back on his bed and felt his heart beat in his temples, burning the phone against his ear. "I agree. Imagine turning my back on Artie Shaw and Benny Goodman and Woody Herman, for what? That imbecile, Gene Krupa? Never."

Diana grumbled, "Fucking Krupa!"

Kronos said, "Between the pet shop and Gene Krupa, we'll be lucky if we live to see twenty-one in a state of sanity. I, too, am anguished by my family." He was conscious of the slight note of pride in his voice, as of one who has Seen Life.

•   •   •

verity stretched out her legs in the passenger seat. "The Vega has a surprising amount of legroom."

Eddie said, "Please. Call her Suzanne."

A cousin in the back said, "I called that butcher shop on Division Street and asked if we could have any leftover parts of their dead sheep shipment, but the guy just hung up on me! Can you believe that?"

"Everybody wants to make a buck," Eddie complained.

They parked a few blocks away from the Empty Bottle on Western and were shocked to see that a line had already formed out the door and around the corner.

"What's the name of this band again?" Verity asked as they took their place in the queue.

"Blüdphaart." Eddie pointed to the flyer in the window. "See? 'From the land of the midnight sun, Blüdphaart brings you the best of Thor-worshipping, Scandinavian Black Metal, in the great tradition of Varg Vikernes and Bard Eithun.' I think you'll really like them, Verity. Of course, they're not on the same altar-of-Satan level as Mayhem, but they're still good."

"Who's Mayhem?"

Metalheads ahead and behind turned in disgust toward the obvious poseur amongst them.

Eddie said, "Old-school Norwegian death metal. Their guitarist was stabbed to death by the bass player, Count Grishnackh, who was envious of the guitarist's more evil reputation."

They bought their tickets when they reached the door, then found a place in the middle of the crowd near the stage. Verity marveled at the Mayhem story; you never heard of this type of show business rivalry involving Herb Alpert or the 101 Strings.

Blüdphaart ascended the stage amid wails, moans, and grunts from the audience. Eddie confided that was the death metal way one showed appreciation for the evening's entertainment. "Clapping's for chumps," he said. Verity shoved her hands in her jacket pockets.

As the opening notes of their first song, "Cool for Cthulhu," rang out, Verity asked Eddie, "Are you sure they're from Norway?"

"Yeah, why?"

"Because the keyboardist is black and the drummer is wearing a T-shirt from Magnificat High School. Which is on the North Side of Chicago. And Catholic."

"Oh." Disappointed, Eddie tried to come up with a plausible explanation. "Maybe they're just in the style of Norwegian death metal, rather than actually being Norwegian themselves. Perhaps they were born in Chicago but honed their craft in Norway." Yet he could not ignore the fact that they *did* have a keyboardist, black or otherwise, which ordinarily was not a staple for Norwegian death metal ensembles.

The cousins bobbed their heads. Eddie watched the performance in rapt concentration. Verity looked all around the club, at the cousins who gave her a thumbs-up for her minimal headbanging, at Eddie who let her stand in front of him because she was too short to see. She thought, *This is kind of like having friends.*

When Blüdphaart came back for their encore, they carried between them a huge object wrapped in a tarp, which they laid on a table off to one side of the stage.

The singer screamed into the microphone in a Colonel Klink accent. "And now a special sacrifice, children!" He tore off the tarp, revealing a large, bloated, rotting . . .

Eddie and Verity stared at the thing, then turned to each other and said in unison, "Sheep carcass?"

It was definitely dead. The smell and the not moving and protruding tongue clued them in. The singer started up a chain saw and invited the audience to partake of the entrails. "Also," said Colonel Klink, "we'll be selling bone fragments after the show, suitable for jewelry and crafts, for ten dollars apiece."

Eddie said, "I gotta get up there, I gotta get that shoulder blade . . ." He pushed his way through the crowd, Verity in his wake. *This is what friends do for each other,* she thought, determined to keep pace with him, determined to help procure sheep parts for the shaman.

The singer brought the chain saw down on the sheep's neck. Some wool flew and Verity thought it would have made a very pretty shawl. The flesh, possibly owing to its being not quite fresh, resisted the motorized blades at first, and the singer plunged the chain saw deeper into the neck with force. Once the saw severed the spinal column, Verity heard a distinct snap and the audience dove for safety, creating a clear path for the projectile. The last thing she saw was the animal's head flying toward her with rocket velocity. *I can't die this way*—nanosecond thoughts flashed in her brain—*my fifteenth-year high school reunion is this weekend and the obituary will sound idiotic.* The room darkened in her sight upon impact.

the sun rose and later began to set when she finally stirred in bed. Earlier, Charlie had anointed her with attar of roses, plugged in a rose-scented Glade air freshener, mumbled a spell, and now sat in anxious and therefore worthless meditation at her bedside.

Eddie hovered in the doorway. "I'll never forgive myself if her medulla oblongata is damaged."

Verity groaned as a thousand tiny Norsemen began to bang their hammers in her skull. She lifted her hand to the throbbing and bonked herself in the forehead with a plaster cast. "Owwww . . ."

Eddie rushed in. "Are you awake? Who's the president? What year is this? How many fingers am I holding up?"

Charlie said, "Verity, what do you remember?"

She croaked, "There was a song, 'I Got Crabs on the Dating Game,' and then . . . I don't know . . ."

The guys thought it best not to bring up the Sheep Incident just then, as it was currently being touted in the *Chicago Sun-Times* as well as within their circle of friends. She drifted into sleep again. It was just as well; perhaps the sudden recollection of the assault by severed head would be too much for her.

"she's going to be fine." Charlie tried to soothe Tex over the phone, but her father wasn't having it.

"I'm coming down there," he insisted.

"Of course you can come, but the doctor did say she would be fine, Tex. Broken wrist, minor concussion, but no permanent damage."

But Tex could no more stay away from his injured child than he could chop off his own head; well, not a good analogy, but he was distressed and not thinking properly. He hung up and phoned Carol, begging her to accompany him into the city. He was not too ashamed to ask her for help. As a vampire lifestylist, perhaps she could offer some insight into this type of injury, which, as he understood it, involved a ritual sacrifice and a group of musical Catholic teenagers.

He arrived within an hour and raced to Verity's bed. When his daughter dozed, he cried, and when she wakened, babbling and insensate, he smiled encouragingly and patted her uninjured hand.

"She's not making any sense," he whispered to Charlie.

"It's the painkillers."

"Have you got my daughter all hopped-up on goofballs?" he demanded.

"The doctor prescribed them. They're sanctioned by science."

Carol, as instructed, kept watch out the front window on Tex's car. Thus far, the hubcaps remained intact. Eddie told her the car would be fine; people did not usually break into the cars parked on Chicago Avenue until at least midnight.

Charlie said, "I have a charm for automotive protection I can use, if you're really worried about the car."

She turned to him. "A charm of protection?"

He lifted his shoulders, ducking his head in a cute display of modesty. "I'm an urban shaman."

Carol laid a hand on her ankh. "I'm a vampire lifestylist." Charlie nodded, recalling their first meeting. Carol made room for him on the couch to discuss the industry.

Eddie, feeling left out, coughed and took a step toward them. He said, "I'm an aspiring hairdresser."

Carol looked at the large Samoan man with the chain-mail tie, gold-framed glasses, and worried expression. "Hairdressing is important to body and soul. If I'm overdue for a color touch-up, I always feel a little lacking in my powers."

Eddie sat on the couch, too, glad for the company. "Lots of our customers say that, so I like to do what I can, in terms of hairdressing, for their well-being. Every little bit helps."

tex's arms went numb from holding one of Verity's hands and clamping an ice pack to her forehead. Dread rose in his chest, then flapped its wings against his heart. He had felt all this before. He wore the flaming tooth sweater vest in spite of the August heat and for the first time in thirteen years he closed his eyes and said, "I'm not a praying man, Lord, but if you can hear me, please hear me."

Eddie knocked gently on the doorjamb. "Mr. Presti? We have an idea."

somehow, it made perfect sense when they discussed it, but now, watching Carol and Charlie adjust Tex on the couch, making him as comfortable as possible before the ritual, Eddie wondered if perhaps these people had all gone mad. Once the Evil Head had been exorcised and he had completely defrosted the sheep's blade bone in the fridge, he would have to reconsider if it was wise to hang out with such unbalanced folks.

"It's really a very simple procedure," Carol said, tucking a pillow under Tex's head. "As an energy vampire, I can capture a bit of your life essence simply by concentrating and holding my hands out over your head as you relax. Then I will take that energy and give it to Verity by a reversal of the process. I function only as a vessel; I will not hold any of the energy for myself. But I must warn you, babe: this may make you a little dizzy now and quite possibly may affect your strength in your elder years."

"Will I still be able to golf?"

Carol considered it, then nodded.

Charlie cross-checked this information in his shaman's handbook and confirmed the prognosis that one's golf swing should not be adversely affected by the transference of energy by a compassionate and humane vampire. "I cannot vouch for your short game, though," he cautioned.

"That's okay," Tex said. "I always get the yips on the green anyway."

Tex allowed himself to sink further and further into relaxation at the sound of Charlie's voice. Meanwhile, Carol crouched over the end of the sofa, closed her eyes, and waved her hands back and forth above Tex's face. After ten minutes, Tex began to snore. Eddie watched, arms crossed over his chain-mail tie. He could have been wrong, but he thought he noticed Tex's face grow pale just as Carol's flushed a deep pink.

Carol then went into Verity's room. "I'll begin the energy transference now," she said. Eddie took this opportunity to call Carl Sandburg and explain Verity's absence tomorrow from work.

"Fine," Carl said. "And I don't even care if you're making all this up, because this is the best excuse I've ever heard. Wish her well."

When Tex awoke, he looked up at Charlie. "Did it work?"

"Carol's still in there. How do you feel?"

He sat up. "Kind of light-headed."

"I'll get you a snack and some water." Charlie opened the refrigerator and saw, on the top shelf, the sheep's shoulder blade and head laid out on a bright orange Fiestaware platter. He closed the door. "I'll run out for hamburgers," he called to Tex.

Verity opened her eyes. The vampire lifestylist hovered over her, hands outstretched, nails sharp and purple. It was impossible not to draw certain Nosferatu associations. "What's going on?"

Tex ran in, Eddie close at his heels. They stood over her bed and questioned her about the president and the year.

She waved off their inquiries. "I'm okay."

Eddie said, "You remember what happened?"

She nodded, then winced in pain at the jostling in her brain. "Unfortunately, yes."

Tex asked, "How do you feel?"

Verity thought about it. "My relationship with sheep is a bit ambivalent. I like them, but not when their heads come flying through the air. I have a headache now."

Relief flooding his face, Tex sighed and sat in the chair by the window. "Frankly, hon, when Charlie told me what happened at the concert, I about fell over. I can't imagine Tony Bennett or Neil Diamond having to resort to carving up dead animals on stage. In my day, we just didn't do things like that. And to think that of all the people there, you were the one to get hit in the head with the sheep. It must have been so frightening."

"It was," Eddie agreed. "Horrible. Very scary." He leaned in close to Verity and whispered to her, "But I just have to say, it was also really fucking *cool*."

charlie pawed through the doughnuts in the staff cafeteria, ignoring the baseball talk all around him. Occasionally, someone would slap him on the back and say, "So: Cubbies in the World Series this year? Whaddaya think?" or "Sosa fired one out clear over Waveland Avenue at last night's game. Is this a pennant year or what?" By the time he had polished off two bear claws, he had had enough of it.

He cupped his hands around his mouth and shouted, "Attention people in the cafeteria, hallways, and around the office: just because I am a man does not mean I understand anything about sports. If you insist on discussing the Cubs, all I can say is, I don't really follow baseball, but it sounds like they've played well this season."

Pete, he of the erstwhile lost Daisy, murmured, "They're not asking you your opinion because you're a man; they want a prediction from you as a shaman."

"Oh." The shaman handbook outlined several reliable prognostication techniques that used hot tea and required the reading of the dregs afterward in an upturned cup. But Charlie did not like tea. Instead, he dumped some Cremora into his coffee, swirled the clumps of powder around, and scanned the mug for messages. At last, he raised his head sorrowfully and said, "Maybe next year."

The chorus of groans followed him back to his cubicle.

"I'm sorry," he said to Pete, who had stopped by his desk afterward. "But I gotta call it like I see it."

"That's okay. I'm really a Boston fan at heart, and even *I'm* not ready for the Cubs and the Red Sox to face off in the World Series. I have a lot of things I want to do before toads rain upon the land and Earth spins into the sun."

Charlie said, "I suppose I was a little gruff with the doughnut crowd, but I've been worried about my girlfriend. She was struck in the head with a—well, never mind that part, but she doesn't feel well and yet she insists on going out to her class reunion tomorrow night, and then we're scheduled for a difficult exorcism a day or two after that. It seemed like a good idea in the beginning, the reunion, that is, but all summer she's been acting like she suddenly wants to make changes in her life, and that's kind of freaking me out. Fat temps who live with their parents get nervous when their girlfriends start making changes." He saw the rather shocked expression on his friend's face and explained, "Even urban shamans have the same ordinary fears as regular people."

Pete said, "But changes can be good. Look at you and the changes you've made, all for the better."

Charlie said nothing. His changes had nothing to do with Verity; if anything, he loved her more than ever, particularly since she had supported and guided him in his shaman quest. But *her* changes? Perhaps hanging out with that tall, lanky KJ in the enchanting world of karaoke clubbing had soured her on the shaman allure. Perhaps at the Hog she would find a slimmer dungeon master at the Sunday D&D LARP tourneys. Perhaps now that she had seen her old high school buds in marriages of varying success, with offspring to boot, she'd look at him and think, *Maybe I can do better than this fat temp who lives with his parents.*

"In fact, Charlie, your changes around here have gotten some attention from the bigwigs. Word around the office is, the project managers have been noticing the extra respect you've been commanding from everyone since you turned shaman, and they've passed some compliments on to the department head. He's been asking about you."

Charlie's jaw dropped. "Really?"

Pete grinned. "I predict a performance evaluation and promotion in your future."

initially, the division head experienced some difficulty in garnering opinions on this temp he had heard so much about. He called in the HR manager.

"What do you know about this Charles Brown person?" he asked, consulting the wrinkled, yellowed résumé from his files.

The HR manager drew her brows together. "Who?"

"He's an IT temp. You sent him to me a few years ago."

"We've had a temp for *years?* That's strictly against corporate policy! I don't know how that fell through the cracks, but someone's head is going to roll for this one."

"Well, I can either fire him or hire him, but I'd like to figure out who he is first."

She stood up. "I can't help you. I don't know anything about him. I can't tell one IT guy from another, if you want to know the truth. I assumed they only came out of the computer room at night to feed at the vending machine."

Her lack of knowledge regarding this IT temp confounded him and certainly added to Charlie's mystique. Well, he had the recommendations of the project managers to go on. They might be little more than babysitters, but at least they knew their underlings.

By the end of the day, he had rounded up a half-dozen employees who knew Charlie, all of whom praised his skills highly. But what skills *were* they? He looked down at the notes he had taken: *He helped find my dog. He plays relaxing zither music on his boom box. He brings in doughnuts. He is a spiritual and kind person.* Though admirable traits, one could not promote a temp to a full-time position based on niceness. Could one? Finally on the last sheet, he found a work-related comment from the head of IT. *Charlie is a diligent systems analyst and works well with others.*

"Works for me," the division head muttered to himself, then pressed his secretary's intercom buzzer. "Lori, please find Charlie Brown in IT and ask him to come see me."

diana cleaned out Taco Bell's cage, gave her a cuddle, and put the dog back in. She adjusted her Petland apron and then waited behind the register for her manager to open the store. The cat guy, as usual, was in the back room, Sharpie-ing his "tag" all over the pet food boxes; the goldfish guy was picking his nose by the tanks; but the rodentia guy was nowhere to be seen.

"Where's Rodentia Guy?" she asked her manager.

He pulled up the giant door that opened into the mall and walked back to the register. "Well, we had to lay him off. I hope you and the cat guy won't mind divvying up the hamster responsibilities and such."

"I don't mind," she said. "But why did you lay off Rodentia Guy?"

"I didn't want to, but the owner just got hit with a lawsuit from the Pet Store Resistance. Something about one of the breeders he buys from, I don't know. But we had to cut back, and the slacker rodentia boy was first to go."

"Not me, as in 'last hired, first fired'?" she asked.

"Not in this case. You take care of the dogs very nicely, you're prompt, and the drawer is never short when you close. I think you have a good future in Petland, for as long as we can stay open."

Diana tidied up the counter next to the register, thinking over her manager's words. In the glass-fronted barkers' kennel, Baskin-Robbins started to howl.

"i'm terribly sorry about your injury," said Laurel. "I read all about it in Bill Zwecker's column in the *Sun-Times*. I don't see why he had to refer to you as a middle-aged sheep grappler, though."

"Yeah, it kind of messes up my mother's decree that one's name should only appear in print three times in one's life: birth, marriage, death. No allowances made for heavy-metal ovine mishaps."

"I called because I wrote a get-well haiku for you," she said. "I can't really include it in my new anthology since it has nothing to do with being Jewish, but I could have Stan print it out for you. Here goes:

> *"O, my sheep brother*
> *Your head, a cannonball*
> *Mine, a target. Ow."*

Verity said, "Thank you. That's exactly how I feel."

Laurel nodded in satisfaction at the quiet power of the haiku. "Are you sure you feel up to coming out tomorrow night?" Laurel asked.

"Yes, I am well protected with painkillers and a cast. I don't want to miss the reunion."

"Stan was thinking everyone could stop here beforehand and, I suppose, have a drink, but God knows I won't be providing any liquor, and then we could all go to the reunion together. Strength in numbers and all that."

"We'll be there." She had barely set the phone back in the cradle when it rang again.

"Verity, it's your mother."

Oh, joy.

"Now, Charlie called me and told me all about your . . . this . . . *thing* that happened. I'm sure that I must have heard him wrong, because he said you were injured by a lobbed sheep head."

"No, that's what happened."

Thelma gasped. "What in the name of God were you doing? Don't you have any sense? At thirty-four, you can't find anything better to do than go to a concert and get pummeled by animal innards?"

Thirty-three. Verity said, "I'm okay, by the way."

"Well, of course I was concerned, if that's what you're implying, but Charlie assured me you were fine and I didn't need to come out. Are you not fine?"

"Oh, I'm fine, all right." Thank God for Percocet.

"Fine." Now that that had been established, Thelma could resume berating her with abandon. "I don't know what you are doing with your life these days, but you should be ashamed of wasting all your talent and potential."

"Didn't we just have this conversation?"

She bulldozed ahead. "Really! Heavy-metal concerts? Working in a store? Not to mention the pounds you've put on in the last year alone, no doubt a side effect of the other depressing aspects of your life, but still. What is going to become of you?"

"Nothing, Mom, nothing's going to *become of me.* This is it. This *is* me. I . . ." It sounded stupid to her own ears, but what the hell—it was the truth. "I like myself."

"I only say it for your own good, because I want you to be better than you are. If it sounds punishing, it's only because I see that you won't punish yourself."

"I've been punishing myself ever since Victory died! I don't do anything, I don't go anywhere, I'm nothing, an un-person. I mean, I *was*. Now I'm trying to just, I don't know, live. Live more. No, just *live*, actually, and be kind of happy. Why do you want me to keep punishing myself, Mom? What do you want me to do, split myself in two and punch myself in the gut? Should I take a crowbar to my head and do some real damage? Sure, why not? I like being in the hospital anyway. And I'd lose some weight, too."

There was a noise; it sounded like a sniffle, then a sob. Oh, God, now Thelma was going to cry? Verity gnashed her teeth for a moment, appreciating the Percocet's ability to let her brux without pain. The snorts and sniffles abated, and she realized she hadn't heard the sound of her mother's tears since the funeral.

Thelma said, "I didn't mean it like that. I don't want you to punish yourself that way."

Verity sank her head onto her wrist cast and slumped down in the telephone chair. "I still miss her, Mom. Nothing has ever been as good since she died. I . . . I used to think that if I killed myself then Dad would, too—like someone had opened the door, given him permission. He and I are both damaged in the same way, afraid of the world, cowards who try to shrink into our own minds—no, not that, *further* than that even—we try to shrink back far enough into the past, so that we'll turn inside out and disappear. Trust me on this one, we have punished ourselves more than you can understand."

Thelma sat silently, petting the pug in her lap.

Verity straightened up in the chair and continued. "But I feel differently this summer. I want to live. I want a future; any future that goes forward and has a little happiness in it. Why does it matter if the happiness comes from a bookstore or a professorship, from a husband and kids and a house, or from a nice boyfriend and an apartment full of junk? Can't I just be happy in whatever way I can be?"

Thelma hugged the pug so tightly in her arms that it panted from lack of oxygen and finally threw itself on the floor. Truly, she wanted to answer her daughter's question, to say, "Yes, please be happy," but she couldn't. It was not in her to do so. So she said, "Your father told Dick that there's pictures of him and Victory all over your bedroom, but none of me. Why aren't there any of me?"

"I have a picture of you," Verity said, not surprised that the emotional conversation had abruptly been detoured onto safer roads. She turned sideways in the telephone chair and gazed up at the corner across from her. "I'm looking at it right now."

"What picture? What am I doing?"

"You're wearing a white blouse. It's Christmastime. Your face is all swollen from getting your wisdom teeth pulled. I'm about nine and I have my arms around your neck."

"Oh, I hate that picture. I look horrible."

"I like it, Mom. That was a great Christmas," she said. "More or less."

Verity stared at the photo. Maybe Thelma's cheeks were puffy, but still . . . it was a good picture. Tex had taken it. When it's your mom, it doesn't matter whether she's glamorous or not. The silver filigree frame looked pretty and delicate against the white wall, above Sleeping Grandpa and below Yawning Dog, there in the Hallway of Strangers.

nineteen

after her third nap, she arose to make herself a peanut butter sandwich. Ugh. Even the idea of getting in the shower exhausted her. Her hair hung in her face; perhaps it would be easier to just cut it rather than attempt styling maneuvers. She hunted for the scissors. Would it be wrong to attend the reunion dirty? Dirty had garnered quite a bit of mainstream acceptance lately, what with the pincushion people and the soiled jeans hanging in the Gap's front window. She thought she could handle a weekend of filth: just one high school reunion and one Evil Head exorcism to go; how hard could that be? Now that the event loomed, all she could do was obsess about it and practice her spiel about her new job. The Hog-butcher was so, so—ah, who cares: *kick-ass*—that she wanted everyone to know everything about it. She washed the sandwich down with a glass of cold milk. Why did she care what others thought? This was new for her, she who had sleepwalked since college, this wanting to share, this . . . well, there was nothing else to call it: this transformation from un-person to person. Not that it was solely the job that had sparked that transformation— no job on earth had that power. It was the act of seeking satisfaction when you thought you were content to be zombified; it was the lassoing of a dream you never knew you had. To think, she was not yet thirty-four and she had already become a person.

Verity shuffled over to the telephone and dialed the number that had permanently engraved itself on her throbbing medulla oblongata.

"Barnes and Noble," the familiar voice answered.

"Hi, Bob, it's me. I've missed you."

"Oh my God!" he crowed. "I don't believe it. Hang on—" he held the receiver away from his mouth and said, "Ma'am, if you'll just wait for one goddamn minute, I'll ring up your silly *Celestine Prophecy* when I'm through on the phone. Well, if you don't like it, then get out. What do I care?" He returned. "Oh, Verity. How the hell are you?"

She said, "Almost human."

"mom, I don't need a babysitter," Kronos said. "I'm going to be a high school freshman in three weeks. I can look after Aura by myself for a few hours."

At odds with herself, Carolyn decided she might have no choice. The college girl across the street who was supposed to babysit had come down with something contagious, and both grandmas had selfishly made plans for tonight.

"I've given her bottles before, Mom. I'm not a moron," he said Craigishly.

Craig nodded. "Yeah, it'll be okay, Carolyn. We'll only be ten minutes away." He took her aside and said, "Come on, this is a kid we've never had to yell at. He's never done anything wrong in his life, and the baby will be asleep for most of the time anyway."

She relented. Kronos was a good boy, mature for his age, dependable. "I guess it'll be all right." She turned to her son and asked, "What will you do to amuse yourself, though?"

"I'm going to practice my clarinet—we're tackling 'Tusk' in band camp this week—and then I thought I'd watch *The Lord of the Rings* and eat a light snack, perhaps celery and peanut butter."

Yes, he was definitely his father's son.

Craig tried to high-five the boy, but Kronos, thinking it was a quasi-militaristic wave, saluted in response. "I know we can trust you, K-Man," said Craig.

Carolyn said, "Please do not call him 'K-Man.' "

When his parents finally left, the boy raced to the phone and dialed Diana's number. "They're gone! Come on over, and bring the beer."

will tripped as he entered the Siko house. "I'm all right, I'm all right," he said, dusting off his knees. He wore dark linen and stank of bourbon. Stan laughed and tried to give him a hand, but Will pushed by.

Verity did not trip when she walked in. She carefully hung onto Charlie's arm as the earth panned beneath her in lazy Percocet circles.

"Why'd you take two?" asked Charlie.

"I got nervous about the reunion. Plus I started reading *Gravity's Rainbow* and one thing led to another."

"So how's the book?"

"I haven't gotten very far, and I won't claim that I understand much of it in even a basic narrative sense, but every once in a while I found myself having read through a section and thinking, 'Hey, I understood that!' My knowledge of math and rocket science is minimal, so I'm merely taking it on faith that it makes any sense."

He said, "Perhaps it has influenced your new hairdo, which, by the way, is quite fetching. It looks very space age, not in a creepy Daryl Hannah *Blade Runner* way, of course, but just very futuristic."

Gingerly, she reached up and patted the uneven bangs that had appeared after lunch. "Yes, that. I remember thinking how much easier it would be to remove the portion that was in my eyes rather than brush it, and the next thing I knew, I had grabbed a pair of scissors and started cutting without strategy."

In the kitchen, Carolyn extolled the virtues of homeopathy and holistic birth control to Laurel, who regarded the information with raised eyebrows and crossed arms. "I'm telling you," Carolyn said, "it's natural and doesn't require taking your temperature or any of that stuff."

Craig said, "It works about as well as my Snickers-wrapper-and-7-Up method, as evidenced by the existence of our two children."

"Shut up," his wife said. "It didn't work with Aura because you didn't follow my directions about the brewer's yeast or the blue cohosh."

Laurel said, "I have to admit, I've never heard of rotten banana peel tea being used as a birth control method."

Craig said, "That's because my wife is a homeopathological liar."

Charlie held Verity tighter and followed Will and Stan out of the kitchen.

Stan led them into his Manly Den and asked, "What can I get you?" He gestured to a tea cart that performed double duty as a well-stocked bar tonight.

"Alcohol in the Siko house?" Will clucked his tongue. "Tsk-tsk. I'm telling Mother."

Stan said, "It's my house, too. It's my sanctuary, my castle." He poured out glasses of Scotch for all, but Verity declined hers, shaking her bottle of painkillers in explanation. "Oh, that's right," Stan said. "How are you feeling?"

The wrist under the cast itched and throbbed, as did the black-and-blue mark on her forehead, which also clashed with her pink-and-white-flowered 1940s rayon dress. But she said, "The drugs have been so wonderful that I'm already thinking of elective surgeries I can one day have."

Will said, "What about you, shaman? Sworn off the good stuff in favor of rotten banana peel tea?"

"Of course not. Benevolent Creator put this stuff on the planet for a reason." Charlie smiled and raised his glass in toast. "What shall we drink to?"

"Who cares?" Stan gulped his.

"Let's drink to excess," Will said.

Charlie put down the glass without sampling any. Every shaman worth his salt knows it's bad luck to drink to a cheap toast. He wandered over to the globe and spun it lazily on its axis. "Black oceans," he said. "Cool." Verity watched the three men in the Manly Den and felt a crackle of electricity in the air.

Sebastian came running down the stairs, yelling and pounding on a toy drum. Laurel steered him back toward the stairs and said, "Sebastian, Mommy told you to put your PJs on. Grandma is going to be here soon and you won't get your snack if you don't have your PJs on."

Stan snorted. "The kid doesn't buy your bluffs anymore. He knows he'll get his goddamn snack no matter what."

"Don't swear, you stupid idiot," she said, shoving her son up the stairs. Sebastian lobbed the drum at his father and then threw himself into the banister, kicking and screaming. Craig emerged from the kitchen, glanced at the scene on the stairs, and refilled his drink at the Manly Den bar, a look of disapproval on his face.

"He's just overtired," Laurel explained, prying the boy's hands from around her neck.

Will said, "It's nothing that a good smack wouldn't solve."

"We're not allowed to do that here," Stan said. "Laurel believes in rewarding this behavior with hugs and toys."

"Wrong, imbecile," she replied. "Hitting him won't teach him to behave, just to be afraid of me."

"I got hit all the time, and I turned out fine," Will said, taking a step toward the bar for a refill. He tripped over an errant train on the rug, swore, and kicked it at the wall, where it left a nick in the paint.

Craig said, "I feel we were lucky with Kronos, we never had any trouble—"

Stan raised his hands to stanch the flow. "Yeah, I know, Kronos was a perfect child, I've heard it from you a hundred times. Ours is not. Ours is subnormal in every way." Laurel's eyes flashed, launching a pair of poison darts at her husband.

Will said, "Maybe it has to do with his name."

Laurel held the spasming child in her arms and spat, "Nothing's the matter with his name!"

Will laughed. "Come on! Sebastian? You're setting that kid up for a life of humiliation, not to mention creating some serious obstacles to future babe-nailing. Why not just send him to school wearing an ascot and carrying a clarinet case?"

Craig said, "And what's wrong with the clarinet? Kronos is a fine—"

Stan said, "Shut up, Craig. 'Kronos' is no prize as a moniker, either." Will laughed and Stan wheeled about to face him. "And what are *you* laughing at? 'Willie' is hardly the type of name to elicit an improvement in your employment prospects, nor does it significantly increase *your* chances of babe-nailing."

"I'm not a 'Willie.' I've haven't been called Willie since I was six years old," he said. "Willie is the name either for a little boy or for someone a rich guy likes to kick around, like a poor black baseball player or an influential blues musician. 'Will' is a real man's name."

Craig said, "First of all, 'Kronos' is rooted in Greek mythology, and you can't get any more manly man than that, and second, 'Will' reminds me only of the kid from *Lost in Space.* But I will give you that 'William' is a real man's name, like a president who gets paid to receive a never-ending series of blow jobs though a sexy, constitutional loophole."

Laurel dragged Sebastian up the stairs, cooing to him in fear, embarrassment, and frustration. The boy kicked a post out of the banister. Will knocked back another drink and spun the globe until its black oceans blurred into the continents. Craig and Stan argued over which of their sons' names would garner him more lifetime bucks and blow jobs.

From upstairs, all heard Laurel shout, "Stop it! Put your pajamas on and stop this tantrum, or I'll really give you something to cry about." Everyone nodded, recalling this generation-old tactic that sometimes actually worked. Sebastian continued to scream and flail in his room.

Stan rose from his chair and calmly ascended the stairs. His voice echoed down the hall. "You heard your mother, Sebastian.

Cut it out." The boy howled in indignation, throwing himself on the floor, and then they heard it: a quick, no-nonsense spank, slightly muffled through clothes and underpants and control. The crying and thrashing subsided, and the two of them got the child into his pajamas. Craig turned up the stereo and was rewarded with looks of relief from the rest of the group.

Laurel held Stan back before they returned to their friends, laying her hand on his arm. She said, "I don't know how to do this, to be a mother. Nothing I try works."

Stan rubbed her shoulder. "Sometimes children need to be a little afraid of their parents."

Charlie and Verity pretended to peruse the bookshelves of the Manly Den. Finally she said, "Speaking of elective surgeries, I've heard that vasectomies are relatively painless." The men stared at her. She said, "I'm just making conversation."

will, half in the bag by eight o'clock, agreed to let Charlie and Verity drive him to the reunion. In his inner pocket was a slim silver flask, which he offered to Charlie as they passed a parked squad car.

Charlie pushed it away. "No, thanks."

Will said, "I didn't drive up here drunk, if that's what you're thinking. I'm six foot two; a couple of slugs don't even affect me."

"I obey all traffic laws," said Charlie. "I can't help it. It's a sickness."

"Not me. I blew off the tolls on the Ike. Well, one of 'em I tossed a couple quarters and a handful of lint and stuff. One of the quarters bounced off and hit the car. I didn't even stop. It was great." He relayed this with a full quota of pride, which depressed the hell out of him.

There it was: Downers Grove South, home of the Mustangs. Reunionees cloaked in varying degrees of business dress, inebriation, and personal failure ambled into the building. Verity followed the guys into the main entrance, where an alumni committee wonk sat bright-eyed behind a long, name-tag-laden table. Will slapped on his tag ("Will Demske—Musicologist") diagonally across his lapel. Verity applied hers ("Verity Presti—Bookstore Clerk") a careful distance above her left breast. Through past name-tag misfortunes, she had learned never to stick one too far down her chest, lest she lose eye contact with the male populace for the remainder of the evening.

"I can't find mine," Charlie said.

The wonk asked for his name, sniggered, as was expected, then shrugged when he couldn't find the appropriate label.

"I'm not an actual alumni, but my girlfriend is," Charlie explained, "so I assumed everyone would get a name tag."

"Oh, here," said the wonk, his brow clearing, "guests' tags are on this side." He handed him a sticker that read HELLO! MY NAME IS GUEST.

"I'll fix that," Verity said and whipped a pen out of her bowling bag satchel. She scratched out GUEST and wrote "Charlie Brown—Urban Shaman," in a slanted scrawl. She decided that altered pain receptors made for lousy penmanship.

"I'm going to find the bar," said Will, and threaded himself through the crowd.

The reunion itself was held on the basketball court, which had changed much since the Class of '88 stumbled out of there high and drunk after their commencement ceremony. The old blue cinder-block walls had been covered over with floor-to-ceiling wood paneling, as though the entire gymnasium was some kind of basement-den conversion. A banner proclaiming, "Go Mustangs!" hung over the bleachers. The girls' teams, known in Verity's time as the Fillies, had never received equal banner treatment. Political correctness, of a fashion, had been instituted at DGS lately, though, because another banner of similar size hung on the opposite wall, cheering, "Go Lady Mustangs!" A smaller championship pennant, mounted with others above the gym entrance, merely announced the victory of the "Lady 'Tangs—1994 Water Polo Class 8A Champs."

Craig and Stan escorted their wives in, craning their heads for glimpses of bullies who had grown fat and hairless, of chicks whose standards had, with any luck, fallen. Laurel crumpled up the generic spousal name tag and took her haiku notebook out of her purse. This place was ripe with inspiration.

"What are you doing?" Stan asked. "More haikus?"

She shrugged. "Gotta find the muse where you can."

Stan grabbed Craig's arm and yanked him away. "Yeah, I agree. I'll go look at the bar."

Craig looked back helplessly over his shoulder, but Carolyn waved him on. She reached into her purse and brought out her cell phone. "I guess I should check on my kids."

Laurel looked up from her notebook and her cheeks burned. "I didn't even *think* to call home yet. I'm a bad mother."

"I know how you feel. I pick up the cell phone and punch in the numbers because I feel like that's what I'm supposed to do: obsess and worry and call them to make sure they haven't been bludgeoned in their beds, that the house has not caught fire, that they're eating the right things and going to bed on time. But I'm not actually *worried*."

Laurel said, "Maybe they'll be okay in spite of us."

"Yeah, we turned out great in spite of our mothers, right?"

Laurel scanned the pages in her hand until she found what she was seeking. She recited her most recent masterpiece.

> *She called me chubby,*
> *Hate my mom, yet I am one.*
> *Not fat, just big-boned.*

"Cool," Carolyn said.

kronos sat on the couch, a can of Bud Light in one hand, a Twix in the other. Candy wrappers littered the floor and the cushions around him, while Diana tried to hide the empties in the bottom of the Kickels' garbage can.

"Don't," said Kronos, "my dad only drinks Belgian beer and will freak out if he sees domestic beer cans in the trash."

"Oh, really?" Diana poked through the wine fridge in the kitchen. The Stella Artois had a pretty label.

"No, don't!" He pleaded when he saw her emerge from the kitchen, bottles in hand. "My dad will know that two are missing!"

"Live a little, Kro," Diana said, plopped next to him on the couch, and guzzled the import. She split a Chunky with him, to take away the sting.

"You don't understand; my dad's obsessed with his beer collection. You should have seen him when my mother tried to hide his special beer glasses. He practically had a nervous breakdown. Any bottle out of place sends him into hysterics." Distressed, he immediately drank the beer without a second thought.

She said, "So he'd be upset that they were gone, but not that you were drinking?"

Kronos repeated, "You don't understand my dad." The chocolate smears dripping down the corners of his mouth gave him the look of a sad, bingeing clown.

"I've got something that'll make you feel better," she said, drawing a joint out of her backpack.

The boy's eyes grew large with simultaneous thrill and fear. "That's marijuana, isn't it?"

"Just one joint. I stole it from the French horn player who always naps through lunch."

Kronos looked around at the Budweiser cans, the candy wrappers, the chocolate stains on his shirt, the marijuana cigarette, and the pretty girl next to him. "I feel just like Rick James," he said, reaching for the joint.

tex opened the cedar chest he had managed to drag into the hallway. He glanced in Victory's room, then turned his eyes to Carol. "I want to, I'm just not sure if I can."

"You don't have to take anything out at all if you don't want.

Maybe you could just go in there and lie on the bed. You know, spread a little of your essence around."

Tex steadied himself, no mean feat in view of his pounding heart and soaring blood pressure. "No, I can do it. I'm really going to try. I'm not getting rid of everything, just some things. It could be an extra bedroom or a computer room, if I ever get a computer, and I could keep some mementos of family and friends in here also. I could have pictures of both my girls, and keep some of Victory's favorite things, like her china dogs and home-made raccoon traps."

Carol said, "I think that's a very nice idea. And then you could have Charlie come bless the room. He has a wonderful stock of urban shaman home blessings."

"But this is the suburbs."

"I think they'll still work."

Tex wiped a tear from his eye, dragged the chest a few more feet, then sat on it with a thump. He felt his heart breaking. His arm began to tingle.

"really," Craig said, "my greatest regret is not knowing what the hell I wanted to do with my life and getting stuck in advertising. I try to justify it by saying it's for a pharmaceutical company, like *that's* anything, but let's face it, all I'm really doing is helping a corporation rake in more money. They stand to make a huge profit off of a new antipsychotic drug that doesn't make patients gain weight like the other ones do—and not like five or six pounds either, but fifty or sixty—plus it doesn't raise their blood sugar, which is good, I guess, because nobody wants to end up fat, diabetic, and schizophrenic."

The reunionees Craig had been railing at inched away.

Aware of his dwindling audience, he snorted—a mirthless, hollow laugh. "Well, Verity, I've driven away our classmates with my sad-sack tales of slaving for Big Pharma. Can you believe what a loser I am?"

She squeezed his arm and leaned against him. "You're not a

loser! And I would express further outrage, but I am heavily dosed on Percocet right now and incapable of expressing anything but fragmented, happy thoughts."

He slung his arm around her and squeezed her shoulder in return. "Lucky girl. You know, if I was working on a cancer cure, or campaigning for a Democratic president, or eradicating poverty from the face of the earth, all this bullshit would be worth it. But it's *advertising;* it makes no difference in the world at all. And yet this is where I spend my days. I know I can't go back in time, but I do wish I had followed a different path, maybe pursued art school the way I wanted to, said no to my father-in-law. I should have made my own way in life. Shame on me."

Stan strode up. "You'll never guess who I just saw. Neal! He's doing great. He funded a pipe-organ club for a Milwaukee charter school, and he's been written up in all kinds of pipe-organ trade publications and profiled in *Young Philanthropists Today.* He's the big hero of the Chibley Middle School Cheesemakers. Now that's something to brag about at a class reunion!"

Craig wailed. "See what I'm talking about? What are we doing with ourselves, when guys like Neal are taking the pipe-organ world by storm? What kind of lives are these?"

"Hey, we have the Lousy Dates. Don't knock that, my friend," Stan said.

"Arrrgghhh." Craig dropped his face into his hands.

Verity explained. "He's upset he's in advertising."

"This again? Look, Craig, I told you before: not everyone can be Neal. Things don't turn out the way you hope they will in high school. That's just life; it is what it is. Every day in my office, I feel like a sponge sitting in a tray of poison, soaking it all up, and it's disintegrating me from the inside. My voice mail light blinks constantly, and it's never good news. But I've got a kid and sometimes he makes life bearable when he's not screaming, and I've got the Lousy Dates now, too."

"And your wife," Verity said.

"Yeah, her, of course."

Being child-free herself, Verity found it depressing that Stan's inane spawn occasionally made life bearable.

"I know," Craig said, raising his head. "It's just that when your work life sucks so much, it affects the rest of your being."

Charlie wandered in then. His pockets bulged with business cards from reunionees seeking spiritual counseling.

Craig went on. "Think about it: a few weeks ago, my old cubemate moved to a new desk in the other wing. Yesterday, I noticed that I no longer socialize with him because where he sits is not along the path between my desk and the bathroom. My whole world is my cubicle. I am becoming my cubicle. "

Charlie closed his eyes. He did not need to consult his shaman crib notes, for he heard in his head the Robert Frost poem about the road diverging in the woods. "You must choose a new path," he said. "The bathroom may yet be your goal, but you must get there by a different route."

verity strolled around the gym by herself. The alumni committee had set up a huge bulletin board display of the Class of '88, complete with blown-up yearbook photos and school accomplishments. They had spelled her name wrong—Verity Presto—which made her wonder if she ought to have become a magician or a spokesperson for kitchen appliances. Her activities were listed just as they were in the yearbook with the addition of "Elder Folk Volunteer," the club that ran errands for area senior citizens. She had forgotten about that. The senior she had been matched up with had helped her fix the mistakes in one of her homemade balaclavas.

Will came up behind her; she smelled his approach. "I never was in the marching band; it was *jazz* band," he said. "Where are they getting their info from? Who the hell's on the alumni committee?"

"I forgot I was in Elder Folk."

"Elder Folk, yeah. I used to drive you to your old person's house, don't you remember?"

She tried, but her brain was hopelessly fuzzed.

He finished his Scotch and said darkly, "I remember everything. Look at the captions beneath my photo: Most Likely to Crap Out Before Thirty, stage crew, AV Club, 'Hey, who took my lunch?' smitten with V.P."

"I always thought that said 'VD.'"

"It's you, dumb ass. I was smitten with *you*. Driving you to old people's houses, playing Hacky Sack even though you *stunk*, but you only had eyes for Siko Boy. You had this way of chewing your fingernails through that mouth guard. You just . . . killed me."

She looked up past the storm on his brow. "I remember some of this, but in different ways."

"People remember what they want to remember."

Her apartment of forlorn objects, the Hallway of Strangers, Tex's shrine—she thought of all this and knew it was true. But memories can regrow themselves, like earthworm segments, like blue-tailed skinks, like starfish chopped up and thrown back in the ocean.

"Listen to that," she said suddenly, cocking her ear toward the DJ on the stage. They turned and saw Craig next to him, pointing at the turntable, waving and smiling. "Young Fresh Fellows, 'For the Love of a Girl.' We could dance," she said, "for old times' sake."

"You know I don't dance. I only pogo."

On the dance floor (the gym floor), littered with streamers and losers and spilled liquor and cigarette butts and ordinary people, he pogoed, she jerked. It was hard to pogo with an astounding rack and a head full of fragmented, happy thoughts.

Charlie found them moments later.

"It was just an innocent dance, shaman," Will explained, holding his hands up, unarmed.

"I know that," he replied. He turned to Verity, one hand holding his cell phone, the other clasping her shoulder. "We have to go now. Carol just called me." He said, "It's Tex."

twenty

the waiting room at good Sam boasted chairs that looked like they had been thrown out of a corporate lobby in 1979 and a digital clock that flashed 12:00 on a table, despite the wall clock's insistence upon 2 a.m. Carol meditated in the corner, while Thelma rested her head on Dick's shoulder. Charlie, having put together a slapdash curative garnish of eucalyptus leaves purloined from the floral display at the hospital entrance and hairs from Verity's scalp, chanted a string of gibberish healing incantations. Cramped and not drunk, not even woozy from the drugs, Verity slumped in a chair next to him.

"I don't even know who this Kronos is," Thelma said. "Diana told me she was riding her bike to a friend's house."

Verity said, "He *is* her friend."

"I assumed she meant a girlfriend."

"Diana doesn't have any girlfriends, Mom. You'd know that if you paid any attention to her." She assured her mother that Diana was in good hands at the Kickels' house for the night.

Carol opened one eye and peeked out at those around her. As a vampire lifestylist, she found that nothing much surprised her anymore, but meeting the fully alive urn resident in the waiting room of Good Samaritan Hospital had surprised her very much indeed.

"You thought I was dead," Thelma said.

"Well," Carol began—how to be diplomatic to a corpse that is not a corpse? "I think he wanted to tell me the truth because the last thing he said before he fell on the floor was 'No one is really dead if we remember them.' "

They spoke then of the urn and all that it had been through, the ceremonies and swinger parties, and Thelma said it was not Tex's fault that he dealt with disappointment the way he did.

Verity half-listened to this, her mind all the while pulsing images of flatline and crash cart. She could not shake the smell of Lysol and fluorocarbons and latex and illness from her nose, and rose to pace the room.

The clock erroneously flashed 12:30, and she felt responsible for what had happened. Cleaning out the damn urn had not been enough; she should have raised him from his melancholy and forced him into the present. Now he was lying in a bed, tubes in him, his heart fibrillating—or was it defibrillating?—all over the place, his eyes closed and unaware. An ambulance had come for him. Her dad in an ambulance. God, how hard it must be to be a patient, to leave your life in the hands of bad drivers, watching your heart thumpthumpthumping on the little monitor. The drivers thought he lived in Clarendon Hills despite Carol's instructions and came ten minutes late; he could have been dead on the floor of Victory's room, his heart flat.

She filled a cup of water from the cooler, 12:41, except in real life it was more like 2:30, except nothing resembled real life on this formerly typical August night. August 4. "Oh, it's my birthday," she said suddenly.

"Happy birthday, honey," Thelma said sleepily.

Her stepfather wished her many happy returns. "I mean of the birthday, I didn't mean of this particular scene—"

"I know, Dick. Thanks," Verity said.

"I have a present at home," Charlie said. He refrained from revealing that he had forgone gum surgery to buy her something.

Thelma said, "When Verity was born, she was red as a beet and bald as an onion. She was beautiful."

"Still is," said Charlie.

Thelma yawned. "But not red and bald anymore," she said, then conked out on Dick's shoulder.

All the Prestis loved to tell the story of Victory's birth, when she had been brought home from the hospital and Verity had asked if they could put her back and get her a brother instead. Everyone always laughed at that story, even Victory had laughed, but Verity had felt guilty about this unremembered event and wished she could tell her sister that she really did love her.

It was November 1990 when she had last paced in this same waiting room with Tex and the Rasmussens, the night that no one had brought them any good news. She sat down and picked the lint balls out of the seat cushion fabric. These were the same chairs. Every year, every fall was hard.

"He's stable." A nurse came into the room. "You can see him now, one at a time." Thelma snored and Verity leaped up.

In his room, the monitor was steady. No lines fluctuated, no obvious sense of panic ebbed from the doctor in the hall or the nurse on duty. Verity pointed to the edge of the heart monitor. "What's this?"

"It's just a loose wire, nothing to worry about," the nurse said. The clock outside must have been flashing 1:00 by now. Who knows what time it was in the real world? The monitor blipped. Verity noticed every little irregularity and asked the nurse each time what was going on, as though she understood how to interpret an EKG.

His pulse, inconsistently 80, 67, 120—Verity asked about that. According to the nurse, movement confused the machine. *That's great. When the machines are confused, we are all lost,* she thought. The nurse was not concerned. With Tex's every breath, little pink lungs appeared on the monitor, with every heartbeat, a little red heart throbbed.

Isn't that an air bubble there? Don't they cause embolisms? She watched her father's head roll back and asked, "Is there an air bubble in his IV?" *Why is a crucifix on the wall? What if we were Hindu? What if we are bad Catholics?* The nurse seemed unconcerned.

Verity drew closer and laid her hand on her father's. He wore a loose hospital gown that gaped open all around his shoulders and chest to accommodate the tubes and tape and saline drip. The pulse monitor read 77, 90, 160. "That just can't be right."

"It's okay." The nurse glanced at the monitor.

"Nothing in this hospital works right! The clock out in the waiting room says it's one in the morning."

The nurse checked her watch. "It's just after three."

Under the tape, peeking from beneath the gown, Verity spied a splotch of red. Red was no good, what was red? She bent down, gently lifted the edge of the garment. Tex's eyes fluttered open.

"Dad," she said, tears running down. "You got a tattoo."

On the left side of his chest was a molar on fire.

He said, "My heart is a bleeding tooth turned upside down."

diana lay awake in the Kickels' guest room. Kronos's mom and dad had been really nice to her, explaining what had happened to Tex and that her parents would come collect her in the morning, and asking her if she needed anything. They weren't even mad that she had come over uninvited—at least, she told them Kronos had not invited her, that she just stopped in on her way home from the pet store to drop off some sheet music.

"What do you play in the band?" his dad asked.

"Clarinet."

"Ah, the ol' licorice stick."

She asked how her sister was doing, and the parents exchanged glances, which told her everything she needed to know. She called Charlie on his cell.

Charlie had handed off the phone to Verity, but she just babbled incoherently. Diana asked how Tex was, how they all were, but Verity kept going on and on about how some clock was blinking 12:00. Diana did not know how to go further in this conversation, or how to end it. Thelma had not raised her daughters to hug, kiss, emote, or be truthful.

"Maybe I'll see you tomorrow, then," she finished lamely.

She turned over in bed. Her parents had never called. Hey, someone would have to let Gin out in the morning. Had anyone thought of that? She had to work tomorrow, but she could stop at Tex's on her way, since Thelma had a key. Diana would make her do it. She closed her eyes.

Oh, fuck it, she couldn't sleep. What was the matter with her family anyway? Why were they all so closed up and weird? Well, okay, she knew why, but still she questioned it. She crept out of bed and stole across the hall to Kronos's room.

"Shove over," she whispered.

Kronos drew the blanket up to his chest, a gesture of modesty even though he was fully covered in plaid pajamas. He did as instructed. Diana's warm body took up more than her share.

He felt it only fair to warn her. "I don't have any protection. Any, you know, devices." His face flamed, and he was grateful for the dark. He had never felt less like Rick James in his life.

"This isn't that kind of thing," she said. Thinking twice on that, hoping to soften the blow of rejection or rudeness, she said, "Not that under different circumstances there couldn't be whatever. But I'm sad and worried now, okay?"

Kronos shifted to give her more room. Diana said it: possibly one day there could be whatever! He was a patient boy; he could wait a long time.

She said, "My family is screwed up so tightly, I don't know if anyone could ever unscrew them. That's why I feel so shitty right now. Your parents are cool, in spite of liking smooth jazz and Gene Krupa, so you probably don't understand."

In Greek mythology, "Kronos" emerged from primordial chaos, a Titan. The myth held that Kronos had castrated his father with a sickle given him by his mother. The father lived, only to be overthrown by Kronos at a later date. The boy often thought about this mythological Kronos, who became ruler of the world—*nice*—yet eventually was dethroned by his own son, Zeus. It depressed him to realize that screwups ran in families, that they passed down inherited anguish as if it were any other faulty gene. He said, "Some of us screw up our parents by just being born."

Diana lay back on the pillow, her arms under her head. Yeah, Kronos might have something there, but still, no parent could be as screwed up as one who has lost a child. "You know," she said suddenly, "nobody ever actually told me that Victory died—not then, when it happened. They had this brilliant idea that it would be easier having me just watch my mother lie in bed weeping, without knowing why. But of course, I really did know why. Death was surprisingly easy for me to grasp." She considered this. "Maybe that's why I always liked Edward Gorey drawings and scary books."

Kronos said, "There are people who believe that stories for children should not have darkness in them."

Diana knew that was true. And there were people who believed that children knew nothing of darkness, period. But she offered up her own childhood heart, full of treachery and deceit and love and longing, as proof to the contrary.

tex opened his eyes early in the morning and saw his family all around.

"What happened?" he asked.

Carol told him he was in the hospital.

Tex asked, "Is it brain cancer from using your cell phone?"

She explained his arrhythmia and atrial fibrillation as best as she could until the doctor showed up.

Tex turned his head from Carol, who looked tired but relieved; he saw Verity, he saw Charlie and his dead tooth and gumboil. Thelma and Dick in the corner, smiling. Thelma. He looked only at her, caught in a stare. No one had seen him meet the gaze of his ex-wife in almost twenty years.

His voice came out thin and reedy. "Thelma," he said. Her eyes widened and she moved forward, touched his toes through the sheet. Though technically a question, he forced it into a statement: "You're not coming back, are you."

He did not mean "coming back to the house for lunch" or

"coming back during the next round of visiting hours." She knew what he meant and said, "No, Tex."

He nodded and closed his eyes, exhausted and sore. Rest was important because he knew he needed to get his strength back. He held hands with whoever reached for them.

with difficulty, Dick managed to cram Diana's bike into the back of his SUV. He had planned to ask his daughter just what she meant by sneaking out to a boy's house, and where was the six-pack of beer that had been in the basement bar fridge? But he couldn't bring himself to do it now.

"Is Tex all right?"

"Yes," said Thelma, "he's going to be fine."

"Good. Hey, don't you think we ought to stop by his house and let his dog out?"

"Verity and Charlie are already going. You better just think about yourself right now and what you did last night, because we're going to have a talk when we get home."

"But I have to work today. My shift starts in twenty minutes. I thought you were driving me to Petland."

Her parents said nothing and stared out the windshield.

"Mom. I have to go. I have a job."

Thelma snorted. "Maybe you do, maybe you don't."

"What's that supposed to mean?"

Thelma turned around in her seat. "I told you I didn't approve of the way that store gets its dogs. I told you I didn't want you to have a job, not with school starting up so soon and—"

Diana put her hand on the door handle. "I swear to God, if you don't drive me there right now, I'll jump out at the next light and hitchhike."

Abruptly, Dick turned the car toward the mall instead of home, as they had originally discussed. His wife threw her hands up and looked out her window, defeated. Dick said, "I'm tired, Thel. I want to go home and sleep."

• • •

in the front window of Petland, the one that held a bay of wiggling pups, was a large cardboard sign reading SALE! STORE CLOSING. Puppies had peed on the back of it in protest.

Diana walked up to her manager with a "What gives?" attitude.

"Another lawsuit from the Pet Store Resistance," he said. "The owner says it's more cost-effective to close this branch. I'm going to the Woodbridge store. That, I can handle. Pet Store Resistance complaints from my own employees' mothers? That I can't handle. This is gonna be your last day."

Stunned, Diana walked into the barkers' kennel and hooked her fingertips through Taco Bell's cage. Her mother? Her mother did this to her? The animal smiled in her usual way, waiting for her paper to be changed and for the daily cuddle.

When Diana regained her composure, she cleaned out all the kennels. Later, a customer asked if she could see Taco Bell and play with her a little. The woman had read the sign about the store closing and asked Diana what she was going to do.

"School starts in a couple weeks, so I guess I should stop working anyhow," she answered. The woman looked sympathetic, and Diana felt the shortage of that feeling in her family keenly. She motioned toward the dogs and said, "I'm more concerned about these guys. I don't know where they're going to go, or who'll be taking care of them." The woman asked Diana her name and said she would pray for her.

One puppy had been sold by the end of the day, Gyro Hut. The others settled down in their cages, quiet stealing over them. They always knew when the store was closing down for the night, when their people, such as they were, were getting ready to leave them.

Diana went into the back room to gather her stuff together so she could go home. She and the cat guy Sharpied graffiti and cartoons all over the supply boxes.

"Why the hell shouldn't we? What are they gonna do?" Diana asked. "Fire us?"

At five o'clock, she made it to the parking lot before she burst into tears. She jabbed Charlie's number on her cell phone. "Can I talk to my sister?"

Verity showed up minutes later and pushed open the passenger door. Diana slid in, wiped her nose, rubbed her eyes.

"Thanks for coming to get me."

"No problem. Charlie let me take his car. He's just hanging out at my dad's, eating everything in the refrigerator."

Diana told her the story of the Pet Store Resistance, of Thelma's role in her job loss.

Verity said, "There's something you have to understand about our mother. She's not a good one. Maybe she can't help it. Not everyone is cut out for motherhood."

"The thing is, I don't care about not having a job or not having money. I care about not having something to look forward to. I liked working at Petland; it made me feel like a better person. I played with animals all day, and I made them happy without lowering my moral standards," she said. Tears brimmed her eyes. "There's something really cool about walking into the store and seeing twenty puppies wag their tails. Cleaning up dog shit is rewarding."

"Maybe you could find another pet store to work at. There's one in Westmont."

"You mean Pet Warehouse? They make Petland look like animal heaven. They stick two dogs to a kennel there and don't vaccinate them against anything. Our store almost took a beagle mix from them, but it died of distemper before they sent it. Distemper, that's fucking easy to vaccinate against, and some family lost their chance at having a really great dog," she said.

Verity took her to Tex's. He was coming home tomorrow, and she enlisted Diana's help in cleaning the house and preparing some meals for him. Charlie roamed the rooms with a bundle of dried rosemary, reciting blessings and plugging Glade air fresheners into the outlets. Then he moved outside to chant and convulse in his ladies' bathrobe, a health-and-happiness jig that resembled an advanced case of Saint Vitus' dance.

"What is he doing, anyway?" Diana asked.

"Distributing health vibes for my dad and freaking out the neighbors."

Diana watched her cut up a chicken. Next year at this time, she'd be packing for Oberlin. She guessed it would be eleven months, two weeks, and one day before she could leave. She looked around Tex's kitchen, remembering the pizza-blotting incident from earlier this summer, and a hard lump grew in her throat. Why did she have to blot his rancid pizza? He was always nice to her. Why couldn't she have just eaten it, unblotted?

Her sister said, "You want to stay with me in the city until Mom calms down about you sneaking off to Kronos's house?"

Diana blinked in surprise. "Me? Oh . . . no, no, that's okay. Mom will have to get over it, the bitch. And I guess I will, too. Plus I don't want to leave Dad; I think he needs me."

"Any time you need to get out of there for a while, you can call me," Verity said, putting down the knife and looking her sister in the eye. "I want you to."

Diana reached for the celery and began slicing it up. She said, "Downers Grove may suck, but it's almost like home to me."

twenty-one

"i can't believe it," eddie Loa said, shaking his head. "What a weekend you had."

Charlie nodded. "Thank Benevolent Creator it's over."

"Are you guys sure you're up to this?" Eddie waved his hand toward the Evil Head. "I got a new crop of boils on my neck this morning, but I'm willing to wait them out if you need some time to recover."

"That's all right. My dad's home now and we're going to visit him later," Verity said. A thoughtful look entered her eyes and she said, "You know, I made it through my fifteenth class reunion. I turned thirty-four years old. I'd like to banish a little evil now, if I can."

Charlie fastened his yellow silk robe and arranged the herbs around him.

Verity said, "I liked that stuff you were waving around at my dad's. Are you going to use any of that tonight?"

"No, that was rosemary. It means 'remembrance' in the parlance of herbs. I strung it up in Victory's bedroom—I mean, the room your dad is going to remodel."

Rosemary is for remembrance, for Victory's remembrance. Verity liked that. She also liked the way he shoved phrases like "the parlance of herbs" into casual conversation.

"Nice urn," Eddie said.

"Thanks," Verity replied. "Once I dumped out Mother's ashes, I thought it might make a nice receptacle to hold the dried plant stuff Charlie's going to use in the exorcism tonight."

Charlie said, "Balm of Gilead—for cure and relief. Bearded Crepis—protection. Calycanthus—benevolence. Just leave the urn on a table or something as long as you live here, and you're good to go."

One of the Loa cousins asked Verity, "You dumped out your mother's burial ashes?"

She said, "It's a long story."

He looked at the other cousin in awe. "She's cool."

the group drove down to the lakefront at Oak Street, that stretch of beach with easy access to the piers and breakwaters. Between the five of them, they lugged the Evil Head out of Suzanne's hatchback, wrapped it in a sheet, and trudged down to the beach. They had to stop every minute to regain their breath and shake out their aching biceps. Four hundred pounds of evil took its toll on five pairs of arms that had never lifted dumbbells. When they finally reached the end of the closest breakwater, they set the Evil Head on the ground and clasped their hands at Charlie's urging.

He began. "I'd like to start with a speech. Ahem. Gods of fire and . . . what is it? Gods of something . . . hmm, I can't remember this. Oh wait, it's on my crib notes. Hang on a sec." He struggled to read the page in the darkening twilight. His perspiring palms did not help clarify the print.

"What speech is this?" asked Eddie.

"It's from one of the all-time great movies with a shaman role, *The Conqueror*."

Eddie laughed. *"The Conqueror*? With John Wayne as Genghis Khan? That's one of the worst movies ever made."

Verity said, "I read about that movie. Didn't a bunch of the cast members eventually die of cancer? Like seven or eight of them?"

Eddie nodded in enthusiasm. "Yeah! The film was shot on a site where A-bomb testing had been conducted, which was hushed up for years. If you could only hear the Duke utter the lines, 'Dance! Dance for me, Tartar woman!' in that twangy western accent. It's the most unintentionally hilarious—"

Charlie said, "I'm trying to conduct an exorcism here."

The group apologized.

"Oh hell, I can't read this thing. I sweated all over my speech." He crumpled it up and shoved it into his robe pocket. "Let me improvise. Hand me the blade bone."

Eddie obeyed, withdrawing the slimy thing from the giant Ziploc bag in his chain-mail satchel. "You want the head, too? Because I brought it."

"The head? Who told you to bring the head? We don't need it. I never asked for the sheep's head."

"Well, now what am I gonna do with it? I don't want it and I'm not lugging it all the way back to the car. Plus it stinks."

"Oh, fine, just throw it into the water then. It doesn't matter."

"This doesn't sound very scientific," Verity complained. Eddie threw the sheep's head off the pier. It floated for a few moments, then sank, whereby interested crappies moved in for a better look.

Charlie took the blade bone from Eddie, bonked the Evil Head with it, then dropped it into the chop of Lake Michigan. "Head, Head, Evil Head, I'm so glad the Head is dead. Now let's toss this bastard in and go home."

The five of them threw the Evil Head into the lake. Only a couple feet deep at the end of the pier, the water clearly showed its ghostly face peering up at them through the murk.

"That's it?" asked one of the cousins.

"No biggie." Charlie rubbed his hands together, divesting them of plaster dust. "All you need is the blade bone, a body of water, and belief. In researching this project, I've discovered that banishing evil is easy; it's creating goodness that's hard."

"Well, if that's it," said Eddie doubtfully.

"Trust me, friend." Charlie led them back to the car. "Hey. Your boils are gone."

Eddie's hand flew up to his neck. He touched here and there, but all he felt was smooth skin and a bit of stubble. "Thank you, shaman! You have a treat in store for you. My aunt made *pea tunuvilivili;* it kicks serious ass."

"Mmm," said Charlie, "is that the chicken in banana leaves?"

Eddie glanced at his cousins. "Um . . . similar. It's awesome. There's enough for all of us." He said no more. Samoan cuisine was hard to explain. Not everyone liked the sound of chargrilled flying fox bats, but everyone liked the taste of them.

laurel said, "There's a haiku slam next week, and I'm reading. Wanna come with?"

"Really? There are haiku slams?" Stan asked. "I had no idea. You always think haikus are so gentle and otherworldly and, like, Asian. You don't think of them getting slammed by people in a bar."

She said, "The Chicago haiku scene is ruthless."

"What about Sebastian?"

Laurel thought about her latest work of art, a haiku that might be a little too sentimental for *Haiku Jew,* yet pleased her nevertheless.

> *My son, the genius,*
> *Throws his trains at my head, but*
> *I've learned to catch them.*

She said, "We'll get a babysitter—your mom or my sister. Sebastian will be fine."

Laurel suggesting a night out, just the two of them, without the kid? Stan hid his surprise. He never thought he'd say it, but he thanked God for poetry.

craig and will crafted a new tune in the Kickel basement. They'd write an easy bass line for it later, something even Stan could handle.

"I have to admit," Will said, "I really like the lyrics he wrote for 'Slippery Steps at the Old-Age Home.' It's kind of creepy that he dedicates it to his parents at every rehearsal, but I still like it."

Craig said, "We need a real audience, though."

"Fat chance of anybody hiring us. I mean, I like our Tears for Fears medley and the tribute to Gary Numan, and even the clarinet solo in 'Turning Japanese,' but what bar owner is going to pay us for that? We'd need to own the bar ourselves."

The light turned green suddenly in Craig's mind. "I have a healthy chunk of savings, Will. Between my cash, your bar connections, Stan's new amp, and our combined cultural capital, I think we may have something here."

Will considered this. "Owning our own bar, the three of us? Maybe it could work. I also have a little money saved, just sitting in the bank. Sad to say, we'd probably have more success in the 'burbs than the city. Property and insurance is too damn expensive in the city and the competition is rough."

"Yeah, the suburbs. Who's out here to compete with anyway, Shadows and Nightmoves? We'd crush them, the pansy dance clubs! Suburban rock clubs are where it's at. Plus the Lousy Dates could play all the time!" Craig nodded in contentment. He felt compelled to add: "It's a risky venture, of course. I don't want to push you into anything."

Will said, "I know it's a risky venture, but so is life. And I'd like to try to have one."

They rewrote that old Housemartins' song, "The Light Is Always Green," incorporating a clarinet part. At their bar, the men decided, they would have all-ages shows. It was important to show the youth of today the mistakes and successes of the previous generation, to show them that in spite of decades of failure, misery, and inertia, of karaoke and cube-dwelling, a light could shine at the end of the tunnel for even the most desperate of men.

carolyn made peanut butter and jelly sandwiches for Kronos and Diana.

"Want more, sugarpants?" She held her hand out for her son's dish.

"Mom, don't call me sugarpants," Kronos whined. "But yes, I'd like another one."

Diana said, "Mrs. Kickel, I think it's really cool how you respect Kronos's vegetarianism. My mother made veal last night. I think she likes watching me gag and retch."

Carolyn said, "As mothers, we have to get our enjoyment where we can."

Kronos said, "The only reason she respects my vegetarianism is because she's one, too."

Carolyn argued. "Not true. If you wanted a steak, I'd grill you one right now. I'd submerge my hands in a bag of raw meat to make you hamburgers. I'd pluck a chicken for you. I'd make mutton."

"You would?"

She considered this, somewhat surprised at the truth. "I would. You're my son; I'd do anything for you."

Kronos liked where this line of questioning had led. He had been shamed by his recent jonesing for greasy flesh and had kept it to himself.

Diana said, "Thanks again for letting me stay here the other night. To be honest, I kind of wanted to just keep on staying. Not run away, exactly. Just not go home again."

"I know that feeling," Carolyn responded. "Sometimes you think your real life would start if you could only ditch your interfering home life."

Diana scowled. "You mean even middle-aged people think this way? How do you stand it? How do you go on, feeling like home is a prison?"

Carolyn heard the strains of "Slippery Steps" from down in the basement. Her daughter cooed in the bouncy seat, the vibrations from the drums jouncing her, a look of supreme satisfaction on her little face. Kronos, nonchalantly heating up a hot dog in the microwave, hummed "Turning Japanese" to himself. Craig bounded up from the basement then, kissed his children on their heads, and grabbed two beers out of the wine cooler.

"Nice! Blanche Steendonk!" he said in surprise, giving Carolyn a thumbs-up. His wide and silly grin caught even him off-guard; his wife had never bought him Belgian beer before.

She smiled in spite of it all. How to answer Diana's questions? Really, you never get over the urge to flee. The trick is finding reasons to stay.

"well? What do you think?" Verity modeled the leopard-skin poly wrap dress, executing what she imagined was the appropriate girlie-twirl.

Charlie drooled in appreciation. Sexy librarian types with glasses and red lipstick, twirling in femmy animal-print dresses? Ohhh . . .

"Three bucks. Hanging hem, but big whoop, I can fix that." The silver glint from her new necklace caught her in midtwirl and she stopped in front of the mirror to admire it, a little silver house on a thin silver chain. "I love my birthday present, CB. It's the best necklace I've ever seen."

"And it's not even from the thrift," he said.

"I know, but I still like it."

When he saw the necklace in the boutique window, he knew right away it was for Verity. A house is a home, right? And what's "home" but a feeling, the security and happiness of belonging. When they had first started dating, right after meeting at Tex's swinger party, he had asked that silly guy question, "How come a cool girl like you isn't taken?"

She had said, "A bad relationship is like a bad house foundation—nearly impossible to fix once it's in place."

"Oprah?" he asked.

She shrugged. "Fortune cookie. But you know what I'm saying."

This girl had made a home out of a rodent flat in the middle of gentry-ghetto blight. She kept a sense of home in her father's house; stuck in the past maybe, but it still felt like home. A house, even a tiny silver one, was the right gift for such a fantastic woman.

Verity opened her bedroom closet door and a cache of crocheted beer-can hats fell on her head. She tried to push the hangers over to accommodate the few new treasures from Goodwill she had brought home, but she couldn't gain an inch. "I don't have enough room," she pouted.

"Maybe if you ditched the portable bowling alley, you could stack up some trunks of clothes in the corner of the living room."

She whirled about in frenzied dismay. "Ditch the bowling alley? *Ditch the bowling alley?* Are you out of your mind?"

"No, I'm just saying if you got rid of some stuff, you'd have room for more."

Verity crossed her arms and shook her head. "No. No way. I'm not throwing out my beloved bowling alley or anything else. If you think I've spent the better part of twenty years amassing this crap just to throw it out, you—"

"No, I'm not suggesting you throw it all out. God knows we don't need to relegate any more abandoned objects to the landfills. I was just thinking you could, you know, rethrift some of it."

"Rethrift it?"

"Yes, take it back from whence it came. Actually, 'whence' means 'from where,' so it's redundant to say 'from whence,' though—"

"Rethrift it," she said again. She rubbed her chin thoughtfully and strolled out of the closet, musing to herself. "Bring it back to the thrifts so that others might get a chance to love it. Restore some decent thrift karma." Suddenly she stopped and slapped her palms together in a eureka moment. "Of course! It's so simple. Avoid the trash heaps for a while longer, spread some of my joy, my lovingly rescued items, to the rest of thriftdom. I don't have to throw them away."

"Set them free, Verity. Return them to the thrifts," he said. "It's the circle of life."

He was the best goddamned boyfriend ever. She hugged him tightly, then settled him on the couch while she went off into the kitchen to whip up some homemade pudding. Not too much would have to go back to the thrifts. Just the stuff that no longer had meaning for her, the things that had served their purpose: appliances, knickknacks, and clothing that had been loved for a while, and then disregarded by their original owners, the stuff that she had eventually ignored, too. A loved thing should never be forgotten twice in life. She'd keep the bowl made out of the Allman Brothers record, naturally, and the bowling alley. And the Hallway of Strangers—she would never get rid of them, nor forget any of their faces. The worried-looking Boston terriers, the grim grandmas, the smiling infants, the houses that no longer stood, the roads that now went nowhere, the gardens paved over, the people who had gone, every fragment of frozen time, all of them would stay with her, a happy family in a happy home.

leslie stella is the author of *Fat Bald Jeff* and *The Easy Hour*, and she has been nominated for a 2004 Pushcart Prize in short fiction. She lives in Chicago with her husband and son. Please visit her Web site at www.lesliestella.com.

Also by Leslie Stella

• • •

The Easy Hour
Catapulted into the role of social trendsetter,
a working-class girl seizes the opportunity
to unleash the next "new thing"—
with hilarious results.

$12.95 paperback
0-609-80972-5